D0052843

GRAVES ON THE FENS

A gripping crime thriller full of stunning twists

JOY ELLIS

Detective Nikki Galena Book 14

Joffe Books, London
www.joffebooks.com

First published in Great Britain in 2022

ISBN: 978-1-80405-691-2

I have the greatest pleasure in dedicating this book to Sue Birmingham. Her extraordinarily moving message touched my heart, made me cry, and gave me a new perspective about the power of books.

Sue, your bravery is awe-inspiring, and if Nikki and Joseph have helped you, even in the smallest way, I'm the happiest author in the world. My love to you for continued strength in the future.

Joy Ellis, December 2022

PROLOGUE

A single scream rang out into the night, rupturing the silence.

Around the small village, people stirred. Some woke from their slumbers.

A nervous wife dug her husband in the ribs. 'What was that?'

'What was what?' he grunted sleepily.

'That awful noise.'

'I didn't hear anything. Go back to sleep.'

In another house, a man leaped from his bed and stared out of the window. All was quiet. Nothing moved, no cars, no figures lurking in the shadows. No lights were on, other than the one in old Emmie Smith's upstairs bedroom, but she always left her light burning. He returned to his bed, wondering if the sound had been the remnant of a bad dream, forgotten on awakening.

A few minutes later, the village of Marsh Enderby was silent again, its inhabitants back in the arms of Morpheus.

All but one woman. She lay sobbing into her pillow, racked with pain and anguish. No god of sleep, of beautiful dreams, visited her bed. He never did. Instead, all that came was the fear of darkness, and what it might bring.

* * *

In another village, not so far away, someone else was awake, but unlike the woman the darkness held no fears for him. He found the night hours energising. He rarely slept but didn't seem to suffer for it. He snatched a few minutes' sleep at odd times when he felt the need to recharge his batteries. It was enough for him.

While the world slept, he was busy working on a gruelling schedule for the following day. He didn't mind the long hours he put in — his work was the most important thing in his life, it meant everything to him.

He stared at a large map of the Fenland area taped to the wall of his "operations room," consulting map references on his laptop and adding a few street graphics so as to get an idea of the look of the various locations he was studying. He planned to take a field trip the following day, to tie everything together.

He printed off what he needed, shut down the laptop and turned out the light. His next job was to get the equipment for his expedition ready. He went downstairs to his boot room, where he selected a tough wax jacket from the pegs of outdoor wear, a Barbour cap and his favourite pair of leather walking boots. He didn't know the area he would be visiting, but one thing was certain, it would be muddy. The Lincolnshire Fens in late winter/early spring were always muddy.

Into the jacket pockets went a selection of things he might need to assist him in his assignment. Satisfied that he'd forgotten nothing, he went to the kitchen and took a Thermos flask from the cupboard, ready for filling first thing in the morning. He made a cheese and pickle sandwich, wrapped it in foil and placed it in the fridge. He threw a packet of crisps and a couple of energy bars into his rucksack, along with an apple and a banana. He had no idea how long this hunt would take, possibly a week, maybe longer. It didn't matter, he had a job to do, and he could do it better than anyone — with the exception, that was, of one other person. The sainted Detective Inspector Nikki Galena, pride of the

Fenland Constabulary. His eyes narrowed at the thought of her, and it was only with considerable effort that he pushed her from his mind.

Concentrate on the job in hand! Repeating the words to himself, he went out to his garage, unlocked it, and gathered up the shovel, the bow saw, the wire cutters and axe that he had placed by his vehicle in readiness.

Into the boot of the big four-by-four went two large tarpaulin sheets, some sacks and the tools. He closed it down and locked the garage.

He stood in the darkness of his garden for a few moments and listened to the night sounds. He cleared his mind and ran through everything he might need, item by item. All boxes ticked, and with a full tank of fuel, he was ready to move out at dawn.

Back inside, he poured himself a small glass of his favourite twelve-year-old Royal Welsh whisky and toasted his coming success. This job would go as well as the last one, he just knew it. He would teach DI Nikki Galena and the rest of the Fenland force how not to give up on people. You didn't do that when the person concerned was so loved and cherished that missing them tore your heart into tiny jagged pieces.

CHAPTER ONE

It was the end of the day. DS Joseph Easter sat at Nikki's desk gazing proudly at three neat piles of reports, congratulating himself on managing to catch up with what had been a pretty daunting backlog of paperwork. He couldn't wait to be back in his own little cupboard of an office in the main CID room with DI Nikki Galena once more reigning supreme from this one. Thank heavens the superintendent, Cameron Walker, would be back from leave next week and things could finally return to normal.

Still, he wasn't complaining. With Nikki agreeing to step up and accept the post of acting superintendent while he covered her duties as an acting DI, they had managed to save their personal relationship from becoming front-page news, which would have resulted in the team splitting up and the two of them moving to different areas. A new superintendent would have spotted their relationship straight away and caused all manner of problems for them, whereas, by holding the fort until Cam's return, their secret stayed safe. Cam was not only their super, he was also their friend. It was him who had suggested this expedient after his wife, Kaye, had to undergo heart surgery and he needed to take several months off to look after her.

Joseph closed the file he had been working on and stretched. Maybe he'd take Nikki a cup of coffee and find out what time she'd be finishing. He was planning a special dinner tonight and didn't want to find she was working late.

He walked up the stairs with a smile on his face. Nikki was a woman of action, not an administrator, and she had dreaded the prospect of filling Cam's shoes during his absence. Even the thought of directing operations from behind a desk had her practically climbing the walls. Now, more than two months down the line, she was bossing it. Not only had she soon learned what was expected of her, she had also made of it a kind of Galena-style superintendence whereby she could oversee operations, get all the relevant reports to whatever bit of gold braid had requested them, while also giving herself time for her precious team.

He knocked, shouldered the door open and carried in the two beakers of coffee.

She gave him a smile of welcome. 'Joseph! Just the person. I've been going over these statistics,' she pointed to her monitor screen, 'and—'

'Oh, sorry. Shall I come back when Acting Superintendent Galena's here? Only you mentioned statistics. And I happen to know she doesn't do statistics.'

She threw him a withering look. 'Very amusing, *Acting* DI Smart-arse. Now listen. First off, as Cam's been so damned good to us, no way am I having him coming back to a shambles, even if that does mean me tackling poxy statistics, and secondly,' her eyes went back to the screen, 'a couple of things here are actually rather worrying.'

She started to explain. At the mention of domestic violence, Joseph gave a groan. Domestic violence was one of the most frustrating and soul-destroying aspects of police work. Time after time, you sat for hours listening to horror stories, tales of cruelty, drunkenness and violence. The victim would swear that they'd had enough. This time he or she would go to court because they couldn't take any more. Then in the morning, the inevitable phone call: 'Oh, he didn't mean it, he's so sorry now. He loves me really, it was just the drink.' Or, 'She is under terrible strain at the moment, and she swears it will never happen again. I have to give her the benefit of the doubt because I do love her.' It was nearly always women who took the brunt of the abuse, but they had come across the odd case in which the husband was the victim.

'I know what you're thinking, Joseph,' said Nikki. 'It's everywhere, and rising all the time — but we've had a big spike right here in the Fens, and it bothers me. It's almost double the national rate — and that's already at six per cent. Hitherto, we've kept pretty well on a level with other areas. I think we need to gather a bit of info from uniform, and who better to ask than our newbie civilian officer in CID?'

'The perfect choice,' agreed Joseph. He grinned at Nikki. 'I *cannot* get used to seeing our Vonnie in civvies! It's such a shock; I mean, we've been seeing her in her uniform since Noah drew up blueprints for the ark.'

WPC Yvonne Collins, or Vonnie, as they always thought of her, had finally decided that retirement was not for her — not just yet anyway — and she had joined Nikki's team as a civilian interviewing officer. She now occupied the desk that had once belonged to Dave Harris, her much-missed predecessor and dear friend. Everyone was delighted that she had decided to stay. Her local knowledge was legendary, and they'd be lost without her.

'Have a word with her in the morning, Joseph. Ask her to see if there's any unusual pattern to what is happening, or some word on the streets about what could be causing it.' Nikki looked back to the computer. 'This other spike, however, is a bit more concerning. We've had far more reports in than usual from women saying they are being either followed or watched, or both. There have been no actual physical encounters or attacks, but these women, all in their late teens to early thirties, have reported being extremely anxious, and a couple of them have said they're too scared to go out alone. I think we need to talk to uniform and take a closer look at this.' She stared at Joseph. 'I've got a really bad vibe about these figures. Have you got anyone free to follow it up?'

Joseph nodded. 'Well, it so happens I've just closed up the paperwork on both the cases I had running, so I'll do it myself, maybe with Cat's help, if she's up to date with her own workload. Ben Radley is on a course for a couple of days, so it's likely she will be.'

Nikki nodded, happy with his suggestion. 'But that's enough for today. I've had it with figures.' She smiled broadly at him, 'So what's on the menu tonight, Oh Great Master of Haute Cuisine?'

He gave her an enigmatic smile. 'That would be telling, Oh Great Eater of Everything I Place in Front of Her. Let's just say you are *really* going to enjoy what I have in mind.'

Nikki chuckled. 'Don't I always? So, what's holding us up? Let's get back to Cloud Fen!'

They still used separate cars to travel to and from work. It was best that way. Most of their colleagues, including the higher-ranking officers, still believed that Joseph lived in Knot Cottage, his house by the marsh, and that Nikki resided alone in Cloud Cottage Farm. To the people it was safest to keep the truth from, they were simply neighbours. Only the team and their closest friends were aware that Joseph had moved in with Nikki some time ago.

Driving home, Joseph went over tonight's meal in his head. He had noticed that with all her extra duties, Nikki had not seen her mother for a while, and it obviously bothered her, so tonight he had invited Eve and her friend Wendy to join them for a special supper.

He arrived just after Nikki. She watched him pull several bulging shopping bags from the boot of his car. 'I know I'm always hungry, Joseph, but that looks like an awful lot of food, even for me.'

'Oh, it's nothing really. I decided to get a few things for the store cupboard while I was shopping, that's all.'

Inside, he banned Nikki from the kitchen and the dining room. He sent her upstairs with a glass of wine, and an order to get out of her work clothes and have a shower, informing her that she had twenty minutes before he wanted her back down again.

'For what exactly, Joseph Easter?' she asked.

'Wait and see. And you're wasting precious time, so go.'

Amused by his little game, she threw him a rude comment and shook her head.

Twenty minutes later he heard her coming back down the stairs, and at the same time, exactly as arranged, a car drew up outside the farmhouse. 'Get the door, would you, Nikki?' he called from the kitchen.

'Who the blazes is calling here at this time?' Nikki marched off to answer the door. He smiled at her squeal of delight. 'Mum! Wendy! Hellfire, I'm going to kill Joseph Easter. He never said. Oh, this is wonderful! Come on in.'

Joseph emerged from the kitchen and instead of killing him, Nikki gave him a kiss. 'I've been feeling guilty about not seeing Eve all this time, so this is perfect. Thank you.' She stared at the closed kitchen door. 'And what exactly is going on in there? There are some rather interesting smells starting to escape.'

He ushered everyone into the lounge. 'Go and get our guests a drink, Nikki, and all will be revealed in due course.'

Joseph happily returned to doing what he loved best — other than catching criminals. He had been dying to do this for ages, knowing it would put a smile on Nikki's face. For years she had been waxing lyrical about the homely food she had eaten as a child, and how so many of the old Lincolnshire dishes were getting lost or forgotten, or adapted to suit the takeaway market. Not long ago, she had been sorting out some old papers of her father's, and had discovered an old family cookbook — the one that now lay open on the kitchen table, surrounded by handwritten recipes scribbled on scraps of paper that she had found folded up inside it.

Joseph smiled. Tonight, he had recreated a traditional Lincolnshire dinner for her, lovingly cooked in the very farmhouse kitchen where Nikki had spent her childhood.

He had added an assortment of other Lincolnshire delicacies and treated himself to a couple of bottles of local craft beer — a perk for the chef.

He had run his idea past Eve first, just to make sure she was okay with it. Eve was Nikki's biological mother, but they hadn't met until the day of Nikki's father's funeral, five years ago, and Joseph hadn't wanted the meal to be painful for Eve, who had missed out on Nikki's childhood. Eve, to his relief, had said it was a brilliant idea, and she would love to join them.

Half an hour later, Joseph ushered his guests into the dining room. Even he was pleased with the look of the dining table. He wasn't exactly into flower arranging, so had bought several bunches of bright yellow daisy chrysanthemums and put a big cluster of them into a water carafe in the centre of the table, and had placed cuttings in a slender champagne flute at every place setting. In the centre of each glass was a little Lincolnshire flag on a stick. He had even snipped off some of the daisy heads and scattered them on the dark blue tablecloth, alongside some paper napkins printed with the county flag he'd managed to find. The whole effect was bright and cheerful, and great fun.

Nikki's face was a picture. He knew that she was fiercely proud of being a "Yellowbelly," a native of Lincolnshire, and it was clear that she was absolutely delighted with what she saw.

'You sly sod, Joseph Easter!' she exclaimed. 'This is brilliant! So, er, what exactly are we having for dinner?'

He made a little bow. 'Your waiter will be along any moment, ma'am.'

He hurried back to the kitchen and returned with the starter. His daughter Tamsin — a vegetarian — would have had a screaming fit at the sight of such an offering, but Nikki would love it, he knew.

'Stuffed chine! Oh, and haslet too! I haven't had this in years!' Nikki picked up her knife and fork eagerly.

He explained to Wendy and Eve, both incomers to this part of the county, about the meal they had in front of them.

'A cold collation salad with slices of delicious traditional meats, including the speciality dish that Nikki mentioned, stuffed chine — that's salt pork filled with herbs, especially parsley.'

Joseph poured them all large glasses of wine, pleased that he'd advised Eve and Wendy to come by taxi.

The meal was a huge success, the high point being Nikki's surprise and delight at her father's favourite main course of Lincolnshire sausages in a delicious casserole with lentils, vegetables and herbs, cooked exactly to their old family recipe. Perhaps it wouldn't have won any Michelin stars, but the old-fashioned meal was wholesome, tasty, and had everyone asking for more.

Now they were eating plum loaf with a selection of cheeses, including the famous Lincolnshire Poacher.

'Okay, Eve, tell us about your next project,' said Joseph, helping himself to some Cote Hill Blue. 'We all know that you two can't exist without something exciting going on in your lives.'

Eve Anderson and Wendy Avery had seen active service in the Royal Air Force, and then gone on to work with the Ministry of Defence. They had remained good friends after retirement, along with two other old comrades, and for the past few years Wendy had been living with Eve in Monks Lantern, her converted chapel home. After their action-packed life, neither were able to "switch off" and take it easy, so they took on a series of ambitious projects.

'Not exactly a project per se,' said Eve slowly, giving Wendy a conspiratorial smile. 'More like a new and perfectly harmless hobby.'

Nikki rolled her eyes. 'Nothing you two take on could be described as a "harmless hobby." And you've got previous for seriously big trouble.' She looked from one to the other suspiciously. 'So, what is this new hobby? Fire-eating for beginners? Bungee jumping for the over-seventies?'

'Eve's right,' Wendy said innocently. 'It's just a hobby.'

'We've bought metal detectors,' said Eve excitedly. 'We're going to be detectorists.'

'We've gone into all the legal regulations, and we've obtained permission from a couple of farmers to go on their fields,' added Wendy.

'And we've also managed to get access to an old airfield.' Eve's eyes flashed with enthusiasm at the thought. 'Can't wait for that little expedition!'

'Whoa!' exclaimed Nikki. 'That could mean digging up live ordnance! Are you both quite mad? What are you thinking?'

Joseph burst out laughing. 'Nikki! These two have handled more live ordnance in their time than you've had hot dinners. I'm betting they know exactly how to go about it. Isn't that right, Eve?'

'Of course, we do. We met this lovely girl called Perrie through an online local enthusiasts' club, didn't we, Wendy?'

'She came over to Monks Lantern to give us some pointers, especially about working abandoned airfields. She's a bit of an afficionado of World War Two relics, and our disused airfields in particular. She's told us how to do the research before we go to the site. We've got plans from the archive at RAF Hendon and we'll pinpoint those areas that are most likely to give us the best pickings.' Wendy took a little more of a cheese called Heart of Lincolnshire, shaped like a heart and coated in a pink wax. 'She also showed us exactly how to go about digging out shells or live ammo safely, so fear not, Nikki, we won't be plunging a shovel directly into an unexploded bomb!'

'And look.' Eve unwrapped a small parcel that had been sitting on the table next to her all evening. 'These are things we found in the garden at Monks Lantern while we were testing out the detectors. They tell you to search in places where people gather for any reason, and as our home was a chapel, whole congregations came and went during its lifetime of use.'

Joseph looked at their finds. There were some coins, several old pennies and a thrupenny bit from the forties, an old metal belt buckle, a brooch with tiny glass flower petals still in place, a silver spoon, and a battered St Christopher medallion. 'That's quite impressive. Certainly better than a load of nails and scrap metal.'

'Oh, we found plenty of junk as well, but we were pleased with these, considering we're only beginners.' Eve fingered the little brooch. 'You can't help wanting to know who owned something like this. Was she sad to lose it, or did she throw it away? Everything has a story behind it, but sadly this is one we'll never know.'

They continued to talk for over an hour over coffee, the conversation, amid much laughter, ranging far and wide, until Wendy looked at her watch. 'I'm sorry to say this but the taxi will be here in ten minutes. Can I take the little flag? It was such a nice meal, I'd like it as a keepsake.'

Joseph took two from the glasses and handed them to her. 'Please do. I love the county flag. Not that I knew what it meant until I bought the flags and serviettes. The old guy in the market gave me a lecture on it.'

'So, what does it mean?' asked Eve.

'Well, as you see, the flag features a red cross, edged in yellow and bearing a yellow fleur de-lys on a background of green and blue quarters. The red cross is St George's, representing England. Yellow stands for the crops grown in the county, and references the nickname "Yellowbellies," given to people born and bred in Lincolnshire, as well. Blue represents both the sea of the East Coast and the wide skies of Lincolnshire, and green symbolises the rich lushness of Fenland fields. The fleur-de-lys is the recognised symbol of the City of Lincoln.' He grinned. 'And there you have it, courtesy of Fred Winters, Greenborough market trader and local historian.'

After Eve and Wendy had been driven away, they stood for a while in the doorway of Cloud Cottage Farm, looking up at the starry indigo sky. Nikki held Joseph closely. 'You must be the most caring partner in all the world. It was so thoughtful of you to make that meal, and I could have cried when I tasted the food. It was perfect, exactly as I remember it as a child.'

'I'm just glad it worked,' he whispered.

The night was utterly peaceful. Beneath the canopy of stars — no light pollution out here — soft night sounds were all that could be heard. No traffic noise, no voices.

Joseph breathed it in, wishing this moment could last for ever.

He wasn't to know it, but this would be the last peaceful night they'd experience for some considerable time.

CHAPTER TWO

Lesley Curtis, Superintendent Cam Walker's office manager, brought Nikki her morning mail and overnight reports, along with a coffee. Nikki smiled, still feeling mellow after her pleasant evening.

'Anything screaming out for immediate attention in this lot, Lesley?' she asked, wondering how a few hours of darkness could generate so much work.

'Not that I noticed,' said Lesley. 'Although I did wonder what this was. It's certainly not official, and it's rather interesting stationery. It's an old-fashioned airmail envelope, isn't it? Who uses those these days? It came by normal local Royal Mail.'

It reminded Nikki of a pen pal she'd had in her schooldays. They'd written every few weeks, so regularly that part of the little girl's address was still imprinted in her brain. Rural Route #Two, Box Twenty-seven, somewhere in Indiana, USA.

Her immediate inclination was to rip it open there and then, but something stopped her, and she waited until Lesley had left.

She sat staring at the thing, resting innocuously on top of the other mail. Only it wasn't innocuous at all, was it? That red, white and blue border, the words *Par Avion* written across it, screamed a warning at her. She knew it wasn't going to blow up or anything like that. All their mail was screened in the mail room before being sent to the various departments. It wasn't that kind of threat that bothered her. No, there was just something about it. That the sender had chosen to use an airmail envelope was weird to start with, and the handwriting with her name and the address of the station, all penned so neatly, looked oddly intimidating.

Telling herself not to be so fanciful, Nikki opened the envelope.

Inside was a single sheet of old-fashioned blue airmail paper, light as a feather and familiar to the touch. On it, just three words: *"You failed me."*

Somehow, this shortest of messages struck home. Who had she failed? And why, when the police received far worse threats than this on a daily basis, did it manage to convince her that something very menacing indeed was about to unravel?

She picked up her phone and rang Joseph in her office. 'Could you pop up here for a moment?'

He was with her in seconds. As soon as the door closed behind him, she handed him the envelope and the note.

Joseph read it and laid it back on the desk with a shrug. 'We fail people all the time, Nikki. We can't help everyone. People need someone to blame when bad things happen to either themselves or a loved one, you know that. The police are common targets.'

She shook her head. 'This is different. Because there is a kind of presence about it. Because he or she has chosen stationery that makes their letter stand out from the other mail. Because it was carefully thought out, not a spontaneous outburst like you get when someone goes down in court. Those three words are so full of hate and accusation that they make my blood run cold.' She stared at him. 'I *know* this is serious, Joseph. Gut feeling. Someone has just introduced themselves to us, and it's not the last we are going to hear of them. This is the opening gambit.'

Joseph knew her well enough not to argue. 'So, we wait for them to make the next move?'

She nodded. It would come, most likely in the form of a second letter. 'There's no point in us trying to guess what this is about, and our opponent will know that. So, as you say, we wait.' She gave him a resigned smile. 'I get the feeling this one is deeply personal, don't you? It's not directed at the force in general, it's directed to Nikki Galena. Looks like I've seriously pissed someone off at some point in my glorious career. The problem is, if I made a list of possible names, I'd still be here a week next bloody Tuesday!'

Joseph sank down into a chair. 'You're not wrong there. With an arrest rate like yours, plus your earlier, well, let's say, "no holds barred" approach to taking down drug dealers, you've disrupted a whole lot of criminals' lives, and those of their nearest and dearest.'

'That's without all the innocent victims' families, the ones we never managed to give closure to, or at least tell them what happened to their loved ones. I get the feeling that's probably the case with this.' She jabbed the letter with her finger. '"You failed me." That sounds like someone who put all their trust in us, or me in particular, and I never delivered.' She groaned. 'Hell, I hate waiting games, but we have no choice with this one. One thing's for sure, I'll be watching the post like a hawk from now on.'

* * *

Yvonne Collins went into Dinah Barrett's garden through the back gate. You rarely used front doors in this village. As she walked up the path to the house, she heard swearing, and Yvonne smiled to herself. It sounded as if the Squirrel Wars were still in action.

Dinah stood on her patio, a large plastic water cannon in her arms, and a look of determination on her face. 'Vonnie! Stand where you are for one moment. If this little perisher takes one step closer to my bird feeders, I'll have him! He's wrecked five feeders this week. Squirrel-proof, my arse! He wrenches the lids off and turns the whole thing upside down. The seed and nuts he wastes are costing me an arm and a leg.'

Yvonne waited. She'd been here many times and it still made her laugh. Over the years, the cute fluffy little Squirrel Nutkin that used to be a welcome visitor to Dinah's garden had morphed into a devious anti-hero, now referred to as vermin — and that was on one of Dinah's good days — a bastard rat with a hairy tail.

A blast of water, followed by the sound of scurrying paws making off along the top of a fence. The battle was won, for the time being.

'I suppose your lot don't have a special unit that deals with *Sciurus carolinensis* and the premeditated criminal damage they commit?'

'A Grey Squirrel Squad?' Yvonne grinned. 'Not to my knowledge, Dinah, but if we did, I imagine they'd be kept pretty busy.'

They both laughed. 'Kettle's on. Come in and have a cuppa.'

Yvonne followed her friend into the kitchen. 'Di, if your students could see you now, a manic look in your eyes and water cannon at the ready, you'd lose all your street cred in one fell swoop.'

'Luckily none of my pupils reside in this village, so hopefully my reputation will remain intact.' Dinah took a couple of mugs from the cupboard.

Dinah Barrett was an old school friend of Yvonne's whom she'd kept in touch with, albeit infrequently, into adulthood. Yvonne had gone into the police force, Dinah into teaching. Now older, and approaching retirement, they had become quite close again.

'So, Vonnie, I'm guessing you have your official hat on today, even if it isn't the one I'm used to seeing.' Dinah passed her a mug of tea.

'Well, let's say I'd like you to keep your ear to the ground for me.' Yvonne sat herself down at the kitchen table and nursed her tea. 'For starters, have you been concerned about any of your youngsters recently? As in something bad going on at home and it's affecting them and their schoolwork?'

'Only around half of them,' said Dinah, and rolled her eyes. 'Our school is in the heart of Greenborough, and we have town kids, village kids and children from every conceivable background attending. Some we know have dark histories, others are from seriously dysfunctional families, and in some we suspect undiagnosed behavioural problems. I see cause for concern a dozen times a day.'

'It sounds like an impossible task, put like that.' Yvonne remembered how many youngsters she'd tried to guide away from a life of crime.

'Can you tell me why you're asking now? Or is it hush-hush?' asked Dinah, opening a packet of digestive biscuits.

'It's twofold really, both to do with statistics that are not playing according to the rules. For a start, rates of domestic violence are higher than they've ever been, and then we might have some kind of predator out there watching women and girls. That last one stays strictly between us, though, Di. It could be nothing, possibly just someone hunting for a missing sister, daughter or significant other, but if you hear anything on your very efficient school grapevine, could you let me know?'

'Of course. And strictly off the record, although I said half the school worries me, just occasionally I get bad vibes about one particular child.' She bit into a biscuit. 'You know what I mean? An unexplained change in a child who is seemingly well balanced and socially well-adapted?'

Yvonne said she understood what Dinah was saying. In the past, she had had dealings with good kids who had suddenly gone off the rails for no apparent reason, and so often the answer lay at home. A marital split, a household at war, these things could have a terrible effect on a child. 'And you have that feeling about a child right now?'

'Two children, actually. Their class teacher brought it to my attention a few weeks ago. It's been bothering her for a while. However, neither of us think it's anything to do with their home life, although you never know what really goes on behind closed doors, do you? Both appear to have supportive parents and responsible siblings, but the work of both girls is slipping way below standard. I've been wondering if it's boy trouble, or maybe bad company? I'm hoping it's just a phase and they'll come through it quickly, as they are both bright, intelligent girls. I hate to see their grades suffer.'

They talked about other things for a while, Yvonne finished her tea, and Dinah promised to ring her if she heard or suspected anything worrying. Yvonne was on the point of leaving when her friend said, 'I've just had a thought. If you have time, call in on old Gladys Chisholm on your way back to the station. She'll be working in the farm shop on the Chisholm Estate this morning. The other day she was going on about her great-granddaughter being stalked. It might be coincidence, or just something the girl made up to attract attention to herself, but you never know, it could be connected to your possible predator. I hope not, but just in case, why not have a word with her?'

Yvonne readily agreed. The Chisholm Farm Estate was only a couple of miles outside Greenborough. 'I had no idea Gladys was still working. She must be in her late eighties to early nineties if she's a day.'

'Ninety-three,' said Dinah. 'Those old-style farming women never give up. She's still sharp as a tack, does all the ordering for that farm shop, and nothing much gets past our Gladys.'

Yvonne thanked her friend, and made her way to her car, the sound of 'Bloody squirrel! Get off that feeder!' following her down the path.

The journey to the farm shop took less than ten minutes. As Di had said, Gladys Chisholm was making her rounds, albeit with a stick, looking at all the shelves, checking what provisions needed ordering, and writing them on a large pad.

'Hello, me duck! It's Vonnie, isn't it? Haven't seen you for a while, girl. What, no uniform? Have they thrown you out at last?' Gladys cackled.

'Retired from uniform, Gladys, but back working as a civilian. Can't seem to let the old job go.' Yvonne grinned. 'Bit like you, I reckon.'

'Ah well, if it's in yer blood, it's what you do, duck. Now what can I get you? Got some nice fresh purple sprouting broccoli just in, straight from our own fields, or if you fancy something quick, our Josh has made up some tasty chicken stir-fry. That goes so fast he can hardly keep up with it.'

Yvonne said she certainly would buy some of that, and some fresh veg, but what she really wanted was to talk to Gladys about her great-grandchild's suspicions that she had a stalker.

Gladys's mouth turned down. 'The police are interested in that, Vonnie? Does that mean other girls have made complaints too?'

Dinah had been right, no flies on this old lady. 'It's all a bit vague, to be honest, Gladys. Just suggestions and fears about being followed and watched but nothing concrete.'

'Bit like my Samantha then. She's sure someone is stalking her, and she's not a fanciful girl. Some of the rest of the family think it's all to get attention, but I know real fear when I sees it, and my Sammie is proper frightened.'

'How old is she now, Gladys? She was a toddler when I knew her.'

'She's coming up to twenty next month, and pretty as a picture. Definitely gets it from my side of the family,' Gladys said.

Yvonne hoped that the girl would inherit her great-grandmother's longevity as well. 'So, what has she told you?'

'Bit like what you said, really.' Gladys scratched her wrinkled chin. 'A shadowy figure that disappears if she looks directly at it. Footsteps behind her, just out of sight. A rustling in the bushes close to where she's walking. All manner of other things too, like the driver of a car slowing down when he gets level with her, then driving off, only to come back a short while later. Never sees a face. She thought he might have a muffler or a scarf over part of his face so she can't get a proper look at him. It's worrying, Yvonne. See if you can find out what's going on, will you?'

'My sarge and one of the DCs are already out taking statements, Gladys. I called in here because Dinah Barrett told me about Sammie. I'll tell DS Easter as soon as I get back to the station and he'll go and have a word with her. Can you give me her address?'

The old lady rattled off the name of a Greenborough street and the number. 'She's working part-time for my nephew for a week or so, so tell your sergeant to call after half past two, she'll be home by then.' She looked suspiciously at Yvonne. 'He's all right, is he, this sergeant? Only she's quite a timid — no, that's not the right word, a *private* sort of girl. I'd be happier if you went.'

Yvonne smiled warmly. 'Don't worry, Gladys. Your Sammie will love my sergeant. He's the nicest man in the force, other than my Niall Farrow, of course. Remember my young crewmate, Gladys? Used to come in with me to buy those big bags of kiddies' sweets? Sammie will be in good hands.'

Yvonne bought some fresh produce, including a generous portion of Josh Chisholm's stir-fry mix, and headed back to base. Having set out simply to ask Dinah Barrett to watch out for signs of domestic problems among her students, she had returned with the name of another possible victim of Greenborough's mysterious stalker. That was the way it often went. In any case, Joseph would be pleased. For all her years, Gladys Chisholm was a shrewd old bird, and wouldn't have told her about Samantha if she didn't think it important.

* * *

As the working day drew to a close, Nikki still found herself mulling over the words from that airmail letter.

"You failed me."

Who had she failed? What did this person want from her? Revenge? Restitution? An apology? Or was she about to become the focus of some scary vendetta?

Nikki tidied her desk, but hung on until she was sure that no more post was filtering through. Then she pulled on her jacket, said goodnight to Lesley Curtis, and made her way down to the CID room to tell Joseph that she was leaving.

She arrived home at Cloud Fen Cottage a short while before him. He had been about to leave when a call came in from one of the women that he had on his list to interview the following day, so she had gone on ahead.

She hung her coat on the hook by the door and picked up that morning's post from the mat. She had expected the flyers, the electricity bill, but she hadn't expected to see an airmail envelope.

Nikki swallowed, gazing at the flimsy, lightweight envelope with its familiar red, white and blue border. She recognised the handwriting immediately. She wanted to tear it open — no, she wanted to wait for Joseph. No, she really wanted to pretend it didn't exist at all, and simply burn the thing.

She went through to the kitchen, slipped on a pair of nitrile gloves from her pocket and, taking a sharp knife, opened it.

The opening message was identical: *"You failed me."*

But this time, below these words, a list of four names:

Alexandra Cornfield
Ruth Baker
Bethany Lyons
Leanne Delaney

Nikki closed her eyes and tried to recall who these women were, but only one of the names meant something to her. The name Ruth Baker brought back an old case from maybe fifteen years back, one she'd had nothing to do with. In fact, she thought it might have fallen under the jurisdiction of the lot at Fenfleet.

Staring at the letter in her hand, Nikki was oblivious to the front door opening, and Joseph's cheerful greeting.

She passed it to him when he came in.

'Ah. Well, I never saw that coming,' he said.

'This person knows my address, Joseph. We've been in this situation before, haven't we?'

'Twice! But this time we have the security cameras up and ready to roll. One click of a mouse and they are activated again, no sweat. In fact, I'll switch on the computer and do it right now.'

He was back in minutes. 'All cameras active. Now, let me see that letter properly.'

He skimmed down the names and pointed to the one she had recognised. 'Ruth Baker, went missing after a quiz night at a local pub in her village.' He squinted, concentrating. 'Can't recall the village, but it wasn't far from Fenfleet. Case still open, and no body was recovered. I think the last update that was sent round said that nothing had been heard of her, no sightings and no credit card use to this day, so it was assumed she had died, most likely murdered, and the case would be regularly reviewed.'

She nodded. That was all she recalled too. 'Joseph, I have to get back to the station.'

'Hold up, Nikki. You need to eat. I'm betting you've had nothing all day apart from a sandwich. We can get the basics about these other women from here, then we can do a full search first thing tomorrow morning.'

'I need to get into the PNC, Joseph. I want background info that only we have on tap. These names can't be random, they have to have some connection to either the person who sent this note, or to the poor soul they believe I failed them over.' She looked at him intently. 'I cannot sit on this all night and do nothing. I just can't.'

'Then we go together, in my car, and only on the understanding that I pick up a takeaway on the way in. Deal?'

She smiled. 'Deal.'

In forty minutes, they were in her old office, along with a bucket of KFC and two coffees. They had intended to split the list in two, but then decided to work together, taking each woman in turn and seeing what they could discover.

After two hours they had amassed everything the PNC could provide.

'All missing persons,' said Joseph. 'All suspected of having been abducted and killed, but no bodies were found, and no answers. Four old unsolved cases that got relegated because something more immediate needed attention.'

'And I wasn't involved in a single one of those cases,' murmured Nikki. 'They're all Fenland investigations, but none of them took place in Greenborough. That's weird.'

'I can see nothing to connect them either,' added Joseph. 'Other than them being unsolved mysteries.'

'Tomorrow, I'm going to request all the case files, and we'll look at them in detail. There has to be a connection somewhere.' She looked at the clock. 'I guess we'd better get home again. I'd hoped for more than this — hell, I'm as much in the dark as when we arrived.'

Joseph stood up and cleared up the remains of their supper. 'And as absolutely nothing we found this evening points to you, I'm wondering if you've been singled out as a scapegoat for the failings of an entire force. Apart from being female mispers, the only other common denominator is that they are all unsolved cases Fenland Constabulary was investigating.'

It made perfect sense. If a loved one or relative of one of these women needed an outlet for their anger at the police's failure, why not pick on an individual to direct it at?

Yes, it did make perfect sense, but Nikki remained unconvinced. In her heart of hearts she knew this one was personal.

CHAPTER THREE

Apart from a couple of minor additions to her reports, Cat was now free of outstanding cases. She was happy to get out of the office for a while and talk to real people. This morning she would be out with the sarge, talking to women who suspected that they were being followed by a stalker and it was making them extremely anxious, if not afraid. That kind of thing made Cat's blood boil. Women had enough shit going on in their lives without being terrorized by some creep. If she had her way, a particularly painful form of punishment would be reserved for such predators.

She knocked on the door to Nikki's office and heard Joseph call for her to come in. It still felt odd to see the sarge behind the boss's desk.

'Ah, Cat, sit down for a minute, would you? I'm afraid there's been a slight change of plan.'

Joseph seemed tense. Cat wondered what was up.

'I'm going to ask you if you would take over interviewing these women.' Joseph passed her a list of names, contact details and addresses. 'I've written appointment times against the ones I've spoken to, so they'll be expecting you. Maybe take Yvonne with you?'

'Certainly, Sarge. But has something occurred? You look worried.'

He grunted. 'To tell you the truth, Cat, we're not sure what we're up against at present, and I have a sneaking suspicion that the shit could hit the fan at any moment.' He took a sheet of paper from a file that lay open on the desk. 'Nikki received this yesterday morning. Followed by this one, sent to her home.'

Cat read the first short note, then the second, and pulled a face. 'I see what you mean. Looks like someone is smarting big-time over an unsolved case or police cock-up, and needs someone to blame. Question is, is this a high-profile campaign to force the police to take a fresh look at an old investigation? Or do we have a raving nutter out there who believes he's a vigilante and is gunning for us?'

'Nicely put,' said Joseph wryly. 'Basically, that's exactly what we were thinking, with one small exception. We think that whoever it is, they're targeting Nikki, not the police.'

'Bugger! Er, sorry, Sarge, I meant, that's not good.'

'Indeed. Anyway, Nikki and I are going to do some in-depth research into the women he listed in his letter. The only one we both know anything about is Ruth Baker.'

'I remember that one, Sarge. And I see he mentioned Bethany Lyons, so if I were you, I'd talk to Sergeant Lucy Wells about her. She was the Family Liaison Officer on that case, I'm sure. There was a massive flu outbreak in one of the other Fenland stations and she was sent to help out with the family of the missing girl.'

'I didn't know that,' said Joseph. 'Thanks, Cat, that's really helpful. So, are you okay to tackle the alleged stalker's victims?'

She skimmed the list of interviewees. 'No problem. I'll go and rope in Vonnie and we'll get straight on to it. By the way, I know one of these young women, and if she says someone is watching her, someone is. She takes no shit from anyone.'

'Good, that's the kind of person we need to give us facts, not fantasies.'

Cat stood up. 'I'll report in directly we get back, Sarge.'

She left Joseph still looking perturbed and went off to find Yvonne.

The first address they visited was that of a Julie Ravenhill. She turned out to be a rather pretty brunette, in what Cat presumed to be her early twenties. She invited them in and offered them a drink.

'We're okay, thanks,' said Cat, knowing that after around six calls they could be awash with tea and desperate for the loo. 'We'd just like to hear what you believe to be happening regarding this person who's stalking you.'

The girl rubbed her hands together nervously.

'I've actually taken a few days off work I'm so upset. I've never done anything like that before. I love my job, but I feel so intimidated I'm scared to even go out.' Julie stared at the floor. 'Dad is working, Mum is out shopping, and I've done nothing but look out of the windows. I'm totally freaked out by this person.'

'Have you any idea who it might be?' asked Cat gently. 'You know, like a jilted boyfriend? Someone who is jealous of a present relationship, maybe?'

'I'm not in a relationship,' Julie said rather bitterly. 'And my last unfortunate attempt at an affair ended with him dumping me, so no, I have no idea at all.'

'And you've never actually seen him?' enquired Yvonne.

'Sounds stupid, doesn't it? But no, I've never seen him properly, just a shadow, a figure that disappears as soon as you notice it. My friend thought I was making it up. She said stalkers like you to see them, to know that they're there and watching you.' Julie looked pained. 'But this is even more creepy, honestly. It's so subtle, it's kind of a mind-bender.'

Cat knew this girl was not making it up. She was well and truly scared. 'How many times have you thought he was watching you?' Cat asked.

'Well, for over a week now, it's been almost every time I've gone out. Here, and in my work's car park, out shopping, anywhere I go.' She looked from one to the other. 'It's far worse at night. I was coming home the other evening after meeting my friend, and I was sure he was almost close enough to touch me.'

'Look, Julie, do you think you can make a list of all the places you've been, and as near as you can, the times and dates you were there? There's a chance he's turned up on CCTV, especially as you say he was in your work's car park. We might just be able to get a look at him.'

Julie nodded. 'Yes, I can do that. Should I email it to you?'

Cat said that would be great and gave the girl her card. 'Be as precise as possible, especially with the locations. CCTV footage can be hugely helpful with something like this.' She looked at her seriously. 'I have to tell you, though, that this isn't the sort of thing CID normally deals with, so we can't promise too much, but we'll do our best for you.'

'I was hoping that others might have reported the same thing, then I wouldn't feel so isolated,' Julie said, a little hesitantly. 'Have they?'

Yvonne nodded. 'Yes, several women have said the same as you, and we are talking to them all. Maybe then we'll get an idea of what he's up to.'

'And the good news is, if he's targeting a lot of women, it's probably not a personal thing. Plus, the more women he goes after, the more chance there is of him being spotted.' Cat hoped she sounded reassuring, though she guessed it would take more than a few platitudes to stop this young woman from being too terrified to go out alone.

* * *

Nikki flicked swiftly through the incoming post, but this time there was no airmail letter. At first, she felt relief, but this was soon replaced by anxiety. All they had was a list of names. This person's motive for sending the letters was a mystery. Was he going to explain, or just leave them desperately trying to make a connection?

She grew angry. Whoever he was, this person was playing with them, manipulating them, and one thing Nikki Galena objected to was being used.

'That's a look I've not seen for a while.' Joseph stood in the doorway. 'But I recognise the emotion behind it. I'm feeling the same myself.'

Nikki indicated for him to come in. 'I have to get my head around this, Joseph, and start behaving like a police officer, not some extra on a film set, their every move directed by some mysterious figure off-screen. I'm not having this bastard pulling our strings for too long.'

'Well, I've phoned the evidence store to see what they have on those missing girls, and there's pretty well nothing. It's certainly not worth requesting it to be brought here, not yet at any rate. We need to concentrate on the reports, and those are all easily accessible.' He placed a pile of printouts on her desk. 'Zena has already printed these off for you, and I've got a set too. They're the original files on Alexandra Cornfield. I've started there as she was first on his list of names. The time span between the others varies. Ruth Baker seems to be the oldest but I thought you'd want to start at the beginning of his list and work down.'

'Absolutely. We'll need to talk to the officers who dealt with these investigations too.' Nikki looked at the first officer named. 'Well, at least this one is still alive. And still working, albeit a little further up the ladder than when he dealt with this.' She smiled. She knew Jim Summers quite well, although since his rise through the ranks in the Fenfleet area, she hadn't seen him for a while. 'He's a nice bloke, even if he is now a chief superintendent.'

'Then, if it's okay with you,' suggested Joseph, 'I'll leave that side of things to you. I'll concentrate on making lists of known facts from this case, then we can run comparisons with the other mispers and try to find connections or links.'

'That's fine, and I suggest you keep Cat and Yvonne beavering away at their enquiries about the stalker and the local domestic violence statistics, while we tackle this between us.' She was about to continue when she was interrupted by a tap on the door and Cam's office manager, Lesley, walked in.

'Sorry to interrupt, ma'am, but a motorcycle courier delivered this to reception a little earlier. It's been screened by the mail room and it's safe.' She put it on the desk and left.

Nikki and Joseph stared at the thick manila package.

'He's not hanging around, is he?' Nikki said quietly.

There was no doubt as to who had sent the packet. Not only was the handwriting the same, but there was also a small bright blue sticker attached: "*By Air Mail, Par Avion.*"

Nikki took a deep breath, opened the package and pulled out a green cardboard folder full of documents.

'That looks like a case file,' murmured Joseph.

On the top was a piece of paper, printed to resemble a newspaper report. The date was today, and the heading read "Fenland Police Discover Body in Remote Location."

She read the rest out to Joseph. *'After receiving information from a member of the public, police today have found the body of a young woman, believed to be that of missing teenager Alexandra Cornfield, who disappeared almost ten years ago. This information led them to an overgrown area of land at the back of a derelict barn on farmland close to Blackstone Fen.'*

She opened the folder, and stared, first at the header, printed in bold, that read "Part One," then at the "article" itself. Joseph had been right. It was just like one of their reports. 'Come and look at this,' she whispered.

Joseph at her side, she flicked through the papers, all neatly typed and printed off, and written in an official manner, as if by an investigating officer. It was signed by someone who referred to himself as "Detective Oliver."

Nikki stared at the name. Oliver? A first name or a surname? She had no recollection of any Oliver. She glanced at Joseph, who shrugged and said it meant nothing to him.

'Oh, my God!' Nikki had turned to the next pages and found what were obviously meant to be crime scene photographs. Pictures of the location — miles of farmland. An abandoned wreck of a barn. A small area of woodland, probably little more than a thicket of windblown, stunted trees and bushes. And an overgrown area of bramble and nettles. Nikki swallowed, dreading what the next page would show.

'What *is* this?' Joseph whispered.

They were staring at the same patch of ground but cleared of overgrowth. The next shot showed it partly excavated. And the one after that showed a shallow grave and what appeared to be a bony hand protruding from the loosened soil.

'Oh shit! I know exactly what we are going to see next,' she hissed.

She was right. Oliver, whoever he was, had carefully removed the soil from around a corpse.

The last photograph showed a gold chain with a tiny heart hanging from it, still in situ around the bones of the neck.

Joseph snatched up the notes Zena had printed and thumbed through them. After a while, he said, 'Yes, Alexandra always wore a heart on a chain. It had been a gift from her boyfriend.'

Nikki's thoughts were a maelstrom, tumbling around in her head.

Who was this Oliver? How had he found the body of a missing girl that the entire Fenland Constabulary had failed to discover in almost a decade? What was his purpose? Did he know where to find her because he was the one who put her there?

Nikki swallowed hard and turned another page. A "pathologist's report," describing what he had noted from the remains, and his thoughts on the manner of her death.

The last page had a small, sealed clear plastic bag attached. In it, the chain and the heart.

'Forensics,' she muttered. 'I want a report on that necklace faster than the speed of light.' She looked at the block capital letters in bold along the bottom of the final page. It read, "PART TWO TO FOLLOW."

What the hell did that mean?

'I think Rory should have the whole thing, don't you?' Joseph said. 'There might be some trace evidence on the paper or the envelope.'

'Absolutely. Let's just try and identify the location, and then you and I, and maybe a uniformed crew, are going to have to take a little reconnaissance field trip.'

'And what will we find when we get there?' said Joseph. 'A hoax? A trap? Or a missing girl?'

'I'm asking myself the very same questions,' said Nikki, standing up and pulling her coat from the back of her chair. 'Well, we won't get an answer farting around here, will we? I'll check out the exact location of this barn at Blackstone Fen, while you bag up the file and get it to Rory. Tell him we need copies of the whole thing to work with, and that the heart and chain are especially important for identification, okay?'

Joseph nodded. 'Got it. I'll pass by uniform and get Niall to give us a crew to go with us.'

'Good. Ring me when you leave Rory and I'll meet you downstairs at my car. Let's move on this.' Joseph was just about to open the door when she added, 'And tell our lovely pathologist that if those photos are the real McCoy, there's a good chance we'll be calling him out to the victim of a ten-year-old unsolved murder enquiry in the next hour or so. That should make his day.'

* * *

Blackstone Fen was an arable farming area about fifteen minutes' drive out of Greenborough. There was no village as such, just scatterings of houses and cottages. Someone looking down on it from the air might imagine that they had been strewn over the massive area like a handful of seeds that had fallen randomly here and there.

Nikki knew it, but not well, and as she drove, she recalled other journeys across these acres of farmland to the marshes. She had a friend, more Rory Wilkinson's friend than hers, the artist, Jenny Jackson. Jenny had helped them with another serious murder case. She liked Jenny a lot. Jenny lived in a remote spot called Malford Farm, in an old ivy-clad Queen Anne farmhouse that sat alone on the bank of a wide dyke lined with willows. If they came unstuck finding the derelict barn, Nikki was certain that Jenny would help them.

'I feel a little apprehensive, don't you?' Joseph muttered.

'I'm not sure how I feel,' said Nikki. 'My overriding emotion is anger towards this person who has us jumping every time he contacts us.' She pulled a face. 'Although deep down I'm certain we're on our way to meet Alexandra Cornfield.'

'Well, the prof said he was almost certain that the images aren't digitally manipulated. So, yes, I'm sure of it too.'

Nikki glanced in her rear-view mirror. The police car behind her was being driven by PC Kyle Adams, Vonnie's former young crewmate, now teamed up with a likeable and reliable officer called Emmie Greengrass. It had been Vonnie's wish before she retired that he be partnered with someone who appreciated his qualities. The lad had the makings of a great copper, and Emmie realised that. All in all, Nikki was pleased to have some backup. She was sure they would find a body, but very unsure about the sanity of this Oliver character. He could have left them more than just a body to find.

Nikki had spoken to several officers who had been this way fairly recently checking out a spate of oil thefts, and she had a pretty good idea where the barn was. What she didn't know was who owned the land, though she had an idea it was up for sale. She had left Lesley making all the relevant calls regarding authorisation to access it and doubted there would be a problem.

'What's that over there?' Joseph pointed across a massive field to a small cluster of buildings surrounding a small farmhouse.

'I'm hoping that's it,' said Nikki, looking for a lane leading to what she believed was the old March Estate.

She found it about a quarter of a mile further along, with a big wooden "For Sale" sign by the driveway. It declared that the land was for agricultural use only, which pleased her. So much land, some of it inappropriate to build on, had been so eaten up with housing that it was changing the face of her beloved Fens. Not that anyone would want to live in an estate out here, with no amenities and no neighbours at all.

The drive was overgrown. Obviously, March Farm had stood empty for a good while.

'I would suggest that those tyre tracks we are following don't belong to an estate agent's car,' said Joseph grimly.

Nikki agreed. It had rained the previous day and the ground was still soft. The impressions looked like those of a pretty hefty vehicle, and it had been here recently.

She pulled up at the back of the house and got out. The sudden blast of cold air reminded her that there was nothing between this spot and the Wash and the North Sea, so the wind could be relentless. She pulled her coat closer to her and set off across the yard to several old barns and what looked like dilapidated stores.

If nothing else, they had the right location.

'I'd say the first photograph we were sent was taken facing this way.' She pointed across the open farmland. 'And the barn in the second has to be that one.' She indicated a building on the far perimeter of the yard, the one in the worst repair.

'That's it all right,' said Joseph. 'And there *is* a scrubby wooded area with trees and bushes to the back.' He looked at her. 'Ready for this?'

'As always,' she returned grimly. She beckoned to Emmie and Kyle who were approaching them. 'This is just a recce, okay? We're only sussing out whether or not we have a crime site. Tread warily and keep your eyes peeled. Don't ask me what for because I have no idea. I simply do not trust the man who has led us here.'

They proceeded across to the ramshackle old barn and walked around the back.

'Careful, guys!' called out Joseph, who was leading the way. 'This place is a dumping ground for old bits of farm machinery. Watch where you walk, some of this junk is lethal.' He pointed to row of rusting tines from an old cultivator sticking up from the ground like sharks' teeth.

Nikki saw a discarded scythe, its blunted blade a sad, dull crescent moon, next to a tangle of dangerous spiked metal that had once been a chain harrow used to aerate the ground and spread soil and fertiliser.

Slowly they picked their way to the copse beyond.

Again, Joseph went first. He had come to policing via a career in Special Forces, and this kind of thing came naturally to him. Nikki never argued. Indeed, she always felt safe when Joseph was "on patrol."

It didn't take long for him to find the trail left by Oliver and, in a few minutes, they were looking at the spot where Alexandra had been buried. Except that there was no open grave. There was nothing.

Nikki stared, bewildered. It was the right spot, no doubt of that, exactly where the partially excavated grave had been in the picture, but it was just an overgrown mat of grass and weeds. She looked at Joseph and saw that he was smiling.

'The cunning bastard! He's filled it in again, Nikki. He stripped off the top layer of thick grass as if you were cutting turf for a lawn, then put it back afterwards. If you look closer you can see the joins. And look, next to it, this flattened area of rough grass is probably where he laid a groundsheet to pile the soil on before refilling the hole. He wants us to do the excavation ourselves.'

Nikki swore. 'And excavate we bloody will. Oh, I do hate jokers.' Though even as she spoke, Nikki knew this was no joke.

Joseph was carefully easing a long swath of carefully cut grass away from the ground. 'Yes, it's loose soil underneath this, so it's definitely been dug very recently. The question is, will we find a body or another surprise?'

Nikki straightened up. 'We have to assume it's a body, so we need the professionals to tackle this. I'm going to ring Rory and get his team to do the delicate bits. And, Emmie? Call in to your sergeant and ask for a unit to bring cordoning, a protective tent and all the relevant gear, please. This is now a crime scene. Let's just hope our Oliver isn't conducting some game of his at our expense.'

CHAPTER FOUR

As soon as he caught sight of their good friend, Professor Rory Wilkinson, loping across the yard, Joseph's spirits lifted. The Home Office pathologist was the best there was, so it was a relief to see that he had decided to join his team at the site.

'Good morning, Rory,' he called out. 'We are honoured!'

'Well, dear heart, presented with such a story, what else could one do? I simply cannot wait to discover what's lying hidden in this shallow grave.' Rory gave Joseph a conspiratorial smile. 'Spike, Cardiff and I have a bet running. Frankly, I think my idea will turn out to be the winner — it has to be a stash of Judy Garland memorabilia. I mean, what else?' Then, more seriously, he said, 'I imagine our beloved DI is not a happy bunny right now?'

Joseph grimaced. 'Neither of us is. Getting those photographs, and then finding that he has filled the grave in again, has spooked us both. He could have replaced that skeleton with anything, including something very dangerous.'

'I'm well aware of that, Joseph. Why do you think I'm heading this one up?' All trace of humour was now absent from Rory's tone. 'Once the first layers of soil are removed, it's going to be me who handles the next stage — alone.'

'I'll assist,' said Joseph immediately. 'And no arguing.'

Rory held up his hands. 'I'd rather you didn't, but I won't object.' He looked around. 'Where's Nikki?'

'Talking to the uniformed contingent. And trying to discover why this spot is already being targeted by the press. We had two reporters turn up within twenty minutes of our arrival.' Joseph frowned. There was little doubt that Oliver himself had tipped them off, but Nikki wanted to know for sure.

'Well, from the look on her face, I'd suggest she has her answers,' muttered Rory. 'Here she comes, wearing an expression cold enough to turn the Mojave Desert to ice.'

'That bloody man is pulling the sodding strings again,' Nikki growled. 'Sorry, Rory, I'm glad to see you, it's just that this damned Oliver, whoever he is, has really got under my skin.' She turned to Joseph. 'As we thought, an anonymous call to the two local rags, telling them about the possible discovery of a body suspected to be that of Alexandra Cornfield. The caller gave this precise location.'

'Then we must procrastinate no longer,' declared Rory. 'I see dear Spike and Cardiff approaching now with all the equipment we need, so we'd better get suited up and digging — gently, of course. Lead on to the site, Joseph, if you would be so kind.'

Using the photographs to ascertain the depth of the grave, Rory instructed his two colleagues to peel the sections of cut turf from the top, then carefully lift away the first layers of soft soil.

The team of three looked like archaeologists unearthing the most precious of ancient historical finds.

'All right, cherubs. Time to retreat to a safe distance and allow the master to continue.'

Spike objected, but after a glance at Rory's face, he backed away. 'Okay, boss, but I'd like it on the record that I'm ready and willing to continue.'

'Me too,' added Cardiff. 'Since I'm certain all we'll find are bones.'

'Duly logged, now bugger off.' Rory shooed them away.

Watched closely by Joseph and Nikki, the latter adamant that she wouldn't be relegated to a back seat, the pathologist brushed away at the loose soil. A tense silence fell.

Then came a sharp intake of breath. 'There's something here,' Rory said. 'Well, I've lost the wager. No sign of Judy, it's finger bones.'

It took him another half hour to reveal the top portion of what looked more and more likely to be the remains of Alexandra Cornfield. Remnants of her clothing still clung to her skeleton. From what he had read, Joseph recalled that the girl had last been seen wearing a very distinctive denim jacket with an embroidered patch on the breast pocket. The years might have melted her flesh and blood to nothing, but the mouldering garments remained, tattered and almost colourless, but still identifiable as denim.

Nikki let out a sigh. 'That motif on the pocket . . .'

It could still be made out quite clearly. 'Crescent moon and stars,' said Joseph. 'It's her.' They would need the forensic evidence, but he knew there was little doubt. Oliver had found the missing girl. Or had he led them to the place where he had killed her? As Oliver himself had said, *Part Two to follow.*

'I don't think this was here when the body was interred, dear hearts.'

Rory's voice broke into his thoughts.

Joseph watched him carefully extricate what looked like a slip of paper from beneath the tattered material of the girl's jacket. It was an envelope. Damp though it was, and smeared with soil, Joseph could clearly see the two words: *Par Avion.*

'It's not sealed,' said Rory. 'I should bag it immediately and examine it only in sterile conditions, but I think you need to know what this says.'

No one objected.

There was a pause while he opened it. 'As before, I'm afraid. It's addressed to you, Nikki, with a single sheet of paper inside, which says—'

'I know,' she said grimly. '"You failed me."'

'As you say.' He slipped it back into the envelope and put the letter in an evidence bag which, since there was no longer any danger, he handed to Cardiff.

'So, what do we know from the body, Rory?' asked Joseph.

'Well, Oliver didn't exhume her any further than this point. He must have decided that this was all the proof he needed to show you what he had found. The ground beneath is undisturbed, and it will take a good while to get this dear girl out of this sad, impromptu resting place and back to my sanctum.'

'Does it look as if she's been here long, as in ten years?' asked Nikki.

'Certainly. And undisturbed until Oliver showed up.' He stood up and stretched his back. 'I suggest that now you good people go and do whatever detectives do at this point. There will be nothing more from me until considerably later. I have a lot of very delicate work to do, and arrangements to make for getting this poor soul to safety at last.'

It was hard to picture this tangle of decaying cloth and bones as the fun-loving girl with a dazzling smile that all the photographs of Alexandra depicted. Joseph thought of his daughter, the beautiful Tamsin. *God, how would he feel if—?* He blocked the thought and pulled himself together. Rory was right. There were things that had to be done.

* * *

Dinah Barrett's morning had been full on. Now, just as she was considering taking a break for lunch, she heard a tentative knock on her door. She guessed who it was immediately, and her heart sank.

Lynette Sims was a young teacher that Dinah rather admired, and she was taking considerable pains to support her in her teaching career. Recently, Lynette had become very concerned about one of her pupils. Dinah's recent conversation with Yvonne Collins about troubled students came back to her, and she had a good idea of the cause of the gentle tap on her door. Dinah called out to her to come in.

Lynette's drawn face said it all.

'More concerns about Ruby Grayson?' Dinah asked, and gestured to a seat at the table.

Lynette sat down. 'I'm afraid so, Miss Barrett. I now get the feeling that she wants to talk to me about something and can't quite bring herself to open up. I'm not sure whether I should actively encourage her, or just be available for her and allow it to happen when she feels the time is right. The problem with the latter is that I could leave it too late, and she won't ever find the courage to speak out about what is bothering her.'

It was a fine line, but if you wanted positive behaviour you needed to know your students. Teachers occupied a unique and privileged position. They could spot, and sometimes diagnose, all kinds of problems and provide help where they could. It got rather more difficult when you suspected trouble at home. In the course of her long career, Dinah had worked with hundreds of different children, some of them troubled. In this time, she had seen radical changes in what a teacher was permitted to do, but communication, she firmly believed, remained paramount.

Dinah felt for the young teacher sitting across the table from her. 'Okay, Lynette, let's look at this methodically and tick a few boxes. Does Ruby show any signs of neglect or abuse?'

'None whatsoever,' Lynette said promptly. 'She is clean and tidy, doesn't wear inappropriate or inadequate clothing, and she's active during sports lessons. There's no bruising or evidence of pain restricting her movements.'

'Well, that dealt with three of my questions. So, any mention of being left alone at night, or parental absence?'

Again, Lynette shook her head. 'She never talks about her home life at all, but she doesn't appear to be tired or suffering from lack of sleep. She certainly doesn't nod off in class. However, her concentration, which has always been very good, does seem to have deteriorated.'

'Which brings it down to a sudden change in behaviour,' mused Di.

'Maybe not so sudden, Miss Barrett. I hope I haven't been remiss, but now that I think back, I suspect this has been a slow process over a matter of weeks.' Lynette looked even more anxious. 'It was her work that struck me first. She'd always been an excellent student, but the quality began to deteriorate. Now it's not just that, it's a distinct lack of interest in subjects she had always been engaged with, and she's becoming more and more insular every day.'

Dinah decided it was time to intervene. 'It's our duty to look out for our students' best interests. We want them to be happy and attain their full potential. I accept that you have raised serious concerns about Ruby Grayson and you'll have my full support. I'm happy to speak to the girl either alone or with you, or if you'd rather, you can make the first advance and hopefully get her to open up to you. She likes and trusts you, I know, but this does need addressing without delay. Since you know the girl better than anyone, I'll let you decide on the best course of action.'

'I'll talk to her, Miss Barrett,' Lynette said. 'I guess I just needed a push in the right direction. I feel better for just talking to you and getting your blessing while I try to get her to confide in me.'

'Then keep me updated, and I'm here whenever you need me.' She smiled warmly at Lynette. 'Don't shoulder too much alone, and remember, if there is something seriously wrong in the Grayson household, it's not down to you to try and rectify it. Neither is it down to you to determine the veracity of what you hear from a child. Any worries, Lynette, you come directly to me, and if we need to report something to the relevant agency, we will do that.'

Lynette was on the point of leaving when a thought occurred to Dinah. 'What about her cousin, young Amber?'

'Back to being more or less her old self, Miss Barrett. I've no idea why, but maybe it was something quite different to what is affecting Ruby.' Lynette paused, her hand on the door handle. 'If anything, she's acting more assertively than before. It's quite odd, actually, she's never been a timid soul, but something seems to have boosted her confidence.' She shrugged, 'I'll watch her for any more changes, for better or worse.'

After Lynette had gone, Dinah frowned to herself. Both girls had registered cause for concern; now Ruby was declining, while Amber had recovered and was apparently thriving. Now more than ever, Dinah wanted to know what was going on in the combined Grayson families.

* * *

When Eve and Wendy decided on a new venture, they didn't stint on the equipment. Okay, it might not be a lasting hobby, but neither saw the point in going at it half-cocked. After all, both women liked nothing better than chasing up old mysteries. Eve had argued that if they found they really enjoyed metal detecting, they would probably find themselves investing twice over by having to upgrade their cheap detectors to something with more capabilities, and Wendy agreed. So, although they didn't go for mega-expensive, all-singing, all-dancing professional gear, what they had was good quality, with coils that could operate underwater, excellent all-round detection and high sensitivity.

'Got something!' Eve called out.

She and Wendy were walking in straight lines across a field, about five yards apart, sweeping the ground in front of them. The farmer who owned the field, which adjoined Monks Lantern, had allowed them a morning to see what they could find, and they had been out since first light.

So far they'd had slim pickings, retrieving mainly junk, although Wendy had uncovered an old Victorian penny, of the type enthusiasts called a "Bunhead," referring to the portrait of a younger Queen.

'How deep is it?' asked Wendy.

Eve looked at the display screen. 'Six to eight inches. And the audio tone says it's silver.' She had trouble keeping the excitement out of her voice. This treasure hunting was addictive! They'd only been searching in earnest for just over a week and they were completely hooked.

Wendy laid down her detector and produced a hand-held pinpointer and her short-handled digger. In moments the pointer's tone and vibration told her exactly where the find would be located. All she had to do now was dig down and find it.

Wendy dug carefully, making as small a hole as she could, putting the plug of soil to one side to replace later. The whole idea was to leave the ground just as you had found it.

'Yes! There's something here all right.' She knelt down and carefully scraped the final layer away with her hands. 'Oh my!'

Eve leaned over Wendy's shoulder and watched her reverently lift a circular object from the ground.

'It's a gentleman's fob watch! And it's silver.' Wendy was brushing away the loose dirt that clung to it.

It was tarnished and would need a lot of cleaning and polishing, but it was their best find yet. 'It's beautiful,' said Eve with a satisfied smile. 'And it's engraved. Look.' It still had the small winder at the top, and although they didn't dare open it out here, it was possible that the watch had been undamaged by its years below ground.

Eve took it from Wendy and felt the weight of it in her hand. 'It's heavy, isn't it? I bet we find a hallmark when we clean it.' Some detectorists preferred to leave objects as they found them, others to clean them up. Cleaning could irreversibly damage the watch, but Eve thought such a beautiful piece would appreciate TLC and gentle cleansers. 'Would you bag it, Wendy, and I'll give the surrounding area another swift sweep, just in case whoever lost the watch lost anything else?'

It wasn't likely, but it had been known to happen. Five minutes later, just as she was about to give up, she had another hit. 'Roughly the same depth and, yes, silver again.' This was extraordinary.

As before, Wendy pinpointed it and dug down.

This time it was a ring, a large silver one, caked in soil but they could make out the kind of Celtic knot band design. From its size it had to have belonged to a man. Eve felt quite overwhelmed. She hadn't expected anything like this, and from Wendy's expression, neither had she.

'We have to take these to the farmer and show him what we've found,' said Wendy. 'Then decide how to proceed.'

'At least Chris is an amenable kind of man,' said Eve. 'He didn't object at all, unlike a lot of farmers.' They knew that the usual practice was to share the discoveries, or in the case of a valuable item, get an estimate of its worth and split the proceeds. 'Perrie said some farmers couldn't care less what you find, others make it clear that anything found on their land belongs to them, end of story. I'm sure Chris won't be like that. He is our neighbour, after all.'

Chris Tate descended from a local Beech Lacey farming family that had been working the land around Monks Lantern for generations. Chris was a born farmer if ever there was one. He lived and breathed his work, and probably dreamed about it too.

'It's lunchtime already, shall we call it a day?' asked Wendy. 'I've taken the coordinates of this spot, maybe Chris will allow us to do another sweep and make sure we have everything there is to find. We can call in at the farmhouse on our way home and see what he has to say about our treasure trove.'

Eve agreed with her friend. Chris had given them a morning, so in any case their time was up. 'Maybe we should get our equipment back to Monks Lantern first, then take our finds over to Homelands Farm.'

They gathered up their things and made their way back across the field to a gate that led into their garden. 'I never dreamed we'd find something as interesting as silver jewellery, did you?' she said, as she secured the gate.

'No way!' Wendy exclaimed. 'I was quite happy with my Bunhead coin! All I'd really expected were nails, nuts and bolts from farm equipment, and bits of scrap metal. Finding that watch just blew me away.'

Now Eve understood what had driven the gold prospectors of old to keep going under terrible conditions. The need to make that one big find, and then search on, in the belief that there were always better, bigger, richer finds.

Fifteen minutes later they were standing on the doorstep of Homelands Farmhouse. Eve felt a bit like an excited schoolgirl, anxious to show her parents a glowing report.

Chris's wife, Maggie, answered the door. Maggie Tate was a typical countrywoman in her late thirties — well-built, with a florid complexion and thick dark brown hair that framed her face in a mass of wild curls. She smiled broadly when she saw who it was.

'Come in! Kettle's on. I was expecting you.'

They followed her into a traditional farmhouse kitchen, obviously the centre of the home. Looking around her, Eve saw the epitome of a typical farmer's wife's domain. When she looked deeper, however, she saw that it was a mass of contradictions. It had everything you would expect to find in such a kitchen but with clever modern additions. There was a proper Belfast sink with a wooden drainer, but an open wooden door showed a state-of-the-art dishwasher behind it. It was clean and tidy, no mugs or utensils left in the sink or on the draining board, yet children's playthings lay scattered across the kitchen table, along with notepads, a laptop and an assortment of incongruous articles, including a table tennis bat and a pair of swimming goggles.

In a few deft movements that would have been worthy of any magician, Maggie had gathered up most of the detritus and whisked it out of sight.

'Sit down, both of you. I'll make the tea. Chris had to go and sort out a problem with one of the tractors, so he told me to look out for you, especially if you were carrying a large treasure chest.'

Maggie smiled, reminding Eve of an overgrown mischievous child.

46

'Well, it's not large,' said Wendy, 'and it's not a chest, but it could be treasure. We did find something; well, two things, actually.' She undid the small pouch that they had put their finds in. 'They need cleaning, but considering we're not long into this hobby, we were pretty excited about them.'

Wendy laid them on the table and unwrapped two small kitchen-paper parcels.

Maggie's reaction on seeing the two artifacts was totally unexpected.

Approaching the table, Maggie stopped mid-stride. The two mugs she was carrying wobbled dangerously in her hands. She put them down quickly and clasped her hand to her mouth. 'Oh, my God!'

Eve and Wendy looked at each other aghast. What on earth..?

Maggie slumped into a chair and stared wide-eyed at the pocket watch.

For a while no one spoke. Then, gently, Eve asked, 'Do you recognise this, Maggie?'

Maggie took a deep breath. 'If that watch has the initials TNT engraved in that decoration on the cover,' she said, 'it belonged to Chris's great-grandfather, Thomas Norman Tate.'

Eve looked closer and, yes, there was a small lozenge shape in the centre. She ran her finger over it, dislodging the fine particles of soil that still clung to it, and saw three letters in script. She could make out a T, and the others, although indistinct, could very well have been an N and another T. She looked at Maggie and nodded. 'From what I can make out, this is the watch.'

Having slightly regained her composure, Maggie passed the tea around. 'I really don't understand this,' she breathed. 'It's bizarre.'

Eve struggled to know why the discovery of an old watch should have had such a dramatic effect on this normally prag-matic and capable woman. 'Why, Maggie? What don't you understand?'

'Coming home one night along the back lane, Tommy Tate was robbed. He was beaten badly and left for dead, but two of his farm workers found him in time and got him back here to be cared for. They thought they knew who had attacked him and went after the man, who was a migrant worker. They were so incensed at the grievous injury done to their employer that they killed him. But when they searched his pockets, and the tiny cottage he rented, they found nothing. The stolen items weren't there. They were never found.' She swallowed. 'Until now.'

'So, they killed the wrong man?' whispered Wendy.

'The migrant wouldn't have had time to hide anything, and they admitted that he denied ever going near old Tommy Tate. Nor had he ever been in any kind of trouble before. They just saw the red mist. Even though they swore they never meant to kill him, they paid the ultimate price for what they'd done.'

'They were hanged.' Wendy's voice was almost inaudible.

It seemed almost barbaric now, the death penalty having been done away with so long ago, but there it was, Eve thought. Murder was punishable by death until capital punishment was finally abolished in 1969.

'So, who stole the watch? And who hurt Thomas Tate so badly?' Wendy asked.

'That's what I don't understand,' Maggie said. 'We assumed that the real thief had made off and sold what he had stolen. Now it turns up in our own field. It's unbelievable.'

Eve's mind was ticking over. Well, well, a real mystery, literally right on their doorstep. She managed to stop the satisfied smile threatening to spread across her face. As far as she was concerned, a mystery should never be left unsolved. Especially one that she and her friend had inadvertently brought to light. It was almost an obligation. On the land that she looked out on to every day, an innocent man had died, accused of a crime that he didn't commit. Someone had attacked and robbed an elderly man and left him to die. Who was it? 'What happened to Tommy? Did he recover?'

'Not really.' Maggie shrugged. 'He lived, but had no memory of what had happened and he more or less took to his bed. He died within a year.'

Still processing the day's revelations, they finished their tea and went home, leaving their precious finds for Chris to see on his return.

Back in their garden, Eve turned to Wendy with a wink. 'Wonderful hobby, this detecting. It opens so many interesting doors, don't you think, Wendy?'

'Oh, it certainly does, Eve. And, personally, I can't wait to unlock this one.'

CHAPTER FIVE

Sitting in her temporary office, Nikki fancied she heard the voice of a dead girl calling out her name, accusing her of failure. It didn't matter that she'd had nothing to do with the original case, the fact remained that a beautiful girl had been murdered. She'd been hidden beneath the ground, away from her friends and her grieving family, and left to rot, and Nikki had done nothing about it. There certainly had been a failure, and as part of the organisation responsible, Nikki felt she must shoulder the blame. However, there was more to it than that. Something about this whole set-up told her someone was gunning for her, Nikki Galena, and no one else.

'You can't take this personally,' said Joseph, reading her mind as he so often seemed to do.

They were now back at the station setting the reopening of the investigation in motion.

'It's hard not to,' she replied a little too sharply. 'It's my name on those damned envelopes.'

'It's not your fault, Nikki, and you know it.' Joseph gave her a searching look. 'Frankly, I'm starting to worry about your reaction to this whole thing. It's not like you.'

He was right. It wasn't, but Nikki didn't feel like admitting it. 'No matter what anyone says, and I'm fully aware that not one of the names on that list were my cases, I'm still bloody certain that this is personal to me. Don't ask me why, I just know it. Earlier on, I was thinking like you, that I'm just the lucky sod who got pulled out of the hat because Oliver, damn him, needs a figurehead, a name to put in the spotlight. Now? No. Something tells me otherwise.'

Joseph pulled a face that could mean one of two things — either he was agreeing with her or he was making a strategic withdrawal.

'I'm sorry, Joseph. I really don't want to feel this way but I do, and it's worrying me as much as it is you. It's one of those basic feelings we get. Call them what you will, instinct, intuition, gut reaction, copper's nose, even after decades in the job they just hit you, and you don't dismiss them out of hand, do you?'

He was forced to agree. 'No, you don't. You get them in the army too. I could sense the presence of a sniper, an IED. Somehow, we knew when an attack was imminent, even a surprise one. It's heightened awareness, I guess, and it comes with experience.' He spread his hands. 'So, I'm hardly going to dismiss your presentiment. The thing is, have you any idea who might be targeting you?'

'Not in this way, not in a million years. This isn't some scrote's mate out for revenge because I banged up his bestie.'

Joseph gave a faint smile. 'For a start, half of them can barely write, let alone in such fine script. Oh well, it's no use guessing who it might be, we'd be better off spending our time making sure that this time we find who killed Alexandra Cornfield now we have a body, and therefore forensic evidence. This time around we'd better make sure her family gets some answers.'

'Or we'll have the media baying for our blood,' Nikki added. 'And here was me saying I had everything tied up neatly for Cam's return. Instead, we find ourselves knee-deep in the cacky!'

'Yet again,' said a deep voice from the doorway.

'Cam!' Nikki cried. 'What are you doing here? You aren't due back for another week!'

'Indeed, but the sound of those jungle drums has reached me, and it's saying things are getting sticky in Greenborough.' He gave them a sheepish smile. 'That, and Kaye is fed up with me playing Florence Nightingale. She says she's better now and could do with less of my loving ministrations. Charming, isn't it? That's the thanks I get for nursing her through one of the most traumatic episodes of my entire life.'

'And I thought it was Kaye having the heart surgery,' laughed Nikki.

'Oh, she took it all in her stride. It was me having the vapours.' Suddenly serious, he said, 'I thought I was going to lose her, I really did.'

'But she thought differently,' said Joseph softly. 'And she's doing well?'

'Amazingly. She's way ahead in her recovery, and she really does want a bit of space. So, can I take some of the pressure off you guys? Maybe not full-time, but enough to make a difference.'

Nikki smiled broadly. 'That, Cam, is the best news we've had all week! Welcome back.'

He dragged a chair over. 'Then let's get straight down to it. Order us some strong coffee, and you can fill me in on what the hell just hit Greenborough.'

* * *

Cat and Yvonne were getting to the end of their list of women to interview, and neither of them felt exactly enthused about their findings so far. No one had actually managed to catch a good look at their stalker. Nevertheless, he had done a good job in scaring them all witless.

'Last one,' said Yvonne, looking at the final name: Samantha Chisholm. 'Is this the great-granddaughter of Gladys Chisholm — you know, the big farming family hereabouts?'

Cat nodded. 'Good old Greenborough name, that. So, what do we know about our Samantha?'

'Gladys said she's not fanciful but she is timid.' Yvonne pulled a face. 'So, who knows what kind of witness she'll be. I only recall her as a little one. Pretty little thing she was, a real sweet kid.'

'Okay, so let's see what she's turned into,' said Cat. 'This is the address we've been given.'

They were standing outside a small, terraced house in a narrow street, a little way out of town. It was well looked-after, but clearly hadn't had a lot of money spent on it. Cat suspected it was a rental property.

Sammie Chisholm opened the door and invited them in. 'Great-Gran rang me and said you were coming.'

As the girl closed the door, she gave the street a quick, apprehensive look, up and down, clearly checking for signs of anyone who shouldn't be there.

'I'm really glad you're here, Officers,' she said when it was clear they were alone, lowering her voice. 'I've been so upset by it all.'

The interior of the little house was much as Cat had expected, plain and utilitarian, and it screamed "rental." Sammie had made an effort to make it more inviting, with some poster prints of the Fenlands depicting waterways, fields of brilliant yellow rapeseed and moody marshes, plus a few green plants and a large teddy bear in one corner, seated on a wooden stool. There was a brightly coloured rug on the laminate flooring, and a fascinating, if somewhat curious, floor-standing lamp in the corner that seemed to be constructed from driftwood and rope and supported a kind of shell-like light fitting. The only other item of note was a classical guitar on an A-frame stand.

Cat and Yvonne sat in the lounge on a low two-seater sofa, and Sammie took the only other easy chair. Both items of furniture were well-used, probably donated by members of her family. Cat wasn't sure that many nineteen-year-olds would be capable of looking after themselves, but Sammie seemed to be doing okay.

This time they accepted the offer of a drink. Their next stop was the police station, so Cat felt quite safe.

Nursing mugs of hot tea, they coaxed the girl into telling them everything that had happened, and to Cat's surprise, Sammie gave them the clearest and most concise account of all of them. Old Gladys had called her timid, but Cat saw an unassuming young woman with very good observational skills and excellent recall. Sammie was obviously frightened, but she was far from hysterical.

Her story followed a similar trajectory to the others — the feeling of being watched and then followed, of hearing a noise behind her but seeing no one. Unlike the others, Samantha Chisholm could list dates and times, and made her version of what had happened sound more like a police statement than a creepy horror story. Cat was impressed.

'Have you considered moving back in with your parents for a while, until this person loses interest in you?' asked Yvonne and smiled. 'I'm sure your mum and dad would feel happier.'

Sammie grimaced. 'To be honest, I'm not sure they believe me. They never thought I'd cope on my own, and I think they'd see it as an excuse to run home without actually admitting that they were right.'

'But you are coping, aren't you?' Cat looked around. 'You've made it very nice.'

Sammie nodded. 'I love it, Detective Cullen. You see, I'm the baby of the family, and everyone treats me that way, even though I'm practically twenty. This is the first time I've had proper space of my own, and it's . . .' She smiled. 'Oh, I know it's nothing special, I can't afford a lot, but I really enjoy living here. Or I did, until this creep showed up.'

Cat felt for her. It wasn't fair. The kid was finally making her own world and this arsehole was spoiling it for her. 'Vonnie here says that your great-gran, Gladys, believes you. Why not stay with her for a while?'

Sammie's face broke into a warm smile. 'If I went any-where, it would be to her. I love her so much. But then he'd have won, wouldn't he? And he might still watch me, and maybe scare her too, and I'd never forgive myself if he did that.'

Cat liked this girl's attitude. Gladys's depiction of a "timid" little creature was beginning to sound like a joke. Nevertheless, Cat was frightened for her. She was vulnerable here, probably more so than any of the other women they had interviewed. If she were a predator, this young woman would be her chosen target. 'Do you mind if we check your house over?' she asked. 'If you are determined to dig your heels in, I'd like to know that you're as safe as possible.'

'Please do,' said Sammie. 'There's not much to see, but I'll show you around my mini domain.'

It was a typical two-up two-down terrace house. Upstairs, a main bedroom at the front, and a much smaller single bedroom at the back that Sammie was using as a storeroom, and a compact bath/shower room. Downstairs, the lounge and a kitchen diner. The only addition was a kind of utility room-cum-lean-to, that most likely the landlord laughingly called a conservatory. This was the weak link as far as Cat was concerned. It was a cheap, flimsy build, and even she could have forced the exterior door without drawing a breath. The connecting door that led into the kitchen was a bit stronger, but Cat saw no key in it. When asked, Sammie said there wasn't one, but that she always kept the outside door locked. Cat didn't want to frighten her but made a mental note of this vulnerable point in the house's otherwise fairly adequate security. Yvonne knew Gladys Chisholm, so maybe she could have a quiet word and see if the old lady might consider paying for a new lock, one with a key. She was pretty certain the landlord wouldn't consider it a priority, that was for sure.

They returned to the lounge. 'And now, Sammie, the million-dollar question,' said Yvonne. 'Have you any idea who this stalker might be?'

'None whatsoever. I've had no arguments with anyone, haven't fallen out with any boyfriends. In fact, there's no one special in my life right now. I get on with everyone at work.' She paused. 'I'm doing a couple of weeks at one of my uncles' businesses to help him through a busy patch. I start a new full-time job in three weeks' time.' She looked anxious. 'I hope you can catch this man before then or I won't be able to do my best. I want to make a good impression, not look like some zombie because I haven't had any sleep.'

Cat said she understood and that they'd certainly do their best for her. 'So, no old feuds either, even going as far back as college?'

A brief flash of apprehension passed over Sammie's face. She shrugged. 'Once, with another girl. Don't ask me what it was about, because I never found out. I guess she just didn't like me, but she was vile. Other than that, no jealous boyfriends, no secret admirers, and all my other mates were great.'

'And you are sure your stalker is a man?' asked Cat.

'Absolutely. The only time I caught a glimpse in the shadows, it was a man's figure that I saw, and I'm pretty sure he had a black scarf over the lower part of his face. Also, once when I sensed he was really close, there was a definite smell of men's aftershave or cologne. Oh, and I could be wrong but I think I heard him, well, kind of giggle? It was weird and really creepy.'

Cat indicated to Yvonne that they were done. 'You've been really helpful, Sammie.' She gave the girl one of her cards. 'Ring me anytime if you see him, and I'll do my best to get here fast, okay?'

The girl looked relieved. 'I'm just happy that you believe me.'

'Oh, we believe you,' said Yvonne emphatically. 'And we'd like nothing more than to get our hands on him, I promise.'

Oh, you have no idea how much I'd like that, said Cat to herself.

As they drove back to the station, Cat said, 'How would you feel about joining me in a little stint on obbo, Vonnie? Purely voluntarily, of course, and in your own time.'

Yvonne gave her a smile. 'You read my thoughts, Cat Cullen. And I'm guessing young Sammie is the one you'd like us to observe.'

'Oh yes, most definitely. I suggest we grab a takeaway after work and find a nice little spot where we can keep a close eye on that little terraced house. Ben is still away on his course, and Byron the cat won't mind, so are you up for it?'

Yvonne agreed immediately. 'What's going on with this creepy guy, Cat? Why target six women, maybe more? It doesn't make sense. Most stalkers fixate on a single woman — or man — but this feels different.'

Cat didn't even want to try and work that one out. Yvonne was right. A lovesick admirer pursued the object of his desires, he didn't haunt half a dozen different women. 'I guess we'll find out one way or another.' She shivered. Suddenly this whole thing felt very sinister. Who knew? Maybe it was just the work of some fruit-loop kid acting on a dare from his idiot mates, but she feared there was much more to this than they suspected. The uncomfortable feeling grew, escalating into real concern, but she kept her anxiety from Yvonne.

She glanced at her friend. No need. Yvonne had reached the same conclusion.

* * *

There was a charged atmosphere about the CID room when they went in. Yvonne immediately noticed that the sarge was back in his tiny office, and DI Nikki Galena was back in hers, busy talking on the phone.

In moments she was out and striding in their direction.

'Glad you're back, you two. So, heads up, we have a situation here, and a change in priorities. I need you to shelve the possible stalker inquiry and get yourselves up to speed on an incident that occurred while you were out.' Her voice was clipped and urgent.

Yvonne stole a swift glance at Cat, who looked as downcast as her. How could they just ditch those terrified women? Especially Sammie, the most vulnerable in her estimation.

Nikki had evidently picked up on their reaction, for she said, 'Look, give me five minutes. I'm having an emergency meeting after which I'll explain everything. Then you can tell me why you both look like I've just stolen the last chocolate biscuit on the plate.'

And with that she turned on her heel and hurried back to her office.

'Sounds serious, whatever it is,' muttered Cat. 'Now it looks as though our extracurricular activities are going to be even more necessary, doesn't it? Are you still game?'

Yvonne nodded. 'Of course. I'm just wondering what's occurred.'

'I'm betting it's something to do with a threatening letter the boss received, concerning several old missing persons cases.' Cat gave her friend a resigned smile. 'If it is, we are definitely going to have to back off our stalker, but on the plus side, doesn't it feel good to have the old status quo back?'

'I wonder who's covering the super's post, though?' Yvonne said.

'That man there,' said Cat with a wry smile, pointing to the door. 'We really do have the old guard back in place.'

Superintendent Cameron Walker was heading directly for Nikki's office, his face set.

'Flung straight into the deep end too,' added Yvonne. 'Talk about hitting the ground running.'

Cat's smile disappeared. 'This must be serious. The super wasn't due back for another week or two. Know what, Vonnie, I don't think we're going to like what the boss has to say.'

Cat's suspicions were soon proved correct. They watched, bemused, while the whiteboard slowly filled up with photographs of a young woman called Alexandra Cornfield.

Yvonne was used to keeping several things in her mind at once, but she found this hard to take in after their interview with Samantha. Bottom line, as far as she could tell, they had a weirdo playing games with the DI. He had sent her a list of female mispers who had never been found. Number one on the list was now a confirmed murder victim, thanks to the letter-writer who called himself Oliver. Did that mean that all the others were going to turn up dead too?

Nikki was winding up the impromptu meeting. As of now they were waiting for forensic reports, and also watching the post for the expected Part Two this Oliver person had promised to send.

Yvonne noted the anxiety in Nikki's voice when she mentioned Part Two, and she could understand the reason for it. What on earth was this man playing at?

'Cat? Yvonne? Hang on for a moment, please.'

The others drifted back to their desks, leaving the three women standing in front of the whiteboard.

'Have you found something regarding this stalker that's cause for concern?' Nikki asked. 'Because you are obviously reluctant to walk away from it — even for a murder.'

Cat explained their fears, especially their uneasiness about Samantha Chisholm.

Nikki looked pensive. 'I quite understand your anxiety about this young woman but the main case has to take precedence. All I can say is, have a word with uniform, see if they can keep her place under surveillance for a while, and do keep in touch with the girl. We can't have her thinking we aren't interested in her safety.' She shrugged. 'Sorry, both of you, but you don't even know if this man exists. Not one of your women has actually seen anyone they could identify. If one of these possible victims has made a big enough noise about what she thinks is happening, other women might fancy they are being targeted too and it has spread like a kind of mass hysteria. It happens, you know.' She inhaled. 'The thing is, our dead woman really does exist, and so do these letters and bogus murder enquiry files and reports. There's no question about what must take priority.'

They were forced to agree, but they both knew in their hearts that this was no case of mass hysteria. Some bastard was out there in the Greenborough shadows watching women. Yes, they would talk to uniform, for all the good that would do considering the workload and lack of bobbies on the beat, and they'd buckle down and do all they could concerning Alexandra Cornfield, but they would not take their eyes off Sammie Chisholm.

Yvonne watched the boss walk away. 'Plan B? Evening classes in observation with special reference to small terrace houses in Linden Road?'

Cat nodded. 'Yeah, I've already signed up for the whole course. So, what kind of takeaway do you fancy?'

CHAPTER SIX

For several minutes, Chris Tate sat as if mesmerised, staring at the grubby, soil-encrusted watch on his kitchen table.

His wife sat across from him, also in silence. She too couldn't seem to take her eyes off it.

After a time, she said, 'There's no doubt, is there?'

He shook his head dumbly. He'd rubbed hard at the engraved initials and examined them with a magnifying glass. TNT. The letters had once been a source of jocularity in the family. Thomas Tate had always had a bit of a temper on him, and when it flared, it could indeed be explosive. Right now, the initials were anything but funny.

'This changes everything, doesn't it, Maggie?' His voice was soft, almost childlike.

'Not really, my love, it can't affect us. After all, it was donkey's years ago. We can't change what happened, and who knows how his watch and the ring came to be in that field? We certainly aren't going to get any answers now, are we?' She reached across the table and squeezed his hand. 'It changes nothing, sweetheart. It's just a bit of a mystery, that's all.'

He didn't reply. She was trying to console him, of course. It wouldn't work. For a start, his wife didn't know the full story. The fact was, this infamous piece of family history had been almost an obsession with him ever since he had heard it as a small child. He had been horrified and yet morbidly fascinated that two loyal farmhands had been so incensed by the attack on their master that they had beaten to death the man they suspected of it. He knew this made them no better than the thief, but there was something in their actions that had held the younger Chris spellbound. Then it had come out that they'd been mistaken. The real thief would have taken his ill-gotten gains and run, no doubt straight to some city pawnbroker. The watch, the ring and the—

Chris blinked. There had been three items gone from Thomas Tate's person. His precious watch, his Celtic knot ring, and a silver cigarette case with the same engraving of TNT. So where was that? Surely an object of that size would have been much easier to detect than a small ring? Was it out there still?

'It's lucky you've never given any of those clubs permission to come on to the fields detecting, isn't it?' Maggie was saying. 'You might never have got it back, or even known about its discovery. I'm sure not every treasure hunter is willing to share what they dig up. At least our neighbours came straight to you with it.'

He'd get Wendy and Eve to go back, he decided. And as soon as possible. The field would be ploughed in a couple of days and the ground disturbed yet again. Farmland could be the richest place on earth for finds, but it was also sometimes desperately disappointing. Heavy ploughs could bring items closer to the surface, but they could also damage them. Abruptly, he said, 'Where's the cigarette case?'

Maggie stared at him. 'Oh. I'd forgotten about that.'

Chris stood up and pulled his phone from his pocket. He must ring the neighbours without delay.

* * *

Lynette Sims hurried along the field path. It saved a good ten minutes to use this back way, rather than sticking to the village streets. Her car had been in dock for two days now, but hopefully it would be ready tomorrow. She hadn't realised how dependent she had become on her car until it broke down. The garage was only a small local one, but she trusted them with her old banger. It was just sad that they didn't have a vehicle available to loan her in the interim.

Her village was only a fifteen-minute drive from her school in Greenborough, but trying to get home using public transport was a nightmare. Buses were infrequent and stopped altogether at 6 p.m., so if you were held up, it was a taxi or nothing.

This afternoon, however, a fellow teacher had been heading in her direction and had given her a lift as far as the outskirts of Fenny Bridge village. Now she was taking the shortcut and wishing she'd put on a warmer jacket. On these open stretches there was nothing to stop the wind blasting across the fen, and sometimes it cut you to the bone. She picked up her pace. At least it wasn't raining.

As she reached the end of the pad and turned left into her end of the village, she thought about her meeting with young Ruby Grayson. She wished she had been able to get more from the girl, but if nothing else, Ruby had let slip a number of indications that things really were not good at home. Lynette wondered if she should have handled their chat differently, but somehow she didn't think it would have made any difference. They had parted company with the girl promising Lynette that she would consider sharing what was bothering her. Frankly, she dared not push her too hard. She had a feeling that Ruby did want to talk but was just not certain that she should.

Lynette walked past the barns that belonged to the big old Fenny Bridge Farmhouse, a rambling old building with several annexes and all manner of outbuildings attached to it in a haphazard fashion. Her mother had always called it Higgledy-Piggledy Farm, and Lynette could understand why.

She had just passed the last old barn when she paused and turned around. For a moment she thought she had heard something quite close by, but there was nothing. The barn itself was empty, and as far as she knew, hadn't been used for many years.

She walked on, now only minutes from her cottage in Pools Lane.

It was one of a row of houses, ten in number, all built on one side of the lane. Opposite lay a pasture where a few horses grazed. Its perimeters were surrounded by overgrown bushes and hawthorn trees, with gaps wide enough to see the view beyond. It gave Lynette a good feeling to come home to the place where she'd been born. It was just her and her mum now. Mum was in her early sixties but still active, despite suffering from the aftermath of a debilitating illness in her thirties.

As she approached her driveway, she heard another sound that seemed to come from the horse field. It wasn't one of the ponies or horses, as she'd seen them on the far side of the meadow when she turned into her road. She made out the sharp cracking of dried twigs beneath the weight of footsteps. Again, she stopped and stared, trying to spot any movement. There was none.

Lynette shook her head and continued up the drive. It wasn't like her to feel this jumpy. She was obviously a bit wound up over Ruby Grayson. Having a troubled child in your class could be pretty stressful.

She let herself in. 'Mum! I'm home. I got a lift to the crossroads. Have you had a good day? Oh, and have we heard from the garage yet?'

Her mother emerged from the kitchen. 'One thing at a time, dear.'

Tessa Sims was a tall, thin woman with iron-grey hair and intelligent dark brown eyes, who was seldom without a smile on her face. 'My day was pants, actually. Celia cancelled our coffee morning at the last minute, the cat ripped up the toilet roll — while I was sitting on the lav — and then the gardener rang to say he still has flu and can't come again this week. Our grass is going to need a combine harvester to cut it by the time he gets back.' She smiled broadly. 'And your car will be ready tomorrow. You can collect it after work, or if you want young Jimmy to bring it here when they close, just ring and tell him.'

Lynette pulled off her jacket and hung it up on the hall coat rack. 'Good news about the car, Mum. Not so good about the toilet roll, though, but Henry's been doing that for the past eight years, so I doubt he'll stop now.' She went through to the kitchen and put the kettle on for tea. 'God, I need this.'

'You sit down, darling. I'll make it. Now, tell me about your problem child. Did you get any further with her?'

Lynette told her mother about the deputy head's suggestion and her ensuing talk with Ruby. 'I wish I could get her to open up, Mum. I just know there's something seriously wrong there.'

'Have you met the parents? Do you know what kind of people they are?' asked her mother.

'Oh yes, several times. I'd say they're the perfect family. On the surface, at least, they appear happy and supportive, which worries me all the more.' Lynette sipped her tea and considered the "happy family." Was it all a front? What if there was some monstrous secret lurking beneath the apparent domestic harmony? And if that was the case, how could she help? What could she do?

'Don't make yourself ill over this, my girl,' said Tessa rather sternly. 'You can't right all the wrongs of this world, and you can't help everyone. Do your best, by all means, but not at the expense of your health. You have plenty of other students who need you, so don't give all your energy to one child.'

'You sound like Miss Barrett,' said Lynette.

'Then she's a wise woman like your mother, so take heed,' Tessa replied.

They chatted about things domestic until, tea finished, Lynette said, 'I'd better take a look at the grass. It'll need cutting if our ailing gardener isn't going to be here again. At least I can do the front, so the neighbours don't think we've gone back to nature, but I'm not sure about the back. That really needs a bigger mower than ours.' The back gardens along Pools Lane were unusually long ones for a small village. Their gardener, a likeable man called Rick, whom Lynette suspected of being a bit of a hypochondriac, always brought his own powerful mowers.

Lynette went outside and unlocked the garden shed. When Rick wasn't suffering from some new and crippling ailment, he kept their old petrol mower regularly serviced along with his own, so it started at once. Lynette decided that if she got a move on, she could get the front lawn cut before her mother had supper ready.

After three or four lengths, Lynette stopped and looked around. She had the oddest feeling. She was sure someone was watching her from close by. Strange. There was no one outside her neighbours' houses. Frowning to herself, she pressed on.

A short time later, the uncomfortable feeling returned. Leaving the mower idling, she emptied the cuttings into the garden waste bin while taking careful stock of the surrounding gardens and the meadow across the road.

From where she was, she could see that the horses were still on the far side by the big five-bar gate, probably waiting for their owner's regular evening visit.

It all seemed quiet and peaceful, even the wind had dropped, yet that disturbing feeling of being watched persisted. Probably her imagination, but she also thought she heard an odd, stifled giggle coming from somewhere nearby.

She finished the lawn in record time, brushed off the mower and locked it away. Then with one last, anxious glance about her, she hurried indoors.

* * *

After everyone else had gone home, Nikki, Joseph and Cam remained, standing in front of the whiteboard and staring up at it.

'What the hell does Part Two mean?' grumbled Cam.

That bothered Nikki too, but she had no definitive answer.

'He's either moving on to the next name on the list, or . . .' Joseph's voice died away.

'Or maybe he's not finished with this case yet, although what more he could do after leading us to her body, I really don't know,' mused Nikki.

Cam stretched. 'Well, as it seems we won't know until our next *Par Avion* communication arrives, I'm off home to my lovely wife. I'll be in tomorrow as soon as I'm happy that Kaye is okay to be left. I'll see you then.'

'It's good to have you back, Cam,' said Nikki with feeling. 'Acting super was an interesting experience, but it really wasn't my thing.'

Cam smiled. 'Actually, you did very well, and I've heard that from on high.' He pointed upwards, meaning from the chief superintendent. 'I'd be careful if I were you. You made a very good impression on the gold braid — probably for the first time in your whole chequered career!' Seeing her horrified expression, he laughed out loud. 'But thank you, Nikki. You kept the boat afloat brilliantly, and I appreciate it.'

'Well, it's all yours again, and you're welcome to it,' she said.

Cam having gone, she and Joseph prepared to leave too. They had attended to everything that had to be done, the worst being notifying the parents of Alexandra Cornfield that they should prepare themselves for bad news. Now there was little more to be done until they received confirmation from forensics.

'Did you notice that Cat and Yvonne left together?' Nikki asked Joseph.

'Er, yes, I did.' He looked at her questioningly. 'And that's a problem?'

'No, unless they are doing what I suspect, which is turning private detective, and carrying on with the stalker enquiries in their own time. I saw their faces when I told them to put it on the back burner.'

Joseph shrugged. 'Nothing that you and I haven't done more than once when a job gets under our skins.'

'True, but I'm going to need every member of the team fully focused on whatever Oliver throws at us next.' She pulled on her jacket. 'Whatever that might be.'

'And they will be, Nikki,' assured Joseph. 'They'd no more let you down than fly.'

She knew that, but "Detective Oliver" had really wound her up. She had to know that at any given moment they'd be prepared to hit back, and hard. She was also afraid that the stalker affair might escalate, and that could mean trouble. DI Gill Mercer and her team were up to their necks in a suspicious death, while at the same time dealing with an ongoing drugs case. So it would be down to Nikki to shoulder the stalker as well as bloody Detective Oliver and his Murder Mystery games.

At least Cam was now back in the driving seat. Even if it did get mega-busy, now she was back with the team they would manage somehow.

She set off down the stairs, turning as she heard the clatter of footsteps behind her. 'DI Galena! Glad I've caught you. This was handed in at reception.'

The civilian handed her a thick brown envelope. Before she'd even taken it from her, Nikki could see the *Par Avion* sticker on the front.

'It's been scanned, ma'am, and the sergeant said to say that the messenger had gone before anyone had time to talk to him. He didn't even wait for a signature. It was a motorcycle courier, but not from a company anyone recognised.'

Nikki thanked her and called back to Joseph, who was just coming down after her. 'Looks like it's back to the office, Sergeant Easter. Let's see what Part Two is all about.'

* * *

Joseph followed Nikki back up the stairs, full of foreboding. He had a nasty feeling that whatever was in that envelope would be something quite unexpected.

Back in the office, Nikki wasted no time. She pulled on gloves, opened the envelope and carefully removed the contents.

As before, so-called Detective Oliver's communication came in the form of an official report file. He had even given it a case number. *Alexandra Cornfield. Case number 0147.*

'I'm wondering if this guy is, or was, connected to law enforcement in some way,' Joseph muttered. 'Or did he just watch a box set of *Line of Duty*?'

'They aren't quite in standard professional style,' said Nikki, 'so I'd go with bingeing on true life crime programmes myself, but even that could be a cover-up. Right now, all options are open. He could be a flake, or he could be an ex-copper, a solicitor, or someone from another department within the force, someone with a grudge, and a big one.'

'So, what have we got, Nikki?' Joseph asked.

She opened the file and turned over the pages, one by one. After a moment or two she let out a sigh. 'It's a full investigation report, Joseph. A list of suspects, witness statements, observations, photographs, various reports . . . until the end. Then we have this single line on a clean page:

An arrest has been made.'

She turned to the final page, which read, PART THREE TO FOLLOW.

Joseph groaned. 'Oh dear. We'll need to read this word by word, won't we? Shall I go and get coffees?'

Nikki looked at the fat file. 'And maybe order a takeaway while you're at it. This is no five-minute job. Sorry, Joseph, but I'm afraid we're here for the duration.'

CHAPTER SEVEN

While Joseph and Nikki pored over "Detective Oliver's" in-depth report, Yvonne and Cat were sitting in Cat's car with a box of KFC chicken nuggets and fries between them.

Samantha Chisholm had told them that she was going to a Pilates class that evening, starting at seven and finishing around forty-five minutes later. So, the undercover sleuths had parked up in a lay-by that gave them a good view of the hall's front doors.

'That girl has some courage, still going out in the evening despite being frightened half to death,' said Cat, taking a handful of fries from the carton.

'She says he can't be allowed to win, and if she cowers at home, she might just as well give up.' Yvonne frowned. 'I like her spirit, but I can't help wondering if discretion mightn't have been the better part of valour, at least for a while. She's at risk, being out of her house at night.'

Cat slowly scanned the area around the community hall. 'All quiet on the western front so far. No shady characters lurking anywhere I can see. Let's hope that, for her sake, it stays this way.'

'At least it's only a five-minute walk from here to her home.' Yvonne watched a cat slink across the road and make for a gap in a fence. 'Even so, I wish she had a friend to walk with her. If it was me, I'd think twice about going anywhere alone.'

They finished off their supper and watched until they saw the doors of the hall open and people start to emerge. Yvonne bundled up the empty food containers and Cat started the engine. Sammie didn't know they were keeping an eye on her, and they wanted it to stay that way. Cat gave her time to get some way ahead of them before she moved forward.

It was a long few minutes. As Cat drove, her eyes firmly on Sammie, Yvonne watched carefully for signs of anyone else paying attention to the lone woman. It wasn't until she was safely inside, the lights came on and the curtains were drawn, that they relaxed. Even so, they parked a little way away and settled down to continue observing the small, inconspicuous terraced house. They stayed watching for another hour, but there was no suspicious activity.

'Well, as we have a big case starting up in the morning, we'd better go home and get some shut-eye,' said Cat. 'Or the boss won't be happy.'

'At least I feel better knowing that she's home and locked up for the night.' Yvonne gave an anxious sigh. 'But this isn't nearly enough, is it, Cat? We can't watch her round the clock, and I am more concerned about this girl than any of the others. I wish she'd go and stay with her great-gran or get someone to move in with her for a while. Surely, no matter how many brave words that kid utters, she must be bricking it.'

'Yeah.' Cat turned on the engine. 'I feel the same, but frankly, Vonnie, we're scuppered. The boss is right about priorities, and if this weirdo who calls himself Oliver is on some crackpot retribution crusade, the team will be run off its feet.' She gave her friend a cheerless grin. 'So buckle up, Vonnie, and I'll take you home. We'd better get some sleep while we still can.'

* * *

71

Nikki and Joseph hardly noticed the hours pass. They barely tasted the food Joseph had brought, so deeply engrossed were they in their files. They were comparing the unofficial document with the original, official police investigation into the disappearance of Alexandra Cornfield.

Finally, her shoulders aching and her neck stiff, Nikki pushed her chair back. 'Enough! My brain can only take so much in. Let's go home, Joseph.'

Joseph eased his aching neck. 'I'm with you there. But it's frightening, isn't it? The similarities, I mean.'

'I can't stop wondering what this man's connection to this case is. What has driven him to go to all this trouble? Producing — single-handedly, I presume — a whole investigation. It's a huge amount of work.' Nikki closed the files and put them into her desk drawer, which she locked.

Joseph put the remains of their supper in the wastepaper bin. 'And I've been wondering what we are actually reading. Was it produced by a professional from somewhere within the world of law and order, or someone outside it with their own twisted agenda?'

'Mmm, some of the jargon he uses convinces me he's a professional, but on the other hand there's nothing in the presentation that couldn't have been gleaned from watching a TV crime series or scouring the relevant sites on Google.' Nikki shook her head in frustration. 'All I do know is that he's fingered the one man who was initially suspected of being involved in her disappearance, but later ruled out through lack of evidence. Neil Weldon, Alexandra's uncle, was repeatedly mentioned in the original police enquiry, then an alibi was established and he was dropped as a suspect.'

They decided to drive home together, leaving Joseph's car at the station, in order to go over what they had gleaned from Part Two. They would be in early, long before the likelihood of a commanding officer deciding to grace the office with their presence.

'And Oliver has disproved that alibi, or says he has,' Joseph said. 'In any case, we'll be forced to follow it up because we're now looking at murder. I'll be very interested to know if he's right, won't you?'

'I certainly will,' Nikki said, 'though I have a distinct feeling that our Oliver's going to be spot on in his conclusion.'

Joseph nodded. 'I reckon we'll be getting to meet Neil Weldon in the next few days.'

They were approaching Cloud Fen when Joseph admitted to having a mild case of the heebie-jeebies. 'I keep wondering what Part Three is going to tell us.'

Nikki slowed as her headlights caught a pair of green eyes in the road ahead. A fox stopped for a second, then disappeared like a wraith in the night. 'It reminds me of the title of that Agatha Christie novel, *Three Act Tragedy*. Whatever the outcome, our case will be a tragedy for someone.'

They didn't mention the case again until they were lying in bed, neither of them able to sleep.

Suddenly, Joseph said, 'Do you think we should take that single line — the one that said "*an arrest has been made*" — figuratively, or literally?'

Nikki opened her eyes wide. 'Literally? You mean bloody Detective Oliver has actually "arrested" Neil Weldon? Like abducted him?' She took hold of Joseph's arm.

'Maybe our first job in the morning should be to find this Weldon,' Joseph said. 'Just in case our bogus detective has gone a step too far.'

Nikki took a long slow breath. 'I hadn't thought of that before, but you're right, dear Joseph. I now have a horrible feeling we may not be meeting Mr Weldon as soon as we'd expected.'

Nikki stared into the darkness. Just how far was Detective Oliver prepared to go? And why the hell was he doing all this in the first place?

* * *

At around three in the morning, Mrs Andrea Smith was returning from answering a call of nature when she heard a cry. She stood on the upstairs landing, frozen to the spot, then ran back into the bedroom, calling for her husband.

'Jed! I heard it again! Someone's in trouble out there!'

Jed Smith, having been disturbed by his wife's trip to the bathroom, was already half-awake. 'Well, I did wonder if I heard something too. You might just be right, love.' He got up and went to the window.

Andrea joined him, but there was nothing to see. They stood for a long time, listening, but all was silent. They heard no more calls of distress that night.

This was the third time that Andrea believed she'd heard something. It was time to report it. She made a note of the exact time the cry had rung out and told her husband what she intended to do.

'Fat lot of good that'll do, but ring 'em if it makes you feel better.' Jed grunted. 'They'll only take action if something serious happens. You know how they are, always shutting the stable door after the horse has bolted.'

'Well, I don't care,' said Andrea firmly. 'It's my duty. At least they'll be aware of it, and if they do get some other complaint, they'll know it's worth looking into. I couldn't live with myself if something happened and I'd not spoken out.'

Jed chuckled. 'That's my public-spirited girl. But don't be hanging by your eyelashes waiting for them to take you seriously. The chances of getting a copper to even set foot in this village are practically zero.' He gave a small snort of derision and went back to sleep.

Andrea remained awake. It had been a woman's voice, she was certain, and she was in pain and torment. She lay listening to her husband's soft snores and decided on a course of action. Unlike Jed, she had great faith in the police force, and was willing to give them whatever help she could. So, from now on, she'd keep watch. She had a vague idea of which direction the cry had come from, and on each occasion, it had occurred between two and three in the morning. She wasn't a good sleeper at the best of times, and whenever she felt particularly restless, she spent the night in the spare room rather than disturb her husband. So, it wouldn't be anything unusual for her to go into the other room. She could go there and wait, watching the street and taking note of any unusual comings and goings. Her decision made, Andrea relaxed and fell asleep.

* * *

In Beech Lacey, Eve Anderson also lay awake. She had slept soundly until something disturbed her at around two thirty, and even after making a hot drink, she found that sleep had deserted her.

The incident with the watch and the ring played over and over in her mind, especially when Chris Tate rang her and asked, no, *begged* her to go back out the next morning and look for another item. Now that really had her perplexed. There had been a strange edge to his voice. Their chance find had evidently had a massive impact on the Tate family. The thing was, it wasn't the sort of excitement she would have expected; there was a different timbre to his voice, one that disturbed her. In fact, if it had been any other situation than this, Eve would have said he was afraid. His anxiety was palpable, even on a not-very-clear phone line.

Eve sat up and rearranged her pillows. Lying down again, she recalled what Maggie Tate had told them about the fool-hardy actions of the two farmhands, and how they had led to the murder of what was very likely an innocent man. Then, how for all those years it had been believed that some robber had sold those precious possessions, which everyone believed was the end of the story, until she and Wendy had turned up and proudly shown her what they'd found.

Wendy had agreed that they should definitely go back into the Tates' field and widen their search. After all, if three items had been lost, why shouldn't the third be there too? There was a very good chance that ploughing had lifted the cigarette case from its original resting place and moved it

75

further from the other two treasures. They both had a feeling that if it was still there, they would find it.

Eve glanced at the clock and sighed. It was only two hours until it would be time to get up. With a great effort, she pushed away her thoughts of hidden treasure and tried to think about other more mundane subjects, like what vegetables to plant for the coming year, and what variety of tomato to try in their newly revamped greenhouse.

It didn't work. When she finally drifted off, she dreamed of sinister men burying ill-gotten gains in a farmer's field.

CHAPTER EIGHT

Having rung Cam and informed him of the latest *Par Avion* delivery package, Nikki and Joseph were standing outside the front door of the Weldon house on the outskirts of Greenborough. It was early, only eight thirty, but they were both extremely concerned about Neil Weldon's safety.

A bleary-eyed teenage boy answered the door. He eyed their warrant cards and made a movement as if about to make a run for it. Nikki quickly said they were here to speak to Neil Weldon, and he relaxed a little. 'Sorry, you're out of luck. Dad ain't here. He's working away at the moment.' He started to close the door.

'And your mother?' asked Joseph, looking at him, hard.

'She's getting ready for work. And she's late, so she won't like it if you hold her up.'

'And I won't like it if you don't shift your scrawny arse and fetch her,' growled Nikki, who was in no mood to hear the excuses of some lippy little oik.

He swallowed and turned to go indoors.

A few moments later, a small, compact woman appeared in the doorway. She had blonde hair cut into a neat bob, and an anxious expression on her face. 'I'm Annie Weldon. I apologise for Shaun, he's at a difficult age, I'm afraid. Not quite mastered manners, but I'm working on it. How can I help you?'

Good luck with that, thought Nikki. 'Mrs Weldon, we need to speak to your husband as a matter of some urgency. I wonder if we could ask you for his contact number, and if you could give us his work address, please?'

Annie Weldon's face clouded over. 'You'd better come in.'

Nikki and Joseph followed her through to the lounge, and she closed the door behind them. She lowered her voice. 'It's best that Shaun and Aidan don't hear this.' She pointed to a leather settee that had seen better days and indicated for them to sit.

When they were seated, she said in a low voice, 'Truth is, I have no idea where he is, and I've given up trying to get him on the phone.' She looked anywhere but at them.

'But you know where he works, surely?' asked Joseph.

She shook her head. 'I don't even know if he is working. Things have been bad between us for a while, Officers. Then, about a week ago he had a call from a number I didn't recognise, packed a few things and took off. He said it was a last-minute job, and that he had to cover for some bloke who'd had an accident. I didn't believe a word of it. The unfaithful sod's been seeing another woman for a while now. I'm guessing he's with her.'

A feeling of dread began to creep through Nikki. 'You'd better give us the address of his workplace, Mrs Weldon. It's really very important that we talk to him. Someone there must know where he is.'

'He works for Carter Hayman, the demolition company based in the business park on the old Wash Road, the Fenlander Enterprise Park. He's a site supervisor and a kind of troubleshooter for the company, so he does travel about a lot,' she paused, 'but that's not the case this time, I'm sure of it.'

'You say he's not answering your calls?' asked Joseph. 'Has he done that before?'

'Once, after a big row.'

'And was there a row this time?' added Nikki.

'Not really, though I was bloody furious with him. Shaun is a real handful, as you probably noticed, and Aidan's little better. Neil doesn't seem to think he should have anything to do with disciplining the kids. He's always been the same, he likes the fun times with them all right, but as to responsibility, he hasn't got a clue. Or just doesn't care. I really don't know anymore.' Annie Weldon looked as if she'd given up on her wayward husband.

Meanwhile, the words *an arrest has been made* were flashing like neon in Nikki's head.

Suddenly Annie Weldon sat up straighter. 'What's this to do with, anyway? Don't tell me it's that old case rearing its ugly head again. My husband was completely exonerated of all involvement in that. Oh God, no. We can't go through all that again.'

Well, it's no use lying, thought Nikki, noting that for all her apparent anger at her errant spouse, Annie obviously still cared about him and the effect this would have on him. 'There is a possible connection, yes, but really we just need to talk to him.' She took a breath. 'Well, I might as well tell you — it'll soon be all over the news anyway. We have fresh evidence, Mrs Weldon, and . . . a body has been discovered. It hasn't been officially identified yet but, well, you should expect to hear that your niece has finally been found.'

Annie Weldon turned pale. 'Do Michael and Amanda know? Have you told them yet?'

'Yes,' Nikki said. 'Alexandra's parents have been informed and advised to prepare themselves for bad news.'

Annie passed a hand across her eyes. 'We don't speak anymore, not after my Neil was accused of involvement in their girl's disappearance. He had nothing to do with it but mud sticks, doesn't it?' Her sadness filled the room as she added, 'I'll ring them anyway. Maybe it will start to heal the rift. I was very fond of them and their company, and I miss them terribly. I can hardly bear to think about what they've had to go through these past years.'

After waiting a few tactful moments, Joseph took down the address of Carter Hayman along with Neil's mobile number.

As soon as they were back in the car, Joseph called the cell phone number. *'Not possible to connect you at this time.'* He pulled a face at Nikki. 'I suggest we get straight round to the Enterprise Park.'

She was already pulling away and heading towards the old Wash Road. 'We've been to the Park before, haven't we? Under some rather unpleasant circumstances.' Nikki was referring to a fire-starter who had once terrorised Greenborough. The business park had been one of his targets. 'I hope this visit turns out to be a bit less traumatic than the last one.'

The receptionist at the demolition company's head office looked somewhat mystified when asked where Neil Weldon was working at present. 'I was under the impression that Neil was at home on sick leave, but I'll certainly check for you.' She checked on her computer, looked up at Nikki and said, 'Yes, back strain. He's been signed off for a fortnight, as from a week ago.'

'I suppose he doesn't have a work phone, does he? As in a mobile used solely for business?' asked Joseph hopefully.

'Only the managers have those now, I'm afraid,' said the receptionist. 'Cutbacks. I'm so sorry I can't be of more help.'

Their expressions grim, they headed back to the car.

Back at the steering wheel, Nikki said, 'So, where is he?' She didn't really have to ask. Wherever Detective Oliver was holed up, she was certain they'd find Neil Weldon, incarcerated and "under arrest."

'I'm wondering if someone knows who the other woman is,' said Joseph thoughtfully. 'Before we throw up our hands to the fact that Oliver has him, we should check that he really isn't shacked up with a new, er, companion.'

'The only person I can think of asking is his wife,' said Nikki.

'Then we should ask her.' Joseph nodded at her phone.

She grimaced. 'I hate to pull rank, Joseph. I mean, you realise I'm only asking you to do it because you are *so* much more tactful than me..?'

Joseph took his phone from his pocket. 'Well, I certainly can't argue with that.'

Listening to him speak to Annie Weldon, Nikki could only wonder at his sensitivity. Not in a million years could she have dealt with such a delicate matter in that way.

He ended the call with a roll of the eyes. 'Thanks for that, DI Galena, I really enjoyed it.'

She smiled smugly. 'Needs must and all that, dear Joseph. So, what did you find out?'

'She said she believes the woman is the sister of a mate of Neil's. Her name is Fiona. The mate's name is Bruce Millard, and he lives in that new development where the old cinema used to be. Hollywood House, apartment seven. And he works from home. So, shall we pay a call?'

Nikki was already moving out of the parking space.

* * *

Wendy and Eve were back pacing the same field as before, this time more carefully. Sweeping the detector from side to side, they made sure to cover every inch of ground, while Chris and Maggie Tate watched eagerly from the sidelines.

After they'd dug up several pieces of junk, Eve was just beginning to wonder if they'd find anything after all when Wendy called out.

'Got something!'

Eve hurried over.

'It's not deep,' Wendy said, 'maybe five inches down, or a little more, but it's registering silver. It's not a very strong signal, though. Have you got the pinpointer?'

Eve began to dig. Even from a distance, she could feel the tension radiating from the watching Tates. Something she didn't know about, or understand, seemed to be at stake here.

Her trowel struck something hard but it proved to be much smaller than a cigarette case. 'Not what you were expecting, I'm afraid,' she called out. 'Looks like a coin, or it could be an old medal.'

She took it from its resting place and brushed off some of the loose soil. She still wasn't sure what it was, but suspected it to be a coin, although it did have a small hole through it. She placed it in her collecting pouch.

She and Wendy continued their sweep, until Wendy called out again, 'Okay, Eve, bring the pinpointer. We have another target.'

A few minutes later they were staring down at an old, battered silver cigarette case bearing the familiar lozenge shape with the three initials inscribed in it. Eve lifted it out, wiped off the surface dirt, and tried to prise it open. Remarkably, with just a hint of resistance, the catch released and she was looking at a few very old cigarettes. How strange it was, she thought, that these scraps of weedy tobacco and the paper they were wrapped in had survived whole all these years, when by now their owner was nothing more than bones and dust.

She took it across to the Tates and handed it to Chris. He received it in silence, and he and his wife remained that way for several minutes, looking at the object. Finally, he thanked them, and told them to come back to the farmhouse, so they could discuss payment for the three items.

Eve didn't want any money nor, she knew, did Wendy, merely a photo for their "finds" book. However, she accepted the invitation out of curiosity, intrigued by Chris and Maggie's reactions to their little discoveries.

'We'll just finish trawling this area, if that's okay with you?' Eve said. 'You never know, there might be a few more small items to be found.'

Chris told them that was fine, but could they come up to the house before lunch as he was out that afternoon?

After the Tates had gone, Wendy said, 'I'm dying to get to the bottom of this, aren't you? I mean, I fully understand their surprise when we showed them we'd found great-grand-father's stolen possessions right here on the farm but is it me, or was their reaction very odd?'

'Oh, I feel exactly the same,' said Eve, 'Let's give it another twenty minutes, then we'll go and see what we can find out up at the farmhouse. Are you up to a little bit of digging of a rather different kind?'

Wendy's grin stretched from ear to ear. 'I certainly am.'

* * *

'That went well,' said Joseph dryly, as they climbed back into the car.

'I'll say,' Nikki grunted. 'And the outcome stinks.'

Neil's friend, Bruce Millard, had been at home, and he'd had a visitor with him — his sister, Fiona. It soon became obvious that the woman was in pieces. Neil Weldon had jilted her, or that was what she presumed. Amid floods of tears on her part and righteous anger on Bruce's, they told Nikki and Joseph that Neil had promised to take her away for the weekend, saying he wanted to talk about their future together. But he never turned up. He hadn't rung either. Fiona was convinced that he had returned to his wife and hadn't had the bottle to tell her.

'Let's face it, Joseph. Oliver has got him, hasn't he?'

'I can't think of any other reason for his sudden disappearance,' Joseph said unhappily. 'And as we haven't a clue as to who sodding Detective Oliver is, I can't see how we can find Neil.'

Frustrated and angry, they drove back to the station. Their only option was to try and trace Neil's movements from when he left home, supposedly to go to work. They had the date and approximate time, and his vehicle registration number. Cameras might well have picked up his car. It wasn't much, but it was something. Even so, it wasn't nearly enough for Nikki, and by the time she entered the car park, she was spitting tacks. Once again, they were reduced to waiting to hear word from this bloody sham detective, and Nikki wasn't good at patience.

'Look, Nikki.' Joseph pointed towards the door. 'Cat and Yvonne are in a hurry. I wonder what they're up to.'

The two women were running towards a parked police car.

Joseph called out. They immediately changed course, and Nikki saw relief on Cat's face.

'Thank goodness you're back, boss,' Cat exclaimed. 'We have an IC1, white European male, found dead, possibly strangled. A court usher on his way to a hearing came across him at the back of the County Court building.'

'Jump in, you two. Let's see what we have.' Nikki tried to keep her voice even, but her sharp mind had immediately made the connection. A body found at the court? She hoped she was wrong, but instinct told her that Oliver had gone beyond the role of detective. They were about to finally meet Neil Weldon.

* * *

A swift glance at Nikki was enough to tell Joseph that she had reached the same conclusion as him. While she drove, he kept seeing that list of missing girls. Was this horrible scenario to be played out time and again, until the last girl had been unearthed? What in hell's name was this avenging angel's mission? And what was the reason for it?

There was a simple explanation, and as far as Joseph could see, it ticked all the boxes. Oliver was a serial killer and he was bitterly disappointed that his work had never accorded him the notoriety that he craved. Oliver was making quite sure that the media couldn't ignore his handiwork this time. He was going to hand it to them on a plate, and in doing so make the police, Nikki in particular, look like incompetent fools.

Well, if that were the case, he, Joseph, would personally take this psycho down. And in doing so, he'd make sure that the world saw him as anything but righteous. They must prove him to be a callous scumbag of a killer, very much *not* an enigmatic, Bundy-type celebrity.

This was no ordinary case — the public's faith in the police was at stake. Oliver was right. The police had failed Alexandra, and he was playing on that. The public needed to believe that the police force didn't give up. They pursued an injustice until they were able to provide answers and bring the guilty to book. Just that it wasn't easy when their opponent held all the aces.

At the courthouse, they made their way through the police cordon. Joseph realised he was holding his breath. Would it be Neil Weldon? He swallowed hard.

Silently, Cat handed Nikki her phone, on which she had a photograph of Neil Weldon, lifted from the police files. Nikki passed it to Joseph, who saw a clean-shaven man with short brown hair and strong even teeth.

They pulled on protective suits and approached the body.

At the back of the court staff car parking area, the lifeless form of a man lay half-turned away.

Joseph sighed. If Neil had meant to leave his new love, he certainly wasn't going back. There was no doubt that the dead man at their feet was Neil Weldon.

Nikki was looking at the corpse thoughtfully. 'I know we're supposed to wait for forensics, but I can see the corner of an envelope sticking out from under his jacket. I need to know what it says.' She looked hard at Joseph. 'Avert your eyes if you think I'm out of line. This bit of rule-breaking is down to me.'

He shook his head. 'No. I want to know just as much as you do.'

When she was sure no one was looking, Nikki quickly slid the familiar envelope out from its hiding place. As expected, it bore the usual airmail sticker. Again, it was addressed to Nikki, but this time it was unsealed. She took out the thin sheet of paper and read, *"As your failure rate is so high, I took the liberty of bypassing the system, one that would no doubt have failed to bring about real justice anyway, and have brought the investigation to a satisfactory conclusion. This case is closed."*

Joseph felt a shiver run down his spine. It was far from closed. The truth was, this case was just beginning.

CHAPTER NINE

Nikki went in person to break the news to Annie Weldon, and to ask if she would be able to make the identification. Annie had rung her sister, who lived nearby, so she could go with her for support. Now they had a formal ID, and another murder investigation was underway. They were now officially hunting Oliver. A second whiteboard was put up in the CID room with the photograph of Neil Weldon at the top.

'We've had a call from Professor Rory Wilkinson, ma'am.' Zena Gardner, Nikki's own office manager, handed her a memo. 'He said to ring him asap on his mobile.'

Nikki thanked her and did so at once.

'Ah, my dear Detective Inspector! I have a positive plethora of news for you about your long-dead girl, and now you throw this at me, a real-life courtroom drama — well, almost, as it's in the car park — complete with sentence carried out. May I beg you to please meet me at the morgue in an hour? I'll be back by then and, as a little incentive, I'll send Cardiff out for proper coffee.'

Nikki hated the morgue but needed the information. 'As long as there's coffee . . .'

'Excellent! See you then.'

She ended the call and saw Joseph approaching her. His expression was strained. 'You've just spoken to Fiona Millard, haven't you?'

'I rang Neil's friend Bruce's number and Fiona was still there,' he said. 'He asked me to tell her about Neil, so I had little option. She wants to see the body, but I explained that it wasn't possible. God, I hate it when these things get messy.'

'It's not our fault if he played away,' said Nikki grimly. 'But it still comes down to us to make all the right noises when things go tits up. Anyway, this should cheer you up. Rory wants to see us at the morgue in an hour's time.'

Joseph visibly brightened. Seeing his expression, Nikki couldn't help wondering what their chosen profession was doing to them when a trip to the morgue was a source of cheer.

'Good,' Joseph said. 'That gives me time to make sure all the right people are notified of Neil's last journey from his home. It's imperative that we find his car and track it.'

'And I need to update Cam about this morning's discovery,' she said. 'See you back here in forty minutes.'

* * *

She wasn't sure if it was because she felt particularly edgy about Ruby Grayson, or because there was a full moon tonight, but Lynette Sims's class had behaved appallingly all morning. It was a huge relief to get away from them in the lunch hour. Then, on her return, she glanced into the girls' locker room and saw Ruby sitting alone. Her shoulders were hunched, and she gave the distinct impression that she had been crying.

Lynette's heart sank. With a soft knock on the door to let the girl know she was there, she went in and sat down next to her. 'I really think it's time you and I had a proper talk, Ruby. You know you can speak freely to me, and if I can help, I will.'

'No one can help,' Ruby said in a listless whisper.

'That's not right, Ruby. It might seem that way now, but if you share your problem, whatever it is, I can help you, and if I can't, I'll find someone who can.' She sat quietly for a moment, waiting. 'Please, Ruby. Don't try to shoulder things alone.'

'I can't talk about it, Miss. It's family stuff, and I shouldn't talk to other people about family stuff.' The girl sniffed.

'Is someone hurting you, Ruby? I really have to know.'

She shook her head. 'No. No, it's not me.'

For a moment Lynette was certain Ruby was going to open up, but abruptly, the girl stood up. 'I have to go.'

Lynette was left alone in the locker room. Well, if Ruby wasn't being hurt, who *was*? Someone was. Someone in the Grayson family was in trouble, and Ruby knew about it. She just had to get the girl to share what she knew.

She had a few minutes before afternoon classes were due to begin, just enough time to have a quick word with Miss Barrett. Lynette hurried through the gathering groups of students towards the deputy head's office.

Luckily, Miss Barrett was alone.

Standing in front of the desk, Lynette told her what had happened. Di Barrett considered for a moment or two, and then nodded slowly.

'Perhaps it's time to reconsider how we approach this, Lynette. Leave it with me and I'll have a think about what's the best way to proceed. Come back after school finishes, if you'd be so kind.'

Lynette felt easier having shared her concern. Not that she'd let it go. She felt a deep personal responsibility for her young, and hitherto most promising, student. Come hell or high water, Lynette Sims was not going to let Ruby Grayson down.

* * *

Looking at her phone, Dinah Barrett had noticed a Breaking News flash regarding the discovery of a body at a deserted farm on Blackstone Fen. They were awaiting a statement from the police but early indicators pointed to the deceased being Alexandra Cornfield, a young woman who had disappeared several years ago.

Dinah couldn't help feeling a stab of irritation. It was a terrible thing, of course, but the timing was not exactly helpful. Her dear friend Yvonne Collins, now part of CID, would be snowed under dealing with it, and would have little time for Dinah's suspicions about domestic abuse in the family of one of her students.

After deliberating for a few moments, Dinah picked up her phone. She was not going to ignore this. Old murder be damned, this was taking place now, and she had a responsibility to both her staff and her children. It was time to talk to Yvonne and, busy or not, she would make sure she listened.

* * *

On her way out of the CID room, Nikki noticed an anxious expression on Yvonne's face. She made a mental note to talk to her when they returned from seeing Rory Wilkinson. Right now, though, she needed to know what the pathologist had for them.

Rory was practically buzzing when they arrived. He ushered them towards his office on his toes, almost skipping in his excitement.

They passed the table on which the remains of Neil Weldon had been laid out, and Nikki was glad it was nowhere near the one bearing Alexandra Cornfield. It had never seemed appropriate to her that a victim and their alleged killer should be kept in close proximity, even in death. Later, she was told that the girl's remains had been removed to "Rory's Retreat," an inner sanctum totally secure from cross-contamination where forensic post-mortems were conducted in minute detail.

Once they were seated, Rory launched into his reasons for calling them. 'You would have had this little diamond of information earlier had you not decided to throw yet another unfortunate soul my way. Naughty, naughty! Nevertheless, this little discovery of mine is quite amazing.' He beamed at Nikki. 'Once again, our dear friend pollen has put in an appearance. Palynology is indeed the Holy Grail of crime scene investigation. And lucky me, my dear friend the forensic ecologist who helped us once before drove over and took some samples from the scene at March Farm. Did you know that pollen can last for millions of years, dear hearts?'

Nikki nodded sagely. 'Yes, Rory, I did, because I was actually listening to your last tutorial on the subject.'

'Were you? Good grief! Wonders will never cease.' Rory looked at her, seemingly amazed. 'Anyway, let's not digress. Setting aside all the scientific detail, the bottom line is this: Alexandra was killed in the old derelict barn and dragged out and buried where we found her. We know this from the pollen of a particular plant species found at the location. She was definitely not murdered somewhere else and transported to Blackstone Fen.'

This was big news for Nikki. It meant they had their actual murder scene, and not just the place where the body had been discovered.

'I can see from your expression that Rory has made you a happy bunny, but wait. There is more to come.' He leaned forward, elbows on his desk. 'Whoever your Oliver is, he will have these very distinctive spores and pollen deposits in his clothing and embedded in the soles of his shoes. What we found in soil samples from that location was pollen in microscopic form, from a particular type of crop being grown in the surrounding fields. It was a new variety being trialled for this season. Even if he washes his clothes, he will not get rid of it as it lodges in seams, collars and cuffs and pockets and lasts for ages. When you find your Oliver, Nikki, I can check him out and tell exactly if it was he who first exhumed Alexandra's body.'

'Believe me, Rory, you'll be the first to know when we do get a suspect.' Nikki wondered what the police had done before forensic science became so advanced.

'Our girl died from a crushing blow to her temple. The shattered bone of the skull proves that beyond doubt. From the kind of circular fracture it caused, I'm looking at a metal object for the weapon, maybe a hammer, but we're doing some in-depth work on that fracture and I'll confirm our findings later.' Rory sat back. 'And, finally, your airmail envelopes.'

Nikki gazed at Rory expectantly.

'We have good news and bad. They can easily be bought online, even vintage-style ones, but those your friend is using are original old envelopes dating from the seventies. It would appear that someone kept a stash of them, even though they're no longer in use.'

'And the good news?' Nikki said.

'Our faithful pollen, my lovely friend. Since we have been using palynology, we have found pollen in threatening letters and ransom notes and, guess what? There is pollen in both of your envelopes. It's not from some rare or exotic plant, in fact it's something often found in the Fens, but it will help to pinpoint where those letters were written. Find Oliver, find his lair, and Rory Wilkinson — along with his trusty sidekick pollen — will tell you if you have the right man, and the right location.'

Nikki had a sudden memory of an old case that had Derbyshire police hunting the county for a magnolia and a tulip tree growing close together. She grinned at Rory. This was all positive stuff, and it added up to solid evidence that would be hard to refute. 'You're right, Prof, I am a happy bunny. And I appreciate what you've told us. One other thing, though. Have you had a chance to look at Neil Weldon yet?'

'You mean, do I believe he's the man who killed Alexandra?' He sighed. 'Nikki, dear heart, I'm the best, there's no doubt about that, but even I don't have a crystal ball. The poor man has only been here an hour or so. Please! At least give this genius time to examine the man!'

'Actually, I was only wondering how he died,' she said, eyebrows raised. 'I was saving your question for later.'

'Oh, right, sorry about that, but I know what you're like.' Rory smiled sheepishly. 'Our Mr Weldon was hanged, and frankly, it was a bungled job. Your Oliver might be some kind of criminal mastermind but he'd make a bloody awful hangman. Even the rope was coarse and thready, so it didn't do its job well at all. Oh, and before you ask, we will be taking as many samples as we can from the deceased, in the hopes that we'll find trace evidence that will indicate where he was killed.'

Hanging? Capital punishment? Nikki felt sick. Oliver had said that he had decided to skip the legal process and cut to the chase, but this was too much.

Joseph cleared his throat. 'I'm starting to believe that this game of his is far more dangerous than just trying to point out our shortcomings and blame us for not finding missing girls.'

'I'm with you there,' said Rory. 'As I recall, there were four names on that list, so you really don't want three more suspects put on trial and disposed of — rather unprofessionally, I hasten to add — by this Oliver person, do you?'

'That hasn't gone unnoticed, believe me,' murmured Nikki. She looked at Joseph. 'We really need to pull our finger out and find out who this bastard is before he creates total havoc.'

Rory added, 'Naturally we will do all we can to try to ascertain if there is any connection between that rather sad young woman and Neil Weldon. But there is little left to work with except the rags that once were her clothes, and her bones, bless her.'

'To be honest, Rory, I'm banking on you finding something on Neil that could lead us to his killer. At the time, there wasn't enough evidence to charge Neil with any connection to Alexandra's disappearance, but Oliver seems to believe he has discovered something we missed. We have to read the case notes very, very carefully so as to fathom out whether there was any real evidence. But right now, we are treating this as the murder of an innocent man.'

'I can't help but think that Oliver is the original killer, and that it was he who buried her at March Farm. That's why he knew where she was.' Joseph looked thoughtful. 'And he's shifting the blame on to Neil who, after all, was our number one suspect for a while.'

Rory stood up. 'Forgive me, cherubs, but although all this hypothesising is great fun, it won't get my post-mortem finished. I have to go and tend to the dead. And you, my dears, have a possibly deranged killer to find.' He smiled benignly. 'Cancel the word "possibly." The man's as mad as a box of frogs.'

The drive back to the station passed in silence. Nikki was busy sorting the team into their various tasks, while Joseph sat staring out of the window. Both of them were wondering how long it would be before another *Par Avion* letter landed on Nikki's desk. She had an idea, however, that Oliver wasn't particularly interested in them or their investigations, he just wanted to lead them through their catalogue of past failures. Basically, he was doing their job for them, or the job that should have been done years ago, and if he really was innocent of involvement in the disappearances and Alexandra's death, then he was doing it rather efficiently.

Scarily efficiently.

* * *

Lying on the kitchen table at Homelands Farm, Chris's great-grandfather's silver watch, ring and cigarette case seemed to tower over the four people who sat drinking tea.

'I'm still trying to get my head around it,' said Chris, shaking his head. 'It's unbelievable to come across them like this after all this time.' He gave Eve and Wendy an almost hesitant smile. 'Look, I know how important these kinds of finds are to you detectorists, but—'

'Chris,' Eve said, 'we enjoy the hunt, that's all. We're both fully aware that these items are precious family possessions.

All we are asking is that you let us photograph them for our book of finds. They belong to you, no question.'

'And we don't want payment either,' added Wendy. 'This is a hobby, just a pastime, and this find has been very gratifying. That's payment enough.'

Chris held up his hands in surrender. 'Then maybe you'd like to use our fields whenever you like — between harvest and planting, of course — without having to ask permission every time. We certainly have enough acreage for you to search — if you want to, of course.'

Eve's eyes lit up. 'That's very kind of you, Chris. We'd love to accept your offer.'

Maggie poured fresh tea. She seemed to Eve to be unusually distracted. Eve glanced at Wendy and saw that she, too, was observing Maggie contemplatively.

'May I take those photographs now?' Eve asked.

'Fire away,' said Chris, and cleared the table around the objects.

Eve had brought her Pentax. She took shots of each item from several angles, close-ups of the engraved initials, and finally a couple showing the three finds together. 'That's perfect, thank you, Chris.' She sat down again. 'Just for our record, you said your great-grandfather's name was Thomas Norman Tate. Do you know his date of birth?'

Chris said that he didn't. He couldn't even remember the year he died.

'You'd have no objection if we checked that out, would you?' said Wendy. 'It's nice to be able to add a little background to our finds.'

'No, no, of course not,' said Chris, looking down at his tea.

Eve hadn't missed the slight inflexion in his voice. It appeared that he did mind. Before going to see the Tates, she and Wendy had discussed whether to come straight out with it, tell Chris they wanted to trace the mystery of the long-lost objects, or ask, as tactfully as possible, what exactly was bothering the Tates so much. Now they were actually here, she reconsidered. They didn't want to upset these people — after all, not only were they central to this strange affair but they were also next-door neighbours.

They drank their tea and chatted about life in the village, and Wendy described the few simple finds they had made in the gardens of Monks Lantern. 'We'd have loved to extend our search into the quiet garden — after all, it's all part of the property — but naturally that's out of bounds, having been a burial ground.'

Chris Tate glanced at his wife. 'We know about that. One of the markers in your garden of remembrance is inscribed with the name Thomas Norman Tate.'

'Oh, really?' exclaimed Eve. 'I thought we knew all of them by now, but I don't recall that name. If we had, we'd have connected it to you immediately.'

'My parents used to look after it when they were younger, but when the chapel closed and was finally deconsecrated, they stopped going there. I know some people had the remains of their ancestors exhumed and reburied elsewhere, but they decided that he was in the soil that he loved, so there he should stay, at one with the land he had tended all his life.' His voice softened. 'You've made a lovely job of that garden, ladies, and it's very generous of you to allow the villagers access to enjoy the peace and quiet. They do appreciate it, you know.'

'Well, they all helped us. If they hadn't rallied round, it wouldn't be what it is today,' said Eve. She recalled the mammoth task of clearing the area and saving it from turning into the overgrown jungle it had threatened to become when she first arrived in Beech Lacey. It had been one heck of an enterprise, but it was now a lovely garden, laid out with trees, glades and grassy paths that the villagers could enjoy when they wanted a bit of respite from the daily toil.

'At least you'll have no difficulty checking TNT's birth and death dates,' added Chris.

'This discovery has really upset you both, hasn't it?' said Wendy suddenly. She was looking at Maggie, who had hardly spoken since they arrived.

Maggie looked down, and it was her husband who answered.

'It comes as a bit of a shock to realise that your beliefs about a very traumatic incident in your family's history are all wrong.' He gave them an apologetic smile. 'I'm nothing more than a simple farmer, ladies. I love working this place. I love my wife and my boys. Yes, my farming methods have evolved along with the technology but my heart and my soul are rooted in the land. The weather, the seasons — such as they are these days — and nature still rule my life. The only thing that ever upset this perfect existence was the wrong done to my great-grandfather. It had a terrible effect on me as a young lad, you know. Besides the horror of Great-Grandad Tommy getting so viciously attacked, one man was murdered and two of his trusted men were hanged, for heaven's sake!'

Eve was quite taken aback by the passion in his words.

'I wanted to know the truth,' Chris went on. 'And I thought I did. Now it seems I know nothing.'

The furrows on his brow reminded Eve of the fields this man ploughed. She chanced a suggestion. 'Erm, Chris, what if we could help? We have time on our hands, we could take a look at what happened all those years ago. There are always records if you know where to look for them. You never know, maybe we could find you some answers.'

Chris hesitated. 'I very much doubt that you'd find more than I did, and I'd hate to waste your precious time, but I suppose . . . if you wanted to . . .' He left the sentence unfinished.

They left soon after that, hoping to get away before he changed his mind. They thanked the Tates, both for the tea and the generous offer of using the fields for their detecting, and hurried off.

They spoke little on the way home, both occupied with thoughts of their new project.

Wendy grinned at Eve as they let themselves into their chapel home. 'Here we go again, my friend.'

'Back into the past,' added Eve. 'But I think it'd be a good idea if we didn't mention it to my daughter.'

'Agreed,' said Wendy fervently. 'I don't have a death wish!'

* * *

Back at the farm, Maggie Tate stood, arms folded, and stared at her husband. 'You oughtn't t'ave said that.'

'Oh? What should I have said?' he bit back. 'If I'd refused, they'd only have wondered why. Anyway, look how long I spent searching. Hours, wasn't it? All for nothing.' He sighed and then tried to cajole his wife back into her customary good humour. 'What can two old biddies find that I couldn't? If they want to waste their time, let them.'

He was about to say that they probably didn't even have any computer skills other than playing solitaire or sudoku, but he remembered the complicated camera that Eve had handled so skilfully and closed his mouth.

Maggie softened, but still didn't look too convinced. 'I just think they should leave well alone.'

'Oh, honey! They'll soon give up on it, don't you worry. It's time-consuming and boring, and all you get are dead ends. Before you know it, they'll be back here, drinking our tea and telling us they're sorry but they hit a brick wall. You'll see.'

At the back of his mind, however, a niggling doubt remained. Did he really believe his own words? He wasn't sure at all.

CHAPTER TEN

Oliver felt as though he had embarked on the biggest roller-coaster ride of his life. Having launched his machine, it was gaining momentum with every passing minute. It was a fast, scary ride but he had it under control. Events were unfolding exactly as planned.

He sat in his study with the day's schedule clasped tightly in his hand. He had no way of knowing exactly how long it would take the "authorities" to react to his revelations, but he had a good idea. By now they'd be giving them priority, pulling as much manpower as they could muster off their other cases to concentrate on him. But they could only progress according to the schedule he had laid down. He was in charge of this operation, not the revered DI Galena. He chuckled to himself. How she must hate it! For someone like her, there was nothing worse than not being in control. He could imagine her chagrin at having to sit and wait for his every new move.

He had been planning his campaign for many years. The groundwork he had covered in that time, the discoveries he had made were little short of miraculous. Just think. He had no facilities, no forensic department on tap, no IT unit ready and waiting and not a soul to discuss his findings with. He had no team, no fawning sergeant to share the load. He was utterly alone.

Alone. He stared at the schedule, wondering why it looked a little out of focus. It couldn't be tears, he never cried. Not since . . .

Oliver mentally shook himself. This would not do. 'Right,' he muttered to himself. 'Moving on to this afternoon . . .'

* * *

The CID room was buzzing with activity. Nikki had called upon all available personnel to try and trace Neil Weldon's last movements, to discover the identity of Oliver and whether his claims might actually be valid. Cam Walker was in, apparently firing on all cylinders, galvanising the troops and bringing in extra help where possible. He had admitted to Nikki that looking after Kaye had been one of the toughest assignments he had ever had. He loved her so much that he overreacted to her every mention of being in pain. Even the little discomforts that had accompanied her recovery had him fussing far too much. They were both secretly rather glad that he was back at work.

Now Nikki and Joseph were heads down in her office, trying to uncover the truth of Neil Weldon's alibi. He had sworn that he was miles away when Alexandra went missing and had furnished the police with an assortment of locations and times — and, most importantly, a witness. This witness had been the main reason for Neil having been released without charge. Oliver, however, declared in his "report" that Neil Weldon's car had been seen on the night in question a mere few hundred yards from where Alexandra disappeared. Not only that, a woman had popped up who was prepared to swear that Neil had been behind the wheel.

'He's given this new witness a name,' said Joseph with a frown. 'Beth Greene. She's a former neighbour of the Cornfields. I'm going to check her out, okay?'

'Be my guest,' said Nikki. 'Although I wonder why she didn't come forward at the time.'

'Oliver says in his statement that she'd been working away, and was only home recently for a brief visit before going back to her job down south. She needs checking, no matter what, even if it's just to confirm her existence. As yet, we have no idea if this whole thing is one huge fabrication concocted by a psycho.'

'Absolutely,' said Nikki. 'And I'm going to look deeper into the original witness's background. From reading the statements, I'm not sure that they checked this man very thoroughly. It looks as if as soon as the alibi was confirmed, it was accepted as gospel. I'm not saying it was sloppy policing but I can't see too much in the way of follow-up.' She stopped. 'That reminds me, I've managed to contact Chief Superintendent Jim Summers from Fenfleet and he's coming over in about an hour's time. He's very anxious to help us.'

'Excellent. First-hand info from someone who was there at the time will be invaluable. Can I sit in?'

Nikki smiled. 'Of course you can. I'm anxious that you do. You might have some questions for him that I hadn't thought of.'

Joseph stood up. 'Then I'll go and find out all I can about Beth Greene.'

After he had gone, Nikki looked up the name of the original witness — Arnold Stone. He had been a workman, employed by subcontractors on one of the demolition jobs that Neil Weldon had been supervising. He had stated that his brother had been a night security officer at the site where they'd been working, and at around nine on the night in question he had stopped by to talk to him about something. He swore that he had seen and spoken to Mr Weldon at around nine fifteen, and that Mr Weldon had told him he had come back for his briefcase, which he'd mistakenly left in the site office. He had only realised it was missing when he got home, but as he wasn't going to be at the site the following day, he'd had no choice but to go back and retrieve it. This was the story that Neil had given the police, and Stone's corroboration had been accepted. Nikki found the home address for Arnold Stone, which was in Fenchester, not a million miles away. The thing was, did he still live there? Ten years had gone by and the man could be anywhere. She looked at the contact details and picked up the phone. The voice that answered was guarded. Yes, Mr Stone still lived at this address but he was very poorly and couldn't speak to her.

Nikki felt her hackles rise. Something about that voice gave her a distinct impression that she was in fact talking to Arnold Stone himself.

'Who am I speaking to?' she asked, rather more curtly than she'd intended.

'I'm his cousin. I look after him. As I said, he's too ill to speak to you, I'm sorry.'

Nikki stared at the phone. The man had hung up.

She glanced at the clock. There wasn't enough time to get to Fenchester and back before Jim Summers arrived, but someone needed to check the veracity of Stone's supposed illness.

Nikki went out into the CID room and looked around. Everyone was busy — on the phone, or staring intently at their screens. Oh well, she'd just have to go herself after they'd spoken to the chief super.

She was starting to worry that bloody Oliver might have been right about that alibi. She went over the statement again and found nothing to corroborate it. Maybe Jim would be able to shed some light on all this.

'I've tracked down the woman in Oliver's report, Nikki.' Joseph was standing in the doorway. 'I've just spoken to her. She's now living in Kent, but she told me a very interesting story.'

She beckoned him in. 'Tell me.'

'Turns out she received a call a short while back, from a detective called Oliver, from CID.' He raised an eyebrow. 'This Oliver told her they were following up new leads in the case of the disappearance of Alexandra Cornfield, and he had been led to believe that Beth might have been in the area on a certain date in January. She said that he sounded very kind and had apologised for contacting her after all this time, but in a new attempt to find answers, he was speaking to old neighbours and hunting down people who lived in the vicinity of where the girl went missing.' Joseph glanced at his sheet of notes. 'He told her that her mother had mentioned that Beth had been staying with her for a family New Year's Day get-together but had returned to the South before the police could question her.' Joseph looked back at Nikki. 'Beth was never interviewed, Nikki. And when her parents rang her and told her what had happened, they only asked if she might have seen Alex, not anyone connected to the family. She only remembered seeing Neil in his car when Oliver asked her about him by name.'

'Did she sound believable?' asked Nikki dubiously. 'After all, it's a whole lot of years after the event. How on earth could she recall who she saw and when?'

'Beth told me that it had been a bit of an emotional visit for her. She hadn't been working away from home long and her job had just been made permanent. So, she was actually leaving home for good. That night she was on her way to say goodbye to her two dearest friends, and seeing Neil Weldon reminded her that she needed to call in and see Alexandra before she set off the following morning. As it was, she was running late, and left without seeing her. By the time news of the disappearance broke, she was gone.' Joseph looked up from his notes. 'I believe her, Nikki. She was definitely on the level.'

'Well,' said Nikki, 'I'm feeling the complete opposite about Mr Arnold Stone. I'm planning to make a surprise visit as soon as we've spoken to Jim Summers. In fact, you should come with me. Mr Stone is apparently too ill to talk to us, but my gut instinct tells me that his supposed cousin, who informed me of the fact, was none other than bloody Arnold himself.'

'Well, if Beth Greene is telling the truth about when and where she saw Neil, your Arnold definitely was lying.' Joseph frowned. 'Perjury carries a hefty sentence. He's probably shitting himself right now.'

'And don't forget, like Beth, he might also have had a call from DI sodding Oliver, and that might well have put the fear of God in him.' She pushed some papers around on her desk until she found the relevant notes. 'He says, and I quote, "Stone should have been marked up as an unreliable witness. Further investigation would most likely have shown him to have numerous gambling debts, and that he would have been more than capable of lying if the reward was high enough."' Nikki threw the paper back on the desk. 'Something else to ask Jim about.'

Joseph looked pensive. 'Didn't the Cornfield investigation have a bit of a reputation? It's not one I'm familiar with, but if Oliver really is coughing up reliable alternative evidence, it doesn't sound too good, does it?'

'You mean was it a total shambles? I hate to say it, but that's the word on the street. I've only spoken to two uniforms who had some minor dealings with the case but they both used the same word for it: "cock-up."'

Joseph grunted. 'Then it's going to be a rather difficult conversation with Jim Summers. He was the SIO, wasn't he?'

'Jim's a good bloke. Even a good officer can find himself embroiled in a messy case that doesn't have a good outcome.' She gave a humourless laugh. 'But fear not, I won't castigate the man without just cause. After all, he's a chief superintendent, and I value my new, shiny reputation among the higher echelons.' She chuckled. 'Frankly I couldn't give a flying—'

'Got the message.' Joseph glanced behind him towards the door. 'And here's your visitor. He's just walked into the CID room.'

Chief Superintendent Jim Summers was a big man in all respects — tall, more than a little overweight, with a thatch of greying brown hair and dark perceptive eyes. He also had a ready smile and friendly manner — unless you were on the wrong side of the law. Jim Summers had a reputation for coming down hard on criminals, and it was often whispered that it was probably a good thing that he wasn't in place back in the seventies, as quite a few villains might have sustained some nasty bruises during their time in his holding cell.

Nikki introduced Joseph, and asked her manager to organise some tea or coffee for their visitor.

Pleasantries over, Jim sat down opposite her and took a deep breath. 'Nasty business, or so I gather. The way that lass's body was discovered wasn't exactly textbook, was it?'

Nikki gave him the whole story, from the first airmail missives to the killing of Neil Weldon.

While he listened, Jim's face grew more and more stony. 'I'll admit it to you two, it was a bastard of a case. If anything could go wrong, it did. It's not an excuse, just a statement of fact, but we were so short-staffed our situation would have been farcical if that lass hadn't gone missing when she did. I'd lost two good officers when that case broke, my best detectives. We did our damnedest to find her, but it was as if the whole investigation was jinxed. Evidence went missing, statements were incorrectly taken . . .' He threw up his hands. 'If anyone tells you it was a screw-up, you should believe them.'

So, we did fail her, thought Nikki gloomily. Sodding Oliver was right about that.

'The thing is,' continued Jim, 'if there's now anything I can do to help, I'd like to do it. That case has haunted me, and if there's a chance of putting something right, I'd be glad of it, even just for my own conscience's sake.' He sighed. 'Even at the time, I had a lot of reservations about some of the suspects, and we always believed that Alexandra had been abducted and murdered. We never wanted to give up on it, but after Neil Weldon came forward with an alibi, our trail petered out.'

'Can we ask you about that witness, sir?' Nikki said. 'Was there any suspicion that Arnold Stone might have been lying?'

Jim Summers frowned. 'No. He seemed perfectly legitimate. He was checked out and his story validated. We confirmed that his brother was on security duty at the site, and he verified that Arnold had called to see him that night.'

'And did the brother see Neil too?' asked Joseph.

'No, but he said that Arnold had told him Neil Weldon had come back for a briefcase that he'd left behind.' Jim's frown deepened. 'Don't tell me you think Stone lied to give Neil a false alibi?'

Nikki handed him Oliver's report, the suggestion about Stone's gambling highlighted. 'Our bogus detective believes Stone perjured himself for a hefty payment. As I'm sure you understand, sir, we are obliged to check everything he says, so I rang him. I was given the brush-off by someone who said Stone was too ill to talk to me. I'm sure it was Stone speaking. He's going to get a visit later today and I intend to do some pretty in-depth checks on his background.'

'I'd like to come with you if I may.'

Nikki was somewhat taken aback but she nodded. 'Of course, sir. Joseph and I were going to leave as soon as we'd finished here, if that suits you?'

'Certainly. I've arranged with DCI Charley Anders to cover for me for a while. She'll notify me of anything urgent that needs my attention. Meanwhile, I need to try and rectify our mistakes of ten years ago.' He hesitated. 'So long as you don't think I'm interfering? This is your case, Nikki, treat me like a consultant, and I'm still perfectly capable of doing legwork or chasing up old records.'

'I'm hardly going to turn down expert help, sir. We'd be very grateful for your input and your assistance.' Nikki meant it. She was already calculating that another pair of hands, even if they did belong to a chief super, might give Yvonne Collins a bit of leeway to keep an eye on her stalker. Both Yvonne and Cat were seriously worried about one of the possible victims, and it would be foolish to ignore the concerns of two respected officers.

'Then I'll go and have a quick chat with your Cameron Walker, and make sure he knows this isn't a takeover bid by Fenfleet!' He gave a booming laugh.

'Can I just ask what your personal opinion of Neil Weldon was?' Joseph said.

'I thought he was guilty as hell. Sadly, I had no proof. He came across as the distraught uncle, desperate for news of his missing niece. He even made an appeal on the local news, but as we all know, that could have been a clever way of distancing himself from blame.' Jim shrugged. 'I thought he was in deep. And I didn't trust him one inch. It was only when that witness came forward that I began to doubt myself. I wondered if maybe I was so desperate to find the poor kid that I was pinning everything on the most obvious suspect, Neil Weldon.'

'What made you think it was him?' said Joseph.

Jim thought for a moment. 'He spent an inordinate amount of time with the Cornfields — by which I mean his sister Amanda and her husband Michael, and Alexandra, of course. Far more than married siblings usually do. I mean, I know some families are very close, but after you get married, you have your own responsibilities — jobs, and heaven knows what to cope with. You don't usually spend more time with your sister than with your own family.'

'That fits in with something Annie Weldon told us,' Nikki said. 'She said Neil seemed oblivious to his family responsibilities. He left it all to her, apparently, and by the way, those kids of his are a right handful.'

'Another thing,' Jim said. 'When he was making good money, and Alexandra was younger, he'd shower her with presents. The Cornfields said he was the perfect uncle, always there for the girl, and had openly admitted that he regretted having only sons. That immediately rang warning bells in my head. If it hadn't been for Arnold Stone swearing on oath that Weldon had been forty-odd miles away when the kid disappeared, I'd have put money on creepy Uncle Neil abducting her.' He sat back. 'Did you know that Alex was on her way to meet a new boyfriend when she disappeared? Well, I reckoned that was too much for Neil and he went into a rage.'

'If I can't have her, no one else will either,' Nikki said.

'Exactly. Jealousy, pure and simple.'

There was a knock on Nikki's door, and Cat stuck her head in. 'Sorry to interrupt, boss, but I've just found out something I thought you'd want to hear.'

Nikki beckoned her over and introduced her to Jim Summers. 'So, Cat, what have you dug up?'

'You asked me to check whether Oliver's claim in his report that Neil Weldon had a connection to March Farm was correct. Well, it was. Oliver was right. Neil Weldon did know the farm where Alexandra's body was discovered. He'd been there several times on behalf of his company, Carter Hayman. The prospective new owners were getting quotes for demolishing the barns and outbuildings and levelling the ground, but they pulled out of the purchase and the place has never been sold. And — here it comes — the reason it never sold, and probably won't, is that part of the ground is contaminated. It's something to do with an old storage depot that was attached to the farm during the second world war. Weldon knew all about it, and that people rarely went there. Sorry, boss, but Oliver is correct, and it puts Weldon squarely in the frame for murder.'

No one spoke for a while. Finally, Jim said, 'Oh shit!'

Nikki remained silent. There seemed little else to add.

CHAPTER ELEVEN

Nikki now had backup in the form of Jim Summers for her visit to Arnold Stone, so Joseph opted to stay behind and keep working. Information about the case was mounting, and it all pointed to "Detective Oliver" having been sickeningly thorough in his private investigations.

Joseph's mobile phone rang.

'Sorry, dear heart,' said the familiar voice of Rory. 'No answer from the lovely Nikki, so you'll have to do. Now, pin back your ears, sweet Joseph, because this is mega.'

Guessing what he was about to say, Joseph nevertheless listened intently.

'I can irrefutably link our dead man, Neil Weldon, to Alexandra. It's a small piece of forensic evidence, and when I say small I mean microscopic, but it's a game-changer. It provides solid proof that he was with her when she died. Now, this will probably sound like science fiction, but yours truly, using a system based on silica membrane columns, has obtained a full DNA profile with balanced peaks, low noise and high reproducibility. And all from a ten-year-old bloodstain that was not Alexandra's. Impressed?'

'With the outcome? Totally overawed! Respect. Though you lost me with all the other stuff.' In fact, Joseph was poleaxed. 'Well, Rory. You've just put the final nail in the coffin, so to speak. Bloody Oliver has found the body, opened a casefile, solved it and topped the guilty party.'

'Look on the bright side, Joseph. He's saving the tax-payer a fortune. Heaven knows what a trial and a full life sentence costs these days. Now, my cadaver awaits. My next task is to find some trace of your industrious Oliver on the body of his victim. Ta-ta for now.'

Joseph stared at his mobile. He should tell Nikki. Or maybe not. If she, and her capable bodyguard, were grilling Arnold Stone, she wouldn't welcome a phone call. He'd wait till they returned.

He didn't wait long. Ten minutes later Nikki arrived back.

'Where's Summers?' asked Joseph.

'Downstairs, enjoying the sight of Stone being marched into the Custody Suite.' She smiled. 'You should have seen it, Joseph. Jim flung the book at him — threatened him with assisting an offender, wasting police time and perjury. Stone recognised Summers the moment he saw him, and looked like he was going to shit a brick! Oh, and we arrived just as he was loading cases into the boot of his car — and he wasn't going on a convalescent holiday either.' The smile faded a little. 'Mind you, we still have to prove it, but I think careful scrutiny of his finances are going to show some pretty damning anomalies, and he's really scared. Jim thinks he'll admit it rather than risk lying again and making things worse for himself.'

Joseph followed her into her office. 'Rory rang while you were out. He's firmly tied Weldon to Alexandra's death. Blood evidence. It pains me to say so, but it looks like Oliver got the right man.'

'Shame he didn't just hand us the file, instead of topping his suspect,' grumbled Nikki. 'He could have saved himself a life sentence. Because I will get the bastard.' She sank down in her chair. 'I reckon we should now direct all our efforts towards hunting for Oliver. If he really is the hotshot detective that he claims, and his record to date would seem to demonstrate, we are wasting precious time in constantly checking what he's already proved.'

'We can't just take everything he tells us as gospel,' protested Joseph. 'He got this right, but that doesn't prove he's infallible, any more than we are.' He smiled at her, head to one side. 'That said, I totally understand where you're coming from. We have to stop him before he turns public executioner again.' Joseph pictured the original list of names and shivered.

'Jim says he can arrange for some more officers to be drafted in to help out. Especially if Oliver goes for broke and the shit hits the fan big-time. He's okayed it with Cam, and I've agreed. Not even my ace A-team can cope with four enquiries at once.' She pulled a face. 'Think of the amount of paperwork just one investigation will generate. It's not a straightforward murder — we have to cope with the original disappearance, then the murder of a girl ten years ago, plus the hunt for Oliver. We need help with this one, and how.'

And Joseph, who was still wondering what was actually driving Oliver, was beginning to conclude that the confusion this overload of work would bring about was exactly what their "detective" wanted.

At the back of his mind was fear for Nikki. She'd always believed it was a personal vendetta and now he was starting to agree with her. If that was the case, was Oliver throwing so much at her in order to burn her out? Or set her up for a fall? Or make her the scapegoat for a whole series of unsolved police investigations? Or did he just hate her for some reason? Whatever it was, somehow Joseph was going to have to find time to do some digging into Nikki's past. At some point in her long and distinguished career, she had done something that had eaten deep into the heart of this man, and now he wanted payback.

* * *

Eve and Wendy stood in their tranquil garden and stared at a worn and mossy headstone. All the ornate, carved freestanding monuments had been left in situ, but the more modest ones like this had been moved to the perimeter of the garden when the ground was deconsecrated, which was probably why they'd missed it.

But there he was, Thomas Norman Tate, along with his birth and death dates.

'Well, it is very worn, and not exactly remarkable either,' said Eve. 'Considering he was the biggest landowner around here, I'd have expected something a bit more imposing.'

'Maybe there's more to Thomas than meets the eye,' said Wendy. 'I must say, I'm looking forward to digging the dirt.' She grinned wickedly.

'Well, no time like the present.' Eve straightened. 'Let's go back inside and hit the Ancestry trail.'

They hastened indoors, made a pot of tea and opened a new packet of Jaffa cakes. Laptops at the ready, they embarked on their search.

'How about you trace the Tate family, and see what you can learn about Thomas?' said Eve. 'And I'll see if I can pull up anything on the killing of that migrant worker. Is that okay with you?'

'Fine.' Wendy checked the printer to ensure it was well stocked with paper.

They were good at this. After all, you don't spend decades working for the MOD and then lose your skills just because you've retired.

The next couple of hours passed in comparative silence, punctuated only by grunts, the odd expletive, and the occasional appreciative chuckle when something fell into place. Finally, Eve got to her feet. 'I was going to suggest more tea, but as the sun is over the yardarm, how about a drop of something a bit stronger?'

Wendy looked up and smiled. 'Well, now you mention it, a Tio Pepe would go down nicely, and then I ought to see about supper.'

The friends took it in turn to cook. They made sure to eat healthily, and both enjoyed their food. They treated themselves to a dinner out once a week, and there was always the hope that Nikki and Joseph would ask them to supper — unlike them, Joseph was a true culinary artist.

Eve returned with two dry sherries. 'How's the work going?'

'I reckon I've got the beginnings of a nice family tree in place, and they certainly were a big family. Brothers, sisters, aunts, uncles, cousins, nieces and nephews, all over this area. I haven't come across anything specific yet, but I have a feeling we'll find quite a few juicy skeletons in the Tate family cupboards. Oh, and I also found an interesting local history site on Google. The historian who produced it published a whole series of articles on well-known Fenland families in which the Tates feature quite heavily.' She looked amused. 'And guess what? According to the author, Tommy Tate was a bit of a bounder.'

Eve sat back down. 'So, he was a naughty boy, was he?'

'More like a lecherous old bastard if this author is correct,' laughed Wendy. 'And his foul temper was legendary. TNT was a very apt initial, it seems.'

'Oh dear, so not the benevolent and well-loved landowner that one might suppose. Maybe there was more to the attack on him than mere robbery.' Eve had already arrived at this conclusion, but would they be able to discover what it was after so long?

'I've sent an email to the historian and asked if he'd be up for a chat about the Tates. He's clearly done a lot of research, so there might be other things that his articles didn't mention.' Wendy sipped her sherry. 'I'm waiting for a reply now. So, how are you doing with the murdered man?'

'Better than expected, actually,' said Eve. 'I found his name, which is Jan Laska, almost straight away. Then I gained a vague idea of what had happened from two, probably highly inaccurate, newspaper reports that I found through a site on sensational murders from the past. I'd already got the names of the two farmhands who committed the killing from local records, plus — and this is the most accurate report

I've found — an entry in the *Encyclopaedia of Executions*. Yes, there is one, and it's a treasure trove of information. It backs up the newspaper accounts to a degree but also provides a mass of other detail. Listen to this regarding the executed men: Name, Age at Execution, Date of Execution, Place of Execution, Hangman, Assistant, Date of trial, Location of Trial, Presiding Judge, Prosecution Counsel, Defence Counsel and Number of Victims. We've got it all!'

'And the victim?' asked Wendy.

'There's fewer details about the victim but nevertheless it's a real stepping stone. It gives name, age, date of murder, place of murder, method of killing, and relationship to killers.' Eve was hugely satisfied with what she had achieved. 'I'll collate it all after supper and we'll have a discussion about how to proceed.'

Before she could answer, Wendy received an email message. 'Oh good, it's the local history guy. Let's see what he says.' As she read, a small smile spread across her face.

It would appear that the history buff was happy to talk. In Eve's book, they usually were. She'd known a couple that could talk for England.

'His name is Jacob Rush,' said Wendy. 'He'll meet us tomorrow morning. He says he knows quite a lot about not only the Tate family but the infamous murder of the migrant farmhand as well. Win-win!'

'Excellent, then we can compare what he says with what I've dug up. Let's just hope he's not one of those dry old duffers who like to lecture and don't let you get a word in.'

'We shall see,' said Wendy, closing her laptop. 'Now, supper. Are you okay with steak, new potatoes, and salad? My head is full of dark mysteries at present, and there's not much room for creativity.'

'Bring it on,' said Eve, suddenly realising how hungry she was. It was clearly doing them good to get their little grey cells working again. She was well aware of the years passing, every month seemed to bring with it some new ache or pain. Well, she was ready to give in to her joints, but she was determined not to let her brain or her imagination atrophy. 'You sort the steaks, I'll do the salad. Then we can get back to work!'

* * *

Listening to Dinah Barrett, Yvonne heard the consternation in the deputy head's voice. Immediately, she booked a new extracurricular activity for the hours after work, and was now, having grabbed yet another fast-food takeaway, on her way to her friend's house. Dinah wouldn't have rung her if she didn't think that Ruby Grayson was in serious trouble.

The finding of a body out at Blackstone Fen was headline news in all the media. Dinah would know that Yvonne would be up to her eyeballs in the case, so she must really need her, and Yvonne didn't want to let her down. If it was a case of a child living in an abusive situation, it should be down to social services to deal with it, not the police. Unless it was serious domestic violence, of course, and then they could step in. In either case, it was certainly not something for CID to handle. All she could do would be to listen to Dinah, advise her as best she could and then take it to Sergeant Niall Farrow. The thought of Niall made her smile. She had nurtured that lad from baby cop to sergeant and was justly proud of her handiwork. He wasn't going to refuse her anything.

So, here she sat, once again drinking tea in Dinah's kitchen. This time, however, there were no squirrel jokes.

'The Grayson family haven't cropped up in our records,' said Yvonne, 'which is a bit of a shame in one way, because if they were trouble, I'd probably be able to quote chapter and verse about them. As it is, I only met them once, something to do with their son and a bit of bother at his school. A something and a nothing in the end as I recall, but I vaguely remember them as a quiet, orderly family — the parents, that son and a daughter. Would that be right?'

Di nodded. 'Yes, Ruby and Daryl. He's quite a bit older than Ruby, around twenty-one by now, I think. And yes, the family do keep themselves to themselves, and they're very supportive of their children. The father is quite different from the mother, he's well read, and I suspect he had a good education. He works away a lot, I believe. Whereas the mother, well, I'm not sure about her background. She seems a bit overprotective.' Di shrugged. 'She may just be a worrier, but I get the feeling that she's always trying to shield her daughter, if you see what I mean?'

'What does the father do for a living, Di?' asked Yvonne.

'He's a designer of some kind, something to do with cars I think. His daughter mentioned that he's in charge of specialist car seats and vehicle interiors. He's based in Greenborough, although he travels between several of the company's factories overseeing new innovations. They live in one of the local villages.'

Yvonne struggled to recall her only visit to the Grayson home. She didn't remember much about the house itself, only that it was in the village of Marsh Enderby. 'So, what it comes down to is that your teacher, Miss Sims, believes that the mother is being abused in some way.'

Dinah sipped her tea. 'All Ruby would say was that it wasn't her, Ruby, who was being hurt. That would imply that someone else was in trouble, and in such cases it's usually the wife, though it could be the son. They both still live at home.'

'Or the husband,' added Yvonne grimly. It wasn't just women who were abused.

'One thing I am sure of is that Miss Sims is a good and conscientious teacher who takes the trouble to know her students. She is truly worried, and that's good enough for me.'

It all sounded so vague to Yvonne, she didn't quite know what to say. 'Okay. Now, as you know them, have you ever had even the slightest feeling of something being amiss in the family?'

Dinah put down her mug slowly, looking pensive. 'Maybe it's because of what Miss Sims has told me, but yes. When I think of it now, I've always felt there was something slightly, well, unreal about them. It sounds silly, but you know what families can be like, especially where their kids are concerned. They can be thrilled at how well their child is doing, emotional, argumentative, defensive, even aggressive sometimes. Their own personalities are revealed in how they talk about their children's futures. Sometimes they disagree with each other, which is perfectly normal. The Graysons, on the other hand, were attentive, agreeable and, yes, overprotective, but they came over as if they were playing the part of dutiful parents, saying all the right things and making the right noises. They gave nothing away about themselves, the family dynamic, or their home life, which is very unusual.' She paused, thinking. 'It was never enough to flag up the slightest concern, but nevertheless, in retrospect, maybe they aren't quite the perfect family they would have everyone believe they are.'

As Di spoke, Yvonne remembered more of her own meeting with them and began to understand what she meant. Little snippets of conversation came back to her. They were conciliatory, appeasing, apologetic, but there had been no real emotion behind their words, no outburst, no shocked indignation. 'When I went there after that trouble the boy got himself into, I left that house feeling no qualms about the family. They were comfortably off, obviously middle class, polite, well-dressed, and they'd been concerned about wasting valuable police time. Only one thing bothered me, it wasn't something I couldn't quite put my finger on.'

Dinah looked at her enquiringly. 'And?'

'It was the boy, Daryl Grayson. I really didn't like him.' She gave a wry laugh. 'Not exactly grounds for an arrest, I know, but it rankled. He had an air about him. We were certain he wasn't responsible for what he'd been accused of, yet we had a feeling that he was looking down on us, laughing at us for some reason.'

'I've never met him,' said Dinah, 'so I can't confirm or dispute what you say, but if you had a funny feeling about him, I'll go along with that.'

'Now you mention it,' Yvonne said, 'even after several years, I can recall thinking how incredibly unruffled they were, how controlled. When I was in uniform, I talked to hundreds of parents about their wayward kids, and there was always some sort of reaction. Some threatened to knock their kid's blocks off, others burst into tears, oh, all manner of emotional outbursts. Sometimes there was a cold rage, and that used to scare me most. It made me anxious about the child in question's safety.'

'I get the same when I talk to parents about a pupil's bad behaviour. That odd placidity is exactly what I mean.' Dinah frowned. 'Now I'm worrying that they're covering something up, hence the pretence of being the ideal family. Ruby is a very intelligent girl, quite a long way ahead of a lot of her class, and whatever is going on in that house is affecting her badly. As a teacher I'm responsible for her well-being while she's in my care, but until I have an idea of what is going on, I can't really call on social services — it could make it worse, for Ruby, or whoever is the victim.'

Yvonne sighed. 'I'm not sure what I can do to help, Dinah. It's not just being so busy with the murders — yes, there's more than one. The next breaking news will feature a second murder, right here in Greenborough. No, it's the fact that now I'm with CID I can't deal with this kind of problem anymore. All I can promise is that I'll pass it on to someone in uniform who I totally trust, and what I will do is run a check on the father, see if he has anything bad in his past. In fact, I'll check the whole family. Can you give me their names to save me looking them up?'

'William and Melanie Grayson, and the name of the house is Pembroke. It's on the Green, in Marsh Enderby.' Dinah drained the rest of her tea. 'And, Yvonne, I do realise how busy you are. I think I just needed you to know about this. I'm not expecting you to wade in all guns blazing, but just in case something bad should happen, at least you're aware of it now, and I've registered my concerns.' She paused. 'And I'll get social services in as soon as I think it's the right moment to do so. The girl's safety is paramount.'

Yvonne was on her way home when a sudden thought occurred to her. The first thing she always did at the start of each day was check all the overnight reports, and this morning there had been a call registered from a woman in Marsh Enderby. What had it been about? She forced herself to remember. Yes. She'd reported hearing cries at night. Yvonne took a deep breath. It was a small village. Could it be connected to Ruby and her family?

Yvonne almost fell through her front door, and before she'd even taken her coat off, she rang the station. A few moments later she had a name: Mrs Andrea Smith, of Twisted Willows, The Green, Marsh Enderby. The Green. This was no coincidence. If there were cries coming from somewhere on the Green, they could only be coming from the Grayson house.

* * *

Frank Ravenhill contemplated his daughter. 'Look, lass, you've not seen hide nor hair of this creep for a couple of days now, and you really need to get back to work tomorrow. I'm on late shift, so how about either I take you in, or I follow you, just to make sure there's no one hanging around? Your mum's said she'll meet you and walk home with you when you finish. Just get back on the horse, my girl, or you'll finish up being one of those poor souls who's afraid to step outside the door.'

'Sermon over, is it?' asked Julie Ravenhill. Deep down she knew her dad was right. Hiding away like a frightened mouse wouldn't solve anything. She just wished that the police would catch this man. She'd sent them details of all the times and places she recalled having seen him, which the detective who'd visited said was very helpful. But having seen the news at teatime, Julie doubted they'd have time for anything as insignificant as a stalker, not when they had two murders to solve. 'Okay, Dad. I'll go back. I won't take the car, it's only a ten-minute walk, but please say you'll follow me and watch out for anyone suspicious?'

Frank nodded. 'Anything for my princess, and I'm glad you're going back to work. They've been very good, but they won't take kindly to you being off for too long. You have to look at it from their point of view, they have a business to run.' He beamed at her. 'Now, your mum's got popcorn, it's family film night, remember? And it's your turn to choose a film, just don't pick anything too schmaltzy!'

'Better than something creepy,' she said with feeling. 'I've had enough of looking over my shoulder for real!'

* * *

Samantha Chisholm turned into her road and quickened her pace. She'd been feeling anxious ever since she'd left the safety of the community hall, and the sight of her own front door came as a relief. She had never seen him clearly, but she was convinced he was still watching her. It couldn't all be in her imagination, Sammie had never been so frightened in her life. She wouldn't have gone out at all tonight, but she'd had a call to say she'd left her purse behind after her Pilates class the other night.

She'd only been gone ten minutes, but her fear mounted with every step. Her house was only a matter of metres away but she knew he was somewhere close. Was that a hint of cologne? A scented plant in someone's garden? A stealthy footstep, or a sound from someone's TV coming through an open window?

Sammie stopped abruptly and turned full circle. 'Leave me alone!' she shouted. 'Whoever you are, just leave me alone!'

She was terrified, but angry too. This pervert had no right to invade her life like this.

Then she heard it. A low chuckle. She froze. It was a horrible sound, the voice of someone insane.

Sammie made a dash for it, her key ready in her hand.

This time it was a kind of childish giggle. It turned her blood to ice.

Yet another sound but Sammie didn't stop to listen. She ran as fast as her legs would carry her. Despite her shaking fingers she unlocked the door first try, and in seconds she was inside and sliding the inner bolt across. Even then she didn't relax. She ran upstairs and looked anxiously out of the window to where the laughter had come from. Staring into the dark, she thought she saw movement among the shrubs in a neighbouring garden, but it wasn't repeated.

Sammie pulled her phone from her pocket and rang DC Cat Cullen.

* * *

'Well, at least we've finished supper,' remarked Ben, who was a glass half-full kind of bloke. 'And my mind-numbingly boring course has left me with a thirst for some proper police work.'

Cat drew up outside Sammie's little terraced house. 'Poor kid sounded frightened to death. She's trying not to let this bastard stalker rule her life but she's in real danger, I'm sure of it.' She locked the car and they hurried up to the door. Cat rang the bell and called out, 'It's DC Cat Cullen, Sammie. You're safe to open the door.'

She heard a bolt being drawn across. The door opened, followed by the pale face of Sammie Chisholm, who peered rather suspiciously at Ben.

'It's okay, Sammie. This is my partner, Ben. Can we come in?'

'He was right there!' exclaimed Sammie, pointing. 'Two doors down! In the garden.'

'I'll go and check,' Ben offered. 'Exactly where was he?'

'You see the detached house that's set back off the road? It has a bigger front garden than these little places. It's called Richmond House. I think he was in the shrubbery close to the front wall.' Sammie spoke more confidently now Cat was there. 'He laughed at me. It was horrible. Oh, please be careful! I think he's mad.'

Ben hurried off to look while Cat took the girl into the kitchen and put the kettle on. 'You need a cup of tea, Sammie. You've had a shock.'

Cat was secretly cursing herself. If only she and Yvonne had continued their surveillance for another night. They hadn't because Sammie had told them she'd be staying in, and things were hotting up at the station.

She was just taking the milk from the fridge when she heard Ben calling to her from the hallway.

'Cat, I need you for a moment.'

She could tell from his voice that he'd found something. Telling Sammie to lock the door behind her, she hurried after Ben, down the street and into the garden of Richmond House.

'Bit of a drastic way of stopping him, but your Samantha won't be troubled by the Laughing Stalker again.' Ben parted some shrubbery and pointed.

In the beam of Ben's flashlight, Cat gazed down upon the lifeless body of a man. He was dressed in dark clothes and had a black scarf wrapped around his mouth and chin. She looked closer and saw that he was quite young, probably in his early twenties.

She looked up. Lights were coming on in every room of Richmond House.

'I've rung it in,' said Ben softly. 'And I've told the house-holders to stay indoors. We'll talk to them as soon as the cavalry arrives. From the wire around this guy's neck, I'd say that this was no accident.'

Though partially obscured by the black scarf, Cat could still make out the deep bloody gouge in the man's throat. 'You stay here, Ben. I must get back to Sammie. She was traumatised enough earlier, but when she hears there's been a murderer at work just two doors away she's going to need someone with her.'

Ben agreed. 'I'll ring and ask for a Victim Support Officer, and perhaps you could suggest that Samantha goes and stays with someone for a few days. She certainly shouldn't be here alone.'

Cat hastened back to Sammie's house, sure she'd have no trouble convincing her this time. She needed another person with her, not a couple of house plants and an acoustic guitar.

She finished making the tea, wondering who could have committed such a crime. Someone close to one of the young women who had decided to take the law into their own hands? But they would have just given him a beating, surely. Whoever had done this had come prepared with a murder weapon in the form of a garotte. He — she assumed it was a he — had meant business. He had fully intended to kill the stalker, not scare him off with a few broken ribs and a couple of black eyes.

Cat had no answers to Sammie's flood of questions, she was as much in the dark as her. It was with some relief that she heard the approaching sirens. Sammie's front room was lit up by blue flashing lights and ten minutes later, she left the girl in the capable hands of a trained VSO.

Bemused, Cat hurried back to Ben. Oh, how she hated being in the dark like this.

CHAPTER TWELVE

Nikki called an emergency briefing for nine o'clock that morning. Cat had rung her the night before to inform her of the murder, and Nikki was wondering just how much more work they could take on before they reached saturation point. The presence of Cam Walker and Jim Summers had doubled Greenborough's staff complement overnight — or at least it seemed that way.

She was very glad to have DC Ben Radley back with them too. He was a valued member of the team, as well as being Cat's live-in partner. Nikki wondered when they would bite the bullet and get married. They were engaged, even lived together, but that elusive wedding date kept moving ever further into the future. Mind you, given her own situation, she was in no position to criticise.

They had moved the meeting upstairs to the biggest conference room. Rarely used, it doubled as a major investigation centre when necessary. Nikki had already made sure that the contents of the CID room whiteboards were transferred on to bigger ones in what was now the MI Room.

Nikki stared around at them, proud and not a little humbled. This was probably the largest gathering of officers that Greenborough had ever mustered. For once, she would be able to allocate uniformed police and detectives to cover every line of enquiry.

She waited until the excited chatter and the screech of chairs being dragged into place died down before she greeted the additional staff. Some she recognised but most were new to her. All were certainly welcome right now, especially after the latest weird murder.

It took her more than forty-five minutes to bring everyone up to speed, and then to discuss who should deal with which specific areas of the investigation. It seemed prudent to allow Jim Summers and his Fenfleet officers to work the Alexandra Cornfield case. Jim's first-hand knowledge of the old investigation would be invaluable. Nikki split the rest of the troops into three units, dealing with the death of Neil Weldon, the murder of the stalker, and the hunt for Oliver. Nikki kept that one for herself. Those letters had been addressed to her in person, so she and Joseph were not about to relinquish the reins to others. She gave the death of the stalker to Cat to coordinate, since she and Ben had found the body. She also suggested they keep Yvonne with them, as Vonnie knew the victims. They would continue to operate from the CID room, thus keeping the cases separate.

Nikki watched the crowd of officers disperse with some satisfaction. Cam had assured her that for once, they wouldn't be working on a shoestring, and for the first time ever, they weren't short of capable officers. True to his word, Jim Summers was doing everything he could to help her close the case that had been troubling him for the past ten years.

'Hellfire! My head's a shed,' muttered Nikki to Joseph on their way downstairs. 'I cannot believe that on top of everything else, someone sodding well tops a suspected stalker! Talk about overload.'

'Sod's law,' said Joseph. 'It always happens when you're pushed to the limit. But that's a really odd murder, isn't it? It's got Cat rattled, at any rate. As she said, she'd understand it if one of the women's nearest and dearest had turned vigilante and had given their stalker a good working-over, but this was nothing less than assassination. There has to be a lot more to it than meets the eye.'

'Unless our hapless stalker picked on a girl who had a pathologically jealous boyfriend,' suggested Nikki. 'Maybe Cat should make that her first line of enquiry. It's the only thing that makes any sense unless, as you say, there's another deeper reason that we're not aware of. But we need to ID the dead guy before we can move forward.'

As she entered her office, she stopped in her tracks. There, in the exact centre of her desk, was a large manilla envelope with a *Par Avion* sticker on it.

* * *

Eve and Wendy met the local historian, Jacob Rush, in a café attached to Greenborough's bookshop. Expecting to find a boring old fart, most likely a good ten years older than her, Eve was considerably taken aback, and more than a little embarrassed at her preconceptions. Jacob turned out to be in his early thirties, with hair — bearing not a trace of grey — cut in the latest fashionable style. It transpired that he was a writer and, having published a highly successful action thriller series, now had enough funds to spend more time on his passion, which was local history.

'I give talks to the Women's Institute sometimes,' he confided, with an almost embarrassed smile. 'And to various other groups like U3A, but it's the research that interests me most. The thrill of the chase, and finding clues to the hidden mysteries of times long past.'

Eve smiled at the young man, who sounded like a kindred spirit. Solving old mysteries was their greatest passion.

'Funnily enough, you're only the second lot to ask about the Tates. Considering that they were the biggest farming landowners in this area, that's quite surprising.' Jacob took a mouthful of coffee and smiled at them. 'So, how can I help you ladies?'

Wendy told him the story of how their new hobby had resulted in the discovery of certain objects that rather turned history on its head.

While she spoke, Eve watched Jacob's expression change from interested to incredulous. Regarding her and Wendy with considerably more respect, he said, 'Perhaps you should come back to my flat with me, if you have the time? I live over a stable block attached to my parents' house. It started out as just a place to write in but over time it's become my home.' He frowned. 'The thing is, I have some research papers that you really ought to see. I don't mind admitting that the Tates and the killing of Jan Laska have been a bit of an obsession with me in the past few years. Maybe it's because of the injustice of it, a man dead owing to a terrible mistake while his killer wandered free.'

'Thank you,' said Eve. 'It's becoming rather an obsession with us too, and we appreciate all the help we can get.'

They finished their coffee and stood up. 'You can follow me home,' said Jacob. 'It's not far, just on the outskirts of Greenborough, at Mere End.'

Twenty minutes later they were parked outside a smart barn conversion with living accommodation above the former stables, now garages. Situated off a narrow lane, it was quiet and secluded, hidden from the main road by the old trees that surrounded it. The perfect place to write, thought Eve. Or to solve old mysteries.

Jacob ushered them into what he referred to as his "work area," an open-plan room whose high ceiling and long narrow windows ensured day-long light. Two walls were lined with bookshelves so high that he had a library ladder in order to reach the top rows. Opposite sat a desk and a computer system, along with filing cabinets and a run of cupboards and drawers. In the centre were two long sofas, at either side of a low rustic coffee table crafted from restored reclaimed wood.

'What a fabulous place to work in!' breathed Eve.

'Beats renting a two-metre-square co-working desk space at the local Artist and Creatives Institute, doesn't it?' Jacob looked around with a satisfied smile.

If you have pots of money, thought Eve.

'But I'm lucky, of course,' Jacob said, as if reading her mind. 'I have a generous and loving family, and my books are selling better than I could ever have imagined. I never forget that. Anyway, enough of me. Let's talk about Tate.'

Jacob produced two box files, set them down on the coffee table and opened them up. Both were full to the brim with papers. 'Like I said, it's become an obsession.'

Wendy let out a long low whistle. 'All that's material on the Tate family?'

'And the mystery of the killing of Jan Laska. I've been looking into it for five years now. Whenever I'm not writing my novels, I'm researching — talking to other historians, dredging through public records and looking up every article I can find.' He looked from one to the other of them. 'And what happens? Eve and Wendy drop into the middle of it all and bring a bombshell with them. You see, what you have discovered is the link, the proof if you like, of my main hypothesis.'

'And that is?' asked Eve.

'Old Thomas Tate was actually attacked by someone who knew him well and wanted him out of the way. There was no robbery. He wasn't assaulted by some vagrant desperate for valuables to sell for food or drink, but someone who hated Thomas Tate enough to want to batter him to death.' He shrugged. 'Okay, he didn't die, but if he hadn't been discovered so quickly, he certainly would have. His valuables were taken only to make it look like a robbery.'

Eve nodded, thinking hard. Jacob had said he had papers he wanted them to see. Did he have something that would point to a suspect? She stifled a giggle. "Suspect!" She was starting to sound like her daughter!

'As a matter of interest, have you any pictures of your finds?' asked Jacob.

'Certainly,' Eve said. 'We're keeping a records book of our treasures. I use a proper camera for those shots, but I've got a few on my phone.' She took it from her bag and showed him. 'Here. One of all three together — the ring, the cigarette case and the watch.'

Jacob looked at the photo almost reverently. 'Well, I'm blessed! After all this time. Who would believe that one day these would turn up again, it's quite fantastic.' He looked at them eagerly. 'I suppose I couldn't see the real things?'

Eve looked apologetic. 'We don't have them, Jacob. We returned them to the family. Although maybe if we can give Chris Tate some answers as to what happened, he might let us borrow them so we can show you. Can't promise, of course, but we can always ask.' Eve noticed a rather strange look come over Jacob's face. It vanished as quickly as it had come, but even so, it had definitely been there.

The smile was back. 'That'd be nice, but no matter. At least I've seen the photos.'

'I can send you JPEGs of the better ones and some close-ups if you like?' offered Eve.

His eyes lit up. 'Please, if you would.' Jacob went through one of the box files, searching for something. 'I had the most amazing stroke of luck, although it came at a price. A woman in our local library told me about this old guy called Frederick Bates. Apparently, his father — and his father before him, also called Frederick — worked for the Tates all their lives. When his parents died, the possessions Fred inherited included old books, as well as some notebooks and diaries. This sounded really interesting, until she told me that Fred was a compulsive hoarder and suffered from some kind of early-onset dementia.' His eyes widened. 'And I mean hoarder! Rooms stacked to the ceiling with, well, junk! The stench was horrific, but the old guy lived quite happily in the middle of it.'

'I've seen reality TV programmes about them,' said Wendy. 'Places that are so bad they need to wear protective clothing to go inside and clean them up. It really was that awful?'

'Believe me, ladies, what the TV series couldn't convey was the smell. It took weeks to get it out of my nostrils!'

Eve laughed. 'But even so, you found the diaries?'

'Two weeks it took me, then another to get him to let me have them — well, borrow them. He wanted them back asap, so I photographed all the relevant bits and duly took them back. He wouldn't let me in! Said he didn't know me and knew nothing about any diaries. Must have been the dementia, I suppose.' Jacob shook his head. 'So, I still have them.'

Eve felt rather sorry for poor old Fred. He sounded in a bad way. But at least she and Wendy might get to look at those valuable diaries.

'But I'm thinking you might appreciate a summary. The books themselves took forever to wade through in order to find the relevant information. Oh, I forgot to mention that there were letters too, in the back of one of the diaries, all carefully arranged in date order. If anything, they were the most informative of all.'

Wendy sat forward. 'Give us the bare bones of what happened, then, Jacob. We can go into more detail later.'

He nodded. 'Look, I really like you ladies, and I'll happily share it all with you, but, er, you mentioned Chris Tate?'

Aha, thought Eve, recalling the odd look on Jacob's face. *So, our friendly farmer is the problem.*

'Oh, he's our neighbour,' she said, keeping her tone light. 'We live in the old converted chapel that borders his farm and he kindly allowed us on to his fields with our detectors. It was a total fluke that we found what we did.'

Jacob hesitated. 'Well, he doesn't like me. He came across my website and paid me a visit one day. He correctly suspected that I was interested in the killing of Jan Laska and insisted that if I ever discovered more than what was already on my site, I must take it to him first, and not plaster it all over the media. He wasn't exactly aggressive, but neither was it a friendly request. He gave me a load of old cobblers about family pride and the like, but I knew perfectly well that it was nothing to do with that. He then tried another angle, telling me he desperately wanted to know the truth. He said he'd been trying to find out for ages to no avail, and that he had the right to know what happened before anyone else did.' Jacob pulled a face. 'That was before I discovered the diaries and the letters, and I've certainly never mentioned them to him. I'm positive that there's something odd about Chris Tate, ladies, but I'm damned if I know what it is.'

That makes two of us, thought Eve. She glanced across at Wendy, who gave her an almost imperceptible nod. 'As we are baring our souls, Jacob, we should tell you that we suggested to him that we might do a bit of investigating ourselves. We got the distinct impression that although he said yes, he, and more to the point, his wife, did not want us doing anything of the kind.'

Wendy added dryly, 'I suspect that the Tates see us as a couple of poor old dears with nothing better to do who haven't the faintest idea of how to conduct a historical search.'

Jacob chuckled. 'Then he's a foolish man. For my part, I suspect you've done this before and are very good at it.' He smiled at them both. 'You have a glint in your eyes that indicates a passion for hunting down the truth, am I right?'

'You could say that.' Wendy returned the smile. 'And, yes, we have done this before.' She glanced at Eve. 'And we saw it through to the bitter end.'

Eve preferred not to go there. Not with that old case. It had got far too dangerous. 'The thing is, Jacob, we'll be happy to keep whatever you tell us to ourselves, unless all three of us agree that it's something that really should be shared with the Tates. After all, as Wendy has said, he won't be expecting us old grannies to come up with anything, so if he doesn't hear from us he won't be surprised.'

'Okay, ladies, I can accept that — apart from the old granny bit, of course.' He grinned. 'So, one synopsis coming up. Thomas Norman Tate, widower, four children — two boys and two girls. Wife died in an accident on the farm. According to one account, she was crushed by cattle, others leave the cause of death open, simply calling it a tragic accident. His two boys, Albert and William, hard workers, followed him into farming, finally taking over the running of the estate upon his death. It proved almost impossible to find anything on the daughters, Maria and Isobel, other than a few rather derogatory comments.' Jacob looked thoughtful.

'I must try to find out more about that pair at some point. I swear there's another mystery there.'

Eve smiled at him. 'I see you also have that glint in your eyes. Addictive stuff, this research, isn't it?'

Jacob smiled back. 'I'm just glad I never went the detectorist route like you. I'd want to know the history behind every single item I unearthed, down to old nuts and bolts and rusty nails.'

Eve saw that they'd found a kindred spirit in this young man. He would have made a good detective.

'Sorry,' said Jacob. 'I sidetracked myself. Back to Tommy Tate. As you may have read on my website, he wasn't the revered and well-loved gentleman farmer that the Tates would have you believe. In fact, Thomas Tate wasn't a very nice man at all.'

'We read that bit,' said Eve. 'But what form did this take?'

'He was a successful farmer all right, but mainly because he was ruthless and calculating. I found many references to his penny-pinching, and his callous treatment of his workers. I've got a *wonderful* letter written by his wife's sister to a friend, in which she suspects him of "bringing shame" upon at least two of the girls who worked for him. This, dear ladies, is one of the reasons I felt the attack to be the work of someone who knew him. Maybe it was the father or boyfriend of one of the aforementioned "shamed" women.'

'That makes sense,' said Eve, 'although why, then, did those two faithful farmhands go after Jan, supposedly outraged at the attack on their beloved boss?'

Jacob Rush nodded slowly, 'Because that story was concocted by Tate's sons and daughters to conceal his reputation from future generations. Those two farm workers didn't kill that man out of outrage at the attack on their employer. They had a completely different motive for murdering Jan Laska and used the attack on Tommy as an excuse. I just haven't found out what it is — yet.'

'My goodness, you have done your research, haven't you?' said Wendy, admiringly.

He shrugged. 'Five years of hunting, fitted in between the day job. And I'm far from being finished with the Tate family history, or so it seems.' He suddenly looked amused, 'You know, I was beginning to wonder if there was actually a point to keeping this hunt alive. There's no doubt that it encroaches on the time I should be spending writing new books and keeping up with all the admin that goes with publishing them, but meeting you and hearing about your amazing discovery has reignited my enthusiasm.'

'Well, we have the time and the inclination to assist you, if you'll allow us to,' said Wendy. 'Don't we, Eve?'

'Oh yes!' she said. 'Plenty of both!'

'So, we form an alliance?' Jacob grinned at them hopefully.

'And between us, we'll unearth the truth,' said Eve, with considerable conviction, 'not just watches and rings and cigarette cases.'

CHAPTER THIRTEEN

Nikki was surprised at how steady her hand was as she opened the latest envelope. This time the contents took the form of a simple letter:

> *Dear Detective Inspector Galena,*
> *I'm fully aware of how busy you must be, but we really need to move on. Having done all the hard graft for you in the last case, I think it's time you started pulling your weight. For Investigation 0148, Ruth Baker, missing, believed murdered, I will provide you with one piece of information as a starting point. Once you have located poor Ruth, you will be sent a full investigation report since we don't have the time for your long-winded and often useless methods. You failed Ruth once, don't do it again.*
> *Find the place that should have offered safety for six unfortunate people only it proved to be anything but safe.*
> *Yours, in haste,*
> *Oliver.*

Nikki threw the letter on to her desk, seething. How dare he turn something as deeply serious as murder into a sodding game. 'Hell, Joseph, he's so convinced of our uselessness.

Well, I'm more determined than ever to catch up with him. And when I do, I'll make sure the arsehole never sees the light of day again.'

Joseph smiled at her. 'That's the Nikki I know and love. But what does he mean with "place of safety"? Any ideas?'

'Nope. Nothing jumps out at me,' she said. 'I suggest we get someone to search for some incident that affected six victims. "Place of safety" could mean any number of things, even a police station. Can you get that underway immediately, Joseph? I need to go and tell Cam and Jim that we've had further contact *Par Avion*, and show them the latest missive.'

'Of course. I'll do it right away.'

Nikki followed Joseph out and hurried upstairs to the superintendent's office. She found Cam alone, apparently deep in thought.

'Sorry to add to your worries,' she said, and held up the evidence bag containing the letter. 'We've got mail.'

Cam pulled on a pair of nitrile gloves and read through the typed sheet, frowning.

'He's not giving us time to breathe,' said Nikki. 'He would have chosen Ruth Baker, wouldn't he? More than all the others, her disappearance was a real mystery. Oh, and it was another Fenfleet one, though not one of Jim's. The DCI who covered that case has now retired.'

'Not Matt Ballard, by any chance?' asked Cam.

'Yes, it was,' said Nikki. 'I've heard quite a bit about him. I've even seen him once or twice, at functions, we may even have met, though I don't remember him. Do you know him well, Cam?'

'Not as a friend but we've run into each other at various conferences and meetings. Nice bloke. He turned private investigator after he retired. I'll get hold of him and see what he can tell us.'

'I'd appreciate it. Maybe he'd be willing to come in and talk to us about any remaining questions, doubts about the case that never made it into the reports. As the officer who was on the front line he could be a big help to us, just like Jim Summers.'

'I'd say he'd jump at the chance. An unsolved case never leaves you, does it? It always gnaws away at the back of your mind, even after you've retired.' Cam gave her a searching look. 'Are you okay, Nikki? This guy is obviously using you as the whipping boy for a whole division's shortcomings. It's not personal to you, I hope you're bearing that in mind.'

Nikki sighed. 'But it *is* personal, Cam. He's made it that way. It's my name on all those communications. Well, he's picked the wrong woman. If anything, it's made me all the more determined to nail the bastard and hang him out to dry. Sorry if that's not what you wanted to hear, but that's how I feel.'

'Honest as always,' said Cam with a wry smile. 'Just don't forget that not one of those cases had or has the slightest connection to you. For his letters to have any effect at all, he had to have the name of a real person to direct them to, otherwise they'd have gone in the bin. He happened to choose you — either for a specific reason or he picked your name out from a list of serving officers. We don't know, and it's not the main issue, which is the investigation. Try not to get sidetracked into searching for some incident in your past that might have caused him to focus on you.'

'Easier said than done,' said Nikki. 'I am wholly committed to getting to the bottom of this, and as quickly as possible, but whenever I get a few minutes to myself, it's there, niggling away. Why me?' She looked him in the eye. 'I really do believe he has a grudge against me; he believes that something I did, or didn't do, justifies his bloody campaign.' She drew in a breath. 'I promise I won't let it get in the way of the case, but when we've finally slammed that cell door on him, I think you'll find I'm right.'

'Then let's proceed,' Cam said. 'I'll ring Matt Ballard, and you put your people on to this new development. Find this "place of safety," whatever that means, and maybe we'll find Ruth Baker.'

* * *

Joseph went into the CID room to have a word with Yvonne Collins, but was diverted by Zena, heading his way waving a large manila envelope.

'Forensic photographs from Professor Wilkinson, Sarge. They're to do with the man found at Richmond House.' She handed them to Joseph. 'He said to say he's already sent them to your inbox but he thought you'd like these hard copies to put on the whiteboard.'

Joseph took the envelope and continued on his way. Sitting at what he still thought of as Dave Harris's desk, Yvonne was busy at her computer. 'I'd like to run something past you, Vonnie. Come over to the board with me, if you don't mind, and I'll explain while I get these shots of our anonymous victim-stroke-alleged stalker pinned up.' He told her about the latest letter. 'So, Vonnie, a place of safety where six people either died or met with some misfortune. I thought you, with your encyclopaedic knowledge of the Greenborough area, might have some idea.'

Yvonne looked thoughtful. 'Some years ago now there was a fire in a village hall. I seem to think it was being used as a temporary refuge for families who'd been evacuated from their homes after one of the rivers burst its banks and flooded part of the village. I'm not sure how many were injured, though. Is that the sort of thing, Sarge?'

'Absolutely!' he said. 'Give it some thought anyway, and perhaps you'd look up that incident you've just mentioned? Get some more details. And it's urgent.'

But Yvonne didn't answer. Joseph looked back from the board, where he'd been pinning up Rory's photos while he spoke. She was staring at them, her mouth open. 'What's wrong?' he asked.

'That's the man who you think has been stalking all those women?' She didn't wait for an answer. 'I know him.'

Joseph shouldn't have been surprised. Vonnie seemed to know the entire population of Greenborough. 'Who is he, Vonnie?'

'Daryl Grayson. His name cropped up yesterday, to do with a child whose recent behaviour has been worrying her deputy headmistress. The girl in question is called Ruby, she's this man's sister.'

Joseph frowned. He never liked it when two different lines of enquiry came together like this, it confused matters. 'Do you know where he lived, Vonnie?'

'In a house called Pembroke. It's in the Green, Marsh Enderby.'

'Better go and find the boss, don't you reckon?'

* * *

Nikki got the picture. Yvonne had always been good at giving a concise account of matters.

'To get yourself murdered, you have to seriously piss someone off, and what better way than to stalk his woman? Did this girl know what her brother was up to, and felt torn between loyalty and what was right? Or was she a victim, as in he threatened to hurt her if she spoke out? Whatever the case, it's no wonder her schoolwork suffered.'

'But who chose to eliminate him?' said Joseph. 'A family member? The wronged man?'

'I met the family once,' said Yvonne. 'On the surface they seemed close, supportive, but I had the oddest feeling that they were playing at Happy Families.'

'Well, Vonnie, now you'll be visiting them again,' said Nikki. 'And this time with Cat. You know the drill, you've done this more times than I've had hot dinners. Break the news, ask for a formal ID, and as soon as we get confirmation that it is Daryl Grayson, you and a CID team are going to find out exactly what's going on in the Grayson household. See if they're still the same Happy Family they were back then. Go to it.'

Nikki watched Yvonne leave the office with a mixture of emotions. The Laughing Stalker wouldn't be terrifying young women any longer but they were left with another death to investigate. It wasn't the best of situations, but at least they had the victim's ID. Meanwhile, she still had Oliver, and now Ruth Baker, to worry about.

'Okay, Joseph, that place of safety. Any clues?'

'A couple of doubtful possibilities, and Vonnie suggested another.' He gave her a resigned smile. 'Looks like it'll be me chasing that one up, since she's otherwise engaged. It's a fire in a village hall that occurred some time ago. If it's okay with you, I'll go and do a search, see what I can find.'

Joseph had just left when Nikki's mobile rang. It was Eve. Nikki gave a little smile. She didn't really have the time to chat, but it was still a relief to see her mother's name on her screen. It reminded her that she had another life. It wasn't all murder and mayhem; there was a small, precious part of it that belonged to family. 'Mum? Not in trouble, I hope?'

'No, darling, far from it. This is just a quick call as I've not spoken to you since our wonderful dinner the other night. I won't hold you up, I realise you're up to your neck, but I wanted you to know that I love you and I'm thinking of you having to work so hard.'

Her words brought tears to Nikki's eyes. 'I needed that, Mum, thank you. And I've always got time for you, you know that. Now, how's the metal detecting going?'

'Fascinating, Nikki! We've made some extremely interesting finds on our neighbour's land, and we are trying to discover the history behind them. We've met this wonderful young historian called Jacob — and I'm telling you, what he doesn't know about local history isn't worth knowing.'

Nikki suddenly had an idea. What if this place of safety incident of Oliver's wasn't recent? What if it dated from some time in the past? 'Mum. This is a long shot, but would you ask this Jacob if he knows of any local story from the past that speaks of a place of safety in which six people were injured or died? I know it sounds weird, but we're anxious to find somewhere that matches that description.'

'I'll ring him now,' Eve said. 'He's coming over at lunchtime, so he can give it some thought, and if he comes up with anywhere that sounds promising I'll ring you straightaway.'

Call ended, Nikki was left with a head full of confused thoughts. There was Cam's warning to stick to the nitty-gritty of police work and not dwell on something from her past that might have given rise to Oliver's campaign.

Easier said than done. She couldn't stop going over past incidents or people she'd met, no matter how hard she tried. 'Come on, Galena,' she muttered. 'Concentrate! Go back to those reports on Ruth Baker, and this time make sure you read every word.'

She turned to her computer and brought up the relevant case notes.

She didn't hear Joseph enter thirty minutes later, until she smelled the coffee he'd brought. 'You angel! That's proper coffee.'

'It is indeed.' He set down a white paper bag. 'And that's a proper pecan and maple Danish. For energy.'

'My hero!'

'And it's also a peace offering because I've come up with precisely nothing on that bloody place of safety,' Joseph said. 'The village hall fire only affected three people, and not seriously, and the other two possibilities were non-starters. I'm now trawling through accident reports involving six persons and, besides being mind-numbingly boring, I get the feeling it's a waste of time.'

'I did wonder if this incident, whatever it is, might have happened back in the past, so Mum is asking a local historian she knows if he has any ideas.' She sipped the coffee and closed her eyes. 'Oh, that's so good . . . Sorry, yes, it could possibly date from the war years, or even further back than that. We can't just assume it was a recent event. All we can be sure of is that it will have taken place somewhere in the Greenborough area, or it wouldn't be of interest to Oliver.'

'That's a fair point, Nikki. Let's hope Eve's historian can come up with something. Meanwhile, I'll press on, just in case it is recent.'

Joseph had barely left the office when there was a tap on Nikki's door and Jim Summers came in. He flopped down in the chair opposite her.

'I'm not sure how to read that expression, Jim,' she said. 'You look half pleased, half disappointed.'

'Both, actually,' he said. 'We now have a watertight case against Neil Weldon for the murder of young Alexandra. There's even a new witness, who swears Alex confessed to being afraid of her uncle and was unwilling to be alone in his company.'

'Why didn't she come forward before?' asked Nikki.

'Initially, she was too scared, and too ashamed. Apparently, Neil tried it on with her too, and then he threatened her, saying no one would believe the word of a dirty little whore like her. He said if she ever went to the police, she'd disappear too. It was only when she heard he was dead that she summoned the courage to come forward. Poor woman's a nervous wreck, Nikki. She said that whenever she saw him around, and she often did, he'd stare at her threateningly. She would have moved away but she has parents who depend on her, so she was trapped. For ten years Neil Weldon ruined her life.' He shook his head, and then brightened. 'Well, there's no question about the man's guilt. I'm relieved that we have the evidence to prove it but I'm sad that it's only happened now, and not back when she died.' He pulled a face. 'Now, with your permission, we'll channel our manpower into helping the other team with finding out who killed Neil Weldon. The paperwork can wait until we have this Oliver in custody.'

It felt odd to be sanctioning the request of a chief superintendent. 'Please, do go ahead, Jim. We have to discover who Oliver is, and since he's admitted to killing Neil, it's our best chance of finding something on him.' She paused. 'Did you have much to do with a DCI called Matt Ballard at Fenfleet?'

'Matt? I know him well, though we were never on the same team, and we weren't there at the same time for long. Bloody good detective, Matt. He's gone into private work now, and DCI Charley Anders tells me he's still a force to be reckoned with. He even assists her on occasion, as a consultant. Why do you ask?'

'It's to do with the Ruth Baker disappearance,' Nikki said. 'Apparently, he was the SIO on her case.'

'Ah yes, you're right, or partly right. As I recall, Matt was only SIO for a short while, until some major crime or other led the powers that be to reallocate him to that one. An officer called Conway took over Ruth's case. He's not only retired but emigrated to Australia.' Jim raised an eyebrow. 'I must say Conway was nothing like Matt Ballard. He and I never got on, I'm afraid. It was all for the best that I took up a new post at Fenchester. I stayed there for eight years, and when I got promotion and returned, I was delighted to hear that he'd left.'

'Any chance he was sloppy with the Baker case?' asked Nikki.

'Every chance!' Jim uttered a sardonic laugh. 'But you won't find any slip-ups where Matt's concerned.' He stood up to go. 'Better go and give my guys the new instruction, then buckle down and help out the team looking for Neil's killer.'

'And I'll pass on anything I get from forensics. I think our biggest hope is that Rory can discover something from the body.' She smiled at him. 'And thanks, Jim. I really do appreciate all the help you're giving us.'

Jim shrugged. 'If we'd got it right all those years ago, there wouldn't be any need. It's the least I can do.'

The door closed behind him, leaving Nikki mulling over the damage an unsolved case could cause. Despite his high rank, Jim clearly still lost sleep over Alexandra Cornfield. It was a sad fact that the proportion of offences actually solved, with the perpetrator brought to justice, was painfully low.

Nikki opened the paper bag and took out the Danish pastry. Her spirits lifted with the first bite. Although they were a long way from understanding who Oliver was, or even guessing at his motive, at least Alexandra was finally back with her family and would be laid to rest with dignity. Maybe the other missing girls would be found too, and their families could find peace. If so, at least some good would have come out of Oliver's crusade. Her only real concern was his end game. Her suppositions as to what that might be sent shivers down her spine.

CHAPTER FOURTEEN

Jacob Rush arrived at Monks Lantern with a small bunch of flowers and a box of Belgian chocolates. Eve was touched by the gesture. It was only a cold, working lunch, certainly not worthy of gifts.

'I've been racking my brains ever since you rang me, Eve, and I've got two suitable candidates for your place of safety incident. One is a better fit than the other but I suggest the police check them both.' Jacob smiled at her. 'Do you get your insatiable thirst for the truth from your detective daughter, then?'

'More like the other way around,' laughed Wendy. 'I'm pretty certain Nikki gets it from her mother. It's a natural instinct with Eve, she can't help herself.'

Eve raised an eyebrow at her friend, the words pot and kettle having sprung to mind. 'So, tell us, Jacob, and I'll ring Nikki, then we can get on with lunch and discuss our own case.'

'Right, my first suggestion is this: back in 1944, an Anderson shelter took a direct hit from a doodlebug. It's a popular misconception that Greenborough didn't get bombed — I've traced at least sixty German Luftwaffe attacks. This one was in the garden of a farmhouse on the edge of town, quite close to one of the decoy airfields that the government constructed to keep bombers away from the town and the real airfields. A mother and her five children were killed outright. The name of the farm is Knight's End, it's situated just off the Saltern-le-Fen Road.' Jacob smiled at Eve. 'That's the one that fits best. My second choice is from a bit longer ago, but it still fits the criteria — though it's a bit creepy.'

Eve was scribbling down notes and directions for Nikki. Her daughter hadn't said what she needed the information for, but given that the news was full of murders, Eve had a pretty good idea.

'There's an old Victorian factory out on the Fenfleet Road,' continued Jacob. 'It's derelict now, and waiting to be demolished — shame, really, it's a lovely old building. Anyway, it was a feather processing factory, one of several in the area that were all part of a large bedding company. The owner, a wealthy businessman named Rowntree, was a philanthropic man who actually cared for his employees. He set up a refuge there, somewhere for homeless people to get a meal and a bed for the night. On the night in question, only six beds were occupied, and someone got in and murdered them all, stabbed them as they slept. The killer was never found, but he was thought to have been an escapee from a local mental institution, what was then called the lunatic asylum.' Jacob spread his hands. 'These are the only two occasions that I know of in which exactly six people were killed. Oh, and if they need more details, especially regarding the old factory, I can give you the relevant websites.'

Well, this was great. Somehow Eve felt certain that Jacob's information was just what her daughter was looking for.

* * *

Within the next half hour, Nikki had instructed two units, each with a detective in tow, to visit the two locations Jacob

Rush had mentioned. She didn't think she'd have long to wait for a result. From the moment she received Eve's phone call, Nikki knew it would be the factory site that contained the remains of Ruth Baker. It was quite unnerving. Even more unnerving was the way it connected to their earlier enquiries into the whereabouts of Neil Weldon. Had he been responsible for Ruth's death as well as that of Alexandra Cornfield? No one had ever looked at Weldon for any other crime, but there it was — the old feather factory had been on Neil's worksheet. He had been advising on methods of demolition. There was a vague possibility that if he had been tailing Neil for some time, Oliver could have followed him to the old factory. Nikki frowned. It didn't make sense. Sure, if either Oliver or Neil had killed Ruth Baker within the last couple of years, the old factory would have been a perfect place to hide a body, but Ruth had disappeared a decade and a half ago. That meant she had no known connection to either of them.

Nikki tapped impatiently on her desk and stared at the phone, willing it to ring. God, how she hated waiting!

* * *

Yvonne, who as a beat bobby had been capable of dealing with anything that was thrown at her, suddenly felt lost. Her mind seemed overloaded with anxieties, and she was starting to think that there weren't enough hours in the day to cover all her many avenues of enquiry.

Seeing Daryl Grayson's dead face staring at her from a forensic photograph had shocked her badly. She had never liked the lad, but still — that he'd been such a prolific stalker was beyond belief. She badly wanted to tell Dinah Barrett, since it would answer all her questions about young Ruby and her reticence to confide in her favourite teacher. She also wanted to talk to the woman who had reported hearing screams in the village of Marsh Enderby, the very place where Yvonne now found herself.

She was sitting in her car outside Pembroke, having gone through the distressing task of breaking the news of their son's death to Daryl's parents. The husband had already gone off with Cat and Ben to make the formal identification, and as a Family Liaison Officer was now with Daryl's mother, Yvonne was taking a few moments to regroup. It was at times like this that she missed her uniform and her old crewmate, Niall Farrow. She smiled sadly. Right now, they'd be sharing a Mars bar and trying to make sense of it. But all that was in the past. Niall was now a sergeant — a bloody good one, too — and she was a civilian interviewing officer. As far as she could see, this seemed to mean that she was just like the rest of the CID team but getting paid a lower wage. Not that she cared. She wasn't ready to stop working yet and be consigned to the scrap heap, so she was quite willing to soldier on until the time came to hang up her cuffs.

Andrea Smith, Twisted Willows, The Green. The name and address came to her in a flash. Yvonne looked along the curve of the lane and made up her mind. Since she was here in Marsh Enderby anyway, she might as well call on Mrs Smith.

Andrea Smith answered the door herself, her face pale and worried-looking.

Showing her ID, Yvonne explained that she was here in connection with Mrs Smith's call to the station. Hearing this, the woman seemed to brighten a little. 'My husband said you wouldn't take any notice, but I knew you would.' She chuckled. 'At least I've got one over on him. Do come in, please.'

Over a cup of tea, Andrea told Yvonne exactly what she had heard, and showed her the notes she'd made of dates and times. 'I've been sitting up for the past two nights, but it's been quiet. I'll not give up, though. It could be important to you, couldn't it?'

'It could indeed,' said Yvonne. 'And you say it was definitely a woman you heard, and not a child?'

'Oh no, it wasn't a child. It was a very different sort of cry, most definitely an adult, and a woman.' She stirred her tea. 'It gave me a real turn when I first heard it, I can tell you.'

'And the direction it came from?'

Andrea pointed in the direction Yvonne had just come from. The direction of Pembroke.

Yvonne took another sip of tea and wondered how much to tell this pleasant and caring woman. She proceeded cautiously. 'Do you by any chance know the Grayson family? They live in a house called Pembroke.'

'Not very well, I'm afraid. I see Mrs Grayson occasionally. She's always very polite but never wants to stop for a chat. The girl — her name's Ruby, I think — is rather studious. I get the feeling Mrs Grayson thinks we're a bit, well, lower-class, having a small house and my husband working in the factory.' Andrea hesitated. 'I, er, get the feeling that the girl's mother is rather overprotective, though I don't know why. Maybe Mrs Grayson is just like that, lots of mothers seem to be these days. The son, well, he never speaks, not that I really want him to. He does nothing but sneer. Most unpleasant.'

Well, he doesn't sneer anymore, thought Yvonne darkly. It seemed that everyone who'd come across Daryl shared her instant dislike of him. Interesting.

Yvonne decided she could let Andrea in on at least a little of what had happened. 'Andrea, I'm telling you this because you're obviously very public-spirited and have put yourself out to assist us. Well, last night Daryl Grayson was found dead. It's an ongoing investigation, so I'm afraid I can't say much more at this time, but there's a good chance you won't be hearing any more cries in the night.'

Andrea Smith gasped. 'Oh my! You mean dead as in murdered? Sorry, you've just said you can't tell me anything more. But my heavens, what a thing to happen! I could never take to him, but still, he was very young to die.' From her expression, it must have dawned on her what this meant. 'You think he was responsible for those cries? As in he was hurting someone?'

'I have no idea, Andrea, but we can't rule out anything at this stage. I'm sure I can rely on you to keep this to yourself for the time being, just until the story breaks?' When Andrea nodded, Yvonne chuckled. 'Though if I know villages, by the time I leave here all Marsh Enderby will know about the police car parked outside Pembroke.'

Yvonne handed Andrea one of her new cards, which still looked to her like they referred to someone else. 'Will you ring me in a day or so, just to confirm that there haven't been any more cries in the night?'

'Of course,' Andrea said, taking the card from her. 'And I'll let you know if I hear anything on the village grapevine. You were right there, Marsh Enderby's jungle drums are like no other. I'll soon get to know any gossip that's circulating.'

Yvonne understood the value of village gossip — so long as you knew how to separate the wheat from the chaff, of course, and after her years on the beat she was expert at that. 'I'll be very grateful, Andrea, thank you. Now I really must go. And thank you for the tea.'

As she drove back to the station, Yvonne went over what she'd heard in her mind. For one thing, Andrea Smith had never once mentioned the father, so he remained an unknown quantity. Since she now knew for sure that the cries had been those of an adult woman, they had to have come from the mother.

Yvonne had spent almost an hour with the Graysons after giving them the sad news of their son's death. Obviously, at such an emotional time she hadn't been able to ascertain if Shirley Grayson could be the subject of abuse. But young Ruby had apparently stated that she herself wasn't being hurt, thereby implying that someone else was. So, who else could it be but her mum?

Yvonne realised that she would have to pay another call on Shirley Grayson, preferably when her husband wasn't around. It wouldn't be easy considering the circumstances, but Yvonne believed it to be necessary. After all, if it hadn't been her son who was hurting her, there was only one other man on the premises — Daddy Grayson.

* * *

When the call came in from the team checking out the old feather factory, Nikki was surprised to be told that they'd found nothing at all at the former refuge, nor anywhere else on the premises. However, the next call was very different.

'Ma'am, we really think you should get over here.' The detective, a young man drafted in from nearby Saltern-le-Fen, sounded pretty hyped up. 'We think we've located a possible burial place.'

Telling him she'd be there immediately, Nikki yelled for Joseph.

'Knight's End. Know it?' she barked, as they headed for the car park.

'It's on the way to Fenfleet. I looked it up after you told me about it,' he said. 'I'll drive.'

Speeding past massive fields beneath the vast flatland skies, Nikki gradually calmed down. 'How on earth does one man solve a case that has baffled the police for years?'

Joseph grunted. 'We don't actually know if he is working alone, do we? We just assumed so. Still, it must have taken many years to complete. Don't forget, too, that he could commit himself fully to the missing girls, whereas the police had thousands of different cases to attend to.' Joseph negotiated a sharp turn on to a long fen lane. 'I'm not making excuses for us, but anyone that single-minded would have had a good chance of success. I know it's not on the same level, but look at your mother. Not that long ago, Eve and Wendy managed to discover what happened to a man who's been missing since Victorian times. Now, to my mind, that's impressive!'

'True,' Nikki said. 'Though I can't help wondering if he didn't acquire a few investigative skills in the course of a former career.'

'Maybe he did,' said Joseph. 'Everyone the police have interviewed so far in connection with the case, people like Beth Greene, has said they only ever spoke to him on the phone and never met him face to face. He's used all sorts of reasons for his queries, but mainly that he's an investigative journalist. Maybe he's telling the truth there.'

Nikki considered this. Joseph had a point. Hacks could be obsessive about a story, always striving for that major scoop, the one that would make their career. What if Oliver had set out to tell the story of an old unsolved misper case which had then grown into a compulsion to find the missing girl himself? Then, having embarked on his "quest," he might have decided to take it a step further and find her abductor. She put this to Joseph.

'And then it got out of control and he decided to conclude the case by executing the accused man,' Joseph added. 'But he couldn't let it go. He moved on to another unsolved missing person investigation.'

'Meanwhile, he couldn't let his brilliance go unnoticed, he had to let us know how clever he is.' She nodded. 'That makes sense, Joseph.'

It took twenty minutes to get to the old farm, where they pulled in behind the police vehicle that was already parked there. Nikki looked around. This place was nothing like where Alexandra had been found. Built on a grand scale for a farmhouse, it looked more like an elegant manor house, had it not been for the stable blocks and the exercise yard adjoining a cluster of large barns.

They hurried over to where the detective, DC Robin Wilson, was in conversation with an anxious-looking woman and a very tall and rugged man.

DC Wilson introduced them to Mrs Martine Knight, the owner of Knight's End, and her farm undermanager, Bryan Calder.

'Mrs Knight told me the story of the old Anderson shelter, ma'am,' Wilson said. 'So, I inspected the area and it's definitely been tampered with recently. Can I take you there now?'

After a brief word with Mrs Knight, Nikki followed DC Wilson across the yard and out towards the door of a walled garden.

Behind the door, she found a dream of a rural country garden. Surrounded on all sides by an old red-brick wall, it was criss-crossed with paths that meandered between vegetable patches, herbs in raised troughs, fruit cages, flowerbeds, and hundreds of different perennials, shrubs and climbers.

'Wow!' Joseph exclaimed. 'How beautiful is this!'

'Surely there can't be an Anderson shelter here?' said Nikki, gazing around her in awe. 'Or a grave?' It seemed incongruous in the extreme.

DC Robin Wilson, who was leading the way along one of the paths, glanced back over his shoulder. 'Let me show you what I discovered, and then I'll explain.'

At the far end of the walled garden, Nikki could see two uniformed officers. As she drew closer, she recognised PCs Kyle Adams and Emmie Greengrass. Both looked apprehensive.

When they reached the wall, Nikki saw just in front of it what looked like a large round cairn made of stones. Rockery plants grew around the base of the edifice, giving it a natural look. The whole thing might have been at home on a Cornish clifftop.

'The old shelter stood right here,' said Robin, indicating the cairn. 'And through that gateway,' he pointed to a small wooden door set in the far end of the wall, 'were two small cottages, what they called the Home Farm Cottages. They were tied, one for the farm manager and his family, the other for the head gardener and his wife and daughter. The manager's home was demolished years ago, badly damaged in the bombing raid.' His gaze returned to the cairn. 'The shelter took a direct hit from a V1 flying bomb. It impacted directly into the door and pretty well vaporised the family inside. Mrs Knight told me the records state that there were no bodies left to bury, so the crater was filled in with soil, and stones and rubble piled on top to form a kind of marker. When the manager returned from fighting in the war, he begged the Knight family to allow him to keep it as a memorial, and when they agreed, he had new stones laid in the form of a small Scottish cairn, as his wife was a Scot, and added some small plants, along with a plaque.'

Nikki looked, and saw the plaque he was talking about. Inscribed on it was simply the name Turner, with six Christian names below. 'Okay, Detective, now the history lesson is out of the way, what makes you so concerned about it?'

Unaccustomed to Nikki's forthright manner of speaking, DC Robin Wilson looked something like a rabbit caught in the headlights. 'Well, um, it's the stones, ma'am. They've been, er, disturbed.'

Nikki gritted her teeth. *Oliver!* 'Show me.'

The detective moved round to the back of the memorial and pointed.

Something — or someone — had indeed disturbed those stones, and recently. To Nikki's untrained eye, it looked like a number of the lower stones had been lifted away, and then replaced with fresh soil pushed into the gaps. At the front of the cairn, lime-green moss grew over and between the plants and made a perfect tapestry composed of stone, leaves and flowers, all mingled together. In contrast, the back was a pig's dinner. 'Call forensics.'

Joseph already had his phone to his ear.

'Shall we go and talk to the owner and see if she's had any calls from a certain investigative journalist lately?' Nikki said, already on her way back along the path.

Martine Knight invited them into her kitchen and asked them to take seats on the high stools positioned around a massive central island unit. The kitchen was like something from a country life magazine feature, with bespoke fittings and hi-tech gadgets that must have cost a fortune. It was impressive, but Nikki much preferred her own cosy and well-loved little country kitchen. A pair of muddy walking boots on her quarry-tiled floor looked perfectly at home. Here, even dust would have been wary of sullying the glistening granite work surfaces with its presence.

The coffee was served from a machine that probably needed a two-year course to master, but it tasted like ambrosia.

'Yes, as it happens, DI Galena, I've had a number of conversations with a young man during the past few months. His name is Oliver. He's not a journalist, although he said he once worked in that capacity. He's now a writer, compiling a book on the Fens at the time of the Second World War. He said he wanted to correct a number of misconceptions, and one of these was the belief that we got off lightly in terms of air raids and bombings. That's how he came to know about the Turner family tragedy.'

Martine Knight spoke like some dowager, Knight's End only slightly less grand than Sandringham. Her terribly upper-class voice boomed slightly and her words were directed at a point slightly above Nikki's hairline. All she lacked was a lorgnette.

'Right, so did you ever actually meet this Mr Oliver?' asked Nikki, suddenly conscious of her Lincolnshire accent.

'No, he never visited, although he did once ask if he could come and take some photographs.'

'And were his questions all confined to the incident of the buzz bomb, Mrs Knight?' asked Nikki.

'No, he was very interested in the history of Knight's End, the farm and the family in general. He showed such genuine interest that one found oneself telling him all sorts.' She frowned. 'What exactly are you looking for in the walled garden, Inspector Galena? Should I be concerned about this Oliver person?'

Thinking that maybe the unvarnished truth wasn't quite applicable in this instance, even somewhat unkind, Nikki said, 'I'm sure the man isn't any danger to you, but he has intimated that there might be something that you are unaware of beneath that memorial. We will have to investigate, I'm afraid.'

A mixture of emotions played across Martine Knight's face. 'Impossible! The gardeners will be devastated if there's any damage done. That's a very special area of the garden. We have a lot of unusual species of plant there, and the greatest of care, not to mention a great deal of money, has been spent on it. It was my late husband's pride and joy.'

Joseph bestowed one of his best calming smiles on the agitated woman. 'Rest assured, Mrs Knight, we totally appreciate what a special place it is. I promise you that we'll be as unobtrusive as possible, but we have to warn you that should we find anything untoward, there could be a considerable police presence on the premises. Meanwhile, I'll do my level best to personally see that nothing is damaged and I'll keep you informed of anything we discover.'

His assured, cultivated intonation wasn't lost on Martine Knight. Somewhat amused, Nikki watched the lady of the house thaw visibly.

'Now, we must go and watch out for our forensics team,' Joseph said, 'and impress on them the value of the plant collection they'll be encountering. Thank you for your delicious coffee, I'll be back later to update you.'

Once they were well away from the house, Nikki burst into laughter. 'You're such a fawning creep, Joseph Easter. And thank goodness. My limited stock of tact and diplomacy certainly doesn't extend to protecting a bunch of obscure weeds when there's a murdered girl at stake.'

'Weeds?' said Joseph, with a mischievous grin. 'Weeds wouldn't dare show their heads in that garden. Anyway, it was worth acting the creep just for a cup of that coffee.'

There was no arguing with that one.

Back in the walled garden, Robin informed them he'd just had a call from the station. 'Forensics are due in fifteen. They'll set up a crime scene as soon as we let them know what we've found.'

Kyle and Emmie were examining the back of the cairn. 'I could be wrong, ma'am, but I'd say these stones have been displaced twice, the first time being many years ago.' Emmie pointed to a couple of the large stones at the base. 'These two, for instance, they look to me as if they were replaced but not nearly as neatly as the stones at the front.'

'Well spotted,' murmured Joseph. 'You're right. A quite different hand set these ones down. The stones around the plaque, and the cairn as a whole, were laid professionally, most likely when the husband built the memorial. Back here it looks like someone, certainly not a stonemason, put them back in a hurry.'

Nikki eyed it dubiously. 'Would it be possible to remove some of the stones, conceal a body in there and the whole thing not collapse?'

'There'd be no chance of it collapsing, it's really solid,' said Joseph. 'But it would depend on what's underneath. If there's nothing but soil, yes, you could. If it's solid stone, then no, probably not. One thing's for sure, no one would think to look here for a body.'

'Someone did,' said Kyle softly. 'Oliver.'

* * *

Across the fields from Knight's End Farmhouse, a lone rambler stepped back on to the verge and gave a friendly wave to the driver of a tractor who had slowed to pass him. He continued along the lane for a while and then stopped and took a pair of binoculars from his rucksack. These he trained on a farm some distance away across fields of rapeseed, focusing on the marked police car and big four-by-four that stood in the farmyard.

Oliver nodded to himself. Even he was impressed at the speed with which Galena had identified his place of safety. Another vehicle appeared in his field of vision, an odd little Citroën painted a ridiculous lime-green colour, heading towards the parked vehicles. 'Ah, the Home Office pathologist himself. Well, I'm honoured! That must be the inimitable Professor Rory Wilkinson.' Laughing quietly, Oliver put the glasses away and strolled on.

This sudden evidence of efficiency on the part of the Greenborough police meant that it was time to submit his report. What would Galena make of — and, more to the point, how would she deal with — his damning indictment of the man who had abducted and killed poor Ruth? He quickened his pace. How he wished he could be a fly on the wall when she read it.

CHAPTER FIFTEEN

Dinah Barrett, deputy head of Ruby Grayson's school, had received official notification of the death of Ruby's brother, Daryl, followed by an *un*official meeting with her dear friend, Yvonne Collins. The news had shocked her profoundly.

Naturally, Ruby had been whisked out of school to be with her family, but Dinah Barrett noticed that Amber Grayson, Ruby's cousin, was still in her classroom. No one seemed to have thought of taking her home. Dinah wasn't sure how close the two sides of the Grayson family were, but she knew that Ruby and Amber had once been thick as thieves. Surely that would indicate that the two families were also close, so it was odd that Amber seemed to have been ignored. She probably didn't even know what had happened to her older cousin, Daryl. Dinah recalled Lynette Sims remarking that Amber was now thriving, while Ruby was becoming more and more introverted. Not only that, they hardly seemed to even talk anymore, let alone hang around together. For two girls who'd once been inseparable, this was odd indeed. Dinah had resolved to have a quiet word with young Amber before the news of Daryl Grayson's death spread through the school grapevine.

Amber Grayson entered her office hesitantly, obviously wondering what she had done to warrant the attention of the deputy head, so Dinah gave her a warm smile and told her to sit down. She began by asking Amber whether she was aware that Ruby had been taken out of school that afternoon.

'No, Miss Barrett, I've been at hockey practice. I've only just changed and got back to the classroom.' She looked concerned. 'Has Ruby done something wrong? Has she been suspended?'

It struck Dinah as rather strange that this should be her first assumption. She shook her head. 'No, my dear, nothing like that. I'm sorry to have to tell you that there's been an accident, and your cousin, Daryl — well, I'm afraid he has died.'

Again, a quite unexpected reaction. Just for a moment, Dinah was certain that she had seen a look of relief, even satisfaction, flash across the girl's face. Surely not!

'What happened to him, Miss Barrett?' Amber asked.

Still trying to analyse what she thought she'd seen, Dinah assumed a non-committal expression. 'I'm afraid we've not been given any details yet, Amber, just that Daryl has passed away. I'm sure your family will explain.' She upped the smile. 'So, under the circumstances, I'm sure you'll want to go home too?'

'No, thank you, Miss Barrett. I've got art this afternoon and it's my favourite subject. I'd rather stay, if I may?'

This might not be the time, given the situation, but questions were streaming around in Dinah's head. One thing was certain, Amber knew a lot more than she was saying about what was going on in Ruby's family. What Dinah did know was that Daryl had been a pervert. Someone in his family — not Ruby, it would seem — was being hurt, and young Ruby was too traumatised to open up, even to her favourite teacher.

'Well, all right. If you're sure?' Dinah said. 'But sit for a few minutes, dear, just in case the shock hasn't quite hit home. And, Amber, I'm very sorry about your cousin.'

Dinah watched for a reaction, but none came. That in itself was peculiar. Young girls Amber's age were prone to histrionics, forever breaking down in floods of tears. Whereas Amber seemed to be completely unmoved, simply saying, 'Thank you, Miss Barrett.'

'I'll leave you for a minute or two, Amber. Just sit quietly, I'll be back in a minute.'

Dinah left the room and hurried downstairs to Lynette Sims's form room. 'I need you in my office, Lynette. I think I should have a second adult present.' She told Lynette of Amber's unexpected response to receiving what should have been some pretty traumatic news.

'I'll settle this lot down and be straight with you,' said Lynette. 'There is definitely something going on between Ruby and Amber. Maybe, since Amber isn't the dominant one of the pair, there's a chance she'll talk to us.'

A few minutes later they were all seated back in the office.

'Amber? Miss Sims is here too. She is very worried about Ruby, and I am too. So, if there's anything you can tell us, anything at all, you won't be telling tales. We're just very concerned about your cousin's safety. Is there anything going on that could cause Ruby any harm?'

Amber shifted in her seat. 'I don't know what you're talking about.'

Oh, but you do, thought Dinah. 'The thing is, since something has happened to Daryl, we're worried about the possibility that something might happen to Ruby as well. Or was it Daryl causing the trouble? Look, Amber, if you know something, you must tell us, or it will be down to the police to make enquiries.' Dinah hoped she wasn't being too aggressive, but the mention of the police brought a different expression to the girl's face. Was it anger? A hint of fear?

'Is Ruby in danger, Amber?' Dinah said again.

The girl tensed, and then shook her head vehemently. 'Ruby isn't in danger, Miss Barrett, not at all. You've got it all wrong.'

Amber bit her lip hard, as if she were furious with herself. She was obviously regretting her words.

'And how, exactly, am I mistaken?' Dinah said, continuing to regard the girl.

'I, er, I meant . . . oh, it's family stuff, we can't talk about it.'

The self-same words that Ruby had used with Lynette Sims. Dinah glanced at Lynette, who nodded. 'Oh dear, oh dear. Well then, we'd better get you home, Amber. It looks like it's time we had a good long talk with your parents.'

This time there was no hesitation. 'No! No! You can't talk to my parents!'

'I'm afraid I can, Amber. I'm obliged to if I believe someone is at risk. It's my duty.'

'We're only thinking of you and Ruby, Amber,' interjected Lynette. 'We care about you both, your safety and well-being are our main consideration. Do you understand?'

For the first time, Amber looked as if she was about to cry. 'Please, don't talk to Mum and Dad. It's complicated.'

'Then maybe it's time you talked to us, and we'll see how we can help.' Lynette's tone was firm but gentle. 'Because we can help, you know. We're not just here to give you lessons, we want to help you through the tough times — all young people have tough times, don't they?'

'Other kids don't have stuff like this to cope with.' Amber looked utterly desolate. And then the tears really started to fall.

Dinah and Lynette looked at each other. Dinah handed Amber a handful of tissues from the box on her desk and patted her shoulder. 'There, there. Now, dry your eyes and tell us what you know. It's best this way, don't you think? With people who care about you rather than the authorities.'

Amber swallowed. 'What will happen to me?'

'If you tell the truth, nothing.' Dinah secretly hoped she'd been right in saying this, and it wasn't an assurance too far. From the look on Amber's face, she wasn't too convinced either.

Amber sat in silence for a while, sniffing. Then she seemed to come to a decision. 'Like I told you, you've got it all wrong. It's not Ruby who's in danger, it's her mother.'

'And Ruby knows about this?' asked Dinah, starting to feel a little queasy.

'Oh yes!' Amber gave a rather unnerving laugh. 'She knows all right.'

More questions began to whizz around in Dinah's head. 'Was it Daryl, Amber? Was Daryl threatening his mother, and was Ruby scared to tell anyone because the abuser was her own brother?'

'No! You still don't get it, do you?' Now Amber was both crying and laughing. 'It wasn't Daryl — though he was horrible and I'm glad he's dead. It's Ruby! She's the one who's terrorising her mother.'

* * *

Contrary to all expectations and against everyone's advice, Samantha Chisholm decided to remain in her tiny house in Rotherham Street. Now that the shock of the murder had worn off, she felt quite exultant. She still heard, often when she least expected it, that maniacal laugh. The other sound, his final gasp before the moment of death, had freed Sammie from menace. The fact that someone had deliberately murdered him — her stalker — was dreadful, but in her book, perfectly understandable. Someone who loved and cherished one of the other victims had to end their nightmare, permanently. She would never condone murder, but she did understand why it had been committed. She also knew that all the other victims of the stalker would breathe easy again once they knew that he would no longer be dogging their footsteps.

Sammie pulled on her jacket and marched out into the afternoon sun. Now she could give her new job the attention it required. It was just sad it had taken a murder to make that happen.

* * *

Rory strolled through the walled garden, enraptured. 'My dear cherubs! At last, you have summoned me somewhere my spirit can soar! Never mind that it's taken nigh on fifteen years for you to do so, but you are clearly learning! I thought the arboretum at your last dalliance with murder was splendid, but this is a rare joy! Oh, do look! Such a marvellous specimen of an *Actinidia kolomikta*! What a wonder of nature that is!'

Joseph looked towards the climbing plant whose green and bright pink foliage was decorating a section of the red-brick wall and had to agree. It was indeed striking. He then said he was sorry, but could they get on with the real reason for Rory's presence as the light wasn't going to hold forever.

'Spoilsport,' muttered Rory. 'Why do these dead bodies have to ruin all my little excursions?'

'Because you are the expert on dead bodies,' threw in Nikki. 'And until you do a little probing for us, we don't even know if we have one.'

The three of them approached the cairn.

'Oh, I say! My latest body is already interred? How quaint!' Rory exclaimed. 'What a clever place to hide a body, in a memorial.' He turned to Joseph. 'Do you think it's a joke?'

'No one's laughing,' Joseph said flatly.

'I bet someone is,' returned Rory with a chuckle. As one of his scene of crime officers laid down protective duckboards around the cairn, he pulled on his protective suit, mask and overshoes. 'Righty-ho! Let's see what we've got — or not got, as the case may be.'

It took a while, Rory being painstaking in his removal of each individual piece of stone. At every stage, his forensic photographer, Ella Jarvis, photographed his progress. All Nikki and Joseph could hear were grunts, muttered curses, and instructions to Ella as to how she should angle the next shot. At last, Rory stood up, his hands on his back. 'I'm going to need a massage tonight, that's for sure.'

'I'll treat you to a bloody spa weekend if you'll just tell us. Do we have a body or not?' called out Nikki impatiently.

'Oh my! You will *so* regret saying that, Nikki Galena! But yes, we do.' Rory exhaled loudly, then said more seriously, 'Although it's not going to be easy to extract it from its resting place. It's firmly jammed in and has been there for some considerable time. I'm afraid we'll have to consult with the owner of this memorial. To bring her out, and I'm certain it is a she, I'm going to have to take this cairn apart, doing my utmost to preserve it to a point where restoration can save and rebuild what remains.'

Joseph saw Nikki looking hopefully at him. 'You want me to go and talk to Mrs Knight, don't you?'

'I sure do. Off you go.'

'Okay, okay. But first, Rory, can you give us a brief overview of what you've found?'

The pathologist scratched his chin thoughtfully. 'I'd say that the cairn was built by a drystone wall contractor. It's a lovely job, no mortar, just carefully stacked layers of stone. Then someone decided it was the perfect place to conceal their heinous murder. They made a valiant attempt at covering up their intervention, and being at the back, it would appear that our murderer succeeded. One would never know, and even if someone did notice, in the course of weeding or clearing the leaves, it could be explained away, I'm sure, by some natural occurrence, like a fox endeavouring to burrow beneath it.'

'And recently, Rory?' asked Nikki. 'Did Oliver's delving around have much effect on the older disturbance?'

'Very little. The recent intervention was minor, just a couple of the larger stones and some soil. I'd say he went no further than to confirm what he already believed, that the cairn had been used to conceal a body.' He held up a hand. 'And no need to remind me, I'm very aware that I must watch out for *Par Avion* as I exhume our latest victim.'

Nikki threw up her hands. 'Sorry, Rory, but that guy is freaking me out with his creepy airmail envelopes.'

'Well, there's nothing apparent yet, dear lady, but as I said, I can see very little. I promise to let you know the moment I find anything.'

Joseph noticed that Rory hadn't made light of the situation, as he normally would, but then the extent of Nikki's disquiet was very apparent. 'Right. I'm off to try and get the lady of the manor's permission to decimate her precious memorial. Wish me luck.'

Leaving the walled garden, Joseph noticed a number of men eyeing him suspiciously. From their clothes, he decided they must be the gardeners. They were probably worried about the havoc the police were about to wreak. No wonder they were looking at him that way. If he'd spent years producing a garden like this, he'd be worried too.

He found Martine Knight still in the kitchen and wondered if he might get offered another coffee. She smiled at him, a little faintly, but it was a smile, so he considered it a good start. Even so, this was going to be tricky.

'Mrs Knight . . .'

'Martine, please. And your first name, Sergeant Easter?'

'Joseph,' he said, starting to feel a tad uncomfortable now he was alone with her. She seemed a very different animal to the one who'd looked down her nose at Nikki. Best not to string this out. 'Well, Martine, I'm sorry to have to tell you this, but we believe that a woman's body has been concealed inside the Turner family memorial cairn, and it has to be removed immediately. Obviously, that will entail a considerable amount of damage to it. Can you tell me if any of the Turners are still in this area, and if so, do they visit the memorial?'

Martine Knight almost fell on to a stool. 'Oh no, this is just awful. My worst nightmare! They'll destroy my beautiful garden.'

'Not at all. In fact, the pathologist who's in charge of this operation is hugely impressed with your garden. He's a bit of a horticulturalist himself, so he'll take the utmost care that his team do no damage, other than to the cairn itself, which is unavoidable.' He was laying it on a bit, but he needed that permission. 'There will be a police investigation, I'm afraid, but I'll do my very best to keep it as low-key as possible. I should tell you that this is an old murder case, not a recent one.'

Martine looked up at him, frowning. 'How old?'

'Fifteen years ago? Something like that.'

She looked aghast. 'You mean we've had a dead body in our walled garden for fifteen years! It's unthinkable! No, it can't be, this has to be some awful mistake.'

'I'm afraid not, Martine. And I'm also afraid that you'll be asked a lot of questions. But we'll be sensitive, I assure you.'

The proud lady of the manor looked quite helpless. 'And it had to be the week my son is away. Oh dear, oh dear, I'm not sure I can do this alone.'

Watching her carefully, Joseph had a good idea that Mrs Knight could probably cope all too well, and was overdramatising for his benefit. 'And the Turner family, Mrs, er, Martine?'

'Oh, they're long gone. There may be one or two distant relatives somewhere around, but no one ever comes here. We wanted to keep it up because it was part of the history of Knight's End. It's part of the walled garden, and we maintain it out of respect for a man who worked loyally for us and lost everything because of the war.' She stood up and walked to the coffee machine. 'I need a drink, and since I can't really take out the vodka bottle in front of a police officer, coffee will have to do.'

Joseph laughed. 'Probably, though I quite understand you wanting something a bit stronger. I'm just sorry to be the bearer of such bad tidings.'

Martine busied herself with the coffee machine. 'I'm just glad dear Gordon isn't here to see this.'

'Your husband?' asked Joseph.

'Late husband, yes. Gordie was the gardener of the family. He devoted the last few years of his life to making that garden into what it is now. That Victorian greenhouse is an exact copy of one he saw in an old manor house in Ireland. He was enchanted by it and had an architect design and build one for us.'

Money no object then, thought Joseph. 'I thought it looked very special.' He cleared his throat. 'Martine, do we have your permission to go ahead and begin work on dismantling part of the cairn?'

She handed him a cup. 'I get the feeling that if I refuse you will only get some sort of warrant and do it anyway, so yes, do what you have to, but please, Joseph, I beg you. Don't let them wreck my garden.'

He accepted the coffee with a reassuring smile. 'I'll take charge of it personally. Tell me, are there lights in the garden, or at least a power source? If not, we'll need to bring in a generator.'

'My gardeners sometimes work late and do maintenance work in the winter, so we have lights all around. I'll get Terry — he's the head gardener — to show you where the switches are. There are also outside sockets, he'll point those out too.'

They drank the exceedingly good coffee in silence. After a while, Martine said, 'About fifteen years ago, you say? Do you actually know the identity of the person hidden in that cairn?'

There was no point in hiding the details from her, it would soon be made clear in any case. 'We aren't certain yet, Martine, but there's a chance that we'll find the remains of a young woman named Ruth Baker who went missing at around that time.'

She looked pensive. 'I recall hearing that name in the news. But why now? What on earth brought you here, tramping around in my beautiful garden?' She glanced at him almost flirtatiously. 'Not that I'm not pleased to meet you, of course, Joseph.'

'Well, that's all I can tell you, I'm afraid.' Joseph decided it was time to go.

CHAPTER SIXTEEN

Yvonne listened intently to Dinah's account of her and Lynette's meeting with Amber. It was a lot to take in.

'And you both believe this young teenager?' she said.

'Absolutely,' Dinah said. 'I've been many years in this job, and I think I'm pretty good at spotting a lie. Amber was not lying. I've discussed it with the head, and we decided that in the light of what happened to Daryl, you really should know about it.'

Yvonne had never seen the unflappable Dinah Barrett so upset. 'What on earth in these children's short lives could have turned them into nothing less than, well, monsters? One a stalker who picks on young women and terrorises them, the other an abuser who victimises her own mother.'

Both fell silent, lost in thought. After a while, Dinah said, 'It may be completely irrelevant, but a short while ago, Lynette told me she suspected that there was someone watching her. According to her, she never saw them but she kept hearing footsteps, and once or twice she thought she saw a figure lurking in the bushes in a neighbour's garden. When all the worry over Ruby came up, she pushed it to the back of her mind. Could it have been Daryl, do you think?'

Yvonne exhaled. 'It certainly sounds like the way he operated according to his victims. We'll only know for certain if it stops now he's dead, but I'm pretty sure your teacher won't be bothered again.'

'I'll tell her that. I know it's been on her mind.'

'Listen, Di, I'm going to report this to my boss. What have you done with Amber?' Yvonne asked.

'She's still here. I'll take her home myself, but only after I know how you'll be dealing with Ruby and the rest of the family. I get the feeling that Amber's parents suspect that there's something amiss in Ruby's home but have no idea about the truth of the matter. Amber's been far too scared to talk to them.'

Yvonne frowned. 'There's one thing that's still puzzling me, Dinah. You told me that Ruby was becoming withdrawn, whereas Amber, whose work had also been suffering, had suddenly picked up. Surely, if Amber were so scared, it should have been the other way around?'

'We wondered that too, Vonnie,' said Dinah. 'But it didn't seem like the right time to bring it up, we'd have been turning what was supposed to be a reassuring chat into an interrogation. Reading between the lines, we suspect that Ruby had been trying to groom Amber for the role of accomplice. I think I've said before that they are both intelligent but Ruby is the brighter of the two. And she's streetwise. After what I've just heard, she's most likely a first-class manipulator too. I think what happened was that Ruby soon realised that Amber just wasn't cut out for it. So, rather than flog a dead horse, so to speak, she decided not to bother with her anymore. I'm pretty certain that her withdrawal from school life was an act put on to make us feel sorry for her.'

Yvonne had seen this often enough in teenage gangs, it was a form of control. How many times had she been told that someone's child had been an angel until he or she got into "bad company" when in fact, the opposite was the case.

'As I said,' Dinah went on, 'once Amber started to talk, it all came flooding out. Apparently, Ruby swore she was feeling terribly guilty about her behaviour. She blamed her brother's bad influence, which had led her into doing things she regretted. However, now she was finished with all that. Even so, she said, for Amber's sake it was probably best they didn't see so much of each other. And they didn't. Ruby left her alone, so after a while, Amber relaxed and went back to enjoying school life again, believing that her cousin was back to being the well-behaved little girl of before.' Dinah gave a little grunt. 'You have to remember that Amber's little more than a child, and it was quite natural for her to believe a girl who'd been her closest friend since birth. Only now has she started to realise just how dangerous her cousin is.'

And some! thought Yvonne, suddenly wondering how the death of a brother would affect an already damaged mind. 'I need to go and take instruction on this, Dinah. Keep the girl safe, and I'll ring you back as soon as I've let the DI know what has happened. Oh, and Di? You've done the right thing in telling me.'

'I had to,' said Dinah. 'For the first time in my professional life I am totally out of my depth. And it's not a good feeling.'

* * *

Cat exhaled. 'The *girl* is allegedly the one doing the abusing? Hell-bloody-fire! We need expert help here, Vonnie. This one is for the guys who specialise in dealing with minors. I'll contact the boss immediately and notify her, then I guess we'll throw it at the superintendent for him to organise.'

'Is it all right if I go over to the school, Cat?' asked Yvonne. 'I have a feeling they could do with some support, and Amber is still with them.'

'Good idea, and stay there until we can find the right people to take responsibility. It's going to need kid-glove treatment, especially since the family has just suffered a bereavement. Daryl might have been a first-class shite, but he was still their son.'

'By the way, my friend told me that Ruby's teacher is also being stalked — or was, since he's dead. Her account is identical to that of all the others.'

Cat gave a low laugh. 'Maybe dear Ruby put him up to it. Who knows?'

'That went through my mind too,' Yvonne said. 'I can hear her now, *nosey Miss Sims is becoming a nuisance, so let's put the frighteners on her.*'

'I wonder how many other women he scared,' said Cat pensively. 'If your teacher didn't lodge a complaint, I'm guessing there are others who didn't come forward either. Not everyone wants the police involved. Right. I'll head off and put the wheels in motion. Off you go, Vonnie, and keep me posted, won't you?'

As soon as Yvonne left, Cat rang Nikki and told her of Amber's allegations. The resulting string of expletives impressed even Cat. Nikki told her that she was tied up at Knight's Farm right now, so Cat should take it directly to Superintendent Cam Walker. Such cases were extremely delicate. The media would be watching avidly and broadcasting every detail to the world.

When Cat returned from seeing the super, she found Ben waiting for her, looking anxious.

'They said you were with the super. Is everything okay?'

'Oh, Ben! You're not going to believe this one.'

* * *

How much more shit was going to be dumped in her lap before the end of the day, Nikki wondered. Normally, she hated having to hand over a case to another team but this one she'd be happy to relinquish, and as soon as possible. They were all trained in handling juvenile crime, but something like this required specialist officers. The youth justice system was complicated enough in a straightforward case, but where the perpetrator was a child, it was labyrinthine. There was even a different framework for the sentencing of under-eighteens. Well, neither she nor her team were sufficiently competent, and anyway, they had enough on their plates with Oliver.

Nikki thought of the cries in the night that seemed to come from the Grayson house, the troubled schoolgirl, the too-bland family and the Laughing Stalker. Well, it could all go, *tout ensemble*, to someone else. Let them fathom it out, and good luck to them.

By the time Joseph came trotting towards her from the direction of the farmhouse, she felt easier about the task ahead. She would now have every officer available fully focused on Oliver, and the conundrum he had presented her with.

Joseph was smiling grimly. 'Yes?' she asked, crossing her fingers.

'Yes. We can go ahead with the cairn.'

'And that rather odd look on your face?' she asked.

'Well, it was a bit uncomfortable being alone with a woman who's suddenly turned into a black widow spider.' He shrugged. 'Still, I got the desired result, and another coffee, so I can't complain.'

She narrowed her eyes. 'Maybe I'll go myself next time.'

'You're most welcome. Not that I think you'd be much of a success with dear Martine. I don't think you're her type.'

Nikki opened her mouth to speak, but saw PC Emmie Greengrass hurrying towards them.

'Please don't tell me that's what I think it is,' groaned Nikki, seeing the thick brown envelope in Emmie's hand.

'A motorcycle courier delivered this, ma'am. It's for Professor Wilkinson. Shall I take it to him, or will you?'

Goodness, she was becoming neurotic about every single envelope. 'I'll take it, thank you, Emmie.' She looked at the PC. 'Was the courier one you recognised?'

'Hard to say about the rider, DI Galena,' replied Emmie, 'what with the biker's leathers and full-face helmet, but the bike was definitely kitted out for the job. Paniers and top box with a logo on them. I'm pretty sure I've seen them around Greenborough.'

Nikki thanked her, and looked at Joseph. 'No *Par Avion*, and it looks kosher. We'll go and see, shall we? And we can tell Rory he's free to start work on that cairn.'

Rory stared at the envelope and shook his head slowly. 'I'm expecting nothing, dear hearts. But I do smell a rat.' He produced a knife from his equipment case, slit the envelope open and pulled out a second brown one, addressed to Nikki and bearing the familiar blue and white sticker. 'Ah, verily, the rat cometh!'

'Shit!' Nikki exhaled. 'Open it up, Rory, and let's read our latest epistle from sodding bloody Oliver.'

It was headed *Case File 0148. Ruth Baker.* Attached was a handwritten note that read:

Respect! Either I'm making things too easy for you, DI Galena, or you really are endeavouring to up your game. Your speed in discovering this one is commendable. Pity it didn't happen years ago when young Ruth was miserably failed by everyone.

However, I have decided to just let you get on with the rest of the formalities, and you'll be pleased to know that after extensive inquiries, the reports of which are attached, there will be no aftermath. No condemned man to find or punish this time. I will be very interested to see what course you take when you read about the perpetrator of this particularly vile murder. Very interested indeed.

Now on to Case File 049. Bethany Lyons. Once again, you failed to find an innocent girl, in fact you failed in every aspect of the investigation. Shame on you.

Oliver

Nikki let out a long low sigh. It was like riding on an ever-accelerating carousel. At some point she was going to fly off and come crashing to the ground. Oliver never gave them a moment to gather themselves. Now, just as they were about to make one discovery, he was throwing the next one at them.

She felt a hand on her arm.

'We will find him, Nikki.' Joseph's voice was low, reassuring. 'He's so sure of himself that at some point he'll give himself away, he has to. He's too fond of his own words.

172

He'll let slip something he shouldn't, and that's when we'll find out who he is.'

'I wish I felt as sure of that as you do,' she said.

'Well, I feel very confident,' chimed in Rory. 'I'm with Joseph all the way. This clever dick of a puller of strings will surely be the instrument of his own downfall, and then I shall laugh like a drain!' He looked puzzled for a moment. 'Such a strange phrase, isn't it, to laugh like a drain, although I wonder if the fact that the French *rigoler*, to laugh, and *rigole*, as in a drain or a channel, look and sound the same might be the answer?'

'It also crops up in World War Two army slang, Prof, but—'

'Boys! Excuse me! We have a body less than two metres away from us. Could we possibly concentrate on that?' Nikki was back to her old self.

The two men threw each other conspiratorial glances, their faces assuming suitably sheepish expressions.

'I take it I'm clear to excavate?' said Rory.

'Go for it,' said Joseph. 'But I've promised the lady of the house that we'll try not to damage her precious garden too much, so do you think you could spread the word to your SOCOs, Rory?'

'If they bruise a single petal, they will be flogged, publicly, in the mortuary car park,' he said. 'Now, what about lighting? I fear my task will carry me into the hours of Stygian darkness.'

'All available, lights in situ, and sockets to plug in any additional halogens directly over the cairn itself. I'll go find the head gardener and sort that out.' Joseph looked towards the gate. 'He should be waiting for me now.'

Nikki indicated for him to go, then added, 'And make sure you tell the flat-footed shower that will be manning the cordon and doing the legwork to watch where they are placing their size thirteen boots, unless you want to upset dear Martine, or should I say, Lady Martine. She's a proper little Vita Sackville West, isn't she?'

Joseph's mouth dropped open. 'I had no idea Nikki Galena knew about that poet, gardener, novelist, biographer, and wonderfully scandalous woman.'

'I'm not a total ignoramus, Joseph,' she said, assuming her most patronising manner. 'Now, go and get the electrics sorted before Rory loses the light.'

Joseph walked away, still shaking his head in disbelief.

Rory regarded her, looking smug. 'So, you really do listen to some of my edifying tutorials then? I'm flattered, dear lady. Not to mention gobsmacked.'

'Yeah, well, I listen to some.' She grinned at him. 'Well, very few if I'm honest, Prof, but that one fascinated me. I couldn't help comparing the Knight woman and her obsession with her walled garden with Vita and her beloved Sissinghurst.'

'You never cease to amaze me, Nikki Galena. Of all the bizarre, blood-curdling, mind-blowing stories and illuminating facts that I choose to share with you, the one you retain is that of a garden designer from the Victorian era.' He looked across the gardens. 'But right now, I see the troops amassing. I have to go and issue my orders along with a few dire warnings of floggings.' He looked back to the cairn. 'And then we bring one young lady back into this beautiful world that she was so cruelly snatched away from all those years ago.'

Moving off, Rory called back over his shoulder, 'I have a theory about this murder, you know. When I've given it a careful mulling over, I'll share it with you.'

'All theories gratefully received,' she said, and murmured, 'because I have very few of my own.' She looked down at the thick envelope she still held in her hand. She needed to read it, and since she wasn't busy at the moment, why not now? She headed back to her car. No time like the present.

Nikki climbed into the passenger seat and made herself comfortable. Intending to skim through it, she soon became immersed in the contents.

Some twenty minutes later, Joseph knocked on the window, bringing her back to the present.

He climbed into the driver's seat. 'Sorted, as much as I can, and the cordon and log are set up. We are lucky, really, as we can easily contain the comings and goings at the site. Only those who are actually needed will go in, which will minimise footfall considerably. That's perfect for us, as there'll be little risk of cross-contamination, and it'll keep Martine off my back.'

But Nikki was only half listening. 'This man. This Oliver. I cannot believe how thorough he's been, and I'm at a loss to know how he has obtained certain facts, unless he was attached to the original investigation in some way. Joseph, I think we are dealing with a police officer who's turned rogue.' She closed her eyes for a moment, thinking hard. 'This needs taking apart, word by word, I've just skipped to the end. I now know why he's wondered how we'll handle this case. Listen to this. Oliver has produced evidence to prove beyond doubt, if everything he states is correct, that the killer was your Martine's beloved late husband, Gordon.'

'Oh shoot! That's going to be a tricky one.' Joseph pulled a face. 'I can't see that suggestion going down too well over another cup of coffee, can you?'

'It would answer why Gordon spent so much time in the garden,' muttered Nikki. 'He was making sure no one else dug her up.'

'And Oliver's irrefutable proof is?' Joseph asked.

'He was seen dragging something towards the cairn.'

'What?' Joseph stared at her. 'And this witness didn't come forward at the time? Why?'

'Oliver says she was a child of eight who was apparently fond of telling tall stories. When she said she'd seen Mr Knight dragging something heavy through the walled garden at night, her mother, terrified of losing their position and their tied cottage, scolded her. The girl was too young to have heard about the disappearance of Ruth Baker, and over the years she forgot about it, until Detective Oliver turned up.' Nikki looked across to Joseph. 'You need to read this. According to Oliver, ever since his visit, she has become haunted by the thought that she'd been witness to a murderer hiding his victim. We'd better talk to her, hadn't we?'

'How come Oliver chanced on this key witness after all this time? Bit of a coincidence, isn't it?' Joseph said.

'Because his enquiries all pointed in the direction of Gordon Knight. He says he spoke to every single man, woman and child who had worked or lived at Knight's End at the time Ruth went missing, all without Martine Knight's knowledge. When he did contact her, he did so under the pretext of writing a book on World War Two.' She raised an eyebrow at Joseph. 'What's more, he discovered a link connecting Gordon and Ruth! We'll have to check it, but a pound to a penny, he'll be right. As I said, he's thorough, and very careful.'

'And you have no doubt of the veracity of his findings, even before you've examined them thoroughly?' he said.

Nikki shrugged. 'I can't help but think he's got it right. After all, he's already located two dead girls, both of whom the Fenland Constabulary failed to find. He may have spent years on this, a decade possibly, but that doesn't matter, he's succeeded where the police did not. If it weren't for him these cases would have been left to moulder in somebody's drawer. Don't get me wrong, the last thing I want is to give the impression I admire this man, because I don't, but I have no reason to think he's wrong. The wrong bit was when he took it too far and executed the man who murdered Alexandra Cornfield.'

Joseph stared out through the windscreen. 'So apart from overstepping the mark in her case, he's doing our job for us. And you're right, he is doing it rather well.'

'And there's another two to go. Will it turn out that he's solved those as well? What is he? Some kind of super anti-hero?' Nikki shook her head.

'He'll be a real hero to the families of those girls,' said Joseph glumly.

'What is his motive, Joseph?' demanded Nikki. 'It doesn't make sense. If it was one girl, it would be perfectly understandable for a loved one to take up a crusade to bring the killer to justice, as well as hating the police for not giving her family and friends closure. But four cases!'

'I think you've got your answer right here, Nikki.' Joseph pointed out of the window. 'Look. The press.'

Nikki saw a big van and two cars slowing down outside Knight's End Farmhouse. 'Oh bugger! Already? We don't even know what's in that bloody cairn yet.'

'This is Oliver's doing. His aim is to discredit us right across the board. Right now, he's just giving them the heads up that something's afoot, but you wait, before long he'll have spilled the beans about the whole thing. I can see the headlines now: "Lone Avenger Solves Cases the Police Have Bungled!" "Why Did the Police Not Find These Murdered Girls Fifteen Years Ago?" and so on and so forth.'

'He can't have had some relationship with all of them. Unless . . .' She watched as the journalists and reporters got out of their cars. Suddenly she grabbed Joseph's arm. 'Go and head that lot off. Tell them no one goes anywhere on this farm and no one accosts Mrs Knight, her family or any of the staff. An official statement will be made, but not until we sodding well know something ourselves. Or words to that effect.'

Joseph got out of the car, then poked his head back in her window. 'Unless what?'

'Unless he *is* connected to one of the four missing women in some way. Maybe he started to investigate one, and turned up all our other failures after he started digging. The venture turned into an obsession and he saw a way to get back at us that would have even wider ramifications.' She pointed to another car that was just pulling up. 'Now bugger off and sort that motley crew out before I do it myself. They really won't like that!'

CHAPTER SEVENTEEN

'I can rarely recall having a more productive day,' said Wendy with a satisfied smile. 'It felt just like it did when we were back with the MOD and found a viable lead in an undercover investigation.'

Eve's friend's eyes shone with the old exhilaration. They had been good at their jobs. It wasn't the kind of work that won you any plaudits but it was gratifying in the extreme.

'If our young Jacob has done nearly as well as us, we'll be breaking open the champagne before long,' Eve added.

'He'll be here in fifteen minutes, so we'll soon find out.' Wendy smiled. 'I hope he likes chilli con carne. I had a feeling we'd be pushed for time, so I took a large one out of the freezer this morning. It was the only thing I could find that's quick.'

'I'm sure he'll love it,' said Eve. 'You make a corker of a chilli.'

She set the table for three, boiled the kettle for the rice and found some tortilla chips in the larder. She was beginning to feel quite nervous. As Wendy had said, their day had been productive but it had brought some unexpected skeletons out of the Tate family cupboard, and depending on what Jacob turned up, they could be looking at a very dark occurrence indeed. What then? Should it be locked away again and left to rest where it lay, or should they bring it out into the light?

When Jacob arrived, his face told her what she wanted to know. He was almost bursting with excitement.

He sniffed the air approvingly. 'Hey, is that chilli? My favourite. I'm so glad I met you two lovely ladies.'

Eve was similarly delighted that they had chanced upon Jacob. 'Jacob, this is nothing to do with the Tates, but could we enlist your assistance if we find any more interesting bits of history below ground? You've been so helpful, and your knowledge of local history is unsurpassed.'

'I'd love to help you, anytime.' Jacob beamed at them. 'This is a real challenge. It's kind of a sidestep from my usual research and far more exciting. Oh, and by the way, were my suggestions for your daughter any use to her?'

'I haven't heard from her, so I'm guessing she's pretty swamped right now,' said Eve. 'I'll let you know as soon as she gets in touch. Now, sit down and we'll dish up supper. Then we can talk.'

Unable to wait until the meal was over, they pitched in almost straight away. Jacob had gone the Jan Laska route, trying to get to why the two farmhands had wanted to kill him, while Eve and Wendy had concentrated on the two Tate daughters and their apparently rather unpleasant dispositions.

'As you said, they were the complete opposite of the two boys,' Wendy began. 'I found some references to them in old man Fred Bates's diaries that you might not have noticed, Jacob, because he never refers to them by name. However, if you look carefully, you can pick up who Chris's ancestor is talking about.'

'Then I checked a website I subscribe to that publishes the full text of old newspaper articles,' added Eve.

'This is brilliant,' said Jacob. 'I never got as far as looking into Maria and Isobel, although they always fascinated me. So, what did they do?'

'You really don't want to know!' said Eve. 'The sisters were definitely mentally disturbed, and although we only have Fred's ancestor's word for it, and some rather melodramatic and probably exaggerated articles, I'd have thought those girls ought to have been in psychiatric care. They weren't just mad as March hares, but if what we've dredged up about them is true, they were outright dangerous. In one incident that was recorded, the sisters held the head of another girl underwater following an argument, and she all but drowned. Another entry in the diaries mentioned a child belonging to one of the farm labourers suffering serious burns after "playing" with Maria and Isobel. And by the way, the family made every effort to quash all rumours or gossip about them.'

'Only once did Fred's diaries infer that the mother's death was no accident,' said Wendy. 'The entry said that the only people close to that cattle pen at the time of her fatal accident, when the cattle trampled her, were her two daughters and a farm worker.' She looked at Jacob, her eyes alight. 'Now, get this. One of the two farmhands who killed Jan was the deceased mother's brother, Tommy Tate's brother-in-law.'

Jacob stared at the table, frowning. Then the light seemed to dawn. 'One of those letters I told you about, the ones from Tate's sister-in-law to a friend, mentioned trouble looming on the horizon, all revolving around one of the migrant workers at the Tate farm. Something had happened, and it was bothering him so much that he was going to take it to the police. She said it would ruin the Tates, but that they deserved it.' His eyes lit up. 'I bet it was Jan Laska! One of his main tasks was to look after the cattle. What if he witnessed the girls shutting their mother into the cattle pen where she was trampled to death?'

'That would be supported by the mention in Fred's diary. It must be the reason why Laska had to die,' said Wendy. 'Very likely.'

'But who attacked Tommy Tate?' asked Eve. 'If the girls killed their mother, could they—?'

'Have tried to kill their father too?' Jacob shook his head. 'I doubt that. I think the men who killed Jan might have attacked Tommy, taking his things to make it look like a mugging and then burying them later, or giving them to someone to bury for them.' Jacob took out his phone and consulted the notepad. 'Or there's another possibility. I've made some other observations about Laska this afternoon. I hadn't known he was married, and one of those letters mentioned that Tommy had his roving eye on a "foreign lady."' He looked thoughtfully from Eve to Wendy. 'The main reason why Laska was deemed innocent of the attempted murder of Tommy Tate was that the stolen goods weren't found on him, and that he wouldn't have had time to hide them. He could have attacked Tommy and left him for dead, and the two men who found him stole his belongings with the idea of selling them at a later date. They then justified their murder of Jan as righteous indignation, although the real reason was that he knew too much about the Tate girls and their mother's death and might have been going to the police.'

Eve was struggling with all that. It was quite possible, but it seemed too complex and too much of it was guesswork. How could they prove anything after so many years had passed? And did they need to? A sudden thought occurred to her. 'Do you know what I think?'

They stared at her, waiting.

'I think Chris Tate already knows all this. I'm not sure about his wife, but I think all that talk of never having been able to find the truth is rubbish. He knows very well what happened. He's just banking on the two old dears giving up and going back to digging up nails and threepenny bits.' She looked at Jacob. 'You said the story about the two devoted farmhands was a fabrication on the part of the Tate sons and daughters to cover up the real truth, and I think you're absolutely right. I also think it's been passed down the Tate family from generation to generation. It's their skeleton in the closet, which has to be protected at all costs.'

Wendy nodded slowly. 'I think you're right.'

Looking somewhat poleaxed, Jacob said, 'So where do we go from here?'

'To Chris Tate.' Eve smiled wickedly. 'This "old dear" is going to change a certain local farmer's perspective on women of a certain age.'

What she hadn't decided was whether to go alone, or with Wendy, or possibly the three of them together.

* * *

As twilight crept over the fen, the walled garden of Knight's End Farm was lit up with bright halogen lights. It had proved far harder than expected to extract the body from the cairn, even more so because Rory Wilkinson had taken it upon himself, along with his right-hand man, Spike, to do all the heavy work himself. Stone by stone, they dismantled the memorial, marvelling as they did so at the expertise of the drystone wall builder who had originally constructed it.

It wasn't until around ten that night that they were able to finally stand back and survey the results of their labours.

The cairn had been constructed using two rows of stones, the gaps between them filled in with smaller pebbles. The centre was hollow. The base was firm soil, rammed down hard, and below that, they knew, was the rubble from the old Anderson shelter and possibly some shattered bones belonging to the ill-fated Turner family.

There lay the twisted and broken body of a woman.

Spike looked angry. 'He wasn't too careful when he shoved her into her final resting place, was he, Prof? Bastard!'

'Indeed,' murmured Rory, staring at the twisted bundle of bones jammed into the cramped space. 'Bastard sums it up rather well. Now, Spike, would you go and find our admirable detectives for me? They need to see what we've discovered, and then they, unlike us, can go home to their beds, as their presence will no longer be required until the morrow, when they join us at the autopsy table.'

Spike straightened up somewhat painfully. 'Sure, Prof.' He looked around at the flowers and plants that shimmered beneath the brilliant lighting. 'This is one of the quietest and prettiest locations we've ever exhumed a body in.'

'It certainly beats most of them,' agreed Rory. 'I suppose that's one consolation. This dear woman did have a beautiful spot to rest in.' He pointed at the contorted limbs. 'But not in that position. To repeat your sage words, dear Spike. What a bastard.'

A few minutes later Nikki and Joseph hurried through the gate and into the garden, their faces radiating anticipation and anxiety at what they might find.

Rory stood back. 'We have the body of a woman, most likely young, she may be around twenty, but that's just an educated guess until we get her back to the mortuary. I'm assuming you have a record of the clothes your girl was wearing?'

Nikki knew them by heart. 'Ruth Baker was wearing blue denim jeans, a white shirt, a tan-coloured suede jacket and blue desert boots. No jewellery that anyone can recall and no wristwatch. She had a mobile phone and a purse made of multicoloured leather patches. That's it.'

'Then unless someone else is wearing her clothes, you finally have the body — or what's left of it — of Ruth Baker.' Rory gave them a wry smile. 'I'm afraid your Oliver has done it again. But just think. Much as this might smart, at least her family finally have something to bury, decently this time.'

'There's one other thing, Rory,' said Nikki, her eyes on the contents of the cairn. 'They recorded a single identifying mark, a deformed big toe on her left foot. It was why she always wore comfortable boots rather than fashionable shoes.'

Rory angled one of the lights and leaned in to where the body lay. Her legs had been folded beneath her, but the bones of her feet protruded slightly. The left toe was certainly deformed.

'Again, we need to examine her properly, but I can confirm an old injury that resulted in a malformation of the left big toe. I suggest we have found your Ruth.'

Just then, Rory caught a hint of fragrance from a night-scented shrub. Some kind of jasmine, he guessed. The contrast between this glorious smell and the heap of bones lying in the dirt in front of his eyes was almost overwhelming. He shook himself. 'Now, my cherubs, Spike and I have work to do. We need to get this poor soul out of this abominable makeshift grave, and restore as much of her dignity as is humanly possible. You may go.'

He watched them walk away, wondering who had the worse job — the pathologists, or the detectives who were about to break the news to a long-bereaved family.

'Okay, Spike, let's do our duty by young Ruth here. She's waited far too long already.'

* * *

At around one in the morning, Nikki and Joseph lay in bed, trying unsuccessfully to sleep. Nikki was pondering the dumb acceptance with which Ruth Baker's father had received the news of his daughter's discovery. He had said later that he always knew she would be found one day, it was just sad that it hadn't happened while her mother was still alive. To her this seemed like yet another example of the police's failure. Now, as she tried to will herself to sleep, she felt terribly low-spirited. She wanted to talk to Joseph, but from his regular breathing, she thought he had drifted off and she didn't want to disturb him. Sleep could be hard to come by in complicated cases like these.

She couldn't stop wondering who Oliver was. As the days passed, she became more and more convinced that he was someone she knew. She was also coming to believe that he had once worked in law enforcement, though he couldn't possibly have had a full-time job in years, not to do what he had done and uncover all this evidence. Before going to bed, she had read his last report in detail, looking for giveaways that indicated an inside knowledge of the police. It was hard to tell, as so much could be gleaned from TV, film and Google these days. He would only have to watch a few of the "crime" reality shows to pick up the jargon.

Nikki stared into the darkness. Maybe that should be her starting point? Compile a list of officers who had left the force and see if one of the names sent up warning flares. She couldn't dispute the fact that she'd made a lot of enemies during her earlier years in CID. She had been a bitch to work with. She had crossed swords with so many officers who in her opinion didn't give it one hundred per cent that for a while she'd been universally disliked. Then Joseph came along. She smiled to herself. Thank heavens he had! She had come a long way since those days, and it would be hard to have to revisit them. Still, a trip down memory lane, unpleasant though it was, might just reveal an individual from the past whose hatred had festered so long and deeply that he had turned murderer.

Nikki started counting faces and, at possible person number twelve, she fell asleep.

* * *

Before they turned in for the night, Lynette Sims and her mother sat in the conservatory with one of Tessa's special hot toddies and had a real heart-to-heart. Lynette told her mother about young Amber's shocking revelations and the fact that Ruby Grayson had managed to take her in that way. She still couldn't understand how a young teenage girl could abuse her own mother. It had shaken her to the core. She had always advocated for the intrinsic good in children, and firmly believed that with good parenting and schooling they would grow into well-adjusted people who were an asset to society, and Ruby's case undermined all that. To all outside appearances, the parents had done their best for their children, yet they'd produced a boy with dangerous predatorial tendencies and a sadistic girl who terrorised her mother. What the parents had not done was admit what was happening and nipped it in the bud.

Tessa listened quietly to her outpouring. 'My darling, you'll see as you get older that not everyone behaves as they should. People will shock and disappoint you, but you need to understand that it might not always be their fault. Circumstances can have terrible knock-on effects. Try not to judge them too harshly, they might be victims themselves. You are a caring and positive person, Lynette, and please, please, stay that way. We need more kindness in this world, and a kind teacher is never forgotten.'

After she went to bed, Lynette lay and watched the numbers on the clock move slowly forward, yet again going over the events of the previous day. She recalled Di Barrett saying that Daryl Grayson had been a stalker, and that her suspicions about being watched were almost certain to have been correct. Daryl had been stalking her too. Now that was a scary thought. In retrospect, she acknowledged that she had been badly frightened. It was simply that all the angst about Ruby had pushed her fear to the back of her mind. Now she recalled the faint sound of dry undergrowth snapping beneath trampling feet, the feeling of someone being behind her, just out of reach. That one time when she had heard again the single, stifled giggle. It had been sinister rather than childish, malevolent and somehow knowing.

Lynette hugged her knees, curling herself into a ball. At least there'd be an end to that now. She dreaded to think what might have happened if it had continued. Daryl might have grown tired of merely watching and grown more daring, perhaps more dangerous. Well, she could forget all that now, thank goodness.

She finally drifted off to sleep, quite unaware of the figure standing in the deep shadows of the trees opposite. He remained there, staring up at her window for a good fifteen minutes before slipping away into the night.

CHAPTER EIGHTEEN

As it turned out, Eve's decision was taken out of her hands. The following morning, Wendy had a dentist's appointment in Greenborough and intended to do a bit of shopping while she was there. So, Eve was by herself, busy at her computer, when a big mud-splattered four-by-four drew up outside the house.

Chris Tate wore an amiable smile, but his eyes were cold.

'Lovely place this,' he said. 'You've done wonders with it, the garden too.'

'Well, I don't mind taking some of the credit for the garden, but the original owner, a dear friend of ours, did the renovations to the chapel.' Remembering Anne Castledine and the way she died always made Eve sad. 'Would you like a cup of coffee? Tea?'

'No, thank you. I just called by to let you know that one of our fields over between Acres Lane and the old mill was to have been ploughed tomorrow, but there's been a problem with the machinery. You're welcome to go hunting there later today or tomorrow morning if you want.'

Eve thanked him and wondered if this was the right time to tell him what was on her mind.

'Had any luck with your detective work?'

He asked casually enough, but his voice sounded strained. Eve made her decision. 'As a matter of fact, I was going to drop by and have a word with you about that.' She smiled. 'Are you sure you don't have time for a drink?'

'Maybe I do after all. Tea, please. Milk and two sugars.' He sat himself down at the kitchen table with the air of a condemned man.

Eve was surprised. She had expected anger, or at the very least, annoyance. While she waited for the kettle to boil, she set about explaining what they'd discovered as tactfully as possible. 'We've found a great deal more than we ever expected to, and it, er, doesn't quite tie in with what your family believes about it. Does that surprise you?'

'No,' he said, 'but it does surprise me how fast you managed it.'

'We've a great deal of experience in sorting out tangled webs, Chris, including those dating far back in the past. We know where to look, and we were lucky with the people we consulted. All we've done is bring together accounts that other people painstakingly documented in order to get to the truth.' Eve emphasised the word "truth." Chris Tate should know that she and Wendy weren't a couple of silly old women amusing themselves with old tales of mayhem and murder.

'Ah, you've talked to Rush then?'

'Jacob's been very helpful,' she said carefully, 'but we've found plenty of other sources besides him.' She pointed to the laptop that sat on the table, its split screen showing a website of old news clippings alongside a detailed family tree. She made the tea and sat down facing him. 'We have most of the basics, but there are still some questions that remain. I'm guessing that you know the whole story, but, er, maybe your wife doesn't?'

A brief flash of annoyance darkened his features, which swiftly turned into amazement. Eve took the laugh that followed to be realisation that he had badly underestimated his next-door neighbours. Suddenly she felt sorry for him. She recalled his impassioned outburst of a few days ago. Yes, he did love his family, his home and working the land, but bore the burden of an unwanted secret that had been none of his doing; one whose weight he had been forced to bear alone. She was reminded of another man whose life had been ruined and finally ended by a family secret. However, Chris Tate was a very different animal to him. Maybe sharing the old scandal would help cleanse his soul and allow him to move forward, unencumbered.

Chris sipped his tea. 'I was told the story when I was a boy. It was just the kind of action-packed murder mystery that would appeal to a young kid and I hung on every word. Soon I came to believe that the attack, and the subsequent death of the migrant at the hands of loyal farm workers, was the gospel truth. It impressed itself upon me so deeply that even now, that's the version that comes naturally to my lips.' He put his hands around the mug as if taking solace from the warmth. 'When I was twenty-one, my grandfather told me what really happened. It turned my whole world on its head. Suddenly my worthy ancestors were tarnished. Even now, my family are not what they seem.' He looked anxiously at Eve. 'What do you intend to do with what you've discovered?'

'That depends on you, Chris,' she said evenly. 'But please understand that we didn't uncover the truth with the intention of hurting anyone. Anyway, I suspect that the harm has already been done.'

He sighed. 'More than you'll ever know.'

'All that stuff about hunting for the truth and not finding it, not staining the family honour . . . All fiction?'

'Yes, it's all part of the deception. The thing is, it still interests people. I've done my best to discourage the curious, but I've always known that one day . . .'

One day an Eve Anderson or a Wendy Avery would come along, she thought to herself.

'And it's not as if it happened that long ago, only three generations back, and that's not including my boys, who are still only seven and ten. So, it's not beyond the reach of a bit of intense research, as you and your friend discovered.' He stared into his tea. 'But I thought the family had covered it up enough to thwart the average mystery hunter.'

'Good old Tommy wasn't a nice man, was he?' she said.

'No, he was a wicked philanderer, and not the most generous or kind boss to work for, certainly not well-liked. On the other hand, he was a damned good farmer, highly intelligent, shrewd in business and clever with money. Thanks to him, we have a solid farming family business, and fortunately, his two sons turned out to be industrious and honest, with a great love of the land. I like to think I've followed in their footsteps, not Tommy's.'

'But the daughters, Isobel and Maria, didn't turn out quite so well, did they?'

If Eve had ever wondered if this lay at the root of the family's shameful past, Chris's face gave her the answer. 'And that is the key to it all,' he murmured softly. He took a long draught of his tea. 'Okay, Eve, I'll give you the truth, then maybe we could talk about where we go from here.'

Eve picked up her tea and gave him an encouraging smile. 'Go ahead, Chris, I'm listening.'

* * *

Having called an early meeting to brief the team on the previous night's discovery at Knight's End Farm, Nikki returned to her office at ten o'clock. She was concerned about Cam Walker who, having been thrown back in at the deep end, was fighting to keep his head above water. The biggest problem was the media. As they had suspected, Oliver was making sure that moments after the police identified a crime scene, the press was there clamouring for answers. He fuelled the fire by making suggestions the newshounds were eager to grab at, and on the strength of which they were hurling increasingly difficult questions at the police. Some of the more canny hacks wanted to know who this anonymous "source" was and, getting no answers, were flooding the papers with increasingly wild speculations. It was Cam's job to throw fire blankets over the dangerous comments, refute the ridiculous ones and offer alternatives whenever possible. It was far from easy, especially with all the other issues he was trying to cope with. At least he had been able to raise a very capable team of specialist officers to take over the Grayson family investigation, so the heat was off regarding that, but he still had a huge case, with many victims, on his hands.

Nikki hoped he would cope. He was still worried about leaving Kaye on her own so much, but Nikki had rung her, and Kaye assured her she was doing well, enjoying some peace and quiet, and had friends on call if she needed anything. She was an understanding and thoughtful police wife who was well aware that from the moment Cam set foot back in the police station, that would be it. He'd be gone. She also knew that if she really needed help, he'd be back at her side in a flash.

Nikki rang the mortuary and was told that an exhausted Rory had gone home for a few hours' sleep but that the dead girl was safely in their care, and he'd be back in later to conduct the post-mortem.

She and Joseph now had the unenviable task of facing Joseph's "black widow," and explaining that she and her family, along with everyone who had worked at the farm at the time of Ruth Baker's disappearance, would have to be interviewed. Her garden was now a crime scene, and whereas they would continue to be as careful as possible, their investigation took precedence over her rambling roses.

Joseph stuck his head around her door. 'Ready when you are. The lady of the house is available now, so I suggest we get this over with.'

Nikki wholeheartedly agreed. 'And what about the eyewitness that Oliver discovered? Have you managed to trace her yet?'

Joseph looked down at his notes. 'Miss Alba Ricci, and she works from home, so we can call immediately after we've been to Knight's End.'

'Nice one. Does she still live locally?'

'About half a mile from the farm, so that's pretty convenient. A little place called Bellmire. As I recall, it's just half a dozen houses strung out along a straight drove. Should be a doddle to find.'

Nikki got to her feet. 'Then fire up the Quattro, Sergeant. I'm done here.'

Nikki wasn't looking forward to meeting Martine Knight again. She was used to dealing with many different kinds of people, but there were still occasions when someone just ruffled your feathers for no particular reason. It couldn't possibly be because the woman had shown rather a lot of interest in Joseph. Could it?

Martine reacted much as they'd expected, offering every objection she could think of, and doing her best to make their visit far more difficult than it needed to be. She showed little compassion for the dead girl found on her property. The whole thing was clearly a terrible inconvenience.

'Who actually owns and runs the farm, Mrs Knight?' asked Nikki.

'I do!' she said indignantly.

'You mentioned a son,' added Joseph. 'Surely he has some interest in it too?'

'Well, yes, my son, James, is the manager but the farm belongs to me, and I make all the final decisions.'

I bet you do, thought Nikki. 'I believe you told my sergeant that James was away this week. He'll be back when?'

'Late tomorrow. He's at an agricultural machinery show, and I have no intention of bringing him back early. This is an annual event and he's sourcing new equipment that we badly need. It's important.'

Nikki gave her a steely look. 'And we have a murder enquiry to conduct, Mrs Knight. Which is *very* important. I must say, right now, I'm not getting the impression that you appreciate the fact that last night a dead young woman was discovered right here at Knight's End Farm, which as you rightly say, is *your* farm and *your* responsibility. I think it's time you considered the implications of this, and how they might impact on you personally.' Her look became icy. 'If you don't feel that we've made ourselves clear, I'm more than willing to spell it out for you.'

Nikki glimpsed a flash of intense dislike on Martine's face, directed straight at her. Then, just as abruptly, it changed, and Martine went from tyrant to simpering victim. Nikki found it quite impressive.

'Oh, I'm so sorry! When I can't cope with something I come across all wrong! Of course, I understand the gravity of the situation. And that poor, poor girl.' She did a rather dramatic head shake. 'And the press! I was horrified. They tried to get their cameras up on the walls to take photographs into our garden. And a drone flew over! I know it was spying on what was going on. It's unbearable.'

This latter was directed at Joseph, Nikki noticed, and tried not to roll her eyes too obviously. It was particularly galling since Joseph was looking as frosty as her. A good old-fashioned liar she could handle, but she had no time for women who denigrated their own gender, nor could she stomach people of either sex who made use of their affluence and position to intimidate others — people like Martine Knight.

Wanting out of this place, Nikki said, 'Right, well, thank you for your cooperation. So, if we could ask you to get a list together of family, friends and employees who were here around fifteen years ago, my sergeant will furnish you with the exact dates, and one of our officers will collect it from you. Regarding statements, we can take them here, or at the station, whichever is more convenient. And as soon as possible where yourself and your son are concerned. We'd like to talk to him the moment he gets back.'

That done, and after a swift trip to check on the crime scene, they were back on the road and heading for Bellmire.

Sycamore Cottage was a bland, featureless semi-detached, typical of the housing the council provided for the lower-paid land workers just after the war and subsequently sold off to the residents.

Alba Ricci opened the door and a look of relief lit up her face. 'I'm so glad you've come! Inspector Oliver said you'd be following up his enquiries, but it's been rather a long time, and I worried . . . Listen to me! Where are my manners? Come in! Please.'

It was a simple home, furnished with all the essentials but not too many home comforts. Alba herself was a young woman with long, raven-black hair, a faintly olive complexion and large dark eyes. She seemed a bit unsure of herself, unused to receiving visitors.

They went into the lounge, and took a seat on a well-used sofa. They refused her offer of tea or coffee, wanting to get straight down to finding out exactly what this woman had seen as a child, in that now infamous walled garden. But first, Nikki was very anxious to know more about "Inspector" Oliver.

'Did you actually meet the man who called himself Inspector Oliver, Alba?' she asked.

Alba looked somewhat perplexed. '*Called* himself? Does that mean—?'

'Did you meet him?' pressed Nikki.

'Well, no. It was all phone calls. I was supposed to meet him but he rang and said he'd been called to an emergency, so we just spoke on the phone.' She began to look anxious. 'Please don't tell me this is some kind of scam?'

With a reassuring smile, Joseph said, 'Please, don't concern yourself about it. It's not a scam as such. We are very glad you have agreed to speak about what happened, but we need to talk to you ourselves, especially in light of certain new developments. Are you okay to start at the beginning?'

Slightly mollified, Alba nodded. 'Yes, yes, of course.'

Her account was pretty straightforward. Alba had been an insatiably curious child, into everything. She loved mysteries, and where there wasn't one, she invented it. Her father, a second-generation Italian immigrant, was a well-respected and knowledgeable gardener who looked after the grounds at Knight's End Farm. The cottage they lived in was a short distance from the walled garden, and she was allowed to play there so long as she did no damage. As she had inherited her father's love of plants, that was never a problem.

'I invented another world inside those walls,' she said dreamily. 'It was my own Secret Garden. That's one of the reasons I did as my mother insisted and forgot what I'd seen, because I was afraid that if we lost our home, it would mean losing my special garden. In the end, even I started to wonder if I'd ever seen it at all.'

Nikki glanced out of the window into the back garden. It was small, as might be expected, but bursting with leafy plants, vegetables and flowers. It seemed Alba's childhood passion had never waned.

'Why were you in the walled garden so late?' asked Joseph. 'You were only eight, weren't you?'

Alba adopted that dreamy look again. 'Oh, Sergeant Easter, that was when it was most special. There were hedgehogs, and a barn owl, and the night-scented flowers gave off a heavenly perfume. My dad would go there some evenings and take me with him. We hunted for slugs and snails by torchlight and, please don't laugh, but he said there were some plants that benefitted from being planted by moonlight. I think he loved it then as much as I did. He knew I sneaked out some nights but he never told my mum. As he said, I was as safe there as in my own bed.'

'Wasn't it ever locked?' asked Nikki.

Alba shook her head. 'No reason to. It was just a garden.'

'Your parents aren't around anymore?' Joseph asked tentatively.

'They split up,' said Alba, suddenly downcast. 'I wanted to go with Dad, but he took a job in the West Country, and there was no place for a child there, so I stayed with Mum.' She brightened. 'Then I met my Harry. We got married when I was nineteen, and here we are. I work for a flower importer, doing the ordering and the admin — two days in the office and three days working from home. Harry drives a lorry for the same company.'

'Okay, so back to the night in question. You were in the walled garden alone, not with your father?' Nikki asked.

'Alone, yes. I went to put some cat food and milk down for the hedgehog and I saw that the owl was hunting, so I watched it for a while, then I realised that someone else was there. I knew it wasn't Dad, as he'd gone to bed early, and I got scared. No one ever went into the garden that late.'

While Alba related her story, Nikki took notes. It was exactly as Oliver had stated — word for word, even down to her mother brainwashing her into believing that she'd invented it all. When she came to the end, Nikki said, 'Well, we should tell you, Alba, that you really did see something, and it's a shame your mother didn't believe what you said. Yesterday, we recovered a woman's body — it had been hidden in the stone cairn. We're pretty sure it's been there fifteen years.'

Alba gasped. Joseph offered to get her a drink, which she refused. After a few moments she seemed to gather herself. 'I knew it! And in my heart, I think I've always known.' She looked at each of them in turn. 'Who was Detective Inspector Oliver?'

'He was carrying out a private investigation, Alba,' Joseph said. 'We don't know more than that. We'll explain when matters are clearer, I promise. Meanwhile, are you certain that the man you saw was Gordon Knight?'

'Absolutely. I recognised him easily from his clothes. He was a big man too, with hair almost as dark as mine. It was him for sure.'

'We are going to need a full statement from you, Alba, and from your mother too, if you could give us her address.' Nikki was still writing.

'She's moved to Italy, I'm afraid.' Alba gave a short laugh. 'Which was pretty ironic. Dad always wanted to go back home to his family, and Mum always refused to go. As soon as they split up, she got together with one of my dad's friends and they moved to Portofino, where Dad was born. Life can be very weird.'

Feeling a little sorry for this young woman, Nikki simply said, 'We can still contact her. Could you give me her number?'

Alba took out her phone and gave Nikki mobile numbers for both mother and father.

'I should never have spoken to that man, should I?' Alba said. 'It was just that he said he was from the police, so I never thought to question him.'

'Probably not, Alba,' said Nikki gently, 'but I'm sure he was very convincing. As it turns out, we're glad you did, or we might not be sitting here now. You observed someone in the act of concealing a murder victim. That makes you a key witness.'

'But Mr Knight? It's unbelievable.' By now, Alba was looking very pale indeed.

Nikki decided that she'd probably had enough for the time being. 'We'll leave you now, Alba, but we'll have to take a statement from you. Would you like us to do it here, or would you prefer to come to the station?'

'I have to go into town this afternoon, so I'll call into the station and get it over with.' Alba stood up. 'I appreciate your understanding. Looking back on it now, I can't believe I let myself be talked into keeping it quiet.'

'You were only a child at the time, Alba,' Joseph said. 'You mustn't blame yourself.'

Just as they were about to leave, Alba caught hold of Nikki's arm. 'Detective Inspector Galena, wait! There's something else, another reason that I knew it was Mr Knight.' She squeezed her eyes shut as old memories surfaced. 'It was his voice! It was definitely him.'

Nikki paused, thinking hard. 'So, he was talking to someone else, Alba?'

'That's right! Mr Knight wasn't alone. He was arguing with someone.' Alba screwed up her face in concentration. 'Yes, that's it. I heard raised voices, one of them Mr Knight, and he sounded really upset. Then everything went silent, and when I dared take a look, I saw him dragging something along the path.'

'Just him? No one else was helping him?' asked Nikki.

'He was alone, she never followed him.'

'She?'

'The other voice was definitely a woman's. And now I think about it, it had to be his wife, because she called him Gordie. Yes, that's it, I can hear her now. Only she ever called him that.' Alba shook her head and exhaled. 'It must be all the emotions this has brought up that's made me remember it now.'

They thanked her, promised to be at the station that afternoon, and left. They sat in the car in silence, contemplating this new development.

'Well,' breathed Nikki. 'Bloody Oliver missed a trick there, didn't he?'

'Oh yes!' Joseph stared ahead of him. 'Alba's little bombshell changes everything. So, is it straight back to Knight's End Farm?'

'No, I don't think so,' said Nikki slowly. 'Suppose we wait till we take her statement? Then we can remind the lady about telling the truth in a sworn statement, since perjuring herself could cost her five years inside, plus fines and probation. You know, I think I'd rather enjoy that.'

Joseph laughed. 'I bet you would!'

CHAPTER NINETEEN

Eve listened to Chris's account of what he'd been told as a young man. She could see it was hard for him, but maybe he'd find it cathartic.

'They had a hereditary mutant gene. It's on an X chromosome, so it mainly affected the women of the family. I only discovered this when I looked into genetic testing. My great-grandparents called it an "affliction." The bottom line is that people with this gene are often mentally unstable, even to the extent of becoming psychopathic.' He looked at Eve sadly. 'It affects some people more than others, and some lucky ones escape it altogether, but Isobel and Maria were at the extreme end of the spectrum. There is no doubt that they engineered their mother's death by locking her in a cattle pen, and then stirring up the cattle.'

Eve frowned. 'From the way you're talking, Chris, it sounds like the mutant gene is still affecting the women in your family?'

'It is, although thank God no one has ever been as badly affected as those two sisters. Direct descendants have a fifty-fifty chance of having the gene, which usually manifests as an absence of compassion. Sufferers tend to be hard-hearted, selfish, and have difficulty expressing consideration for other

199

people's feelings, which means they don't interact properly with other individuals. My sister has it, but mildly.' He gave Eve a rather pathetic smile. 'Most of the time, she comes across as a hard-nosed cynic. Anyway, I convinced her to get herself tested, and it was confirmed.'

'You must have been mightily relieved to have two sons then,' remarked Eve, wondering if in his place, she'd have dared produce children at all.

'Trying to decide was a nightmare, Eve. We desperately wanted children, but we couldn't make up our minds about the justification for it, knowing that if it was a girl, she could be born with the condition. In the end, we decided to risk it, and when the scan showed it to be a boy, we were over the moon. We stopped at two — the wheel of fortune wasn't going to spin in our favour for ever.'

Eve knew Chris needed to speak, but it was the history she wanted to hear, the answers to her questions about Tommy Tate. 'So, do you think the migrant worker, Jan, did see something incriminating, which involved Isobel and Maria?'

'No, that's not why he died.' Chris Tate drained his tea. 'It was quite simply Tommy Tate's inability to keep his hands off the women, and the effect it had on the people around him. The "loyal farmhands" were actually the farm manager, Reg Bourne, who was Tommy's brother-in-law, and his assistant, John Remnick, a lad of limited mental capacity who adored Reg and would do anything he asked of him.' He pulled a face. 'Yes, even murder.'

Eve frowned. It seemed that things might not be quite as she had supposed.

'Reg had been conducting a secret affair with Jan's sister, Maja, and they planned to marry, but they hadn't told anyone yet. Then great-grandfather Tommy raped her. Maja was traumatised, and too afraid to speak out. She refused to see Reg anymore. He was devastated, he couldn't understand what had happened.' Chris took a deep breath. 'He mistakenly believed that Jan was behind her rejection of him, and over time, his hatred increased.'

Eve puffed out her cheeks. 'Phew! This is getting nasty.'

'It's unforgivable, but you can see why the family sanitised the whole thing.' Chris heaved a sigh. 'Because of what Tommy had done to her, Maja took her own life. It was the breaking point for Reg. He was convinced she had killed herself out of a broken heart, because Jan wouldn't allow her to see him anymore. One night, having had too many beers, he decided to confront Jan. During the argument that ensued, he lost all reason and, aided by his faithful shadow, John, killed him. The irony of it was that in the moment of death, Jan gasped out what he believed had really happened to Maja. With his last breath, he accused Tommy Tate of rape.'

'Oh my! So Reg and John went after Tommy?' Eve asked.

'This time Reg really saw the red mist. Tommy had destroyed his plans for marriage and had brought about the death of his beloved Maja. He had even indirectly caused Reg and John to kill an innocent man. They found Tommy and beat him mercilessly. They took his things to make it look like robbery, then took him back to the farm with the intention of saying they had found him on the footpath. However, faced with his two sons, Reg broke down in a fit of remorse at what they had done to the innocent Jan. He handed over Tommy's possessions and confessed everything.'

Eve had a good idea of what happened next, and Chris confirmed it. 'The brothers, Albert and William, realised at once that publicly acknowledging that a member of their own family had committed a murder would ruin them all. No one would do business with a family capable of committing such a heinous act. Not only that, they also had the secret of the hereditary mental condition. Reg, however, overwhelmed by guilt and shame, insisted on confessing and facing the punishment.'

By now, Chris was looking exhausted. He ploughed on. 'My father told me that having spent the entire night going over it, they finally reached a compromise. There would still be a furore, but the laundered version that became our stock story allowed Reg to take the blame as he demanded, while being less shocking than a deliberate premeditated murder. It also kept the stigma of Tommy's lecherous behaviour, and that of his deranged daughters, from the world.'

'And Reg agreed because he was still part of the Tate family,' Eve said.

Chris nodded. 'He was. He didn't want John involved, but it was inevitable. John had been part of it. He did, however, agree to remain silent throughout the proceedings. John didn't say a word, not even when he was sentenced.' Chris looked up. 'And that, more or less, is it.'

'And the watch, the ring, and the cigarette case? Your shock at seeing those items was real, wasn't it?'

Chris gave her a rueful smile. 'It was. I'd never even seen them until you brought them along. When my father made me promise to keep the secret, he also said I'd never have to worry about Tommy's things, they were gone forever.' He shrugged. 'I thought he'd sold them or destroyed them, not that he'd buried them in his own field.'

Eve was beginning to think it might have been better if they'd never found them. Not all mysteries have satisfactory endings when they're solved. 'In a way, justice was done, wasn't it? The right men paid for murdering Jan, and it sounds like Tommy got his rightful comeuppance too. Do you really think you have to keep this a closely guarded secret anymore? I mean, there's no one left to be hurt by it.'

'If it was just me and my wife and boys, I'd agree, but we have a very big extended family. It's that mutant gene, you see.'

Eve didn't understand his reasoning. 'Surely forewarned is forearmed? I'd want to know if there were defects in my genetic makeup. Science has moved on from a time when the only answer to a mental problem was an asylum.'

'Oh, we know that. Everyone is fully aware of it and the various families monitor their children's behaviour very carefully. It's the outside world we don't want knowing about it. Think about it,' he said. 'It would only take one curious individual, someone who'd heard about that mutant gene, to do exactly what you've done. It might lead them to the story of Maria and Isobel murdering their mother, and from that to what Reg and John did. In no time the Tates would no longer be respected farmers but a brood of dangerous psychopaths.'

Eve didn't think that would be the case at all. To her mind, most people would feel nothing but compassion for a family afflicted with a hereditary disease. She was also pretty sure she'd never convince Chris of that, so she kept it to herself.

'But what now?' he asked. 'You're the first person to learn the truth. What do you intend to do with it?'

Eve had been wondering the same thing. 'I'm going to talk to Wendy, but I'm pretty sure the answer will most likely be nothing. It's not for us to share your family secrets if you yourself want to keep them that way. Knowing my friend, I think she'll agree with me, and we'll close the book on it. We'll put it down to an exciting find with an interesting but unconfirmed story behind it.'

'And Jacob Rush? What will you tell him?'

'He knows most of it already, Chris. He's not a threat to you, he's just passionate about local unsolved mysteries. He's a nice young man when you get to know him, and he loves this county and its past. I suggest that Wendy and I discuss what to say to him and keep it to a minimum. I'm sure he'll agree that there are some things you have to just drop and leave well alone, they're really not our business.'

Chris looked a little less perturbed. 'So, you'll let me know?'

'I'll talk to you this evening, I promise.'

Chris stood up. 'Thank you. I appreciate it.'

As he was about to open the door, Eve called after him. 'Why didn't you tell your wife the whole truth, Chris?'

He stopped. 'It's always been that way. Stick to the story that everyone knows, then you can't make mistakes. She knows about the gene, naturally, but not about what the sisters did, or what really happened on the night Tommy was attacked. It's for the best. It's passed from father to son when they reach the age of twenty-one, and that's how it will stay.'

Eve was left wondering what planet Chris Tate was on! She had considered him a down-to-earth practical farmer, yet he had these odd, outdated beliefs that didn't belong in the world of today. It was like he was in his own little bubble, locked in the past. These days people didn't give a damn about what someone's ancestors had got up to. Not only that, there were plenty who'd love to have murder and mayhem in their family tree, and the more notorious the better.

Eve put the kettle on for more tea, her mind buzzing. She was quite relieved when she heard Wendy's car draw up outside. After a brief recap of her dentist's visit, Eve sat her friend down with a cup of tea and told her the whole story.

When she got to the end, Wendy let out a little whistle. 'All because we asked Chris Tate if we could go metal detecting in one of his fields and made a lucky find.' She grimaced. 'Well, maybe not so lucky. Seems we've opened a can of worms.'

Wendy reacted just as Eve had to the next part of the story. Chris Tate was living in the past. 'Passed from father to son!' she said. 'For heaven's sake! When it's the poor women who suffer. How damned sexist can you get? Talk about keeping the little woman in her place, poor thing couldn't cope with a nasty thing like this. It's positively antiquated, and bloody ignorant!'

'Which doesn't exactly fit in with what we know of him, does it? It's well out of character.' Eve was thinking hard. She sat in silence for a time, while Wendy quietly seethed. 'I think . . . I think that everything Chris told me was true, except for one statement.'

Wendy blinked. 'And which statement was that?'

'He said that the Tate descendants didn't suffer so badly with the condition, that their symptoms were mild, none of them anywhere near as disturbed as the two sisters.'

'And?' Wendy looked puzzled.

'What if he was lying? What if there have been more recent occurrences? What if some of the Tate women are still danger-ous?' She smiled. It was all just slotting into place. 'I believe Chris Tate wants it kept secret not because of his family's dark past, but because of the present. Maybe the future as well.'

'Bloody hell, Eve!' Wendy looked aghast. 'That's one nasty supposition. And it gives us even more problems, the main one being — what do we do now?'

'I haven't got that far yet, but I guess my first thought is that whatever we decide, we keep it to ourselves. The last person we mention it to is—'

'Chris Tate.'

* * *

Nikki and Joseph returned to CID to be greeted by Zena, who handed her a long list of requests, phone messages and memos — all urgent, of course. With a groan, Nikki carried them into her office, while Joseph disappeared into his tiny den to decide what to proceed with in the interim.

Aware that Nikki's main bugbear was the question of Oliver's identity, he decided to start with that. She was certain they were looking at a former police officer, though Joseph wasn't convinced, but as he had no better ideas, he decided he might as well start there. He began by contacting the two detectives who had been charged with looking for possible connections between the missing girls on Oliver's list. He was soon told that their paths had never crossed. None had friends, families, witnesses, or suspects that related to the others. In the words of one of them — nix.

But they hadn't checked on the police officers who'd been involved, so that was Joseph's next port of call.

He got himself a coffee and sat down at his computer. Pulling up the case reports, he checked the names of the SIOs in charge, then, starting with Alexandra Cornfield, he went slowly through the file, making a note of the names as they arose.

The resulting list was extensive. Some he knew personally, some he had heard of, but most meant nothing to him. Well, at least he'd be able to furnish Nikki with a list of names to work with. He made a note to remind himself to check if any police officers in the Fenland Constabulary had either been relieved of their duties in the last fifteen years, or had left under a cloud. That would be a bit of an undertaking, since a number of them had probably left of their own accord, in which case the reason for their departure wouldn't have been recorded. Maybe he could enlist HR's help on that one. He knew of one or two cases of cops who'd gone bad, but all of these were out of the picture. One he knew to be incarcerated in a maximum-security prison, one had died and another had fled abroad.

He sat back and scanned the list, hoping he wasn't wasting his time. After all, it could so easily be someone with a very different kind of grudge, something they knew nothing about. Joseph was still of the opinion that Oliver had either had a very close connection to one of the missing girls or was conducting a campaign directed solely at ruining Nikki's career. Well, he had to start somewhere, so he picked up the phone and asked HR for their help. One of the operatives, a woman called Chrissie, who he vaguely knew by sight, offered to check their files for him. He thanked her and hung up.

He glanced across to Nikki's office but the door was still closed, so he turned to the file on Bethany Lyons. He'd identified the police officers who were involved but he hadn't read the full report yet. He did recall Cat saying that Sergeant Lucy Wells, their FLO, had something to do with it, so he made a note to talk to her about it.

He watched the file download with a sigh. *Here we go again, another police failure, no doubt.*

'Sarge, sorry to bother you, but I think you'll like this.' Cat stood in the doorway, looking pleased with herself.

He pointed to the only other seat. 'Carry on, I could do with some good news.'

'Oh, you'll love this!' she said. 'We've had some luck, and I thought we'd share it with you and the boss before we pass it on to the specialist team.' She leaned on his desk. 'Although Ruby Grayson is now out of our hands until an official statement is made about Daryl, we're still fielding calls from women who had been frightened by the stalker. We had one that came in a couple of hours ago from a young woman who lives about half a mile from where Daryl was murdered. She and her dad live in a little bungalow on a corner plot, and it has a big wrap-around garden. Twice during the past week or so she's had a feeling that someone was out there at night — her bedroom faces the back garden, so she doesn't always pull her curtains. On the very night Daryl was killed, she actually saw someone. She described him as tall, dressed in dark clothes, with a black scarf covering the lower half of his face.'

'Exactly what Daryl had on when he was found,' said Joseph. 'There's more, isn't there?'

'The girl — she's called Emily Teal — yelled for her dad. They went out after the intruder, but he took off through the garden. Emily said he gave a sort of giggle, which sounded dead creepy. Then they heard a car start up and move away.' Cat's eyes sparkled. 'Now here's the best bit. Next morning, she goes to have a look and finds a boot print, in the exact spot where he'd been standing. They'd been watering the garden the evening before and the ground was soft. Clever Emily grabs one of her dad's garden cloches — you know, one of those little covers that you put over plants to protect them from frost — and she puts it over the boot print. I shot over there and took a picture of it, and, guess what, Sarge?'

Joseph beamed at her. 'It was a perfect match for the boots Daryl was wearing?'

'Identical! A SOCO is working on it now. It's a good three-dimensional impression, so they'll photograph it and make a cast. I know the CPS will need more than that to pin the stalker case on Daryl Grayson, but I have a very good idea that more and more evidence will come in over the days to come. We have one other thing already. As you know, we have Daryl's car in the pound. The SOCO told me that there's a good chance they'll find soil samples in the footwell that match that in the Teals' garden. More solid evidence that Daryl Grayson was definitely the Laughing Stalker.'

'Well, that's good news indeed. The specialist team will be overjoyed. It's probably still not quite enough, but the evidence against him is building up nicely.' He smiled at her. 'I'm glad we've still got an ear to the ground, even though the case is off our hands.'

'Vonnie has an old mate working it too, so we're getting updates.' She stood up. 'Better get back to the day job. I'm going through Oliver's statements and comparing them to what we've found.' She looked at him. 'This Oliver bloke's a copper, right? All the jargon, all the reports and forensic detail. Has to be, doesn't he?'

'Nikki thinks so,' said Joseph.

'But you don't?'

'I'm not sure, Cat. Maybe. The jury's out as yet.'

'Oh, he's a copper, all right.' Cat edged her way out of the cramped little office. 'Betcha.'

CHAPTER TWENTY

When classes broke for lunch, Dinah Barrett called Lynette Sims into her office and told her to sit down.

'I've had some news about Ruby, and I thought you deserved to know, since you took such pains with that girl. It's not much, a friend told me about it, under the counter so to speak.' Dinah looked her in the eye. 'This is not for anyone else's ears, okay? I can't afford to get my friend into trouble. She knows full well that she shouldn't be talking about the case at all, but she also knows how worried we are.'

Lynette nodded furiously. 'Of course, Miss Barrett. I'd be very grateful to hear it. I'm really worried about what's going on with Ruby.'

'Apparently, things aren't going smoothly at the Grayson house. It's such a complex case that they've brought in a specialist team to deal with it. It seems the Graysons are still denying that Ruby is in any way responsible for injuring her mother.'

Lynette looked shocked. 'But Amber didn't lie, Miss Barrett, I *know* she didn't.'

'I agree with you, and I'm told this kind of thing is typical in cases of domestic violence, the victim refuses to press charges.' Dinah sat back. 'However, Mrs Grayson has injuries on both of her forearms, which were definitely not inflicted by her, nor did they result from accidents. She still refuses to say who inflicted these injuries, just that they had nothing to do with her daughter.'

'Could we be wrong? Could it have been Daryl?' asked Lynette.

'The husband categorically denies that his son was responsible, which is odd, isn't it? If they'd wanted to shift the blame from Ruby, Daryl would have been the perfect fall guy, since he's no longer around to contradict them. Oh, and the family refuse to believe that Daryl was a stalker, so perhaps Mr Grayson's trying to protect his son's reputation.' She shook her head. 'No, Lynette, we aren't wrong about Ruby. Amber told the truth. Heavens, we, more than anyone, know when a child is lying, and that girl was too upset to give us anything but the truth. My friend tells me it will take some time to sort it all out, they have to be extremely careful in such a delicate and potentially volatile situation. Anyway, that's all I have for now. I'll let you know immediately there's any more news. Oh, and by the way, the Graysons aren't aware that it was Amber who brought the matter to light. It will come out later, I'm sure, but not at this stage.'

'What a horrible mess,' said Lynette. 'It's hard to get your head around. They seemed such a tight-knit family.'

'Well, you know what they say about not knowing what goes on behind closed doors,' said Dinah grimly.

Lynette smiled. 'Thank you for letting me know, I appreciate it — and I won't say anything.'

After Lynette had gone, Dinah sat and pondered what her unofficial source — her old friend Yvonne — had told her. Sounding uncharacteristically downbeat, she'd said she only knew what she did because she had a colleague on the specialist team, who had told her that there were so many unproven accusations floating around, so many grey areas, that they could see the whole thing "disappearing down the plughole."

Dinah bestirred herself and went to get some lunch. How difficult and frustrating it must be to know something for certain but be unable to find hard evidence to support it. It was tough enough being a teacher, but she couldn't imagine doing the job Yvonne Collins did. If the Crown Prosecution Service required such incontrovertible proof of every single assertion, how did Yvonne and her colleagues ever get anything done?

As she stood in the queue waiting to be served her tuna mayo sandwich, she could see why her usually chirpy friend seemed so low. There was something hateful going on in the Grayson household, and Yvonne knew it. She also knew they'd need a miracle to prove it. And then what?

Her phone buzzed with a message.

Turning point! Will update when I can. Vonnie.

Dinah's spirits lifted so much that she added a large iced bun and a cappuccino to her order.

* * *

Nikki set down the receiver. She'd never worked alongside the retired DCI Matt Ballard before, although she'd seen him a few times at meetings and knew of his reputation as a real terrier. Now she was about to meet him. He had been away on holiday for a few days and had only just seen her message about the reopening of the Ruth Baker investigation. As Cam had said, Matt was willing to do all he could to help.

Nikki wondered what he'd think when she told him about Oliver and his unofficial investigations into Matt's old case, and also about the new witness who had thrown a dirty great spanner into the works. She couldn't help crowing over the fact that Oliver could fail too. She could hardly wait to point it out to him.

Nikki was just about to go and tell Joseph about Matt's imminent visit when the desk phone rang.

'It's your favourite pathologist, dear lady, and even if said professor is *totally* exhausted, he has unselfishly found time to ring and update you. What a hero!'

Nikki chuckled. 'You are indeed a superstar, Professor. Now, what have you got for me?'

'I had expected more of an accolade than that, but there you go. Well, firstly, our lovely young woman was strangled. How can you make such a deduction from a many years-old corpse, you might well ask?'

'Because the hyoid bone in her throat was fractured?' suggested Nikki, trying not to giggle.

'Good grief! You really do listen to me, don't you?' exclaimed Rory, sounding positively amazed. 'And you're right, of course. What you don't know, though, is that we found something buried with her — a narrow leather belt that had been fastened around her ankles. It was still in situ when we released her body. I believe the killer either used it to make it easier to drag her along the path, or they could have bound her feet while she was still alive, to stop her kicking and struggling.'

'A man's belt?'

'Aye, well, there's the rub, Nikki. That's in dispute. Cardiff calls it unisex, but I'd say it's a woman's belt. It's not very long, but made of good quality leather. It certainly wasn't something you'd pick up in Greenborough market, that's for sure. And it didn't belong to the victim. We found what appeared to be a cheap, coloured elasticated webbing belt still in the loops of her jeans.'

Nikki made a careful mental note of this. It was the second indication of a woman possibly being involved. 'Does it have a particular pattern in the leather, Rory, or a distinctive buckle?'

'It is, or was, very classy. Handcrafted, with a slightly domed profile and stab-stitched along the outer edges. The buckle is white metal, and rather elongated. It's certainly identifiable, you can be sure of that. I'd say it would take such genius detectives as you are about five minutes to find the manufacturer and the supplier.'

Nikki was already making a note to request family photographs, to confiscate phones, SD cards and computers — anywhere pictures could be stored. In particular, she'd be scrutinising a certain Mrs Martine Knight's fashion accessories and going through her wardrobe.

'Finally, I think she was badly beaten prior to being throttled to death. We've noted a broken front tooth, and there is considerable dark staining on the remains of her jacket and her blouse. We haven't tested it yet, but it's obviously blood.' There was a short pause. 'This is, of course, just a friendly update, we've barely started on sweet Ruth herself, but . . .' She heard a loud yawn. 'But a preliminary report, followed in the fullness of time by my customary extraordinarily informative and technically perfect official post-mortem report, will wing its way to you. I bid you good day.'

Before she could even thank him, the line went dead. Nikki was left staring at the phone and harbouring dark thoughts about Martine Knight, and her possible involvement in a young woman's murder.

* * *

'So, we are about to meet the famous Matt Ballard?' Joseph looked at Nikki with interest. 'Well, whatever you do, don't mention any of his other old cases. Stick with Ruth's.'

'Sorry?'

'He was involved in two of the worst cases imaginable — one of which left him injured and his sergeant, Liz, now his partner, at death's door. Remember? It sent shivers through every station in the division. After that, Matt retired. It was rumoured that he just cleared his desk and walked out of the station.'

'Joseph Easter! You're worse than a mess room of gossips! Besides, I can recall cases where I've been sorely tempted to do exactly the same, clear my desk and bugger off.'

Joseph laughed, though he secretly hoped this wouldn't be one of those cases.

Matt arrived, looking younger and a lot more relaxed than the last time she'd seen him. Civvy street must suit him, thought Nikki. He was a tall man, fit-looking and attractive, with iron grey hair and a ready smile. No wonder his old sergeant was now his partner, he looked like the kind of man you'd want to hang on to!

After the introductions and the ordering of coffee, they settled down in Nikki's office and she gave Matt a brief overview of the disquiet Oliver's airmail communications had caused. At the mention of Ruth Baker, Matt Ballard shook his head.

'Well, that was a nightmare of an enquiry if ever there was one. That girl just disappeared into thin air. But you say you've found her body?' He looked pained. 'In one way I feel relieved, especially as you'll have answers for her relatives and friends, but I'm quite devastated too. I always believed the girl had planned her own disappearance, ran away, and started a new life somewhere, maybe even out of the country.'

'Can you tell us a bit about what happened at the time, Matt?' asked Nikki.

'Of course. It's one of those cases you never forget.' He sat back and crossed his legs. 'On the night she disappeared, Ruth had been at a quiz night at the Moon Gazer pub in her village. She lived just a ten-minute walk from there. Her friends saw her walk off, in the direction of her house, at exactly ten o'clock that evening. She never got home. We talked to everyone who was there that night, and they all swore that she was in good spirits, showed no signs of being worried about anything, and as her team won the quiz, she left on a high. The only odd thing about it was that she left half an hour earlier than she usually did. Generally, she stayed on with her friends until half ten, and then a couple of them walked home together.' Matt frowned. 'She gave no reason for going early, even to her best friend. Her exact words were — and I recall this clearly — "Gonna slope off now, mate, see you tomorrow." Apparently, her friends went to the door with her, trying to persuade her to hang on a bit longer. They had talked another friend into singing a couple of songs before they closed. However, she said she'd had enough excitement for one evening, and they watched her walk away.' He shrugged. 'That is the last time Ruth Baker was ever seen.'

'Until now.' Nikki sighed.

'How did you interpret the part about wanting to leave early, Matt?' asked Joseph.

'We checked with her friends and family, and she wasn't in a relationship, even a casual one. But we did wonder if she was meeting someone in secret.' Matt drank a mouthful of coffee. 'But if that was the case, she had certainly kept it to herself. Her best friend swore that was not the case. She said they shared everything, even the bad stuff, and it wasn't in Ruth's nature to be secretive. If she hadn't, in fact, planned to run away, we came to conclusion that she left the pub early because she wanted to get home to check up on her father, who'd been unwell.'

'And the name Gordon Knight never came up in your enquiries?' asked Nikki. 'We certainly didn't see it in the case file.'

'No, it didn't. He's a farmer, isn't he? Owns a lot of the land between Greenborough and Fenfleet?'

'He was. He's dead now, and his wife, Martine, holds the reins at Knight's End,' Nikki said. 'And she holds them very tightly indeed. But I think it's time to move on to what has happened in the last twenty-four hours.'

Nikki told him about the gruesome find in the cairn, and about the new witness and what she had heard in the garden that night.

'How on earth did this Oliver make a connection to Gordon Knight?' Matt said. 'As I said, he wasn't mentioned at the time. Sure, we didn't manage to solve the case, but I swear we were as thorough as it was possible to be.'

'We are guessing that this is an obsession with Oliver, who obviously has all the time in the world to delve into these old cases.' Joseph raised an eyebrow. 'A lot of the people here think there's a strong possibility that he's a rogue copper. If that's the case, he might have had legitimate access to the enquiries at some point. We're trying to identify him, but it's far from easy. Anyway, somehow, he discovered that there was a connection between Gordon and Ruth, because

Gordon had offered her a job a month or so before she disappeared.'

Matt looked astonished. 'That certainly never came to our notice.'

'Oliver professes to have also discovered that she worked in the farm office for a trial period of a week, but for some reason never took up the job. Oliver says that when he investigated further, it transpired that Gordon had tried it on with her and Ruth had initially rejected him. It seems he really had the hots for her, and persevered until she weakened. He confided in his farm manager, who was a close friend, that she had accepted his invitation to accompany him to a three-day trade exposition in Holland.

'This is merely what Oliver says in his statement, Matt. We've only just got officers out checking the veracity of what he wrote, but the little that's already filtered back to us shows he was on the right track.' Nikki smiled faintly. 'If it turns out to be true, we'll be conducting a very interesting interview with Martine Knight, which is something clever dick Oliver never did. So far, we have three separate incidents where Martine lied to the police, albeit by omission, but she'll have some serious questions to answer.'

Matt leaned forward. 'You think she was actively involved in the murder? Like an accomplice?'

'Absolutely. For one thing, someone overheard her using a pet name no one else used, arguing with Gordon when he was engaged in dragging something heavy towards the cairn. Then a woman's leather belt was found wrapped around Ruth's ankles. It was expensive, and certainly didn't belong to Ruth. Thirdly, there was massive local and national media coverage at the time and several announcements on TV begging the public to notify them of any sightings of Ruth Baker, or any other information relating to her disappearance. When we spoke to Martine after finding the body, she said she didn't know her. If Ruth had been working in the office, even temporarily, Martine would have known, she had to. So, she lied.'

Matt let out a long low whistle. 'Then was she the killer, and her husband covered it up?'

Nikki sat back. 'That is what we plan to find out.'

'Look, I know I'm not a serving officer anymore,' said Matt, 'but if I can help in any way, my partner Liz Haynes and I are completely at your disposal as private investigators. We occasionally work for DCI Charley Anders in that capacity, and she'll vouch for us.'

Joseph smiled. Matt Ballard needed no one's endorsement.

Nikki thanked him. 'There is something. With Cam Walker's permission, I'd like to ask you to spend a bit of time here, Matt. It would be hugely beneficial to have the SIO of the original enquiry present to bounce our queries off. Half the time we are struggling to get a handle on what really happened outside what was reported in the official documentation.' Her face darkened. 'We have to stop this man, Matt. He's very dangerous. Apart from anything else, we can't dismiss the possibility of this being a personal vendetta against me. I'd never forgive myself if innocent people got hurt because of something I was involved in back in the past.'

Joseph's glance at her was solicitous. This was at the root of Nikki's desperation to know who Oliver was, a feeling of guilt that somewhere along the line, this had all been her fault.

Matt took the words from his mouth. 'You mustn't think like that. The blame lies entirely at Oliver's door, Nikki. No matter what's happened in his life, you are not responsible for the way he has reacted to it. You know as well as I do that he's off the rails. He is dangerous, and if he's not a calculating and ruthless criminal doing this for monetary gain, which I seriously doubt, he's probably mentally disturbed. *That's* why you need to catch him. This is *not* your fault, Nikki Galena.'

Very nicely put, thought Joseph, though Nikki looked a long way from being convinced.

'If Cam agrees, I'm very happy to help in any way I can,' concluded Matt.

While Nikki went upstairs to talk to Cam, Joseph took Matt out to meet the detectives who were working on proving or disproving Oliver's claims regarding Gordon Knight's involvement. They had been told not to question Martine Knight. Joseph and Nikki themselves would be off to Knight's End shortly, to bring Martine back to the station for interview.

CHAPTER TWENTY-ONE

Not wishing to appear unsettled by what they had learned from Chris Tate, Wendy and Eve decided to take him up on his offer to let them use their detectors on Acres Lane field. It was important to them that Chris believed them when they said they weren't going to share his dark family secret with the world. They would go that afternoon and, as they normally would, take any finds to the farmhouse. They had no intention of actually letting sleeping dogs lie, but they needed time to think over their suspicions about the modern-day Tate women.

They were just loading their equipment into Eve's car when another vehicle drew up beside them. Jacob Rush got out.

'Glad I caught you ladies! I've found something!' he said, looking pleased with himself.

'Let's go inside, Jacob,' Eve said, shutting the boot lid. She and Wendy had decided that they would tell him the basic truths but leave out their suspicions that Chris Tate had told a lie. 'We were just about to have a cuppa before we went hunting.'

Once settled, Jacob asked, 'Any updates from your side of our investigation?'

'Oh yes,' said Wendy. 'We were going to ring you as soon as we got back later this afternoon. You'll not believe this, but a few hours ago, Eve actually wrung the whole story out of our neighbour.'

Jacob's expression went from awe to disbelief. 'And you believe what he told you?'

Eve nodded. 'It's the truth, Jacob. It all fits together, and I could see from the way he spoke that it hurt him to tell me. Now he's terrified about what we'll do with it.'

She gave him the story, from the terrible mistake Reg and his sidekick John had made in killing Jan to Chris Tate's feigned surprise when they presented him with Tommy Tate's stolen possessions. She explained that the Tate brothers had kept it secret to protect the two mad sisters from being committed to an asylum or jail for the murder of their mother. She remained silent about their suspicions regarding the Tate women.

'Wow! So that's it. It all fits together now,' said Jacob, 'and answers all our questions.'

Wendy looked at him. 'You said you'd found something, Jacob.'

'Yes, and it very nicely brings the whole thing to a conclusion.' He delved into the tote bag he'd been carrying and produced a photograph. 'This is your copy. It was just a snapshot I found in one of those old diaries and then enlarged.'

Eve stared at the grainy black and white photo. It showed a bride and groom standing in front of a church door surrounded by a large group of people in their Sunday best.

'Tommy Tate's wedding. The whole family are in it. I identified this man straight away.' He pointed to a man standing with the bridal party. 'His face was immediately recognisable because he was hanged for murder. It's Reginald.'

Eve stared at the figure. He looked handsome, in a rugged sort of way, obviously uncomfortable in his best clothes. She noted the slightly ill-fitting suit, probably only brought out for weddings and funerals, the flower in his lapel, and the waistcoat with a pocket watch chain looped from one of the buttons. Eve squinted at the chain then, with a little grunt, went to a drawer and took out a small magnifying glass.

'What have you seen?' asked Wendy.

'I'm not sure . . . Well, I'm damned!' Eve turned and went into the dining room. On the table was a large tray with their recent finds laid out on it. One of them was the coin with the hole in it that had been the first item they'd found in Chris Tate's field.

Hurrying back to the others, she placed the coin beside the photo. 'Look, it's Reg's coin. It was on his watch chain, probably a lucky token. And we found it with Tommy's things, buried in that field.'

There was no doubt about it. But why had it been disposed of along with Tommy's treasured possessions? Maybe it hadn't. Men wore their pocket watches even in their working clothes. Reg was out in the fields all the time, so maybe it was just coincidence that it had been lost in the very field where Chris Tate's father had buried the incriminating silver articles. She smiled to herself, thinking that if she'd been a superstitious woman, she might have seen the finding of that coin as a sign from the Other Side, telling her to look further in that particular place. But she wasn't superstitious, and this was just one of those small mysteries that crop up every once in a while.

'So, we've come to the end of our investigation,' said Jacob, rather sadly. 'May I ask how you left it with Chris Tate?'

'If you agree, Jacob, we'd rather not take this any further. We've got more than we ever dreamed of when we unearthed that watch, and that's enough for me. It's up to the family how they deal with it, and it's really not our business. If I were him, I wouldn't want my family secrets broadcast far and wide by someone I hardly knew. Plus, at the end of the day, he's our neighbour and we have to get along with him.'

Jacob nodded. 'Well, when you put it like that, I have to agree. Normally, I'd update my website, fill in all the gaps and add the gory details, but under the circumstances, I'll leave it alone. I'd never have discovered half of this without the help of you two lovely ladies, especially since Chris Tate and I aren't exactly the best of friends. I know the truth, and that's what counts, so I'll draw a line under it.'

Eve was hugely relieved. 'I'm sure you have plenty of other interesting stories waiting for your attention.'

Jacob nodded. 'Actually, I've got this really baffling little mystery concerning one of the old airfields. I reckon it's time I started looking into that, and I could possibly even use the help of a couple of metal detectorists?' He raised an eyebrow. 'We won't lose touch, will we?'

'No way!' said Wendy. 'In fact, we'd like to be able to call on your help if our trusty detectors turn up any other mysterious finds — if that's okay with you?'

'Oh yes!' he said. 'Same here! I may well need some expert help in the future.'

'You know us,' said Eve, 'born nosey. We'd be happy to help.'

After Jacob had gone, Eve and Wendy locked up and went out to the car. 'Chris will be relieved when we tell him Jacob Rush won't pursue it any further.'

'He will,' said Wendy. 'That just leaves us with how we proceed from here.'

Eve got into the car and started the engine. 'I suggest that after our trip to Homelands Farm, we have our supper, a very large glass of wine, and get back on the computers. You start looking up anything newsworthy that relates to the name of Tate, and I'll start hunting for female criminals in the area. It'll take a while as the women could be married, so we'd need to trace their maiden names. How does that sound?'

'Sounds like a plan.' Wendy grinned at her. 'Meanwhile, let's hope we don't dig up anything else on Tate land that has a mystery attached to it!'

* * *

Lynette Sims was feeling somewhat easier now that the problem of the two Grayson girls had been handed over to the authorities, though she couldn't help thinking that she should have noticed something amiss long before now, in which case she could have done more.

As she parked her car in the driveway, she caught herself surreptitiously glancing around. She told herself not to be so stupid, Daryl and the threat he posed were long gone.

She locked the car and went up to the front door. She was just about to put her key in the lock when she spun around. The old feeling of being watched by someone hidden just out of sight flooded back. She shivered and jammed the key into the lock. *Stupid woman.*

After accepting a large mug of tea from her smiling mother, she began to feel better, but the conversation soon turned to Daryl Grayson.

'If what I read in the papers and see on TV is true, that kind of behaviour usually escalates over time,' said Tessa thoughtfully, stirring sugar into her mug. 'You can't help but wonder what he might have become if he had lived.'

'I've seen several documentaries on serial killers. They all started out as peeping Toms,' said Lynette. 'Well, someone certainly stopped him in his tracks. I wonder who it could have been?'

'Obviously a man who discovered what Daryl was doing and went ape,' her mother said. 'It could have been a boy-friend, a fiancé, a husband, or even a father. My bet would be on the last. I've known many a man who would commit murder for his daughter, including your own father. I have no doubt that he would have taken on any man alive if they'd threatened you.'

Lynette gave her mum a sad smile. Her dad had died suddenly when she was eighteen, and not a day went by in which they didn't talk about him. When she was little, Lynette always called him her teddy bear, and his bear hugs were the panacea for all her woes. 'I'm sure he would. And you could be right about it being someone who followed him and caught him watching their loved one. After all, he would only have had to pick on a woman with a very jealous other half, and it'd be curtains for Daryl. A jealous man in a rage . . .'

While Tessa got their supper together, Lynette went upstairs and changed out of her work clothes. Now all her worries were over, she must get her head back into her normal routine. She had plenty of other students who needed her attention, and recently far too much of it had been taken up by Ruby Grayson. She'd learn the outcome soon enough. Meanwhile, she should be back doing what she loved — preparing interesting lessons and projects for her kids, getting into the pool for a regular swim, and maybe even going out jogging again.

She ran down the stairs to be met with the delicious aroma of her mum's toad-in-the-hole. She told herself there was nothing more she could do for the Grayson family right now, and life must go on. She'd still fret over the cousins, but their problems were out of her control.

* * *

The Martine Knight who sat in the interview room was nothing like the haughty lady of a few hours ago. But the austere interview room was hardly a bespoke farmhouse kitchen, and the plastic cup of water somewhat different to coffee from a machine that probably cost as much as Nikki's first car.

The moment Martine was arrested and cautioned, all her arrogance had disappeared. Now she looked lost and scared.

As expected, she had asked for her own legal representation who, thus far, had been pretty reasonable. He hadn't kept them waiting, and had listened politely to Nikki and Joseph when they had their customary private word with him prior to the interview. Stephen Wray was not a name they knew, and he didn't come with the usual reputation. Much to their surprise, he hadn't displayed the usual contempt for the police when they explained why Martine had been arrested. Rather cynically, Nikki wondered if his true colours would come to light when they began questioning his client. Wray went on to advise his client to answer their questions and give her own account, rather than take the "no comment" route. That could mean one of two things — he was either absolutely certain of her innocence, or he was wary of the poor impression her refusal to provide information would give if the case did go to court.

After the introductions, Nikki opened the interview with a straight question: 'Mrs Knight, why did you tell us that you didn't know Ruth Baker, when in fact she'd spent a week working in your office?'

The question seemed to take her aback. She glanced at Wray, who nodded. 'Er, well, I suppose it was my husband who took her on. I don't recall ever actually meeting her. Back then, it was Gordie who hired and fired, I had little to do with the running of the farm. Staff came and went, often without my knowledge.'

Nikki raised an eyebrow. 'And no one brought it up when she went missing a few days later? Given all the media coverage, and human nature being what it is, I'd have thought it would have been the talk of the entire farm. You said yourself that you saw it on the news.'

Martine looked down. 'Maybe. It was a long time ago. I don't remember.'

'Okay.' Unconvinced, Nikki turned to Wray. 'I'm sure you will have advised your client that perjury is a serious offence, Mr Wray, and that making a false statement can incur a severe penalty?'

With just a hint of a smile, Wray said, 'Mrs Knight will answer your questions as truthfully as she is able, and she is fully aware of how harsh UK law can be in cases of perjury or the like. I must remind you that *fifteen years* have passed since the event you are investigating. You are asking my client to recall details that time may have clouded or distorted. Memory is rarely perfect, Officers.'

Nikki watched Martine grow pale. It was clear that she was totally unprepared for what was taking place. She was fully in charge in her little empire, but here she was way out of her depth. Nikki was also surprised, having expected Martine to react with her usual self-assured arrogance. She had interviewed plenty of powerful women who, in just this situation, had responded to Nikki's questions with vitriol and aggression.

'Mrs Knight, we have a witness who is prepared to swear that she saw your late husband in the walled garden at Knight's End Farm, dragging something heavy along the ground, and stopping when he reached the stone cairn, which is where we discovered the body of Ruth Baker. She saw this on the very day Ruth went missing.' Nikki paused, watching her reactions carefully. 'He wasn't alone, Mrs Knight. There was a woman with him and he was arguing with her. She called him by his pet name of Gordie.'

'Who is this witness?' interjected Wray.

'The daughter of the head gardener,' replied Nikki.

A look of pure hatred flashed across Martine's face. Wray shook his head at her in warning.

'I'm sorry, Detective Inspector, but are you referring to a child?' he asked.

Keeping her eyes on Martine, Nikki said, 'She was eight years old at the time, but at twenty-three, she has perfect recall of exactly what she witnessed. And she is prepared to swear to it in a court of law.'

'What a child may have imagined is hardly evidence, is it?' For the first time, Wray's voice had a condescending edge to it.

'The thing is, Mr Wray, we have also spoken with the girl's mother. Her daughter told her what she had witnessed, and her mother, Mrs Ricci, confirmed the date. She remembered it so clearly because it was her husband's birthday.' Nikki frowned. 'You see, what bothers me, Mr Wray, is the timing. The witness reported this fifteen years ago, and it was dismissed as the fabrication of a child, which is why no one ever tried to verify it. But we have pulled a fifteen-year-old dead body from the exact spot the child described. Now I'd say this meant she was telling the truth, wouldn't you?'

'None of this concerns my client. It certainly seems to point a finger at someone, but not Martine Knight. This man, if he existed, could have been arguing with anyone, if indeed he was arguing at all. The child might have seen *something*, and having a vivid imagination like any eight-year-old, concocted a dramatic story around it.' He shrugged. 'As I said, it has nothing at all to do with my client.'

Nikki decided to keep the part about the leather belt to herself for the time being. Right now, she had people checking out the Knight family photographs and Martine's extensive wardrobe. She'd wait until they had more on that. She changed tack. 'Did you and your husband have a good relationship, Mrs Knight?'

'Exceptionally good.' Martine seemed to be on more secure ground. 'Ask anyone.'

'And you trusted him completely?'

Her eyes flashed with a dark, bitter look. That look said something very different to the answer she gave Nikki. 'My husband was faithful to me all our married life. We loved each other and our son, and we were justly proud of the successful business that under our stewardship we had seen develop from a small concern into what you see now.'

'Mmm,' Nikki said dubiously. 'So, if I told you that certain respondents have indicated that he was less faithful than you appear to believe, you would be surprised?'

'What exactly has my client's relationship with her late husband got to do with the finding of that body, Detective Inspector?' asked Wray before Martine could reply.

'Because it's been brought to our notice that Gordon Knight had been planning to take Ruth Baker with him to an exposition in Holland, and the trip wasn't entirely for business purposes. We're checking all Mr Knight's movements and travel plans around the time of the murder.'

To Nikki, Joseph and Stephen Wray's surprise, Martine let out a string of expletives, consigning her "beloved" husband to the fieriest pit in hell.

Wray held up his hand. 'If you please, I must request some time to speak with my client.'

For the benefit of the tape, Nikki said that she and Sergeant Easter were leaving the room, gave the time and stopped the recording.

Outside the room, Joseph gave a low chuckle. 'Oops!'

'Indeed,' Nikki murmured. 'But you can see where this is going, can't you?'

'Sadly, yes. She'll throw the whole thing at her dead husband, and it will probably be impossible to prove that she had any involvement at all. She could be the killer for all we know, and hubby was just clearing up her mess, but without a lot more hard evidence, it will come down to him.'

'And as the man is well and truly deceased, sweet innocent Martine will probably get off scot-free.' Nikki groaned.

'Unless,' said Joseph thoughtfully, 'we can take the stories of Gordon's infidelities a bit further. We might be able to find more witnesses — people who can attest to his wife's jealousy. It's a long shot, but who knows?'

Nikki was doubtful. 'Under normal circumstances, I'd jump at the chance, but with all we're having to contend with right now, it's a low priority. Let's see what happens when we go back in there, shall we?'

* * *

Having had enough of trying to placate the media for one day, Cam Walker mounted the stairs and went into the former conference hall, now the Major Investigation room. He would have laughed if the matter hadn't been so serious. In one corner, Fenfleet's legend, ex-DCI Matt Ballard, was in earnest conversation with a small team of seconded detectives, while across the room, animatedly explaining something to his cohorts, stood Chief Superintendent Jim Summers, also from Fenfleet. Cam had seen some collaborations, but never one quite like this. All it needed was the next missing girl to have been found in the Saltern-le-Fen area, her case headed up by DI Rowan Jackman, and they'd have a full house.

'Any updates?' he asked the assembled officers. 'DS Greene?'

Cam looked towards an older woman detective who was part of the specialist team looking into the murder of Daryl Grayson and Ruby's alleged assault on their mother, Shirley.

'Yes, sir. Information obtained from Daryl's acquaintances all seems to indicate that he'd been sailing very close to the wind for some time. We've spoken to several women who said they would have registered complaints about his unacceptable and lewd behaviour but had been discouraged by either friends or family, who didn't want any fuss. One said that he'd scared her badly, she felt quite guilty about not reporting him to the police at the time. Another said that a man with a black scarf over the lower part of his face exposed himself to her on two occasions. She was sure it was Daryl Grayson — she knew him from school — but she couldn't prove it. She said she had a lot of respect for his parents, who according to her were thoroughly decent people. The case against him is building up, sir. We have also contacted all the women who did report being watched, and not one of them has had occasion to worry since Daryl's death. There is little doubt that he was the stalker, and had targeted up to twelve women that we know of, plus heaven knows how many more who haven't come forward.'

'And the alleged attack on the mother?' Cam asked. 'Any progress there?'

'Ah, that's still a pretty delicate situation, sir. They had a bit of a drama earlier, when the girl started blaming an uncle for her mother's injuries. Naturally the man was checked out, and as far as we are concerned, he's not likely to have been involved, but even so, Ruby Grayson is adamant that someone is trying to blame her for something she didn't do, so further enquiries are being made. I'll update you as soon as we have anything more, sir.'

Jim Summers strolled over. 'It's worth noting, Cam, that although we've pretty well sewn up the Alexandra Cornfield/ Neil Weldon part of the enquiry, there are still reports coming in, all damning for Weldon. Once we've finally got an ID on his killer, aka Oliver, and sorted all the paperwork, we'll have a very strong case against him. One hateful old investigation that has haunted me for years finally put to bed.'

'Looks like my old nightmare is coming together too,' called Matt Ballard from across the room. 'I just wish it wasn't thanks to this sicko. Still, we need to put these poor women's families first, so no matter how galling it is to us, something good is coming out of it.'

'He's certainly doing wonders for our clear-up rates,' said Cam dryly, 'but I'm sweating bullets over what Oliver expects to get out of all this. And why did he choose Nikki as the one to target?'

'That scares us too,' said Matt. 'Doesn't it, Jim?'

Jim Summers nodded. 'Yes, we were talking about it earlier. Both of us reckon it stinks of something personal. This could be the hate campaign of the century. It's our bet that sometime in the past, Nikki made a serious enemy of someone, even if she isn't aware of it.'

Cam laughed. 'Given that woman's track record, the total will probably hit three figures! She was the number one bad girl for any number of years. Back then, there wasn't a drug dealer in the Fens who didn't tremble at the name Galena.'

'We reckon it's more personal than that, Cam. This guy's more than some pusher who did a stint inside. It feels like bad blood that has festered over time, finally sending him on a private vendetta that will end who knows where.' Matt frowned. 'And he's very impatient, isn't he? He can't wait for us to finish one thing before he throws us the next. He's already got us racing ahead on the Bethany Lyons disappearance while the report from Ruth Baker's PM is still pending. For some reason he's really rushing us.'

'I wonder if he only has a limited amount of time to bring it all to a head?' said Jim thoughtfully. 'Like Matt said, he's in one heck of a hurry.'

Cam hadn't thought of that. It was more than possible.

'Another thing I thought of,' said Matt. 'I have a wide network of contacts — my private agency relies on them.

Since there's an entire police team looking into Oliver's identity, and I'm sure Nikki and her sergeant are going back over her past with a fine-tooth comb, how about I try from the other side of the fence? If this guy has any connection with the criminal world, someone on the streets will know about it. A small offering in the form of a twenty-quid note, and we could get a lead.'

Jim nodded appreciatively. 'That's a smart idea, Matt. I've got a few sharp ears to the ground too. What do you think, Cam?'

Cam didn't hesitate. 'Go for it. And we've got an officer here with a photographic memory who also happens to know more about Greenborough and its inhabitants than anyone around. With her input, together with all our snouts and contacts, we might just hit on a pointer. Anything's worth a try. I fear for Nikki with this maniac on the loose.'

'And he's in command,' added Jim grimly. 'Apart from missing out on the wife's involvement in the Ruth Baker case — impatience again, maybe — he's efficient and totally in control of our every move.' His face set hard. 'And I hate that with a vengeance.'

He wasn't alone. Cam and Matt agreed wholeheartedly. 'Then let's do that,' Cam said. 'Let's hit every contact we can, and as fast as possible.'

As he strode out of the MI room, Cam heard Matt and Jim both talking on their mobile phones. Maybe Matt's idea would prove to be the breakthrough they needed.

CHAPTER TWENTY-TWO

Oliver had been working for fifteen hours non-stop when he sensed his thought processes becoming a little less sharp. Time for a quick nap? Bed, and a complete rest? He ran through his workload for that night and the following day. Given the scale of what he wanted to achieve in the next twenty-four hours, he would have preferred just to shut his eyes for a few minutes and take a nap, but the task he was about to embark on depended on absolutely fine timing, added to which was the possibility of an unknown factor creeping in at some point. No, he needed to be as sharp as possible. Three hours of proper sleep it would have to be. He couldn't remember exactly when he had discovered this remarkable ability to exist on very little sleep, but it had been of enormous benefit to him, especially now. He exhaled slowly, closed his eyes and immediately fell into a deep sleep.

* * *

There had been several interruptions to the progress of their interview with Martine Knight, some arising from the regulations, others down to Stephen Wray, her solicitor.

Nikki was becoming increasingly irritated. As the interview ground on, she was more and more certain that it was a waste of precious time. It was never going to bring Ruth back, and the probable killer was dead anyway. It was certainly important that this woman shouldn't be allowed to get away with murder, or even with abetting one, but there was so much more going on. The real danger lay in the here and now, not in something that happened fifteen years ago.

While Martine conferred with her solicitor during a drinks break, Nikki received a text asking her to ring Cat as soon as she was free.

Cat sounded excited. 'I've been doing a bit of research into classy leather belts, boss, and guess what? The leather belt found around Ruth Baker's legs is an exclusive design only available at a particular London boutique, with which Mrs Martine Knight has an account. It cost a mere one hundred and thirty-nine pounds, would you believe. And we have photos of her wearing it. Ben's just found several in the pictures folder on her laptop.'

Nikki thanked her, but before she could hang up, Cat added, 'The prof sent me a close-up of the belt retrieved from the cairn. Ben, meanwhile, has enlarged a photo of Martine wearing what looks like an identical one, which we can now confirm is the same belt. Her initials are tooled into the leather, and there's a tiny gouge in the metal of the buckle in both the picture and the real thing.' Cat gave a little chuckle. 'I'd like to be a fly on the wall of the interview room when you tackle her on that one!'

Nikki told Joseph, but despite their relief at being able to confront her with something concrete, they both knew what Martine would say.

She didn't disappoint them.

'I had no idea what happened to it! All I know is that it went missing from my wardrobe. I have no idea how it got where it did.' Martine seemed to have gained confidence following her last consultation with her solicitor. 'And that child was a little liar! She probably made up the part about an argument, just for attention. She could never have heard me in that garden because I wasn't there! And if there was a woman, then you need to look somewhere else. Yes, Gordon did have other women. I tried to ignore it for the sake of my son and the farm. We put up a very good show of being the perfect loving couple, but the fact was, dear Gordie played away, always with younger women.'

'Like Ruth Baker?' asked Joseph.

'Exactly like Ruth Baker.'

'So, you remember her now, Mrs Knight?' asked Nikki.

'Not specifically. There were several young women on the scene around that time, and I'd had enough. I gave him an ultimatum. I threatened to divorce him and take James, and that we'd have to sell the farm. It was a bad time, Inspector Galena, made worse by his diagnosis of prostate cancer.' She looked down. 'I still loved him, you see, despite his infidelities. So, I looked after him and ran the farm until he died. That's what loving someone does to you. I never forgave him, but nor did I stop loving him.'

'And do you believe that he killed Ruth Baker and hid her body in the cairn?' asked Joseph.

Stephen Wray jumped in. 'My client can't possibly answer that. She's just told you that she loved her husband and cared for him through a terminal illness. That's hardly the behaviour of someone who believes their husband to be a murderer.'

'Your client was none too polite about her loving husband earlier, when she was told a witness had seen him in the walled garden,' said Nikki. 'In fact, I distinctly remember her cursing him for letting himself be spotted dragging that "heavy weight" towards the cairn. I can play you the recording if you like. Maybe you missed it?'

Wray turned to Martine and said, 'You don't have to answer that.'

Martine, however, said she wanted to, and proceeded to say exactly what Nikki and Joseph had anticipated.

'Yes, Officers. In answer to your question, I'd like to alter my statement. The child was probably correct about what she saw, though incorrect about what she heard. Gordon came in very late that night and immediately had a shower. The clothes he put out for the laundry were filthy and his jacket was missing. So was my belt. I've never found either. He acted very oddly the next day and, yes, I did wonder if he might have had something to do with the missing girl. I kept quiet about my suspicions because the day after that we received the news about his cancer.' She glanced, all wide-eyed innocence, at Nikki then Joseph, her gaze resting on him a fraction too long. 'He had always left the care of the walled garden to the gardeners, but from that day forward he spent nearly all his spare time in there. He had always loved it, so I thought it was probably a way of distancing himself from his illness. After what you discovered under the cairn, I now realise he was making sure no one paid too much attention to the damned thing.' With her eyes still on Joseph, she said, 'Yes, I do believe that Gordon killed Ruth Baker and concealed her body. But I had nothing to do with it. That is all I have to say.'

She stared down at the table.

Nikki said everything expected of her and concluded the interview. Outside, she said to Joseph, 'Unless Rory comes up with a miracle, or we find another more reliable witness, we'll never prove otherwise. For now, we walk away from this line of enquiry. When this whole thing is finally over, and please God it's soon, perhaps then we can renew our acquaintance with Martine Knight.'

'I agree,' Joseph said. 'It's not our priority. Finding Oliver is. Let's go.' And he marched off.

* * *

Back in his office, Joseph plunged back into the search, looking for possible candidates for Oliver among the police officers from Nikki's past. He was immersed in his pool of candidates when all of a sudden, Cam Walker's broad figure filled his doorway.

'Just a word, Joseph.' He eased himself into the small room and closed the door. 'I thought you'd like to know that Jim Summers, Matt Ballard and I have extended the search for someone with a grudge against Nikki into the criminal fraternity. We're getting in touch with every snout we have between us. Matt's very useful here, since he has a lot more contacts than us, on both sides of the law. It's just another angle to try, but we need to ID this renegade before he gets to his end game, because we're all getting increasingly concerned for Nikki's safety.'

As was he. Joseph was glad of *any* new angle, and using their networks sounded like a bloody good idea.

'I'm down here now to have a word with your Yvonne Collins. I'm certain she's already thinking along these lines herself but I want her to know that she has our full backing to make as many undercover inquiries as she sees fit, and I'll make some cash available to her so she can smooth the way for a few lips to flap.' He stood up. 'I just wanted you to know that we too are looking out for Nikki.' He gave Joseph a rather anxious smile and was gone.

Joseph was touched. How lucky they were to have Cam as a friend. It was good to hear that the big guys were watching Nikki's back as much as he was.

His phone rang.

'Hello, Eve. Are you okay?'

'Yes, I'm fine. Look, Joseph, we know how busy you are, but you still have to eat. Can you and Nikki meet us tonight at Mario's restaurant? It's five minutes from the police station, so it won't take any more time than getting a takeaway.'

'You sound a bit anxious, Eve. And I get the feeling that it's not totally connected with our diet?'

There was a short silence, then Eve said, 'We've stumbled across something that could be of importance to your investigations at some point. It won't take long, honestly, but Wendy and I think you should know about it.' She gave a little dry laugh. 'It's probably nothing, and mainly it's because I'd like to treat you hard workers to a decent meal that you don't have to cook yourself. What do you say?'

Knowing Eve, if she had picked up on something, it would be worth hearing about. 'What time?'

'Excellent! Would six thirty or seven suit you? Mario can fit us in any time before eight.'

He glanced at his watch, it was almost six now. 'We'll be there at seven. See you then. And, Eve? Thank you.'

* * *

'Oh Joseph! I wanted to press on tonight. If we don't move on to Bethany Lyons, sodding Oliver will be barking at our heels. It's very sweet of Mum, but—'

'Enough.' There were times when Joseph could be positively severe. 'Eve is well aware of how busy you are. It's not going to be a long piss-up of an evening, just a good meal, and you need that to keep going. Plus, she wants to talk to you about something. Okay?' She made to protest but he held up his hand. 'Cat and Ben have now finished wading through the contents of Martine's dressing room, and they've volunteered to stay on this evening. They'll be gathering all they can from the old reports on Bethany Lyons. When we've finished with Eve and Wendy, you can come back and see what they've uncovered. No arguments!'

Nikki exhaled. 'Well, okay.' Thoughts of Mario and his delicious menu were already gaining ground over her firm decision to work late. 'What does she want to talk to me about? Did she say?'

'No, and I didn't press her. She just said that she and Wendy had come across something that she felt we ought to know about.'

Nikki let out a groan. 'That mother of mine! Can't she manage to keep away from trouble for five bloody minutes? I bet it's something to do with that new hobby of hers. Detecting buried stuff, I ask you.'

Joseph grinned. 'Maybe she's detected something quite unexpected. You can ask her yourself soon.' He returned to business. 'Oh, and I've just spoken to Niall. He says he has all available officers keeping an eye open for motorcycle couriers. He's already spoken to the local ones and none of them have delivered packages to this address. Anyway, they've all been alerted and will ring in if anyone tries to get something to you.'

Nikki hadn't expected anything different. Oliver was far too clever to use the official companies. He'd probably pay over the odds to get an outsider to come in and deliver his mail or pay even more and get some chancer with a fast bike to pose as a courier. She favoured the last option. Whatever he did, he'd use a phony name. Still, every avenue had to be checked out. They couldn't afford to miss a single possibility.

'Talking about Bethany Lyons,' said Joseph, 'I'm guessing our next little *Par Avion* epistle will be with us shortly, along with some stupid bloody clue telling us where to look for her body — the one he discovered ages ago. Even that's disgusting. Finding these poor kids and just leaving them there so he can use them to taunt us. That's really sick!'

'Sick as hell,' said Nikki. She stood up. 'Well, I think I'll go and tie up with Cat and Ben, then nip upstairs and see if anything new has come in while we were interviewing Martine. Then we'll go and meet Batman and Robin. Who knows what my mother and her trusty sidekick have got themselves involved in this time. It doesn't bear thinking about.'

As she walked away, she distinctly heard someone sniggering behind her.

* * *

This early in the evening, the restaurant was quiet. Eve had been able to choose a table tucked away in an alcove where no one was likely to overhear them. After Nikki introduced her to Mario's, Eve had become a regular customer, and she and Mario were now on very good terms. Tonight, there were two dry sherries waiting for her and Wendy, courtesy of the man himself.

'So, how are we going to tackle this?' asked Wendy, sipping her drink.

'Head-on, no messing. It's the only way with my Nikki.' Eve pulled a face. 'I can't say I'm exactly looking forward to it, but she has to be told.'

'And now is your chance.' Wendy pointed to the door, where Nikki and Joseph were being greeted by Mario.

Having made their choices, Eve, knowing her daughter's time was limited, launched straight in. 'We've discovered something that we feel we ought to share with you both — as members of the police rather than family. Hear me out, and then we'll discuss it properly.'

Nikki opened her mouth to say something but instead sighed and sat back.

Eve told them what they'd found in Chris Tate's field, and how his reaction had led them into tracing the objects' history. Keeping it brief, she spoke of the story they'd unearthed with the help of Jacob Rush, ending with Chris Tate's revelation of his family secret, about which even his wife knew nothing.

Here Nikki broke in. 'He never told his wife but he did tell you? How come?'

'Because he underestimated us,' said Wendy.

'He certainly did,' said Eve. 'He thought we'd swallow the story that the family had concocted over the years to forestall any inconvenient questions that might have arisen.'

'Big mistake,' muttered Joseph, trying unsuccessfully to hold back a smile. 'I assume he didn't know what you two used to do for a living?'

They shook their heads, then, before Eve could continue, the food arrived and they busied themselves distributing condiments and garlic bread.

Everything sorted, Eve sat back and surveyed her daughter and her partner. 'What we are about to tell you may be of no use to you at all. However, we both felt that if we're right, then you should at least know about it.' Before Nikki could speak, Eve held up her hand. 'Just please be aware that we are talking about our next-door neighbour, who we have to get along with. We like the Tates and we get on well with them, but we believe that their "family secret" might still be affecting the present generation.' She stared at her daughter. 'We may be wrong, and if we are, you can forget the whole thing.'

'Come on, Mum! Spit it out.' Nikki laid down her fork and eyed her mother impatiently.

Between them, Eve and Wendy explained about the mutant gene many of the Tate women inherited, which sometimes led to insanity and had caused the two sisters to engineer the death of their own mother.

'And he admits that the female side of the family are still affected?' asked Joseph.

'Oh yes,' Eve said. 'I'm certain that everything Chris Tate told me was the truth, apart from his assertion that the symptoms are no longer as severe as they used to be.' Eve spread her hands. 'And that's it. Can you see why we wanted you to know this?'

For once, Nikki didn't remonstrate with her mother. 'Just like us, you were taught to spot a lie, weren't you?'

'We were good at it too,' said Wendy. 'We had to be. If we got it wrong, the entire country could have been at risk.'

'I guess we thought that just in case you have any old cases, possibly involving violence on the part of a woman, that seemed too incongruous to be true, you might like to check and see whether she's a member of the extended Tate family,' explained Eve. 'As you probably know, Tate is a well-known name in the county, there are Tates everywhere, and not just in the farming community.'

'It doesn't affect them all of course,' Wendy added. 'Like a lot of hereditary conditions, some are lucky enough to escape it, and some have a mild form that just makes them appear somewhat lacking in empathy, but—'

'But there could still be the odd woman who is unfortunate enough to be seriously affected. It's happened in the past, so it could happen again,' Eve concluded.

As if by mutual agreement, they all turned their attention to their food. For a while, nobody spoke.

Then Joseph looked at Nikki, a glint of excitement in his eyes. 'I suppose you aren't thinking what I'm thinking?'

Nikki returned his gaze. 'You know what? I think I probably am.'

Eve glanced at Wendy, and both stared at Nikki.

'Ongoing case, Mother. We can't discuss it, but your story would answer one hell of a big question that's been hanging over it.' She looked reflectively at Eve. 'Not that I'm sure how we can use this knowledge without causing an eruption of volcanic proportions.'

'We were thinking of old cases, not something in the present,' Eve said disappointedly. 'I really don't want a war with my next-door neighbours.'

Nikki smiled at her. 'Forget the volcano bit. Leave this with us, Mum, we won't drop you in it. There are ways round everything. It might not even be relevant.'

Eve had seen the look her daughter had exchanged with Joseph. Whatever they were considering, it was serious. She wondered if she'd made a mistake in revealing the Tates' secret. It had seemed morally right to do so, but perhaps she should have stuck to the old adage about silence being golden.

Nikki stood up. 'I'm just going to make a call, won't be a moment.'

Eve's heart sank. What had they done? She looked at Wendy and saw her own anxiety reflected in her friend's face.

'Hey, you two! You did the right thing. It'll be all right, don't worry. As Nikki said, we can't discuss it just yet, but this could be the answer to something that is causing massive concern and ruining a whole lot of lives, some of them young. A simple check can tell us if we are on the right track and if we are, believe me, you'll have made a huge difference to a lot of people. And,' he gave her his warmest and most disarming smile, 'none of this need come back to you.'

She supposed he was right, but his words did nothing to lift her mood. She kept hearing Chris Tate declaring his love for his family and the land, and she felt as if she'd just stabbed him in the back. Well, she couldn't turn the river back now, she'd opened the floodgates and she'd have to take the consequences.

* * *

Thanking whatever powers there might be for speedy computers and clever algorithms, Cat got straight down to it. She told Ben what the boss had asked her to do. 'This is just between us, Ben, and no one else. The boss says it's very sensitive and she'll explain fully when she gets back.'

Ben pulled an imaginary zip across his lips. 'Interesting. I've heard of such rogue genes, in Huntington's disease and the like, but never as part of an actual police case.' He leaned over her shoulder to look at her screen.

Within minutes, they were staring at the answer.

'Mrs Shirley Grayson's maiden name is Shirley Annette Tate. Poor Shirley, it looks to me as if she's gifted young Ruby with a nasty little rogue gene.'

'And she's paying the price in silence,' added Ben. He exhaled loudly. 'Thank heavens we have a specialist team dealing with this, it's one case I'd hand over like a hot potato.' He went back to his desk. 'Are you going to be ringing the boss?'

'No. She said they'd be back within the hour, she doesn't want to talk about it in the restaurant.'

Cat printed off the marriage certificate that had given her the answer. She didn't know the story yet, but at least if the child Ruby was suffering from some kind of hereditary mental illness, it would answer so many questions. 'Ben, you said you'd heard about rogue genes, do you know if they can affect males as well as females?'

'You're thinking of Daryl, I suppose,' said Ben. 'Well, I'm no expert, but women have two X chromosomes, while men have one, from their mother, and a Y male specific from their father, so if the mutant is attached to an X, whereas it would be far more likely to affect women, I reckon it's possible for a male to have it.'

Cat nodded thoughtfully. If there was a DNA test for it, then at least it could be proved that the Graysons weren't just wicked kids, born bad. If anything, they were born unfortunate.

Cat returned to her work on Bethany Lyons. They were struggling through myriad enquiries right now, but hopefully this new information of the boss's would take the Grayson case off their hands. They could certainly do with it, because at any minute *Par Avion* would land another old murder on their desks, and frankly, extra hands or no extra hands, it was getting to everyone. It was a difficult enough case as it was, but with the media watching their every move, it was like trying to concentrate with a road drill hammering at your side. They couldn't take a step outside the door without having a microphone thrust at them, or a camera shutter clicking in their faces. And dear Oliver was stoking the flames, inundating the papers with suppositions and not-so-veiled suggestions that past failures aside, the Fenland Constabulary were really not up to the job.

Cat's fury mounted. She relieved her anger with fantasies of what she would do if left alone with this Oliver bastard in a locked room. She glanced at the clock and got down to the next question. *Now, Bethany Lyons, whatever happened to you?*

* * *

By eleven that night, Nikki had had enough. She and Joseph returned to Cloud Fen. They had accomplished a lot on their return from the restaurant. Eve's news had made the unplanned dinner well worth taking the time for. Nikki had been lucky enough to get a word with the psychologist who was evaluating young Ruby Grayson and her family. She had found working with Julia Tennant difficult to start with.

She'd only recently replaced the well-loved Laura Archer as force psychologist, and memories of Laura were still fresh, but Nikki believed she could trust her, so she told her of her belief that there was a rogue gene running through the Grayson family on Shirley Grayson's side, that of the Tates, which had never been admitted to or spoken about. She also told Julia that she trusted her source completely but couldn't divulge their identity. Julia had assured her that in light of the dead brother's possible tendencies, she had already requested that Ruby too should be tested. She had wondered if there might be some hereditary cause for such violent abnormal behaviour occurring in two out of two siblings. The problem would come if the parents refused to allow their daughter, who was still a minor, to have the tests. However, they could impose no such restriction on forensic tests done on the body of Daryl Grayson, and if a rogue gene showed up in him, it might shine a different light on the whole thing. This, Julia said, could be a way of keeping Nikki's suspicions and her "source" out of the equation.

Feeling immediately easier, Nikki called Rory, put him fully in the picture, and asked for his help. Aware that the credit for making this interesting and unusual discovery would go to him, he said he'd be delighted. He said that he was waiting on the full results of Daryl's pathology tests, and was still running others, so he would be looking very carefully into the DNA. He would ring her the moment he knew anything definite.

Nikki was keen to ring Eve with all this, but as it was almost midnight, she settled for a text. She told her mother that any major breakthrough would come from forensic testing rather than information received, and that she could relax. There would be no mention of an outside source. If anyone found themselves in the spotlight following the discovery, it would be Professor Rory Wilkinson, or possibly the psychologist, Julia Tennant. Certainly not Eve Anderson.

That done, Nikki drew a mental line beneath the Graysons, just as she had done in the cases of Alexandra

Cornfield and Ruth Baker. The reports and other paper-work would be dealt with later. Their focus now was Bethany Lyons and identifying and capturing Oliver.

Nikki fell asleep thinking of Oliver. It wasn't a restful night.

* * *

Still awake, Eve read the text and nodded to herself. It was the best she could expect, but she felt no better about what she had done. She also knew in her heart that Chris Tate would still suspect her and Wendy of passing his story to the police. How could he think otherwise? He had confessed his secret to the mother of a detective heading an investigation involving a Tate woman and, hey presto, they were checking the family's DNA.

Eve was still awake at three in the morning, sipping a hot drink and waiting for the dawn chorus.

CHAPTER TWENTY-THREE

Par Avion.

The envelope was the first thing Nikki saw as she entered her office. At once, she was gripped with the strange mixture of fear and anger that Oliver's letters always evoked.

'How the hell did that arrive? Certainly not via the post office at this time in the bloody morning,' she muttered.

Joseph picked up a memo that lay beside it. 'It looks like there was an influx of rowdy kids at around midnight. By the time they'd been escorted off the premises, the desk sergeant found this in the foyer. Oliver must have paid some kid to act pissed and sneak it in.'

'Then he'll be on CCTV,' growled Nikki. 'Not that we'll ever trace him. If he's a street kid, he'll have been wily enough not to look at the cameras and certainly not to be noticed leaving that.' She indicated to the envelope. 'Okay, let's see what the bastard has to say this time.'

They read the letter together. It was headed with the usual refrain, *You failed me.* It went immediately into a description of Case No 0149, Bethany Lyons. In very concise wording, he stated that the twenty-two-year-old, a receptionist in a local doctor's surgery, had called in sick one morning and then disappeared. She was last seen by a member of the public getting into her car and driving away from her home at around ten in the morning. The car was later found abandoned in the parking area of a remote and little-used bird reserve close to the marsh. Oliver then proceeded to berate them for conducting a sloppy and ineffectual investigation in which they missed a vital clue that would have led them to an answer within days — if it had been followed up properly.

Joseph frowned. 'Is it me, or is he sounding more, I don't know, disparaging certainly, but the letters have an air of desperation too. I keep getting this overwhelming impression that he's running out of time and that he wants this over for some reason.'

Nikki threw up her hands. 'Hell, we can't possibly move any faster than we already are. We have half the Fenland Constabulary out searching, day and night. He's spent years getting his sodding crusade together, while he expects us to deal with the shit he throws the minute it lands on us!'

'I know, I know,' Joseph said. 'But why? Why is he bombarding us day after day? Is he trying to wear us down?'

'If he is, he's succeeding,' muttered Nikki. 'Okay, let's see what his next commandment is.'

They began to read:

In the hopes that you can get it right this time, I'm going to give you the one clue I discovered and that you, unsurprisingly, missed. From then on a kid could work it out, but even that doesn't fill me with confidence.'

Nikki looked up from the letter. 'Whatever you do, promise me you won't leave me alone with this man after we catch him, I won't be responsible for my actions.' She returned to the letter.

'If you can manage to focus for five minutes, look again at her calendar and what she was doing on the Tuesday night before she disappeared, and this time check it out properly. Then talk to a man called Tyler. You have twenty-four hours, and if you can't find her within that length of time, Nikki Galena, there will be repercussions, so I'd get to work if I were you. The clock is ticking.

Oliver.'

Joseph groaned. 'Jesus Christ! He's putting even more pressure on us.'

'On me, actually. For the first time he's made it clear that I'm the one he's gunning for.' In her whole life, Nikki had only truly hated two individual people, both of whom were long gone. There were plenty she disliked, and she often hated what people did, but pure hatred was a terrible, destructive emotion that damaged the hater as well as the hated, and Nikki had no capacity for that. What worried her was that Oliver had deliberately omitted an important part of his threat. Silently, she finished his sentence for him: *There will be repercussions, Nikki Galena, so watch your nearest and dearest. I'd get to work if I were you. The clock is ticking.*

She looked at Joseph and saw that he too had understood the implications. 'Then let's get to work,' he said. 'I'll go and see if Cat and Ben are in yet. They know most about the Bethany Lyons case, having spent last night cramming it. The first thing we'll do is go back to what she was doing on that Tuesday night.' He looked at Nikki. 'We're not fools, no matter what he says. If his clues are accurate and we hit the ground running, we'll do this in no time, and fucking Oliver can stuff his ticking clock up his arse!'

Even in her present state, Nikki had to smile. Joseph rarely swore, and when he did, she always found it funny. 'Okay. I'll go and leave Cam a memo to let him know what's up. You're right, we can do this.'

* * *

Upon entering the CID room, Joseph saw Ben and Cat peeling off their jackets, obviously just having arrived.

'Sorry, guys, Oliver has dumped on us again, only this time he's imposed a time limit. I suggest you grab a coffee and we get this thing moving.' He gave them an uneasy look. 'It seems he really is directing his threats to Nikki — this letter mentions her by name — and that could extend to the people she cares about. We need to pull our fingers out. He's told us to look at what Bethany was doing on a date he has given us.'

'I'll get the coffees.' Ben was already heading for the vending machine.

'I'll pull up the report and find the date. What was it?' Cat was already seated at her computer and logging in.

As they waited for it to load, Joseph asked, 'Who ran this case?'

'A detective called Rodgers, Sarge. Sadly, he's brown bread, so there's no bringing him in to help out unless you happen to have a Ouija board on you.'

'Sorry, I left it at home. Where did all this occur?' asked Joseph.

'On the borders of Harlen Marsh and Fenton village. There used to be a police station at Fenton at the time Bethany went missing. It closed down years ago, but the search was originally based there. Harlen Marsh assisted, but,' she raised an eyebrow, 'well, we all know what a load of shysters that crew were, especially their illustrious leader, Superintendent James Cade.'

The very name brought a bad taste to Joseph's mouth. Cade had been an evil bastard, and if it hadn't been for their colleagues at Saltern-le-Fen, he could be ruining lives even now. 'So, basically, we are on our own, with just the case notes and media reports to go on?'

Cat was peering at her screen. 'At least those are pretty good, Sarge. Rodgers was methodical and very meticulous.'

'Oliver disagrees. He said a vital clue was missed, and it involves something she was doing on the Tuesday night before she went missing. Oh, and a chap called Tyler.'

Cat pulled a face. 'There's no mention of any Tyler, but she did have an actual calendar — it was mentioned several times. It was one of those wall jobs with a square for each day.' She hit a key. 'Yup, here it is. Tuesday, you say?'

Joseph nodded, and thanked Ben for the coffee he'd just put down in front of him.

'Got it.' Cat read out the entry. 'Owl Watch, 2200 hrs WEBR.' She glanced at Joseph. 'Oh yes, she was into bird-watching, and wildlife conservation, I think. Sergeant Lucy Wells, who was the FLO, said the family told her she was passionate about it.'

'Okay,' said Joseph, thinking hard. 'So, what did Rodgers find out about this Owl Watch? Like where was it, and who did she go with? And what does WEBR mean?'

Cat scrolled down, closed the report and accessed another one. 'Here we are. It seems that the location varied, as well as who attended. Their group had around twenty-five members, but they often went out in small groups or even in pairs.' Cat read on. 'Ah yes, Rodgers said she was going to the Wash End Bird Reserve, so that's your WEBR, and she was going with three friends, er . . . Yes, two girls called Lisa and Ava, and a guy called Artie. They wanted to get some night photos of a barn owl, but they cancelled as the weather was bad and the conditions too poor for photographs.'

'No Tyler,' mused Joseph. 'How about on the list of members of the club?'

Cat shook her head. 'No, definitely not.'

'The next day, her car was found in the car park of a bird reserve. Was it the same one, Cat?' asked Joseph.

'No, it was found at a small place right at the bottom of Carters Drove, near the marsh. It's called Saltmere Reserve, but it's seldom used and has never been properly maintained. According to Rodgers, the hides were falling to bits, it was well overgrown, and the car park was a dump. I heard that a burnt-out stolen car was found there a week or so ago, so I guess it hasn't changed.' Cat looked up. 'So, where's this glaringly obvious clue we're supposed to have missed, Sarge? It looks to me like Rodgers was pretty thorough.'

Joseph shrugged. 'That's what we have to discover, and fast. Something is apparently wrong with her calendar entry, so get hold of those birdy friends of hers, if they're still around, and try to find a discrepancy.' He frowned. 'I'll dig out uniform's report on her car. You never know, there might have been something odd about it, like some indication of a struggle? It's a bit tenuous, but worth a look.'

Twenty minutes later, Joseph looked up from his desk to see Cat hurrying breathlessly towards his door.

'I think we've got it, Sarge! I've just spoken to her friend Ava. She lives in Corby Glen now, but clearly remembers Bethany and what happened.'

Joseph pointed to the other chair. 'Brilliant! So, what did she say? And a little slower perhaps?'

Cat grinned back sheepishly, 'Sorry, Sarge. Well, I got her to tell me everything she could recall about their Owl Watch — the one that was cancelled. She said they discussed it on the phone and decided to go another night after the weather improved. It was all exactly as Rodgers notes, but then I asked her to tell me a bit more about Bethany and how she got on with the other members of the group. Ava said she was well-liked, almost fanatical about conservation, especially the protection of wild birds.' Cat raised her eyebrows. 'But she wasn't reliable. She often failed to turn up when she said she would, or backed out just before a planned outing without giving any excuse. Ava called her lovely, but deep, and said she often wondered what was going on in her life.'

'And so?' There was more, Joseph could tell.

'And so, I spoke to Bethany's next-door neighbour, a Mr Tucker. He said he saw her car leave at ten the morning after her disappearance.' Cat leaned forward. 'This is where Rodgers, or whoever questioned the neighbour, slipped up. Tucker was asked when he saw her last, and he answered truthfully. He was *not* asked about the previous evening. Another neighbour, an elderly lady, had seen Bethany's car parked outside her house at nine thirty, and it was assumed that, because the Owl Watch was cancelled, she'd stayed at home.'

'But she did go out?'

'She did. Tucker saw her drive away at around ten fif-teen, and he thinks he heard her car engine again at around one in the morning. He's pretty sure he's right, and as it was parked outside her house when he woke up, he thought no more of it.'

'So where did she go?' asked Joseph.

'That's where we are now, Sarge, trying to find out. But we know one thing — she took her camera. Tucker said that he saw her leave carrying it on a strap over her shoulder, as it always was when she went birdwatching. There's a street lamp right outside, and he saw it clearly.'

'So, she went anyway? Even without the others and in bad weather.'

Cat stood up. 'To be continued. I'm off to see where Ben's at.'

'That camera, Cat. I've just checked with uniform, and it wasn't in the car when it was discovered. We need to look at the inventory of her house. If it's not there, where is it now?' Joseph could feel himself beginning to tense up with excitement. 'I'll get on to that, you keep on following Bethany's movements.'

It didn't take long for Joseph to discover that no camera had been found in Bethany's home. He closed his eyes for a moment. *Okay, concentrate! How did Oliver move on from here? And where does this Tyler come in? A girl goes out at night, taking her camera. She returns home late, then the following morning goes out again and is never seen again. The car is found, but no girl and no camera. Ergo, she kept it with her.*

Joseph exhaled. Where to go from here? To get better picture of where Bethany's car was found, he looked up Saltmere Bird Reserve on the internet. The images all showed a dreary-looking spot that flanked a river and ran into the marsh, the river's edge and a sea-bank walk that stretched away into the horizon. Getting to it involved tramping across miles of fields.

He wondered why Bethany would have gone there. He was about to get Cat to ask one of the birdwatching group when something on his screen, a blog on birds seen in the Saltmere area, caught his eye. According to the blogger, because it was so little disturbed, a number of particularly lovely specimens had chosen it to build their nests. You had to know where to look for them, though, the blogger added. Joseph had a good idea that Bethany would have known exactly where to go. At the bottom was a Q&A section. Joseph read one or two posts that advised keeping quiet about it, or they'd have hordes of people invading the place. Some said if more attention was paid to it, the RSPB might put up some usable bird hides, and sort out the overgrown paths. Joseph idly wondered if this blogger had known Bethany. He glanced at the name and did a double take.

Joseph could have punched the air with delight. He jumped up and ran down to the IT department.

He was greeted by Spooky, the IT chief, who looked at him in amazement. 'Excuse me, but what's happened to the suave, imperturbable Sergeant Easter this morning?'

'He's busy,' Joseph said. 'Spooks, I need your help! I need to find the address of a blogger. Is it possible to trace it? It's urgent.'

She grinned at him. 'Just give me the site name.'

A few minutes later, Joseph came hurtling back through the doors to the CID room. Nikki's office was empty and he guessed she was still with Cameron, either up in the MI room or discussing their next move.

'Cat? Ben? I've found Tyler, and I want one of you to come with me when I pay him a call.'

Ben jumped up. 'Where's he at, Sarge?'

'He's in a caravan park called Willow Acres, about three miles out of town on the Fenchester Road. Know it?'

'Yep! Pass it regularly,' Ben said. 'Not a bad place either, it's more like upmarket static homes than caravans these days.'

Joseph told Cat to watch out for Nikki and tell her what they were doing, and he and Ben hurried down to the staff car park.

'Fill me in on what you know on the way,' Ben said. 'This is falling into place faster than I'd expected. I just hope it's fast enough for matey-boy Oliver, that's all.'

Joseph had no answer to that.

CHAPTER TWENTY-FOUR

Dinah Barrett put down her desk phone with a frown. Lynette Sims had not arrived for work. The head had rung down to find out if she'd called in sick but she hadn't.

This was most unlike Lynette, who was the most conscientious of teachers. Di wondered anxiously if she'd been involved in an accident. She was loath to phone Lynette's mother, Stella, for fear of alarming her. Now, her first priority was to get someone to take her class. Mr Hendricks had a free first period today, so she'd ask him to cover, and then they'd just have to fill in where they could. If necessary, she'd take a couple of lessons herself.

Dinah hurried out of her office and began reorganising lessons and rescheduling teachers. After an hour with still no call from Lynette, she became really concerned. Not knowing who to turn to, she took a chance on ringing Yvonne Collins.

'Sorry, Vonnie, I didn't know who else to ask. Have there been any traffic accidents reported in the area this morning?'

Yvonne hadn't heard of anything serious but said she'd check for her. A few minutes later she reported that there had been a bit of a shunt at some temporary traffic lights but there were certainly no casualties. 'Why the concern, Di?'

'One of my teachers, Lynette Sims — I think I mentioned her to you once — she's not turned up for work, and she hasn't called, which isn't like her at all. I'm really worried, especially after all this bad business with the Grayson family.'

'Is she the one who thought she was being stalked, and we wondered if Ruby had put her brother up to it?' Yvonne asked.

Dinah said that it was. 'I don't like to ring her mother — the last thing I want to do is scare the woman. Maybe I should check the hospitals?'

'I think you *should* ask her mother, Di,' said Yvonne. 'Maybe something's happened to her, like a fall or some accident at home, and the mother hasn't had a chance to ring you. Contact her and let me know what she says.'

Dinah did as advised. 'She left as normal,' she told Yvonne. 'Her mother said she went for a half-hour jog, came back, showered, had breakfast and left for work at the usual time. She's heard nothing from her.'

'I'm going to tell my boss, Di.' Yvonne sounded anxious. 'Considering Miss Sims's involvement in the Grayson business, this doesn't sound right, does it? It could be a simple problem and she'll be with you in no time. Things do happen after all, cars break down, phones run out of charge and so on, but do keep me posted. Meanwhile, I'll pass it on to my boss.'

With a sinking feeling in her stomach, Dinah went to the head's office to bring her up to date. With every hour that passed she became increasingly certain. Something was terribly wrong with Lynette Sims.

* * *

Having snatched a few moments to get himself a hot drink, Cameron went back to the MI room. So far, not a single one of his or Jim Summers's contacts had come up with anyone with a grudge against Nikki Galena — or at least one big enough to act upon. It was now down to Matt Ballard to come up with something. He looked around the busy room which was humming with voices, ringing phones and the noise of printers whirring, but couldn't see Matt.

'Don't get your hopes up, Cam.' Jim was striding towards him, holding a sandwich with a large bite out of it. 'But Matt's off visiting a contact in what he said is a last-ditch attempt to discover what this Oliver is up to.' He sighed. 'I had such high hopes of getting to a snout with a lead, but none of mine have heard a thing. They were just as much in the dark as we are. Matt said he got the impression that his contact might be able to find something out, and if he managed to ensure that he understood the gravity of the situation, this guy could put out feelers for him where it counted.'

Like Jim, Cam had little hope of the contact coming up with anything. 'Oliver has given Nikki twenty-four hours to find the body of Bethany Lyons, or . . .' The full weight of it bore down on him. 'Or there will be repercussions. I dread to think what he means by that.'

Jim swallowed a mouthful of his sandwich. 'It could mean a whole lot of things, depending on Oliver's state of mind.'

'Or the intensity of his hatred for Nikki Galena.'

'Or of the entire Fenland Constabulary,' added Jim.

Cam took a mouthful of his tea. 'I've asked the force psychologist to pay us a visit. I can't think how it will help, but I can't afford to miss a trick, can I?'

For a moment neither man spoke. They were both thinking about the terrible loss to the whole constabulary of their well-liked and highly respected Laura Archer. Her sudden death, and the effect it must have had on their Saltern-le-Fen colleague, DI Jackman, had been felt throughout the entire division. Cam had been advised that her replacement, an older and very experienced psychologist named Julia Tennant, was eminently capable, and given her status in the field of forensic psychology, they were very fortunate in having her join them. He knew that Nikki had spoken to her and had been pretty impressed.

'Indeed not,' said Jim, coming out of his reverie. 'Oliver's actions so far, along with his various communications, might well speak volumes to a professional. She might not be able to point us to the man's identity, but it would be a great help to us if we could get an insight into how he might act.'

Cam's phone rang. 'Matt? Anything for us?'

Down a line that kept breaking, he made out the words, '. . . told to look to our own . . . Whisper that another police officer is going after DI Galena . . . watch out . . . intentions far from benign . . . Find out more and get back to me.' Then, more clearly, 'Bad signal. I'm on my way back now.'

Cam relayed the message to Jim. 'We can't rely on some whisper, can we? We still need to keep all avenues open while we concentrate on police officers, past and present. Agreed?'

'Agreed.' Jim threw the remains of his sandwich into a bin and hurried back to his team of borrowed detectives. 'We're on it, Cam.'

* * *

Tyler Morton came as something of a surprise. From reading his blog and having been told he lived on a caravan site, Joseph had expected someone quite different to this short, stocky, fortyish man with short, salt-and-pepper hair. Only his clothes were what a birdwatcher might wear, though even these were far from scruffy. He saw a Barbour logo on the gilet, and those cargo pants were certainly not cheap. Joseph noted that he dragged his left leg slightly when he walked.

Joseph and Ben had accepted the offer of a drink, which was made and brought to them by an elderly man who introduced himself as Tyler's father, Simon. The static caravan they lived in was a luxury model, with a spacious, open-plan lounge and central heating radiators. He said they loved their life there, away from the town centre and close to the countryside.

After the old man had left the room, Joseph turned to Tyler Morton. 'You had a visit from a man named Oliver, I believe.'

'Not a visit, Sergeant. He rang me.' Tyler spoke in a cultivated voice. 'Initially I was suspicious, I wasn't sure if he was who he said he was, but he gave me a number to ring him back on. It put me through to the police station, and I was connected to his office, that of DI Oliver of Greenborough.'

Joseph gritted his teeth. Clever sod! He must have rigged that one up pretty cleverly.

'He said his sergeant would contact me at some point, and here you are.' Tyler smiled expectantly.

Wondering where to start, Joseph glanced at the walls and saw a number of excellent paintings, mostly studies of birds of prey.

Tyler smiled. 'My father is an artist. Like me, he has a passion for birds.'

'These are very good,' breathed Joseph, wanting to look closer. 'But I mustn't waste your time. We are here about Bethany Lyons, as you are aware. Can you tell us why you didn't contact us after she went missing five years ago?'

Tyler set down his mug on a coaster. 'As I told the inspector, I was in Scotland, on the island of Jura, and I didn't hear a thing about it.' He smiled at them. 'My real love are the raptors — hawks, eagles and falcons. Twice a year I travel to the islands of Jura or Islay, which are a haven for birds of prey. When I got back I heard some talk of a girl going missing, but I had no reason to think it could be anyone connected to me.'

Joseph knew it hadn't been a high-profile case. People went missing all the time and few made the headlines. There was also a strong possibility that Bethany, who had been a habitual runaway when younger, had found something difficult to cope with and had done a disappearing act. Of the four missing person cases Oliver had picked on, Bethany's was the least publicised. 'And your father? Did he not make a connection?'

Tyler shrugged. 'Why would he? I barely knew her. I might never have even mentioned her to him. He says I didn't, and I'm sure he's right.'

'Tell us what you do know of her, sir,' said Ben, making notes on his phone.

'I met her at Saltmere. There was a marsh harrier that she was trying to photograph. We watched it together for a while and chatted a bit, about birds and the reserve there. I thought that she was a bit, well . . .' Tyler paused, frowning. 'Strange? I'm not sure if that's the right word. Anyway, she knew her birds all right, and I got the feeling that she was very much committed to ecology and the protection of birds. I saw her briefly a couple of times after that, once just to wave to from a distance, and from what DI Oliver told me of the date it happened, it seems that I saw her the night she disappeared. The next morning, I left for Scotland.' He looked from Joseph to Ben. 'I never even knew her name.'

'Was she alone when you saw her that last night?' asked Ben.

'Initially I thought she was. She'd been alone on the other occasions I'd seen her, later I was forced to wonder if someone else had been around somewhere. I only spoke to her for a moment or two to ask if she was okay, it certainly wasn't a good night for photography.'

'What did she say to you?' asked Joseph.

Tyler shrugged. 'I've told all this to DI Oliver. She seemed distracted, said something about having seen a short-eared owl, which I thought was a bit odd, as they prefer to hunt in the daytime. She then said that she'd been waiting in the Hidey-hole, which is the only usable bird hide, but needed to get home. And off she went. That was it.'

Joseph frowned. 'Did she have her camera with her? I know it's a long time ago, but can you remember?'

Tyler Morton bit his bottom lip. 'Camera? Well, she always carried it with her. It was a good one too, not one of those flashy things with a forty-foot lens like some obsessed birders lug around, but a decent one, a Pentax, I think.' His frown deepened. 'I could be wrong, but as she hurried off, I don't think she had it over her shoulder. No, Sergeant Easter, now you mention it, she definitely didn't.'

Joseph's mind began to buzz. 'Tyler, you said you now wonder if someone else might have been there that night. What made you think that?'

'It's hard to explain, Sergeant. It's just that when you know a place and are really familiar with it like I am, you kind of recognise subtle differences. Even after she'd driven away, I still had a feeling that I wasn't alone there. It could have been my senses fooling me, but I thought I could smell a hint of cigarette smoke. I never smoke, never have, and to a non-smoker that smell is quite distinctive.'

'But you didn't see anyone?'

Tyler shook his head. 'No, sorry. It was just a feeling, but what with Bethany's unease and the smell of cigarette smoke, I'm still pretty certain there was someone else on the marsh that night.'

So am I, thought Joseph. *Someone who probably killed Bethany Lyons the very next day.* Time to tell this man the truth about DI Oliver. He gave him a brief outline of what had been happening and watched the colour drain from Tyler's face.

'Not a police detective? He was lying about everything?' Tyler said, aghast. The shock on his face could not have been feigned.

'If it makes you feel any better, he's been fooling people for years. He's very, very good at it,' Joseph said kindly.

'But to what end?' exclaimed Tyler.

'We wish we knew,' said Ben grimly. 'He's dragging the police through the mud all right, we just hope it's nothing more sinister.'

At that point Simon Morton came back into the room and spoke quietly to his son. While they talked, Joseph said to Ben, 'From what we've just been told, it's my opinion that Bethany left the reserve because she was frightened of something and ran off, leaving her precious camera behind. I think she went back for it the next morning and someone was waiting for her.'

Ben nodded slowly. 'We need to check out this Saltmere place, don't we?'

'We certainly do,' said Joseph. 'Immediately.'

'With him?' Ben nodded towards Tyler.

'Who better? It'll save us a whole lot of time, and time's at a premium, what with Oliver's ultimatum. You ring for a crew to meet us there, we'll go direct, hopefully with a guide.'

As soon as Simon had left the room again, Joseph asked Tyler for his help.

Tyler stood up. 'I'll just go and tell Dad and then get my boots on.'

* * *

Yvonne went to tell Nikki that the teacher who had first flagged up Ruby Grayson's issues had left for work that morning but had never arrived. The news almost floored her.

Outwardly calm, Nikki was screaming inside. It wasn't fair, it really wasn't. Having to cope with the shit Oliver was throwing at her was bad enough, and now this. She had been certain that with the death of Daryl Grayson, the whole stalker thing was over.

'I'm concerned that this is still something to do with the Grayson family, although with the stalker son dead and the disturbed daughter being watched round the clock, I cannot think how,' Yvonne said.

Yvonne looked drawn, older than Nikki had ever seen her. Their workload at present was affecting every last one of them, which only served to make Nikki hate Oliver even more.

'I understand your concern, Vonnie,' Nikki said, 'but first we need to rule out all other possibilities. Contact the local hospital, and if you get no joy there, we'll need someone to check all the available cameras along the route she takes from home to school, okay? I assume someone has tried her mobile?'

'Di Barrett did that, and there's no connection at all. That's something else I didn't like the sound of.' Yvonne stood up. 'I'll go and make that call to the hospital, and I'll let you know the outcome.'

'Please do, Vonnie, and I must say, even though we have to do these checks first, I'm with you on suspecting the Graysons.' And like Yvonne, she had no idea who or why. Okay, the teacher had opened a can of worms, but she had meant no harm, quite the opposite, she was only trying to help. Now she had vanished.

Yvonne went out, leaving Nikki thinking about the Graysons. What a perfect family they had seemed! Little had they known. She hadn't yet received the forensic report on Daryl Grayson's DNA, but she was certain it would show that he had inherited the rogue gene. She was also sure that Ruby possessed it, and by the bucketload. As they had expected, Mr Grayson had vetoed any suggestion of Ruby being tested, but there was nothing he could do about Daryl's post-mortem report.

Nikki tried to imagine a mutant gene that took away someone's human kindness. What could their family do? It was a scary thought.

She was certain there'd be no one at the hospital matching the teacher's name or description. Their best hope lay in the traffic cameras and CCTV along Lynette's usual route to work. Then pick up her car and follow it. But where to? Nikki dreaded to think.

CHAPTER TWENTY-FIVE

Saltmere turned out to be an even more miserable place than the pictures Joseph had seen of it. The rather eerie and otherworldly quality it had seemed to possess was nothing of the sort. It was merely grey, the most depressing place Joseph had come across.

'I know what you're thinking,' Tyler said with the hint of a smile. 'But for birdlovers it's a real diamond, though I admit it's set in a necklace of paste. There are rare birds here that can't be seen anywhere else in this county.' He took out his phone and showed Joseph a photograph. 'Spring this year. This was the first time I'd ever seen one for real.'

Joseph looked at a big, long-legged bird with a long, curved beak and streaks of brilliant colour running through its dark chestnut feathers. The colours across its back and wings were almost metallic, with tones of bronze, green and violet.

'It's a glossy ibis, and we have a pair here.'

Joseph felt a nudge in his ribs. Ben whispered, 'That ticking clock?'

Joseph nodded and turned to Tyler. 'Incredible. I'd love to hear more when this is over, but right now . . .'

Tyler put his phone away. 'Sorry, I tend to get a bit overenthusiastic about my birds. What do you want to see?'

Good point, thought Joseph. 'Could you show us exactly where you saw Bethany on the night when you smelled the smoke? And that bird hide that you called the Hidey-hole?'

Snagged by brambles and stung by the tall nettles, they followed Tyler along an overgrown path until they came to an area of murky lagoons. The water looked dark and oily, and Joseph could see slow swirls of movement in it, as if unseen creatures were moving languidly in the depths. It might be a paradise for a bird, but they were welcome to it as far as he was concerned.

'I met her here, close to the river,' said Tyler. 'On this rise of dry land. There's a good view of the estuary, and it's particularly beautiful in moonlight.'

'So where had she come from, and in the dark?' Joseph wondered what the hell she had been thinking of, coming to this godforsaken place at night.

'Over there, at the Hidey-hole.' He pointed to a ramshackle wooden structure on a higher point, a little way away. 'And it's a safe path if you are familiar with it. She had a flashlight, of course, and she knew the place as well as I do, or she would never have come here alone.'

'Forgive me, Tyler, but I cannot imagine *anyone* coming here alone at night. It's madness.' Ben sounded exasperated.

'It's because you're not passionate about birds that you feel like that,' said Tyler. 'We all visit wild places, day and night. Nocturnal birds are wonderful to watch. It's what we do.'

And Bethany made it home safely, thought Joseph, *only to go missing the following day, in full daylight.* Nothing made sense. 'Let's go and take a look at the hide.'

The path here was wider, and much clearer than the one they had arrived by. Joseph began to realise that if she had known the area well, and had a good light, it was perfectly possible for Bethany to get to the Hidey-hole and back fairly safely. He'd trodden far worse ground in the past, but of course he had been a soldier, not a young and vulnerable woman.

Tyler opened the door to the hide and a musty stink hit them.

'It is a bit gross,' he admitted, 'but we've patched it up so at least it doesn't leak, and the viewing flap works. It could be worse, and it does have great views across the wetland, right to the water's edge. I actually saw a bittern from here earlier in the year.'

But Joseph wasn't listening. He had a body to find, and he wasn't getting anywhere.

A sound behind him made him swivel around. The crew of two uniforms had arrived and were making their way towards them. He left Ben with Tyler and went to meet them.

'I'm going to get you guys to liaise with the man talking to Ben. His name is Tyler Morton and he knows this place well. He tells us there are two other bird hides here, both in disrepair. I want you to check them out really carefully, and if you see anything that looks at all suspicious, don't touch it, just call it in. It'll be down to forensics to check it out properly. We're pretty sure that this is where Bethany Lyons came, possibly to look for a camera that she left behind the night before. I'm certain she never left this miserable place.' He looked at the two young constables. 'Ben and I will search this one, although we don't hold out too much hope. The only place a body could be hidden is under the floorboards, and as the bird enthusiasts have been working on it, I doubt we'll find anything much, but we can't afford not to look. Let's go.'

While Tyler took the uniformed officers to the older hides, Ben went back to the car, fetched some tools and began to prise up the floorboards. 'There's nothing under here, it's just empty space. I guess they raised it a bit to keep it off the damp silty soil, otherwise it would rot. The only way we'd discover a grave beneath this stinking shed would be if we dismantled the whole floor and removed it. And we'd need help for that.'

'Then we'll get it,' said Joseph. 'I'm going to ring Nikki and get her to organise a team.' He stared at Ben. 'I am totally convinced that this is where Bethany died, and that her body was concealed here somewhere.'

'But surely the place was thoroughly searched at the time, Sarge?' Ben said.

Joseph shrugged. 'You read the reports, Ben. The overriding belief was that she had engineered her own "disappearance" and simply ran away for some reason. I also got the impression that they concluded that if she had been abducted, whoever did it used this remote spot simply to dump her car and the girl herself hadn't come here at all.'

Ben stared down into the gap between the flooring and the ground beneath. 'You're right. And knowing that Harlen Marsh was responsible for searching this area, they'd have been pretty cursory about it.'

'My thoughts precisely. That is why we're going to rip these hides to pieces if we have to.' Joseph went outside and searched for a spot with a half-decent mobile phone signal.

About five minutes after he made the call, one of the young constables came crashing down the path, calling his name. 'DS Easter! We've found something! Oliver's been here!'

Joseph's heart leaped. Without a word, he and Ben hurried after the retreating uniform.

The hide they came to was a wreck. One wooden wall had rotted and caved in. The four steps that had led to the door still stood, but the door itself lay in the tangle of damp and splintered wood that was the collapsed wall. Remarkably, part of the flooring was still intact.

Joseph took all this in at a glance, while his gaze went straight to the object that told him all he wanted to know: the muddied and grime-caked camera hanging by its leather strap on a rusty hook on one of the three remaining walls.

They were standing over the place where Bethany Lyons had been buried.

* * *

Lynette Sims couldn't remember ever feeling so disorientated. But the nausea that gripped her was nothing compared to her fear. She had no idea what had happened, no recollection of anything since getting into her car and heading for work. Worst of all, she didn't know where she was.

Her head throbbed mercilessly and she fought back the urge to be sick. She had to get herself together and stop panicking. Whispering to herself to get a grip, she began to take deep breaths, the nausea gradually abating and her heart pounding less hard. Time to assess the situation.

She didn't seem to be injured in any way but she suspected she'd been sedated. She knew she was lying on the floor, in a room that was almost dark. It probably had blinds or thick curtains. She also realised very quickly that her wrists and ankles had been bound.

With difficulty, she eased herself up into a sitting position and leaned against the wall. From this position it was easier to make out where she was. The floor she was lying on was carpeted, so she couldn't be in a basement, or a barn somewhere in the back of beyond. It smelled a bit musty, but it was the smell of disuse rather than dirt. As her eyes adjusted to the deep gloom, Lynette made out a narrow single bed, a wardrobe, a drawer unit and a bedside table. Like a monk's cell, it was bare of all ornament. On one wall the barely discernible outlines of two heavily draped windows, and facing these a single door.

A door meant a way out, escape, even though there was zero chance of it being unlocked. Still, she couldn't just sit there and look at it.

She took a deep breath and forced herself to re-evaluate. She peered down at her bonds. Her hands had been secured in an intricate manner that left a kind of short plait of soft rope between each wrist. It enabled a certain amount of restricted movement. Her ankles were tied the same way, firmly secured but with enough leeway to allow her to shuffle if necessary, only this time some kind of leather restraint had been used.

So, she wasn't totally immobile. Rather than stand and edge her way to the door and risk losing her balance and falling on her face, she shifted along on her buttocks.

As she had expected, the door was locked tight, and the whole exercise had been a waste of energy. Next, the windows. If she could just see out it might give her some idea of where she was, and if she knew that, maybe she could fathom out who had done this to her.

Stupid. It didn't really matter, did it? You didn't snatch someone, bind their hands and feet and lock them up out of loving kindness.

Lynette curled herself into a tight ball and wept. It looked like they'd got it wrong. Daryl Grayson might be a thoroughly nasty young man but he wasn't her stalker. Whoever had been watching her had taken it a step further. She didn't dare imagine what he would do next.

* * *

Nikki gazed out over Saltmere and shivered. 'Jesus, what a dreary place!' Sure, the sky was overcast but she had a feeling that even shafts of heavenly sunlight wouldn't lift the depressing atmosphere pervading this corner of the Fen. If that poor girl had indeed been left to moulder here, no wonder she'd never been found.

'Tyler Morton thinks it's a diamond of a place,' said Joseph flatly.

'What is he? Some kind of a moron?' she said.

'Nope, he's a birdlover, and this place is home to rare species, so it's special to him.'

'Well, he's welcome to it. Now, where are we heading?'

'Over to the left, and watch out for the brambles and nettles along the first path. The rest is easier.'

Joseph led her to the ruined bird hide. Uniformed officers stood a little distance away, one holding a reel of striped police cordoning. 'As we suspected, she's beneath what's left of the floor,' Joseph muttered in a voice as sombre as the sky above them. 'Sometimes I hate this job.'

Nikki squeezed his arm. 'I know. But at least we can do what's right by her now, can't we?'

'Yes, of course.' He briefly touched her hand with his. 'The prof's on his way, and I'm pretty sure he won't be as ecstatic about this crime scene location as he was the last one.'

A constable and a SOCO were laying stepping plates around the outside of the hide to stop the spread of further contamination.

'She was buried in a shallow grave towards the back of the hide. The killer then pulled bracken and other greenery over it. It wasn't visible at all from the front or sides, and as most of the back was just an overgrown tangle of bushes, no one ever thought to look any closer.'

Nikki peered inside the cabin and at once saw the mud-caked camera. 'The bastard certainly knows how to create a dramatic effect.' She glanced around. 'No *Par Avion* apparent?'

'Not as yet, and I don't think he did too much excavating at the grave site either. It appears that the killer buried her without disturbing anything, then threw the camera in at the last minute to get rid of the evidence. I think Oliver did a bit of rooting around and dug it up, then just checked to make sure there was a body there. He never actually exposed the remains.' Joseph looked at her. 'We've certainly got in well before his deadline, so maybe he'll back off a bit now he knows we are, in fact, on the ball.'

'I doubt it. He's more likely to increase the pressure. And who killed this poor kid? He hasn't started waving that in front of us yet, has he?' She exhaled. 'I can hardly wait.'

'Ma'am?'

Nikki looked round to see a uniformed officer standing by the newly positioned cordon.

'We thought you should know that the press are already trying to get into the reserve, and there's hordes of them.' He looked anxious. 'My sergeant says to tell you that Oliver is already lashing out big-style at police incompetence.'

It was no more than they'd expected, but it was irritating all the same. It hampered their movements and it was bad for morale. More than anything, it put increasing demands on

269

Cam Walker, who had to keep them at bay and try to swing public opinion away from this psycho and back behind the police.

Nikki thanked him. 'Just keep them out, Constable — and they mustn't be told a thing, okay?' She turned back to Joseph. 'I'm going to ring Cam, though he's probably already aware of what's happening. Then, as soon as Rory arrives, I'm getting back to base. If Oliver is operating at full throttle, I'm expecting to find a *Par Avion* letter on my desk. Or if we are really lucky, a case file.'

'Delivered by some devious and untraceable method, no doubt,' added Joseph grimly. 'It will be another major operation to extract the body — Rory will be well pleased with us.'

Nikki gave Joseph a wry smile. 'Oh, he'll probably dine out on it for months. I can hear him now, regaling his audience with the way we make him work his delicate fingers to the bone, and in the most difficult of situations—'

'Glad you can, dear heart, even though your description of my precious and incredibly talented digits was sadly lacking in creative imagination.'

It was obvious that Rory was grinning broadly beneath his mask. 'Don't creep up on people, Professor — if this case gets any worse, it's likely you'll hear much worse than that.'

'Oh, I know! But it's such fun! By the way, the press and the media really need to be made aware that their presence in busloads is obstructive in the extreme. When time is of the essence, they are a blasted pain in the nether regions.' He glowered over his shoulder. Turning back to Nikki, he said, 'You've certainly chosen an inaccessible location to find your latest corpse in, haven't you? Well, I'm here now, just please don't tell me this stinking hovel is my next excavation site. It is, isn't it?'

'Well, yes. Deeply sorry as we are to admit it, this is it,' said Joseph. 'She's in a shallow grave beneath the floorboards.'

They regarded the ruined hide in silence.

'I'll need some willing assistants, preferably with plenty of muscle. This thing will have to be dismantled. I can't afford for it to collapse into the burial site and destroy what remains there are. Can you sort that for me? I'll get a couple more SOCOs down here too.'

'Already done, Prof,' said Nikki. 'We guessed that's what you'd want. We have a unit all prepared to get this thing down — under your supervision, of course.' But Rory was deep in thought. 'We'll leave you to it, then. Any nasty surprises, ring me.'

'Of course, dear lady. Now, to work. Spike! Cardiff! Centre stage, if you please!'

CHAPTER TWENTY-SIX

While the others were busy at Saltmere, Matt Ballard received a rather important call. 'Hi, Bernie. Have you got something more for me?'

Unlike a lot of Matt's contacts, Bernie Wetherby had a foot in both worlds. The respected owner of a gourmet restaurant, he was just as much at home in the criminal underworld, where he engaged in various shady dealings. He was also a damned good friend.

'Probably the best bit of info you'll get, Matty my boy, and it's hot off the press, so pin back those ears.'

Matt gripped the phone tighter. Bernie's information was always reliable.

'One of my customers happened to mention — in passing, so to speak — the situation you were enquiring about. You know, involving a certain DI.'

'Go on, Bernie.'

'He doesn't know the full story, but he said your DI would do better to look at *women* she'd once crossed swords with, rather than any men.'

A woman? For a moment Matt was lost for words. 'But, Bernie, Oliver can't be a woman! It wouldn't fit at all. All the people Oliver contacted during his unofficial investigations said they'd spoken to a man.'

Bernie gave a little chuckle. 'You misunderstand my meaning, Matty. What my customer said was that your DI should look for another female, possibly a copper, that she'd either gone up against for some reason, or been involved with somehow, and this woman would lead her to Oliver.'

'I get it. This woman, whoever she is, has a champion!'

'Exactly! I'll get no more than that from my man, Matty, so it ends here as far as I'm concerned, but good hunting. Hope it helps.'

He thanked his friend, saying he really owed him one this time, and ended the call.

For a while he sat in silence. It did make sense. All that intensity, all the vitriol and the bitterness, was all for a woman, probably someone he had loved and lost for some reason. And Oliver blamed Nikki Galena for it.

On the other side of the big room, Matt saw Cameron talking to Jim Summers. He stood up and made his way over to them. This was something they really needed to know.

His colleagues stared at each other, amazed.

'Well, I've just heard from Nikki,' said Cam. 'They've found a body out at Saltmere, the place where Bethany Lyons's car was dumped. Oliver had definitely been at the site, he left Bethany's camera on display at the spot where she was buried. She's on her way back here now, and we can ask her.' His face brightened. 'If she can come up with the name of this woman, it might finally lead us to that son of a bitch, Oliver. Well done, Matt! It was a bloody good idea of yours to throw it at our contacts.'

Matt smiled. 'Well, I needed to justify being allowed to participate in a proper police investigation again.' He sighed. 'I have to say, I do miss it.'

Cam, having just spent months away from his own job, said sympathetically, 'We don't stop being coppers when we retire, any more than we do when we go on holiday or take sick leave. Once a copper, always a copper, I'm afraid.' He clapped him on the shoulder. 'Well, I'm glad you're here, and once again, well done.'

Cam went off to wait for Nikki, while Matt and Jim had a coffee.

'It's not going to be easy for our Nikki, is it?' said Jim, as he rifled through his pockets for some change. 'She's got a reputation that takes a bit of beating when it comes to ruffling feathers and telling it like it is.'

'So I've heard,' said Matt, holding out a couple of pound coins. 'But I wonder if it isn't a bit of an urban myth — you know, vastly over-exaggerated.'

'If anything, it got played down. She was a proper virago, believe me!' Jim said. 'At one really low point in her life, a time when her only daughter was hanging on to life by a thread, she almost got thrown out. Even she says that if Joseph Easter hadn't turned up when he did, she'd have been history.'

'Then it's lucky he did,' said Matt. 'Imagine if we'd lost her. Her arrest rate is bloody awesome!'

They strolled back to their desks, both wondering who the woman could be that Nikki had hacked off so badly. Matt hoped she'd rattled fewer women than men, but knowing Nikki Galena she wouldn't have given a shit about their gender. In which case, he sincerely hoped she had a really good memory.

* * *

Nikki was standing in her office staring at the all-too-familiar envelope on her desk when Cameron called to her from the doorway. 'We've got some info for you, Nikki. Come upstairs as soon as you can.'

Saying she would, she picked up the envelope and opened it, for once, not waiting for Joseph to join her.

Detective Inspector Galena,
There is no Part Two. If you want to know more, you'll have to do some work unaided, if you can cope with that. Suffice it to say, if

274

you ever do trace the man that caused her death, you'll never put him on trial. He's dead. Oh, and it wasn't down to me, it was natural causes this time. End of story as far as I'm concerned, and if you have any sense, you'll make it the same for you. You, Detective Inspector, are about to find yourself with one last chance to go down in a blaze of glory. At this point I wish I was talking to you face to face, because I'd like to look into your eyes when I tell you what comes next. Maybe we should talk? I'll have a think about that.

Meanwhile, you are now expecting to move on to Case 0150, Leanne Delaney. Don't bother — unless you feel like it — trawling the streets of Glasgow looking in shelters and shop doorways. If you do, her street name is Red, and she has a cute little mongrel dog with her — it helps to get the passers-by to act more generously. No, forget all that, you have much bigger fish to fry . . . Now, shall I correspond in my usual manner, although I fear it's getting boring, or shall we speak?

I'll get back to you on that.

Oliver

Nikki swallowed hard and tried to assimilate what he had said. "Forget" the last girl, this Leanne — so why had he even mentioned her? *You have much bigger fish to fry.* Hadn't she completed his list of four girls? Apparently, they were just a foretaste.

She picked up the letter and, yelling for Joseph, left her office and headed for the stairs. 'The super has something for us,' she said, as Joseph caught her up. 'And I have this.' She waved the airmail letter. 'I'll let you and Cam read it together, it'll save time.'

Nikki was wondering how much longer she could hack the pressure her unknown adversary was putting on her. It was unrelenting, mentally draining and physically exhausting. She guessed that was the whole point, to wear her down, but to what end? He sounded like he was going to throw one last mammoth task at her. Would she be up to it? Meanwhile, Cam was speaking, and he looked excited.

'Before you show me that nasty little envelope, Nikki, I need you to put everything else aside and concentrate on a new lead that's come our way.' He leaned forward. 'Matt Ballard has picked up some possibly vital information from a contact of his.'

'A snout? Is it a reliable one?' Nikki couldn't quite understand why her relationship with Oliver should be of interest on the streets.

'It's not a snout, Nikki, it's a friend with dubious connections. And yes, he is reliable. If Matt vouches for him, you can be sure of that.'

'And this new avenue?' asked Joseph.

Cam repeated, word for word, what Bernie had told Matt.

'A woman!' Nikki looked as amazed as they had been.

'It appears you had a major falling out, a disagreement or something, with a woman, and someone who cares for her has taken umbrage, to the extent of putting together this god-almighty great production in order to pay you back for whatever happened to her.'

Nikki swore. 'So, all these hours of going over possible candidates for a rogue male officer were wasted. Shit! A woman!'

'It must shorten the list of candidates, surely?' said Joseph hopefully.

Nikki closed her eyes, suddenly struck by a terrible thought. 'So, it *is* all my fault. All this because I probably got into a strop and bollocksed someone out. An incident I can't even recall, but it meant so much to Oliver that he's made it his life's work to make me pay. This is awful! I can't get my head around it.'

'Not quite correct, Nikki,' said Cam gravely. 'One, it's no good assuming anything at this point, while we actually know nothing and, two, even if you did give someone hell, they probably deserved it. It's no bad thing to expect other officers to give a hundred per cent, and if you picked on someone with a pathological partner, that's hardly your fault. I suggest you postpone your guilt trip until we have some facts. Hard as I might sound, I need you at the top of your game, not wallowing in self-pity.'

Cam's uncharacteristically harsh words had the same effect as being doused with ice cold water. It hurt, but it did her good. They needed the old Nikki Galena to bring this man down, not some pathetic loser that even she didn't recognise. She apologised, something she rarely did, and found it quite unnerving.

Apparently, Cam and Joseph did too. Cam raised an eyebrow at Joseph, and said, 'Well, that's a first!'

The moment over, they all smiled. 'Just remember, both of you, this is no star-crossed lover, this is a psychopath we're hunting, and we have only one clue to work on. You *have* to identify a woman, probably another detective, or even a uniformed officer, who Oliver believes you, or a situation that involved you, caused a great deal of distress to. It might not even be a direct confrontation between you and this woman, it could have been something like a promotion where she got overlooked in your favour, we have no idea. It's all up to you now, Nikki. Search your memory for anything that might fit the bill.'

'Understood,' she said. All her previous resolve, along with her intense loathing of Oliver, had returned. 'Now it's your turn to find out what matey-boy is planning next, because I have no idea. I can't make head nor tail of this one, I really can't.' She handed Cam the airmail envelope.

Cam read it carefully and handed it to Joseph. 'You're right, Nikki, it's not clear at all. One thing's for sure, we have to take his next move very seriously indeed, whatever it is. I don't like what he says about going out in a blaze of glory, that indicates something on a grand scale.'

Nikki grunted. 'In the last ten minutes I've interpreted that in several, and all very scary, ways, and not one of them leaves me unscathed.'

'All the more reason to do the one thing that Oliver won't expect, and that is identify him.' Cam tapped his fingers on the desk impatiently. 'We have to find him before he can launch his next twisted scheme.' He sat back. 'Now, while you were at Saltmere, I had a visit from Julia Tennant, the psychologist you spoke to about Ruby Grayson, Nikki. I agree that she's very easy to talk to, and she seems like a very clever woman indeed. I've given her all we have on Oliver and left it with her to mull over. I have to say that I didn't like the expression on her face at all. It was pretty dark. Anyway, she's ringing me later today, and I'll pass on anything useful she says to you both. Now, off you go to delve into your memory, Nikki Galena, and find the woman behind it all.'

* * *

Rory was feeling unaccountably low. He surveyed the marshy land, the pools of dark, brackish water and the grey sky, and decided that it was the location that was bringing him down. That, and the fact that he had to wait for the old hide to be dismantled before he could exhume the poor girl.

Finally, he and Spike were unwinding the remains of her clothing. Rory noted a padded anorak, a wool jumper in a faded yellow colour, and black stretch jeans. All matched the description given by Bethany Lyons's neighbour, who had seen her drive away from her home. The camera found in the hut was most definitely hers, having been identified by a man named Tyler Morton, another birdwatcher who knew Bethany slightly. Apparently, Morton had spoken to her on several occasions and had led Nikki and Joseph to this miserable place. Rory had been curious about this man, and asked one of the uniformed officers if Morton was still on site. A few moments later the officer returned with a sombre-faced man in tow.

'Mr Morton?'

Tyler Morton nodded and moved closer to the tape. 'Yes. Can I help?'

Rory introduced himself and found his usual enthusiasm returning. 'So, did the young lady who disappeared come here a lot? I mean, it's quite a dismal spot, isn't it? There are far more beautiful places in this area to watch birds in.'

The man, clearly happy to find any excuse for talking about his great passion, started to explain in great detail what drew true wildlife lovers to Saltmere. After a while Rory began to regret having asked, so he quickly threw in another question. 'How many people would you say came here regularly at the time of her disappearance?'

Tyler Morton screwed up his face. 'Not very many. Maybe half a dozen regulars, and the odd visitor who found Saltmere by accident. Most people don't stop. They want more these days — good usable hides, sometimes even a visitors' centre.'

'Was Bethany friendly with anyone in particular?' asked Rory.

'Sorry, but I didn't know her well. I didn't even know her name, and I only saw her a few times, so I really couldn't say. All I can tell you is that when I did see her, she was always alone.'

Rory considered this. He didn't like the idea of a young woman coming alone to a place like this, and sometimes at night. 'Mr Morton, you mentioned some regulars — did any of them come here after dark, like night naturalists?'

Again, Morton stopped to think. 'Only one that I knew of. Bit of a loner, a much older man. I think his name was Ron something. Yes, Ron Chivers! That's it. A really committed bird man, and quite zealous about keeping this place from becoming known to too many visitors. He said it was best for the birds, that their nesting grounds ought not to be disturbed, so we should leave the place as it is.'

'Does he still come here? Especially at night?'

Morton gave a little grunt. 'Not unless he haunts the place. He died of a heart attack about two years back. Now I come to think of it, I never actually saw him here after that girl disappeared. Funny, really, he was a real regular, knew all the birds and their haunts and the best spots to view them from. It was only after he stopped coming that I dared to patch up the Hidey-hole so we could use it without the fear of it collapsing on top of us.'

Rory thanked him and returned to where Spike and Cardiff were silently removing soil from around the woman's corpse. He moved away, and rang Nikki Galena.

'A little bit of advice, dear friend, to check out a dead man. A certain Mr Ron Chivers, last seen out here in the Slough of Despond at around the time Bethany went missing. He had been a regular visitor, but after she vanished suddenly stopped coming and never returned. I know it's not the most important thing on your mind at present, but it's my belief that the killer was a local who knew exactly the best spot to bury our body where it wouldn't be discovered. He also believed they should keep other birdwatchers away — and here's the good bit, Nikki — he didn't want anyone to renovate the hides. Now I'd say he needs a little posthumous investigation, wouldn't you?'

Nikki thanked him. 'Oliver stated that the killer is dead, so I think you're spot on. I'll get some officers to follow it up, then maybe, after we have all your findings from the post-mortem, we can draw a line under this one too.'

'Well, I assure you there'll be no delay at this end, the sooner I'm away from this dreary place, the happier I'll be. So, *au revoir*! Rory has to crack on.' He rolled up his sleeves and crouched down beside his assistants. Three pairs of hands would be better than two.

* * *

When any of the team wanted to escape the hubbub of the police station, they sometimes went down to the basement. Years ago, they'd been forced to vacate the CID room due to some urgent repair work, and had allocated themselves an old storeroom to work from. Cat had turned scavenger and kitted it out with a few home comforts, including a sofa and a potted plant, and they grew rather fond of the place, which became known as "Galena's Grotto."

Nikki and Joseph sat opposite each other across a desk, a packet of biscuits between them, and went through all the old cases she had worked on, the old disputes she'd been involved in, people she'd competed with for promotion.

It went on for over an hour, with Joseph making the occasional note of anything that needed following up.

Taking her third biscuit from the packet, Nikki said, 'It's rather depressing to think of the number of times I went head-to-head with people back then, and not so far back either, if the truth be told. I must have been a total nightmare to work with.'

Joseph grimaced. 'No comment.'

Nikki laughed softly. 'I gave you a hard time too, didn't I?'

'Well, I can't deny you were less than warm and fluffy, but that doesn't take away from the fact that you were a good copper. It was always the desire to make things right that drove you, and still does, you just no longer go for the jugular when you run up against a wrongdoer.' He paused. 'Unless it's needed, and I guess Oliver is going to encounter that side of you when we get him.'

'You can bank on that,' growled Nikki. 'With knobs on!'

They continued their discussion.

'Who would you call your real bête noire among the women coppers you've met? Someone you just could not relate to on any level?' asked Joseph.

'How long have you got?' said Nikki miserably. 'At one time, I couldn't even relate to myself.' She frowned, then her eyes widened. 'Adele Jacoby. We were both DCs, at the same station but in different teams. Talk about a clash of personalities, I swear there were times when we nearly got physical. They moved her to Fenfleet in the end.'

'Do you think she holds a grudge? Or might someone she's close to think he's doing her a favour by taking on her old duelling partner?'

Nikki shook her head. 'No. She's a DI now, up county, happily married to another detective from a neighbouring division, a woman called Fiona. I've spoken to her since those days, and we're both different people now. She's got herself a great record since transferring out, and a good team under her — I could almost admire her. When we spoke, I got the impression she felt as I did, that we'd both grown up and moved on.'

'Anyone else?'

'There was another detective, a bit younger than me, who was pretty envious of my position. I can't even recall her full name, but her surname was Jones, I do remember that. She was really spiteful — the toadying type, you know? A right brown-nose and happy of any opportunity to drop me in the mire. Which she did, on many occasions. I bloody hated her!'

'The sort to hold a grudge,' suggested Joseph.

'Probably, but I can't see Oliver wanting to take up her cause. He's too intelligent, too bloody clever. For a start, she wasn't at all likeable. It wasn't just me either, she had very few friends and I never recall hearing about a boyfriend. Oliver must have really admired someone to take his campaign this far, and that just wouldn't happen with DC Jones.'

After another half an hour, Joseph looked up from his notes. 'There are a few possibilities here. Maybe I should go upstairs to my computer and get searching for more details?'

Nikki was deep in thought. 'I can't help but think that while we've been digging up my past, somewhere along the line we touched on something that should have rung bells.'

'But it didn't.'

'No, but something should.' She bit hard on her bottom lip, trying to recall what case or person they had been discussing. Nothing materialised. 'Shit! That is so annoying!'

Joseph agreed. 'But you know what they say, try to put it out of your mind and then it'll come to you.'

'Easier said than done. Oh hell, Joseph, whatever this is, I'm sure it's relevant.'

'Would another coffee help? I'll go get one and bring it back down. You stay here and try to go over what we've discussed.' Joseph stood up. 'Maybe a few moments on your own might allow you to clear your mind a bit.'

She thanked him. 'It's worth a try, and I wouldn't mind another coffee anyway.'

After he'd gone, Nikki sat with her eyes closed tightly, going over every case and every name they had considered.

* * *

When Joseph arrived back in the CID room, he was practically jumped on by Cat and Ben.

'Sarge, we didn't like to interrupt, but the boss needs to know that Lynette's car was picked up on CCTV, and then seen, parked and empty, in a lay-by just 500 metres from the school. Someone recalls seeing her talking to a tall man through the window of her car, then she got out, locked the car, and hurried after him in the direction of the recreation ground on Laurel Drive. That's the last time anyone saw her. We believe he's abducted her.'

Joseph cursed silently. He needed to keep Nikki focused entirely on Oliver, and not get distracted by separate incidents. 'Go and tell the super. He knows Nikki's pretty involved with something else at present. He'll make sure this is dealt with in the proper manner.'

'Has Nikki come up with any suggestions for Oliver's ID yet?' asked Ben hopefully.

'Not as such, but something has touched a nerve somewhere, and she's trying to fathom out what the hell it is.' He looked at them both, 'She's pretty sure we discussed something that should have set off alarm bells. I'm getting her a strong coffee, and I'll keep you posted.'

He bought her a chocolate bar too, and went back down to the Grotto, where Nikki was pacing to and fro.

'Joseph! I think I've got it! It could be a complete crock of shit, but things are starting to make sense. I think I know who Oliver is!'

He put the drinks down, spilling some, and stared at her. 'Tell me!'

'Sit down, please, and I'll explain.' She flopped into her chair, and picked up her beaker of coffee, clasping it in both hands and staring into it as if into a crystal ball. 'Remember we talked about a messy case where tempers ran high, and there were several fallings out among the officers, with me at the heart of one or two of the disagreements?'

'The missing boy, who was found to have been drowned?' Joseph queried.

'That's the one. But this is the thing. It wasn't the actual case, but something else that was going on at the time, and it involved a DC called Sharon Kelly. Lots of the guys called her Shaz. She was drop-dead gorgeous, Joseph, and one of the most likeable women you could hope to meet.'

'Even by you?'

'Yeah, even me. In fact, we were practically best friends. We talked a lot, and unlike most, Shaz actually valued my opinions. Anyway, she was going out with a detective from over Louth way. To start with, she was pretty enamoured. He was very smart.'

'Brain or wardrobe?' Joseph asked, trying to get a picture of the man who might turn out to be Oliver.

'Both, as it happens, but I'm talking intelligence. He was sharp as a razor. And he fell hook, line and sinker for DC Sharon Kelly. After a couple of months going out together, he proposed.' Nikki pulled a face. 'But Shaz wasn't ready for that, nor was she prepared to start juggling her career with a marriage, so she backed off.'

'Ah, and this detective didn't take it well.' Joseph had seen this kind of thing before. Some men were not good with rejection and simply couldn't accept it.

Nikki puffed out her cheeks. 'Didn't take it well is an understatement! In the end, Shaz told me she'd become scared of him. Apparently, he was talking all kinds of rubbish — couldn't live without her and he'd be better off killing himself, or her, or better still, killing them both. Shaz was in pieces.'

Something, he wasn't sure what, told Joseph that she had correctly identified Oliver. But what could possibly have happened for him to feel so hostile towards her?

'One day I had a visit from this man. Sounding perfectly reasonable, calm and collected, he tried and tried to make me take his side. He even asked me to advise Sharon to stay with him, said that he truly loved her and would care for her. Hell, Joseph, by the time he'd finished I could almost hear the words "Until death us do part."'

'I dread to think what you said to him!'

'Actually, I was thinking of Sharon, and how, if she wasn't mistaken about him, shooting him down in flames, as I was tempted to do, would only make things worse for her.' Nikki sighed. 'He was obviously obsessed with her. So, I told him that it might be better if he just cooled off a bit and let Sharon have some space. Receiving a proposal was a big thing, women needed time to think it over, especially those with career prospects and a job they loved.'

Joseph was surprised at Nikki's tact, given that it hadn't been evident at other times in her stormy past. 'And how did he take that?'

'Badly, even though he endeavoured to cover it up. He said he'd hoped that as Sharon's friend, I'd help him persuade her to see sense. I tried reasoning with him, even though all I wanted to do was chop him up and feed him to the fishes, but he just walked out and I never saw him again.'

Joseph thought about it. 'That's not nearly enough for a vendetta on this scale, Nikki. What happened after that?'

Nikki looked perplexed. 'This next bit is odd, because I was certain he couldn't know about it. Anyway, Sharon told me she needed to get well away from him. She talked about going to Australia, that's how frightened she was. She knew that there was no lateral transfer agreement between the UK and Australian police services — sadly "police officer" doesn't qualify you for an immigrant visa. However, before entering the force, she had trained as a social worker, which was on the list of preferred occupations.' Nikki took a gulp of her coffee. 'Her plan was to get a sponsor and emigrate, work for as long as it took, then apply for the police as an Australian citizen.' She looked up at Joseph with a pained expression. 'I got her the sponsor, a distant cousin of mine whose wife worked for social services, but we made sure never to speak to anyone else about it, so how her rejected lover found out that I was involved in getting her away, I have no idea.'

'Maybe he didn't, Nikki. Perhaps he just thought you encouraged her. The idea could have built up in his mind and got out of control, until he decided you were entirely to blame.'

'Mmm. Maybe.'

But Joseph read her expression. 'This doesn't have a good ending, does it?'

'The worst. And I've never got over my guilt at having helped her, however irrational it may be.' She stared down into her soothsaying coffee mug. 'Oliver, whose real name I suspect to be ex-DC David Pelham, went right off the rails. He had a glowing career ahead of him, prospects most people would have given their eye teeth for. His commanding officer believed he was one of the most astute and perceptive detectives that he'd ever come across, and David blew it all.

'When he learned that Sharon had left the country, though he had no idea where she'd gone, it affected him so badly that he screwed up a case, and another officer was seriously injured as a consequence. He handed in his warrant card and left the force.'

'He lost everything, then.' Joseph exhaled loudly.

'More than you think.' Nikki sounded about as sombre as he had ever heard her. 'All went well for Sharon, she settled in and enjoyed her new job, though she couldn't wait to get back into the police. She took a holiday and went backpacking with two new friends. In short, there was a freak accident, Sharon got hit by a piece of metal that somehow sheared off a massive truck and trailer that was passing them as they crossed a bridge way out in the middle of nowhere. It practically decapitated her and she died instantly.'

Joseph hardly knew what to say.

'I know,' said Nikki. 'Floors you, doesn't it? It took me months to even talk about it. She was such a beautiful woman, Joseph, it was a terrible waste. For ages I kept asking myself if she'd still be alive if I hadn't got her that sponsor.'

'You know the answer to that, Nikki,' said Joseph softly. 'If that man hadn't made her life hell, she'd probably be here now, with a fantastic career under her belt. If it hadn't been for David Pelham and his obsession with her, she would have had no need to run away at all.'

'I often wondered about Pelham, and how he took the news. It was all over the local papers, and even on the TV, so he couldn't have missed it. I mean, if I felt bad, how the hell did he feel?'

'Whatever he felt, it had nothing to do with personal guilt, even though he was solely responsible. He looked for someone else to blame, and you fitted the bill nicely. My God, Nikki! You've got this! You've identified Oliver. Even the airmail envelopes make a kind of sense now. He's reminding you that you helped get her away to another country. We have to take this to Cam!'

Nikki stayed where she was. 'I should have thought of this long before now.'

'Why? We were looking for rogue officers, and both Sharon and Pelham were exemplary by the sound of it. We assumed it was someone you argued with, or you got into trouble, or plain disliked, but Sharon was your friend. Why would you even think of her? And David Pelham never threatened you, did he? Not then. You said yourself you tried to be understanding with him, and you simply never saw him again. It's a miracle you chanced on it at all.' He smiled gently at her. 'But we really do have to go and find Cam. He needs to put out an attention drawn to David Pelham, aka Detective Oliver.'

CHAPTER TWENTY-SEVEN

Nikki and Joseph hurried up the stairs and into the CID room. Even before the door closed behind them, Nikki was calling to the team. 'Okay! Heads up, everyone!'

Phone calls were put on hold, keyboards fell silent and all looked at Nikki. 'There's been a development. Would you all please make your way immediately to the MI room for an update.' With that, she turned on her heel.

The "Big Three," as Nikki liked to think of them, were all together in Cam's office.

'Nikki Galena!' Cam said on seeing her face. 'You've done it, haven't you?'

'We're almost certain, Cam, but we have to make absolutely sure of it before we go too far. Hear me out, and if you feel the same as we do, take action as soon as you consider it appropriate.' Meaning, of course, *as fast as you bloody well can.*

The Big Three, along with Nikki and Joseph, went up to the MI room, where Cam called on everyone to listen up. An expectant hush fell over the room.

Nikki, with Joseph's help, gave them a shortened version of the story of Sharon and David. Relating it like this served to confirm her belief that she'd drawn the right conclusion. Oliver was David Pelham. He just had to be.

As she drew to a close, she noticed a lone figure standing at the very back of the room, listening intently. It was the new force psychologist. The smile Julia Tennant gave her was grave and full of sympathy. Nikki determined to talk to her at the earliest opportunity.

Cam took her place in front of the whiteboards. 'Okay, everyone, we're going to run with this. In a moment, I'll be allocating the tasks, but first there's something you need to be aware of.' He looked around the room. 'As you all know, we have a missing young woman, who happens to be a teacher at the school attended by the two Grayson girls. We cannot rule out some sort of involvement on the part of that family, but open minds are required for this one. Now, I know it doesn't solve all our problems, but we now know for sure that Daryl Grayson was the stalker, and that he did follow our teacher, Lynette Sims, but as he was dead when she was abducted, it certainly couldn't have been him. Forensics have confirmed his guilt from prints left at several of the sites he was known to have visited, including Lynette's, all a match for the boots he was wearing when he was murdered. Also, pollen traces on his car correspond exactly to that found in the gardens of at least two of the victims. Next, his trademark giggle, something the women victims found horribly unnerving, has been confirmed as a habit of his. His work colleagues have testified to this, and one man even had a recording of it on his phone. Finally, and this is of some importance, it has been suggested that Daryl might have possessed a mutant gene, a hereditary condition that affected his behaviour. This is not the case. There was no rogue gene in his DNA — Daryl Grayson was simply a dangerous deviant bearing all the hallmarks of a rapist, and possibly a killer.'

The officers began to mutter among themselves, some whose words were audible expressed relief that the filthy bastard was dead.

Cam raised a hand. 'Just remember, it wasn't Daryl who abducted Lynette, so save your loathing for whoever has taken that poor woman. Daryl was murdered, and we have to investigate that as we would any other unlawful act. But right now, we have two priorities — finding Lynette Sims and David Pelham.'

While Nikki, along with the other senior officers, discussed how best to allocate their men and women, she kept an eye on Julia Tennant, in case she left before she had a chance to talk to her.

She needn't have worried, the psychologist was just as keen to talk to her, so at the end of the meeting, Julia Tennant went up to her. 'DI Galena, there's something I thought you should know, considering it was you who suggested that the Grayson family, through the Tate side, might be suffering from a hereditary condition.'

'Well, that got blown out of the water, didn't it?' said Nikki apologetically.

'Not at all. That's what I wanted to tell you. I went to the Grayson house earlier, in a last-ditch attempt to get them to allow Ruby to be tested, and to my surprise, Mr Grayson agreed. He said he'd been going to contact me anyway to sanction the test.' Julia shook her head. 'People do have the capacity to shock even me. It's quite refreshing, stops us getting complacent.'

Nikki found something very likeable about this woman. Apart from her looks, which resembled those of a beautiful Oscar-winning actress in her later years, she had a commanding presence, which was very reassuring.

'I will of course let you know the result as soon as it comes back, but I'm confident it will be positive. Daryl, being male, was unlikely to have inherited it anyway, but I suspect, from observing her behaviour and her responses to certain questions, that our Ruby is one of the unlucky recipients of that mutant gene.'

'I wonder what made him change his mind?' said Nikki. 'He was so adamant that he didn't want it done.'

'I'm sure it will be made clear before long.' Julia looked at her encouragingly. 'Now, what did you want to ask me? It was written all over your face when you saw me back there.'

'Ah, yes. How about you come down to my office where it's a bit quieter?'

'Lead on, please.' Julia looked about her. 'I'm not yet acquainted with the layout of this particular station, only having been here a couple of times.'

Nikki beckoned to Joseph. 'Come with us, would you? I need a few words with Julia and I'd like you there. Maybe you could organise Zena to get us some refreshments?'

When they were seated, Nikki explained what was worrying her. 'I'm fairly certain that David Pelham *is* Oliver, but what if I'm wrong? What if we find David and accuse him of waging this terrible vendetta and he has nothing to do with it? How would it affect him, knowing his history?'

Julia looked at her shrewdly. 'Superintendent Walker gave me the story, and I listened carefully to what you told the meeting just now, and in my opinion it fits seamlessly with Oliver's scheme. Don't waste your energy worrying whether you are right or not. It is my belief that David Pelham is an obsessive who became deranged upon the loss of the object of his desire. He has completely exonerated himself of all blame, and needing someone to hold accountable, he's transferred it to the police, personified by you, as his lost love's best friend. Don't forget that he is also dealing with another grievous loss, that of his career, which could have been stellar. He never even considered the fact that the loss of both the things that gave his life meaning was entirely down to his obsessiveness and his controlling nature.'

Zena appeared with a tray of drinks and offered them around. When she'd left, Julia continued. 'You can see, I'm sure, that he is using his skill as a detective — which was never in doubt — to show you all just what you lost when he left the force.'

Joseph looked at Nikki and nodded. 'That sounds spot on, doesn't it?'

She agreed, though her apprehension didn't leave her entirely. A small voice at the back of her mind whispered that they weren't infallible. She couldn't bear to send an already damaged soul over the edge.

Stirring sugar into her coffee, Julia mused, 'I'd be interested to know why he called himself Oliver. There's always a reason.'

That was it! Nikki smiled broadly at Julia. 'Thank you! You've just dispelled all my doubts about Oliver's identity. He calls himself Oliver because that was the name of Sharon's beloved dog! It was an old Labrador that died not long before she left. She always called it Ollie, and she adored it. Apparently, David had expressed his jealousy of Oliver because she loved the dog more than him.'

'Then, my dear, I suggest you tell your superintendent to look no further for a suspect,' said Julia. 'You know your man, now you just have to find him.'

* * *

It took the terrified Lynette some time to get over the initial shock of what had happened to her. Having got herself over to the bed, she sat on it and tried to think of something she could do to help herself. Now that she was calmer, her biggest concern was her mother. They had always been close, and Tessa would be out of her mind with worry. If only for her mother's sake, Lynette had to get away from this place, wherever it was. Okay, first step. She would try and see if there was any possible means of escape.

It wasn't easy finding anything in this intense gloom. She had already discovered that beneath the heavy drapes, which had been tightly sewn together, there was another sheet of material tacked and stapled firmly to the wooden window frame, and which was impossible to remove with her hands tied. She had even tried tugging at the drapes to bring them down, but the fittings were strong and defied all her attempts. At least, even though there was no natural daylight, the window's faint grey light meant she could make out what was around her.

Still on her buttocks, Lynette shuffled around the room, checking everything she came across. The chest of drawers had two low flat baskets on top of it which, on closer inspection, turned out to be two packed lunches. The first consisted of three little packets of biscuits like the ones left for guests in hotels, a single pack of sandwiches, a packet of crisps, a banana, some red grapes and a bar of chocolate. The second basket contained an identical meal. Along the back, and close to the wall, she found a row of bottles of still water and two small bottles of orange juice. 'Look on the bright side, Lynette,' she whispered to herself. 'At least I'm not going to starve.' Although if this was two days' rations, she'd have to eke it out very carefully. She continued her investigation, making one further discovery, tucked into a corner with a dust sheet thrown over it.

She stared at the portable camping toilet with some relief.

Lynette shuffled back to the bed and sat down again. From what she had found, she guessed her captor wouldn't be back for at least forty-eight hours, or why leave the food?

She stared at her tied wrists, suddenly very angry. She refused to sit here and wallow in self-pity. She was going to get her hands free, rip off that window covering, put something heavy through the glass and get out!

* * *

Hearing the doorbell ring, Eve glanced out of an upstairs window and saw Chris Tate's big four-by-four parked outside. She called down to Wendy that Chris was here. At the bottom of the stairs, her friend met her with a look of mock horror.

Eve was concerned that her decision to tell Nikki about the Tate family secret had been a big mistake. The thought that she and Wendy might have set their next-door neighbour against them filled her with dismay. Nikki had promised that it wouldn't come back on her, but you could never be really sure.

When she opened the door to him, Chris looked kind of strange. He simply said, 'May I come in?'

'Of course.' Eve held the door open for him. 'Come into the kitchen.' She led the way through with a sinking heart and offered him a seat at the table. She and Wendy sat down facing him.

'I'm not sure where to start,' he said, staring down at the table. 'It's all a bit overpowering, really.'

Eve sneaked a look at Wendy, who was managing to keep a neutral expression. She was tempted to prompt him and get it over with, but for once in her life she held back.

'Well, ladies, the crux of the matter is this: I need to give you both a big thank you.' Like a sun rising, his face broke into a smile. 'Today has been something of a milestone in our family, and like I said, I'm finding it all a bit overwhelming, but I wanted to come and tell you about it.'

'I reckon it's time to put the kettle on,' said Wendy, getting up and heading for the sink. 'Tea or coffee? Or something stronger?'

They settled for tea, and while Wendy made it, Chris explained the reason for his visit. 'I think your discovery of those old relics belonging to Thomas Tate was a kind of sign that things were about to change. And change they have. What you said about it has been haunting me. Last night, I lay awake practically till dawn. Like a modern-day Scrooge, I was visited by the ghosts of my ancestors, and was shown the past, the present and the future.' He grimaced. 'And I didn't like how I felt about that future. I realised that I'd been locked in the mindset of people from a past era, and it was time for the Tates to put aside our ridiculous belief that we have to cover up past sins. For heaven's sake, they're not our sins, are they? We're just paying for them. Anyway, early this morning, I rang my brothers, my sister and our other relatives, and we have all agreed — especially as one member of our family seems to be seriously affected at present — that we should admit to having a problem and make sure everyone gets tested rather than wait for the hammer to fall, and get help where necessary. We are dragging the Tates out of the shadows of the past and moving them into the twenty-first century at last.'

Eve could have cheered. 'That is so good to hear, Chris. I can't tell you how worried we've been for you and your family.'

The farmer gave a merry laugh. 'I feel like a massive weight has been lifted from my shoulders. It's as if we were a family of outcasts, and now we are free. People will understand, won't they?'

'Oh yes,' Wendy assured him. 'And those that don't want to aren't important anyway. Oh, I'm so delighted you've had the courage to put a stop to all that secrecy. Now the Tate women who are unfortunate enough to have inherited that gene will have a chance of obtaining good treatment and hopefully a better life.'

Chris said he should get back to the farm. He thanked them again. 'And your friend, what's his name, Jacob? Well, you can tell him that if he wants to add to his website, he's welcome, so long as he does it sympathetically.'

Eve thought about that. 'Do you know, I think he'll probably leave it as it is. It's up to you to decide how and when you want the world to know. There are plenty of other mysteries out there for young Jacob Rush to investigate. I think it's time for him to move on to them, and leave Tommy Tate and all his nasty secrets right where he is, buried in our garden!'

* * *

As evening approached, a strong wind began to blow in from the North Sea. Cold and unrelenting, it tore across the flatlands, whipping the few trees and scattering everything in its path. It seemed to Nikki like a manifestation of the frenetic, highly charged atmosphere that ran through the police station.

Knowing Oliver's real name had given them direction. They, and every other police force in the county, and even beyond, were on the alert for a sighting of David Pelham, onetime ace detective constable in the Fenland Constabulary.

At the same time uniformed officers poured out on to the streets carrying photographs of Lynette Sims and started knocking on doors in and around the area where she had last been seen. Cam had already booked a slot on local TV and put out a plea to the public for their help in finding this popular and dedicated teacher who appeared to have been snatched just metres from her school.

The CID room was redolent with the smell of pizza and chicken nuggets as detectives and civilians alike worked round the clock, making and fielding phone calls and scrutinising the internet and the police databases, in order to follow every possible avenue that might lead to the whereabouts of either David Pelham or Lynette Sims.

At around nine o'clock, Nikki escaped to the relative calm of her office to grab a few minutes alone. Speaking to Julia Tennant had been a turning point in the way she perceived this horrible case. None of it was down to her at all, they were dealing — once again — with a disturbed mind. A man who was so far off the rails that he had lost sight of reality. A tiny part of her felt almost sorry for him.

Nikki sat at her desk and held her head in her hands, remembering the time when Sharon had started going out with David.

They had seemed the ideal couple — attractive, compatible, happy together. Each had the prospect of a fine career ahead of them, especially David. Sharon had confessed that he possessed a rare quality. 'It's really hard to describe, Nikki. It's a kind of clarity of thought that gives him the edge over everyone else in an investigation. He could go right to the top if he wanted to, though he prefers the thrill of the chase to mingling with the gold braid. I think he'll call a halt at superintendent.' She had laughed. 'And I'll still be a humble detective constable!'

How wrong her friend had been. Sharon ended her short life as a civilian social worker, and David? Who knew where he'd ended up, but it wasn't going to be as a superintendent.

Nikki was sure that they'd genuinely loved each other, but Sharon had needed time. She wanted their relationship to develop slowly into a real commitment that would allow them both to continue with the jobs that were so important to them. If David could only have controlled his intense emotions and been patient, it might have worked.

Under the relentless pressure of David's demands, Sharon's love began to wane, while David's grew stronger as he grew ever more desperate to hold on to her. It took months for this to become apparent, but as the chasm between them widened, it became clear to everyone but David that the relationship was a lost cause.

And the rest, as they say, is history. Now David Pelham was back in the CID room, not as a respected police officer but as a picture on a whiteboard.

* * *

Nikki and Joseph arrived home shortly after midnight. Joseph was exhausted, mentally rather than physically. Initially, the excitement of discovering who Oliver was had set them all off on a high. Now the adrenalin had worn off, and he felt wrung out. For once, they had driven to Cloud Fen together, as the night had been so wild. Everywhere there were branches down, and in one place an old horse chestnut had toppled over completely, landing across the road and blocking it. At least Cloud Cottage Farm was undamaged, and by the time they were ready to turn in, the wind was beginning to drop, much to Joseph's relief. Weather like this did nothing to help when they were hunting for a missing person.

They had just locked up and were about to go upstairs when Nikki's phone rang.

'What now? I'm out on my feet.'

While she listened to the caller, Joseph watched her expression change. 'Send it to my private email address, right now, please.' She ended the call. 'He's contacted us again. One of the detectives on the night shift has scanned it and is sending it to me.'

They put the lights back on and went into the dining room where Nikki's laptop sat on the table. She switched it on. 'It seems it was delivered via a crew that were out canvassing near the school. This motorcyclist drew up level with a uniformed constable, thrust an envelope at him and said, "Get this to DI Galena!" then roared off.'

A few moments later they were staring at the letter.

There were no preliminaries.

This is the last time you will hear from me. No clues, no suggestions. This one is your case to solve, so let's see how you detectives deal with The Last Missing Person.

Case No 0151 Lynette Sims. Went missing on her way to work at Ferndale School, Greenborough.

The difference with this one is that you are on a time limit. You have thirty-six hours to find her alive. The clock will start at six am. After that, if you do find her, she will be dead. Like so many other beautiful women. All failed by you. Unless you all want to live with nightmares for the rest of your lives, don't fail Lynette.

'No signature,' breathed Joseph, 'and he doesn't single you out this time, Nikki. I think you've served your purpose, and now he's finished with sending letters, you're no use to him anymore.'

'But he's got Lynette Sims! Oh my God! I don't get it! Why her?' Nikki looked pale.

Joseph had no idea, but he did think he now understood why Daryl Grayson had been murdered. 'Consider this, Nikki. We don't yet know why Oliver picked Lynette, but if she was special to his plan and he saw that little pervert Daryl watching her . . . Catch my drift?'

'Yes, perfectly. Daryl had to go in case he messed up whatever Oliver had in mind.' Nikki nodded slowly. 'And we're no longer looking at two separate searches — find one, we should find the other. Lynette is now our only priority, and as we know he has her, we concentrate on finding Oliver and his lair.' She picked up her phone. 'Cam needs to know.'

'And then we grab a few hours' rest before the clock starts. Thirty-six hours isn't long, but it'll be a damned sight longer if we get no sleep beforehand.' To his surprise, Nikki didn't argue. She passed the message on to Cam, closed her phone and put the light out again.

'We get up at five. We go in to work, and are fully functioning by six. Agreed?'

Joseph followed her up the stairs. 'I'll set the alarm.'

CHAPTER TWENTY-EIGHT

Like the rest of Nikki's team, Yvonne Collins had received the alert about the thirty-six-hour deadline issued by Oliver. She now knew his name was David Pelham, but they had lived with Oliver for so long it had stuck in her head. Even when they charged him and locked him up, as she firmly believed they would, he would still be Oliver to her and those who had hunted for him.

The text had simply asked her to present herself as early as she was able, so at five thirty, with a large mug of builder's tea and two slices of toast under her belt, she sent a message to her next-door neighbour, Ray, asking him to please look after her precious dog for as long as it took. Both pet and neighbour were used to this convenient arrangement and enjoyed it to the full, Ray delighted to have the company and her rescue boy, Hobo, relishing the extra treats his temporary dad always provided.

At precisely six o'clock, Yvonne marched into the CID room.

Nikki gave her a quick smile of appreciation, which she extended to Cat and Ben, who must have followed her up the stairs. Yvonne, too, smiled warmly at them. How privileged she was to be a part of this team. It had certainly been a culture shock. She had been a foot soldier for decades, part of the army of uniforms that often harboured a poor opinion of detectives, considering them a bunch of desk jockeys and pen-pushers, although she never heard DI Galena's team referred to in those terms. And look at her now. Die-hard street bobby WPC Yvonne Collins had joined their ranks.

'Vonnie, a minute, please?'

Joseph was beckoning to her from Nikki's office, and she hurried over.

She noticed at once that Nikki seemed different somehow. She had a more commanding air about her. Gone was the recent rather haunted expression, the hesitancy of the past few weeks.

'Vonnie, you know the basics — thirty-six hours to find Lynette Sims in, or . . . Actually, let's ignore that last word. We have thirty-six hours, and we need to make every minute count. Now, if I'm not mistaken, you have a friend who knows Lynette well — the deputy head teacher at Lynette's school.'

'Dinah Barrett, ma'am. An old and trusted friend.'

'Right, well, do you think she'd help us?'

'Like a shot, ma'am,' said Yvonne.

'Then I'm going to ask you to pick her up and go with her to see Tessa Sims, Lynette's mother. The woman is understandably stunned and desperately worried about her daughter, and I think that in this particular case, you two women, who are more or less contemporaries, may be of even more help than an FLO. No one knows more about Lynette than her mother, and she might be able to tell you something important that she considered a trivial detail.' Nikki paused, looking at Yvonne. 'Yvonne, I swear Oliver had a particular reason for choosing Lynette Sims as his "Last Missing Woman," as he puts it. Do your damnedest to find out what that is, because it could lead us to him, thereby saving Lynette's life.'

'I'll ring her now.'

Nikki glanced at the clock. 'It's only just after six, you know.'

'No matter. If I know Di, she'll be up and dressed and probably filling her water cannon as we speak.'

'I'm curious to know what a schoolteacher is doing with a water cannon, but it'll have to wait, unfortunately.' Nikki shook her head. 'Right, off you go.'

Yvonne left the office feeling the weight of what was being asked of her, but determined to do her best.

* * *

Nikki's Big Three were also in early, busy going through the overnight reports in the hope of finding some small clue as to what had happened to Lynette.

Cam was frustrated that nothing of the vaguest importance had shown up. 'We have one big advantage, the fact that we have identified David Pelham as Oliver, but other than that, it's a total mystery how that young teacher could have just disappeared. She was there one minute and gone the next.' He looked to his two colleagues. 'Suppose we focus our attention on tracking Pelham, from the moment he left the force to the present day. What do you think?'

They nodded, and Jim added, 'Uniform will continue looking for anyone who might have seen Lynette, so CID should definitely do as you suggest. Is Nikki okay with that?'

Cam said that he'd already agreed it with her. 'She's also got a friend of Lynette's helping out with the teacher's mother, just in case she can give us anything useful. All bases are covered, so let's get down to chasing up Pelham's movements after he left us.'

'One thing, Cam,' said Matt. 'I hope this isn't the case, but David Pelham was well-liked back in the day. There's a possibility he still has connections within the force. It's unlikely, since he left under a cloud and very bitter, but maybe a close friend, someone who really cared about him . . .?'

'Mmm.' Cam considered the point. 'That could be either a godsend or a disaster, couldn't it? If this friend cared about him enough to warn him, Pelham could find out that we are looking for him all too quickly, or,' Cam shrugged, 'if the friend is a decent, conscientious copper, he or she could lead us to him.'

'Maybe I should check with people who knew him at the time,' said Jim. 'See if he had any special mate or buddy who might fit the bill?'

'Yes, absolutely, Jim. Find anyone from his CID days, and even further back when he was in uniform. An old crewmate would be your best bet. You talk a lot stuck in a car together on long hours of obo.'

'That's very true. I'll never forget those dark nights sitting in a car that smelled of fish and chips and farts!' Jim pulled a face, then hurried away to rally his small team into action.

'I seem to recall reading an article about David Pelham in *FenBeat*, the Fenland Constabulary newsletter,' said Matt thoughtfully. 'It was a while ago, but the editor has been producing it for eons, so maybe he could tell us who wrote it. It was pretty in-depth as I recall — you know, one of those "Where are they now?" things. What I'm wondering is, did anyone ever respond?'

Cam nodded slowly. 'As in, "Oh yes, he lives next door to my auntie in Skeg" kind of thing.'

'Exactly. Worth a try, I guess. I'll give him a bell.'

Matt went back to his desk, and Cam was left wondering where to begin. Something bothered him, and he was sure it was to do with what Nikki had mentioned about the last case David had dealt with, the one that saw him leave the force.

'I'm not sure if that look is reflective or distracted,' said Julia Tennant softly.

Cam had been so deep in thought he hadn't noticed her approach. He gave a rather rueful smile. 'It's just the expression of a man who is wondering if he's been in this game too long, and is mildly concerned that his thought processes are no longer quite as clear as they used to be.'

She smiled. 'Anyone juggling a case of this magnitude should be allowed more than a few moments of fuzzy thinking. But you know that, Superintendent. If it helps, just remember that tests done on the working memory show it to be capable of only holding around seven items at a time, sometimes only three or four. So, I suggest you accept that your mind is overloaded, and frankly you are dealing with it better than most people would. I've been watching you, and believe me, you are quite exceptional.'

Cam was both touched and encouraged by Julia's words, but before he could respond, she said, 'Is there anything I can help with?'

'Actually, there is, Julia, and by the way, you can call me Cam. We tend to save the titles for the gold braid.' He pointed to a chair. 'Please, sit for a moment. I could do with your opinion on something.' It had suddenly come to him, the memory he had been searching for. 'It's about David Pelham's final case. Nikki told me he messed up, resulting in another officer being badly hurt, which led Pelham to resign. At least, that is the common belief, but I seem to recall some talk among his commanding officers that suggested otherwise. I need to look it up, but I'm pretty sure the SIO didn't believe Pelham brought about the injury to his colleague.'

Julia narrowed her eyes. 'So you're wondering why Pelham acted in the way he did? As in taking the blame when he knew it would cost him his beloved career.'

'I think we should have another look at his record. It may have nothing to do with anything, but knowing more about his behaviour at the time might shed some light on how his mind works, don't you think?'

'Absolutely,' said Julia. 'I'd be very interested to take a closer look at his career history. I also wonder if he'd always been prone to obsessive behaviour or it started with his relationship with Sharon Kelly. Can you get hold of his file for me? I'll get to work straightaway.'

Cam reached into his desk drawer and removed a folder. 'This was going to be my next task when I had a few minutes to myself.' He handed it to her. 'Use my office if you'd like a bit of peace and quiet.' He looked around the big room that was alive with the sound of telephones, printers, voices.

'Actually, I'm fine here,' replied Julia. 'I spend a lot of my time in relative seclusion, conducting one-to-one consultations, and I'm finding all this quite invigorating.' She stood up. 'For now, at any rate. If something really interesting comes up, I might take myself off for a little quiet contemplation.'

She made her way to an empty desk, while Cam took out a duplicate of the same folder. The more he thought about it, the more he was sure that Pelham had left the force under a cloud of his own making. Had he engineered his own departure? Why? Cam opened the file and began to read.

* * *

Yvonne and Dinah were full of admiration for Lynette's mother. Consumed as she was by anxiety about her daughter, Tessa Sims spoke sensibly, and her answers were considered. She told them she refused to give way to emotion because she'd be no use to her daughter as a pitiful wreck.

They asked Tessa if Lynette had mentioned anything that might explain why she had been abducted. Initially hesitant, in case she alarmed Lynette's mother, Yvonne decided to ask Tessa if she knew a David Pelham.

'I can't say I do,' Tessa said. 'Why? Is he the person who took Lynette? Do you *know* who has my daughter?'

'There is a chance this Pelham has her, but we have no idea where he lives or what his reasons are for taking her. Can you try and recall whether she ever mentioned him?'

Tessa sat for a while in silence. Suddenly she burst out, 'Surely, given all the technology available to you nowadays, you'd be able to trace him. They do on the television, why can't you?'

This was the first time Tessa had allowed her emotions to show. 'We are using every possible means, believe me, but he disappeared years ago, and tracing someone who doesn't want to be found is difficult.'

'But who is he?' asked Tessa, and a tear rolled down her cheek.

We know who he is all right, we just have no idea where to find him, thought Yvonne. 'Think hard, Tessa. We are certain this man hasn't chosen Lynette at random. Are you sure she hasn't mentioned a David?'

But Tessa was adamant. Lynette hadn't, or she'd have remembered.

Trying a different tack, Dinah said, 'She hasn't had a particularly easy life, has she?'

Tessa sighed. 'No, poor lamb. Losing her father in her teens was devastating for her. Then she lost her closest schoolfriend to a bone tumour. And if that wasn't enough to cope with, her godmother, who she adored, was killed in an accident.' She shook her head. 'No, my girl has had more than her fair share of heartbreak in her life.'

Something — she had no idea what — made Yvonne ask about the godmother and what happened to her.

'Even after all these years, it still makes me shudder. It was a freak accident. She was killed on a backpacking holiday in Australia.'

Yvonne thought her heart had stopped. 'Was her name Sharon, by any chance?'

Tessa stared at her. 'Yes! Sharon Kelly. Kelly's my maiden name. She was my eldest brother's only girl. How on earth . . . Oh my God! David! Of course! It was because of him that Sharon left the country.'

Yvonne stood up. 'Excuse me a minute, Tessa, I need to make a call to my DI. Then I'll explain.'

Yvonne hurried outside and rang Nikki. 'Boss! Lynette does have a connection to David Pelham, although I still don't know why he should have taken her. I just thought you should know immediately. Sharon Kelly was Lynette's god-mother, and her cousin, I think. Tessa Sims tells me Lynette adored Sharon.'

Nikki gave a low whistle. 'Okay, Yvonne, get back in there and try to find a possible reason for David abducting Lynette.' She began congratulating her on making the connection, but she'd already ended the call.

Back in the house, Dinah Barrett was in animated conversation with Tessa.

'So, after Sharon died, the whole family took up arms against David?'

'They blamed him for driving her out of the country, we all did. Lynette was devastated, and that made it worse.' She hung her head. 'To be honest, it wasn't fair on him, I see that now. He did love her and being rejected must have just pushed him over the edge. But the family needed to hold someone accountable for our beautiful girl dying like that.'

'Was Lynette particularly vindictive towards him?' asked Yvonne.

'Oh no, she was too young and too kind. She was just bereft at losing the one person she really looked up to. The vindictive one was Sharon's mother, Ellen. She would have torn him to pieces if she'd laid hands on him. My brother was little better. He actually confronted David, and accused him of as good as murdering her. It was a very bad time for us all.'

So, David Pelham had cause to hate the Kelly family, but why take Lynette? Before Yvonne could think further, Tessa asked if it really was David who had her daughter.

Yvonne couldn't lie about it. 'It looks that way, Tessa. Although I can't think why he should take Lynette and not someone from your brother's side of the family.'

'Sharon and Lynette were the only girls. All the rest were boys. Maybe he felt . . .' She swallowed hard. 'Maybe he still hates us. Maybe he's taking this opportunity to pay us back for accusing him of murdering the woman he loved.'

Sadly, that was all too likely. 'We don't fully understand his motive, but we have people from three different areas all hunting for David Pelham, and for your daughter. We'll get him, I know we will.'

What she didn't know, and certainly wouldn't be saying out loud, was whether it would be in time to save Lynette. Thirty-six hours didn't give them nearly long enough to catch a killer.

CHAPTER TWENTY-NINE

Nikki reminded Joseph of a tigress on the prowl, stalking from desk to desk in the big MI room, checking what had come in, and then checking again. Joseph glanced around and his gaze came to rest on Jim Summers, who was just setting down his receiver. Jim's expression told him he was on to something. Joseph hurried over. 'Have you got a lead?'

'Maybe. It's certainly a possibility.' Jim beamed at him. 'I've just spoken to a retired detective who was a rookie DC with David Pelham. He's given me the name and address of someone he referred to as a really good mate of David's. According to him, if anyone is still in touch with David, it'll be this guy, Adam Ross. They went through training together and remained friends even after Ross moved to Cambridgeshire Constabulary. He had to retire on health grounds, and he now lives in Peterborough.'

'Good. That's not far away.' Joseph beckoned to Nikki. 'Are you going to see him?'

'Damn right I am! And at once. I'll take my chances on catching him in. I can be there in just under an hour if I put my foot down.'

'Be where?' asked Nikki, hurrying towards them.

Jim explained.

'You go straightaway, Jim. I'll square it with Cam, he's bound to say the same as me, and we don't have much time.'

'Whatever it is, Jim, if Nikki says go, you go,' said a voice from the doorway.

Jim grabbed his car keys and left the room at a run.

Cam strode over to them, and Nikki explained what Jim had been told.

'And you, Nikki, what's your next move?' the super asked.

Before she could answer, a voice rang out, 'Ma'am! Got a minute?'

All three went over to the desk where one of the young Fenfleet detectives was seated.

'I've been checking Pelham's domestic arrangements.' DC Kim Peters picked up a print-out. 'David Pelham had two residences, one of his own, and one left to him by an uncle. He sold his years ago, but the uncle's property is still in his name. It's out in the sticks, somewhere between Cloud Fen and Fenny Marsh village.'

'I know that part well,' Nikki said, 'and it is remote. What's it called?'

'Mallards, but there's no road name given. I'm checking for a postcode now.' Kim looked at her screen and read out the location.

'I'll drive, you navigate,' Joseph said.

Cam nodded. 'But take some uniforms with you. It could be where he's holding her, though probably not — he's too clever to use a place that's so easily found. Still, you never know.'

Joseph agreed. In any case, they had to check. They couldn't risk dismissing the smallest link in case it led them to Pelham and his hostage.

In five minutes, they were driving out of Greenborough. Joseph knew the area pretty well by now, but not nearly as well as Nikki, who had lived there all her life. 'Do you know Mallards?' he asked.

'I'm pretty sure it's one of two properties on a winding lane that leads nowhere, other than to a series of ditches and fields. The sat nav won't find the place, it has trouble with Cloud Cottage Farm, let alone somewhere in the middle of nowhere.'

It took them less than twenty minutes to find Nikki's winding lane. About a quarter of a mile away, Joseph could see a farmhouse, partly surrounded by a windbreak of trees and fencing. 'That one?' he asked, indicating the lone property.

'No. *That* one.' Nikki pointed to what appeared to be a ramshackle barn, again partially surrounded by trees, as were all the buildings out here — they needed the protection from the Fenland winds.

As they got closer, Joseph realised that the barn had obscured another building, an old and almost derelict-looking house. A weather-worn board, the paint peeling from it, bore the name *Mallards*.

They pulled into a weed-choked drive, followed by the patrol car. They all got out and stood staring up at the old building.

'Surely no one still lives here,' murmured PC Reg Jenkins. 'It's a dump!'

Joseph silently agreed. They'd just wasted a precious hour on a wild goose chase.

'Okay, let's not piss about. Check it out and we'll get back to base,' Nikki barked. 'It looks like a crock of shit, but who knows? Be careful, guys.'

Joseph went up to the front door. It was locked as expected, but he noticed that a side window wasn't fastened securely. He slipped his hand into the narrow gap and lifted the latch. 'Access point,' he said to Nikki. 'I'll go in first, and if all is clear, I'll open the front door.' He knew she wouldn't object, it was how they worked. After all, he was best at this.

The interior was in as bad a condition as the outside, but it took only seconds to realise that this place had seen visitors, and recently. Among other signs was a tiny area of dust brushed from an old wooden hall table, a partial footprint on the bottom tread of the stairs. Small things, certainly, but they put him on high alert.

He opened the front door and held a finger to his lips. He whispered to Nikki that there were signs of recent disturbance and he needed to do a recce of the whole house, especially the upstairs rooms.

She nodded, and whispered back that Reg and his partner, PC Bob Tinker, should take the downstairs, while they checked the upper floor.

He sensed they were alone in the place, but nevertheless they moved cautiously. He knew from experience that you should never assume anything. Doing so could cost you dearly.

The place smelled musty and damp, and it was probably many years since anyone had actually lived there, but even so, Joseph kept noticing those small indications that said they were not the first visitors to have been here of late.

It was a strange place, sad. The furniture was old and shabby, but looked as though it had once been comfortable and well loved. The place had been a legacy, and it was clear that the last occupant had been the person who wrote the will. No one had moved in or tried to renovate it after the owner's death, and the house looked as though it hadn't been touched since the funeral director's black van had driven away.

They went from one grimy room to another, Joseph wondering what reason someone would have for coming here, leaving footprints and disturbing the dust.

'There's nothing here, Joseph. We should abort and get back.'

As Nikki grasped the brass handle of the last door along the landing, Joseph noticed another footprint, pointing towards the door she was about to open. 'Stop,' he hissed. 'Let me go first.' He pointed to the floor and Nikki stepped back.

'Someone's been in here?' she whispered.

With a nod, Joseph gently turned the handle and flung the door open.

No one lurked there, nor was there anywhere to hide.

It was a child's room, still containing a single bed with a cover on it depicting the faded but still recognisable figures of the Wombles. The room was empty, there was no doubt about that, but Joseph knew it had been the focus of the previous intruder.

'Look.' He pointed to a shelf that held some tattered boy's adventure books and a model Spitfire.

Nikki moved closer. 'There've been other things on this shelf that have been removed, circular imprints of . . . what?'

'I'd say toiletries, wouldn't you? Given the shape, they were most likely something like cans of deodorant, shaving foam cannisters, or maybe toothpaste.' He leaned close to the shelf and sniffed. 'There's a hint of some pleasant fragrance. Can you smell it?'

'Vaguely,' said Nikki thoughtfully. 'And that means someone has actually stayed here.'

'There's even an indentation on that bed. Sure, they threw the cover over it, but . . .' He pulled it back. 'Look, that pillow is new, and it's slightly flattened in the centre.' He looked around again, this time noticing a number of slight disturbances. 'Why this room?' he mused. 'Out of the whole house, why pick a child's room?'

He heard a noise and saw Reg and Bob standing in the doorway. 'Someone has been in the kitchen, ma'am. There's no mess or anything, but the sink has been cleaned, and a small table and chair have also been dusted and wiped over.' Reg gave a short laugh. 'People rarely break in to do a spot of cleaning, it's usually to trash the place and piss up the walls.'

'Oliver, or should I say David Pelham, has been here,' Nikki said thoughtfully. 'But why?'

'A place to crash for a short time, where no one would recognise him or even see he was there? Maybe he didn't dare use a hotel, but needed to be in the area for some reason?' Joseph too was nonplussed. It was odd. 'I suggest we do a second sweep. There's not enough evidence here to bring in forensics, and little point either. If he was here, fine, but he's gone now. Even so, we need to check that he's left nothing behind that could give us a clue as to where he went when he left.'

'I agree, but we have to do it quickly. We can't afford to spend too long here.' Nikki turned to Bob and Reg. 'When we're through, go down the lane to the only other house in the area, I think it's called Ransome House Farm, and ask if anyone saw lights out here, or maybe a car heading towards this place. If they did, I want to know when, okay?'

The two constables nodded, then Reg said, 'Shall we check out that old barn and the outbuildings before we do that? One thing's for certain, he needed transport to get here, and the barn would be a great place to hide a car.'

'I'll do that now,' Nikki said. 'You two get down to Ransome House. It won't take four of us to do a second sweep, Joseph can check the house, and I'll do the barn. Let us know if you find out anything, but if not, keep moving and we'll tie up again back at the station.'

Starting in the kitchen, Joseph moved slowly and methodically through the whole house, constantly on the lookout for something that didn't fit or caught his attention for some reason. He concluded his inspection having found nothing that might help them track down Oliver.

He finished up back in the boy's room. He had the distinct feeling that Oliver's stay had been brief, maybe only one or two nights, and that apart from getting a snack and making a drink in the kitchen, he had spent all his time in this one small room.

Joseph sat on the edge of the bed and tried to put himself in David Pelham's head.

Okay, so the house belonged to him, bequeathed by his late uncle. He had every right to be here. So why not use the master bedroom? It was a bit austere and outdated, but a nice big room nevertheless. Yet Pelham had chosen the child's room. As he waited for Nikki, he wondered why he was so convinced that it was David Pelham who had camped out here. It could have been anyone, couldn't it? No, not really:

whoever came in used the front door and had a key. That narrowed it down considerably. Pretty well to David Pelham.

A sound from downstairs brought him from his reverie. He stood up, took a last look around, and went down to meet Nikki.

'Definitely signs of a vehicle having been driven into that barn,' she said. 'But nothing anywhere else. None of the outbuildings have been touched for years. I'm considering getting a SOCO to come down here and take an imprint of the tyre tracks I found. It could possibly tell us what vehicle he's driving. I've taken some shots on my phone, in case getting forensics is a waste of time. Did you find anything more in here?'

'Nothing to help us, so I suggest we get back. I think we need to take a really in-depth look at David's personal life, I mean his family history. He was here for a reason, and it might be linked to where he's holed up now.'

'Okay, let's go.'

They hurried back to the car, and as they drove away from Mallards, Nikki said, 'Reg rang me, he said there was a vehicle seen driving this way about a week ago. The people at Ransome House saw it just the once, and didn't notice it leave, or return. They couldn't identify it, just that it was a dark-coloured SUV, although their young son reckoned it was a Volvo. They wondered if someone was finally going to live at Mallards, or whether it was going to be bulldozed and the land sold off.'

'Well, one thing's for sure,' said Joseph soberly. 'After we've caught him, David Pelham won't be residing at lonely old Mallards, and he won't be alone. He'll be sharing his new accommodation with a lot of other men, mostly murderers.'

Nikki just grunted.

'We'll catch him, Nikki. And I believe we'll do it soon.' Joseph felt strongly that they were getting very close to bringing this case to a conclusion. He just wasn't certain how it was going to end.

CHAPTER THIRTY

At twelve fifty-five precisely, three different people experienced a moment of epiphany.

Julia, having read everything available to her on Pelham's last case, was convinced that David Pelham had not been to blame for his fellow detective's unfortunate injuries. Reading deeper into his history, she came to the conclusion that it had suited him to leave when he did. His obsession with Sharon had become all-consuming, occupying all his waking hours. She was certain that until she rejected him, Pelham had been an energetic and astute member of his CID team, and dedicated to his career. Sharon Kelly's refusal to marry him, followed by her departure for the other side of the world, which culminated in her unfortunate death, sent him completely off the rails. He left the force in order to spend all his time waging a deadly campaign against those he considered had been to blame.

Julia considered the picture that was forming. It was troubling to say the least. It showed that the man they were hunting was dangerous in the extreme, someone there would be no reasoning with, which put his hostage at serious risk. She stood up and hastened over to Cam Walker's desk.

* * *

At the same time, Jim Summers was seated in a rather shabby lounge. Across from him, and looking everywhere but in his direction, sat retired police officer Adam Ross.

Jim was pleased he'd thought to arrive unannounced. He was almost certain that if he'd phoned ahead, Adam Ross would have either done a runner before he got there or refused to answer the door. As it was, after a rocky start, Ross appeared to be slowly coming round to the idea that his friend was no longer the man he'd once known. It was hard going, and Jim might have commended his loyalty if it wasn't so imperative that they find the man.

'Come on, Adam! You were a copper long enough, and a good one too, going by your record. David is not the man you once knew. Just think what he's done. He's already killed two men, and now he has abducted a young schoolteacher. He's given us thirty-six hours in which to find her, Adam. A young, innocent woman. If we don't, she dies.' He glared at Ross. 'And if you withhold any information you have on where your friend might be, that makes you as guilty as him.'

'I don't know where he is, I swear, except that he's somewhere in Greenborough.' For the first time, Ross looked Jim in the eye. 'Yes, I have kept in touch with him over the years, and yes, I've noticed him change. But the poor sod hadn't a friend in the world except me. I was all he had left. Sharon leaving, and then her dying like that, well, it just destroyed him.'

'Adam, listen to me.' Jim gazed at him. 'Your "poor sod" set himself up as judge, jury and executioner and hanged a man. He didn't make a good job of it either. He then went on to strangle someone else. I know David's history and it's heartbreaking what happened, but surely you can see that he hounded Sharon Kelly so that she had to run to the other side of the world to get free of him. You say he loved her, but the truth is that his obsession with her sent her to her death. Now he's making others pay for what he did. He's screwed up so badly he probably believes the world is flat and UFOs cause crop circles, and we, Adam Ross, need to catch him before he kills an innocent woman.'

Adam groaned. 'Okay, I'll tell you everything I know, although it really isn't as much as you might imagine. He talked a lot — and I listened — but it was nearly always about how much he loved Sharon and how, if it wasn't for others, she'd have realised her mistake and come back to him. He repeated the same old story again and again, and nothing I ever said was the slightest help.'

'Okay, well, let me ask you a few questions, and let's see if you can fill in some blanks for us.' Jim was beginning to feel rather sorry for this unhappy man. 'You're doing the right thing by David too, you know. We have to stop him before he makes things even worse for himself.'

'Yeah, I see that now,' Ross said. 'What do you want me to tell you?'

Jim had been thinking of little else but what to ask him, but he pulled out his notebook anyway. He didn't want to forget a thing. 'Places, Adam. Anywhere that was special to him. Where does he live, for a start? The woman he's got with him will be hidden somewhere. Where would he take her?'

Ross looked pained. 'I honestly don't know where he's living now, he's been cagey about it for months. When we were mates, he lived in his father's house in Lane End, Greenborough, a big drum called Cairngorm. His parents were divorced, and David stayed with the father until the old man decided to move to some fancy retirement complex in Spain, giving the house to David.'

'But David sold it?'

'Yeah, and he sold it for peanuts,' Ross said.

'How long ago was that?' asked Jim.

'Three years? Something like that.'

Jim frowned. 'Why did he let it go so cheaply?'

'He said he couldn't wait for a good offer. He had important things to do and wanted a quick sale, by which he meant his campaign against the force, I suppose.' Ross shook his head.

'Most likely,' Jim said. 'So where did he go after that?'

'Here and there. He even dossed down here for a week or so. He said his stuff was in storage. He then told me he was in digs in one of the Greenborough villages. See, the thing is, he always came to me, I never visited him.' Ross looked thoughtful. 'He did say one thing that was a bit odd. I asked him what he meant but he wouldn't tell me. He said he couldn't have found a better buyer for his home. So, I said, did he mean the new owner would look after it, and he laughed and said, "Oh yes, he'll look after it all right, just as carefully as I did."'

Jim wrote that down. He'd have a word with these conscientious new owners and also check out the local storage facilities. 'Did he ever mention an old place that an uncle left him?'

'Yes. Mallards, out Cloud Fen way. I said it was crazy to keep that old dump and sell Cairngorm, which got him a bit shirty. He said Mallards was special to him, and he couldn't possibly sell it.'

'Maybe he lived there for a while?' Jim asked.

'No, I don't think so,' Ross said. 'Though the last time I saw him he did mention needing to visit the place again. He said it had been his happy place in his childhood days. His father was always working and he pushed David hard with his schoolwork, but the uncle just let him be a little boy and have fun. Anyway, David said he had a few very important things to do, after which he'd be moving away permanently.'

'When did you see him last, Adam?'

'About a month ago, and for the first time, he scared me. He'd lost weight and looked kind of weird, sort of distracted, yet calculating. It was like he was working things out in his head all the time, counting through them. He didn't stay long, and frankly I was glad to see him go. I was even more worried about him after he left. I guess I knew then that he needed help, the kind I couldn't give him.' He looked Jim in the eye, defiant. 'He was a bloody good detective, and it's a wicked, wicked waste that he's finished up like this. I don't regret trying to stick by him.'

'I won't knock you for that, Adam, and I appreciate your help. However, the situation changed when he turned killer. So, last question. You know him better than anyone, where do you think he's gone? He has a hostage with him, don't forget.'

Ross sat in silence for a while. 'I . . . I honestly can't think. If he'd still had Cairngorm, I'd have said there, as it was well away from the other houses on that lane. Or, second thoughts, probably Mallards. Very few people know that old place is even there, and it's right out in the boondocks. Unless you know the area well, you'd never find it. Yeah, my money would be on Mallards, it's the kind of place where no one would hear you scream.'

Jim didn't like what that implied and said so.

Ross merely shrugged.

Jim stood up. He knew that Mallards had been checked, and if anything of interest had been discovered he would have been notified so, frankly, Ross was wrong. Still, it was worth enquiring about the new owner of Cairngorm. He didn't know why, but he was getting those odd little messages in his head that always heralded an important breakthrough.

As soon as he was out of Adam's house, he called his team. 'Find out all you can about a house called Cairngorm in Lane End. It belonged to David Pelham, who subsequently sold it. Then speak to the super and get him to send some men round there to talk to the new owner. Tell him to make sure they're very careful — I'm wondering if Pelham has an accomplice.'

* * *

Matt Ballard set down the receiver and stared into space, wondering if what he had just heard was a red herring or a bloody good lead. Either way, it needed following up. He went over to Cameron Walker's desk. 'Okay to pop out and have a swift talk with a local, Cam?'

'Certainly. Something helpful, is it?'

'I won't know till I get there, but I've a feeling it might be.' Matt hurried out into Greenborough almost at a run. He had a good feeling about this.

He found the offices of the local newspaper in a cobbled lane just off the main high street. The receptionist smiled at him. 'Matt Ballard? Mr Cooke is expecting you.' She pointed across the room to a door marked "Editor." 'Go straight in. Can I get you a coffee? Or a chocolate? We've run out of tea, I'm afraid.'

Matt said he was fine, thanks.

Johnnie Cooke was a big man with a wide smile, dark-rimmed glasses and a mop of dark hair that badly needed taming or shearing. 'I heard from my friend Lucas who edits your *FenBeat* magazine that you're trying to hunt down David Pelham. Is that right?'

Matt said it was. 'We are very anxious to find his whereabouts, sir. Do you actually know him?'

'I did, certainly. My family home was also in Lane End, so I knew him when we were boys. We weren't very close, but we spoke often enough. And I saw him, oh, maybe a month ago. He came asking for access to back issues of my paper. He told me he was writing a book about unsolved cases involving missing persons. It was nice to catch up a bit but, hell, had he changed!'

'How so?' asked Matt.

Johnnie Cooke puffed out his cheeks. 'Phew! He was intense. Kind of driven, if you get my drift. He'd always been laid back, calm, in control, oh, and very shrewd, but when I saw him this time, well, I wondered if he was on something. I thought maybe the writing bug had well and truly bitten him, and this new book had become a bit of an addiction.'

Matt smiled inwardly at that. *Something certainly had, but it wasn't a book.* 'Did he tell you where he was living, Johnnie? We know he sold the house in Lane End.'

'Damned shame that was. When I saw that board go up, I was quite sad. The Pelhams had lived there for three generations, as had my family, but mine still do. But in answer to your question, he didn't say where, just that he was still local.'

'And the new owners of his old house? What are they like?' he asked.

'No idea, I'm afraid. I married six years ago and I now live just outside Beech Lacey. I visit Mum and Dad regularly but I've never seen the new people, and my parents have never mentioned them.'

'What about a car? What does he drive?' Matt asked hopefully.

'A Volvo,' Johnnie said. 'A black SUV XC40, a nice motor. He's always had Volvos since way back. He told me his first car was a beat-up old Volvo 200 series and he's never wanted to drive anything else.'

Well, that was something. Matt scribbled it down, but before he could say anything, Johnnie's face lit up.

'I do know one thing! Talking about that car made me think of it. He can't live far from his old home, because my dad told me he'd seen his Volvo in Cedar Avenue, which is round the back of Lane End. My dad reckoned he rents a garage from one of the householders there, as he'd seen the car a couple of times, and always outside Clem Smith's place. Clem has a couple of old barns that he converted into garages and rents them out.'

'You've made my day, Johnnie! Thank you. Now I've got to get back to base. Forgive me for rushing off, but this is important.'

He was almost at the door when Johnnie called out, 'Keep me updated, won't you?'

With a brief wave, Matt kept right on going. Without pausing for breath, he called Cam and told him about the car.

'Get yourself back here, Matt! A whole lot has happened and we're having an emergency meeting. We'll hang on for you.'

Matt speeded up. Really, he was far too old for this.

* * *

Nikki looked around at the assembled team. Only Jim was missing, being still on his way from Peterborough. Cam gave them a brief rundown of recent activities — the visit to Mallards, Jim's interview with Adam Ross, and what Johnnie Cooke from the local rag had said about Pelham's car. He finished with Julia's warning. David Pelham was in a very dangerous state of mind, and it would be futile to try reasoning with him.

'Anything to add, anyone?' asked Cam. 'Any new intel?'

A young Fenfleet detective called Izzie raised her hand. 'I've found the estate agent that handled the sale of Cairngorm, sir. It's a Bruce Penny, who says the purchaser was a man named Ian Barton. He was the first person to view the property, and David Pelham himself showed him around. The sale was agreed immediately and the house was taken off the market. He said that Pelham basically gave it away for well under the price they'd valued it at. All he seemed to want was a quick sale to take it off his hands.'

'He knew him, didn't he? whispered Joseph, from just behind Nikki.

'Oh yes, I'd say so,' murmured Nikki. 'I think we'd better pay Mr Barton a visit.'

'I've also found that Barton was friendly with David Pelham when he was in uniform,' continued Izzie. 'Barton was a security guard at the shopping precinct in Fenchester. Apparently, they shared an interest in cricket. They were both Yorkshire fans and went to matches together.' The detective looked up from her phone. 'That's all I have so far.'

'Bingo,' hissed Nikki. 'He *did* know him.'

Cam thanked Izzie. 'So, to summarise, we have the make and colour of his car, and possibly where he keeps it. We have a person living in his old house who is definitely known to him, and who may be an accomplice of some sort. We also know from his friend, Adam Ross, that he has a list of things he needs to accomplish in a very short space of time, because he is going away permanently.'

'I wonder,' added Julia Tennant sombrely, 'just what that means. "Going away permanently" probably signifies death. I think you should consider that when David Pelham's agenda is completed, his campaign will close with his own demise.'

'So, he has nothing to lose?' said Nikki.

'Nothing at all, which makes him doubly dangerous. As I said, there is no reasoning with him, so don't even try.'

'Then we need to act swiftly,' stated Cam. 'I suggest we hit both places simultaneously. Do you agree, Nikki?'

'Absolutely. Joseph and I will go to the house and confront Barton, while Cat and Ben get around to this Clem Smith's place, and hopefully seize the car, or at least make sure that's where he keeps it.'

'Can I add that we send a crew to keep an eye on Mallards?' added Joseph. 'It seems that it's a part of this list of his, and I'm not sure if he's already done what he needed to by visiting it recently, or if it's a work in progress.'

Cam nodded. 'And we'll press on with dredging up all the intel we can on Pelham — past and present. Okay, Nikki, off you go, and keep us posted.'

Nikki and Joseph didn't need telling twice. Nor did Cat and Ben. In minutes, their two cars were speeding out of the station car park in the direction of Lane End.

CHAPTER THIRTY-ONE

'Wow. This is some place,' breathed Joseph, regarding the elegant Victorian frontage with some admiration. 'And well kept.'

'The Pelham family must have been enormously wealthy for Daddy to hand this over to David, then bugger off for a life in the sun,' Nikki said.

'And David sells it for well under the market value.' Joseph frowned. 'So that had to be part of his plan.' They got out of the car and approached the front door. 'Let's see what light Ian Barton can shine on it all.'

Joseph rang the doorbell but to no avail. The house was silent. 'Damn it!' Nikki said. 'Maybe he works.'

'Wait a minute. I can hear a lawnmower.' Joseph started off around the side of the house. 'Yes, someone's cutting grass in the back garden.'

Through a side gate, they came upon a long sweeping lawn, surrounded by trees, a shrubbery and flowerbeds. On a ride-on mower sat a slender man in canvas trousers and a green sweatshirt with a silver logo on the back.

They walked quickly across the lawn, Joseph muttering, 'How does an ex-security guard afford the upkeep on this place?'

'Good point,' said Nikki. She held up her warrant card and the man on the mower cut the engine and stepped off.

'Mr Barton?'

'Oh no, I'm just the gardener. Alan Kennett's the name. Can I help at all?'

'We need to talk to Mr Barton as a matter of some urgency. Could you tell us where we might find him?' asked Joseph.

'I'm afraid he's away. He went a week ago today, visiting relatives in County Wicklow, Ireland. He paid me upfront for three weeks.'

'And the house is locked up? No one staying there while he's away?' asked Nikki.

'No. He's not that kind of man. Doesn't like anyone coming into his house. I'm not even allowed in for a cuppa, or a wee for that matter, and I'm here for three hours at a stretch.' The gardener rolled his eyes. 'Bit of an oddball really, if you get my meaning. I rarely see him. He pays well, but he's not exactly sociable.'

'How long have you worked for him?' asked Joseph.

'I came here when he first moved in, must be three years back now.' He frowned. 'He's not in any trouble, is he?'

'No, nothing like that,' said Nikki quickly. 'We just want to talk to him about someone he knows, that's all. Do you have a contact number for him by any chance?'

'I do, but it's his house phone, so that won't help, will it?' Alan said.

'I'll take it anyway,' said Nikki, scribbling it down in her notebook. They both added Alan Kennett's mobile number to their contacts, in case they needed more information at some point. 'How did he go to Ireland, Mr Kennett? Did he say if he was getting the ferry, or flying?'

'Flying, definitely. He mentioned getting a car to East Midlands Airport, and had a moan about the cost.'

They thanked the gardener, Joseph complimenting him on how well looked-after the grounds were, while Nikki tapped her foot.

Joseph smiled. 'Keep 'em onside, Nikki. Good relations can pay dividends.'

They hurried back to the car, Nikki in a state of intense frustration. 'I'll drive. You ring base and get Yvonne to check if anyone by the name of Ian Barton flew to Dublin a week ago today.'

The moment Joseph finished the call, another came in. It was Cat.

'We have his garage, boss! And his licence number. This bloke, Clem Smith, is a right canny businessman, he keeps a record of all his clients' car numbers. I'm not sure it's a totally legal set-up, but I'll save that for another day. The thing is, Pelham took the Volvo out two mornings ago and hasn't returned. We've got a contact mobile number from Smith, but as you'd guess, it's unobtainable. Ben's just requested an attention drawn for that licence number, but I reckon the bastard has probably either dumped it or hidden it somewhere. We're now on our way back to the station.'

Joseph thanked them, ended the call and glanced at Nikki. 'He's tying up loose ends in preparation for the final performance, isn't he?'

'Whatever *that* might be, and as my mind doesn't work like a sodding psycho's, I'm not even trying to guess.' She sped up, and they drove on in silence.

By the time they were back in the CID room, Nikki had regained her composure. Before the door had even closed behind them, Yvonne was waving to them.

'I've confirmed that Ian Barton did fly into Dublin with Ryanair a week ago, and he has a return ticket booked for two weeks' time, ma'am.'

'Sod it, that means he's no use to us right now,' Nikki grunted. 'Thanks, Vonnie.' She turned back to Joseph. 'I'll bet you anything you like our clever ex-detective treated him to a trip to see the rellies so as to get him out of the country and away from our reach.'

'We can always call in the help of the Gardaí,' suggested Joseph. 'I'll ring them now if you like?'

'I'm not sure it'll help. If he is in cahoots with Pelham, he'll have been well and truly briefed, and sure as little apples, he'll give us some cock and bull story intended to send us on the wrong trail. It'll be a waste of time. Cross Cairngorm off the list of priorities.' As she said this, she noticed Joseph's expression. 'Okay, you. What's the problem with that?'

'I'm not sure,' said Joseph slowly. 'Probably nothing. It's just a feeling I have about the whole set-up there. It doesn't ring true to me. Can you give me a few minutes to try and unscramble my thoughts?'

'If you can do the unscrambling while operating the coffee machine, sure.'

'It's as good a place as any.' Frowning, Joseph turned and made his way along the corridor.

Nikki returned to her office. So, they had Pelham's vehicle make and number, but very little else. She had hoped for more. Much more. For the umpteenth time, she looked at the clock. Twenty-six hours to go. Twenty-six hours in which to save a life. They needed someone, anyone, to give them a lead — fast.

* * *

Lynette Sims had always been a glass half-full kind of person, but now she couldn't summon a single positive thought. Her earlier determination to get out of her prison at all costs had faded, she was just too incapacitated. Whoever had put her here had prepared well. The room was escape-proof.

She was plagued by thoughts of her mother. How desperate she would be, not knowing if her daughter was dead or alive. It would be tearing her apart.

Lynette's other fear concerned her kidnapper. Why had he taken her, and what was he planning to do? He couldn't have done it for ransom. She had very little money, and her mother was far from well-off. That left some very scary scenarios, which Lynette tried not to dwell on.

She ate sparingly, partly because the thought of food made her feel sick, and partly to spread out the rations in case he didn't give her any more. And what if something happened to him? An accident? Or he might even get himself arrested and refuse to say where she was. A sob rode into her throat, and she swallowed it. This was doing her no good at all. She had to think of her mum, and all her precious students, and find a way out.

'I can do this,' she muttered to herself, and repeated those words until she could think of nothing else.

* * *

Oliver felt calm, very much in control. He now thought of himself as Oliver, it was better that way. David Pelham belonged to another life. The good detective Pelham had dealt with his last case, let him rest in peace. It was Oliver's turn now, and it was as Oliver that he'd bring the long painful episode to its conclusion.

Oliver glanced at his watch. Not long to go.

* * *

Joseph arrived back in Nikki's office with their two coffees just as Cam hurried in. Nikki glanced up hopefully, but Cam's expression conveyed nothing but concern.

'Neither traffic, nor the CCTV camera operators have seen a single sign of Pelham's car over the last two days.' He flopped down on to a chair. 'I'm coming to the conclusion that he's stashed it away somewhere, or else he'd have been seen leaving town.'

'He wasn't seen because he never did leave town.' Joseph stared from Cam to Nikki. 'This is only a hypothesis, but my gut tells me I'm right. Nikki, can you give me time to make two phone calls, and then I'll explain?'

'Go.'

He saw her trusting expression and hoped that he was right.

Back in his tiny office, he picked up his desk phone and dialled a number from his contact list.

'Alan Kennett, Garden Maintenance, how can I help?'

'Alan, it's DS Easter, we spoke earlier. Listen, I'm going to send an image to your phone. Would you be kind enough to confirm the man's identity? It was taken a while ago, but I'm certain he still looks basically the same.'

'Certainly, Sergeant. I'll wait for it.'

Joseph sent it off.

'Oh, yes. As you say, he looks older and he's a lot thinner now, but I certainly recognise him. That's Ian Barton, no doubt about it.'

Joseph thanked him and made his second call. This one wouldn't be so easy. He asked to speak to Bruce Penny of the Penny Estate Agents on a matter of some urgency. After a few moments, in which he heard whispered voices, apparently in dispute, the deep voice of Penny told him he was due at a viewing and Joseph would have to be quick. He gritted his teeth. 'Mr Penny, my call concerns the abduction of an innocent woman whose captor has threatened to kill her. If you are late for your appointment, get your secretary to phone and apologise. Now, I want you to tell me about the sale of Cairngorm and the transaction between David Pelham and Ian Barton.'

'But I've already told you about that,' said Penny.

'No, you haven't. For a start, it wasn't exactly a standard transaction, was it?' Silence. 'I'm waiting, Mr Penny.'

'I . . . I mean I don't know what mo—'

'Mr Penny. If you have trouble discussing it on the phone, I'm quite happy to collect you from your agency and take you to the station so we can talk more formally. I presume you have your own solicitor, or shall I call the duty one?'

'All right, all right. Just let me close my office door, and then I'll tell you what I know.'

Joseph smiled grimly to himself. It didn't suit him to be a hard guy, but time was short.

Bruce Penny picked up the receiver and began to speak, keeping his voice low. 'Yes, you're right, it wasn't exactly standard procedure but, well, at the time, things weren't too good for me, and his proposition was, how can I put it—'

'Mr Penny, let me make one thing clear, I'm not interested in whether you went by the book or not. All I want is to find this missing woman, and I have very little time before something terrible happens to her. Just give me the facts and there's a good chance that if we catch David Pelham before he acts on his threat to kill her, your involvement will be neither here nor there. Just tell me one thing. Did you actually sell Cairngorm to Ian Barton?'

'No, they decided on a private arrangement. We took it off the market and the sale was never completed. However, Mr Pelham said he was a fair man, and he didn't want to see me lose out on my percentage after we'd done all the marketing.'

Joseph closed his eyes for a second. 'Say no more, Mr Penny, that's of no concern at present. Thank you for your cooperation. Oh, one more thing. Do you still have all the details about the house, you know, the brochure, photos, floor plans?'

'Yes, we always keep them on file.'

'Then email it to this address, and immediately, please.' He gave Penny the address, hung up and hastened back to Nikki and Cam.

Nikki looked at his smiling face. 'Positive news?'

'Yes, absolutely! I know where he is, most likely Lynette too. Cam, you need to organise a unit that can deal with a hostage situation. Not only did David Pelham never leave Greenborough, he never left his home. The sale was a hoax. I've just confirmed with the estate agent that the sale never went through.' He showed them the image he had forwarded to Alan the gardener. 'Alan Kennett positively IDed this man as the owner of Cairngorm, Ian Barton.'

Nikki stared at the photograph. 'But that's David Pelham!'

'Exactly. All along I've kept thinking that the situation stank. A security guard with a place like that? And the fact that a likeable man like Kennett wasn't even allowed in for a cup of tea or a wee. The owner wasn't just a bit eccentric, he didn't want anyone seeing what was going on inside Cairngorm.'

'Surely the neighbours would have seen him come and go?' said Cam.

'You haven't seen the place, Cam,' Nikki said. 'It's set well back, maybe three hundred metres off the lane, and it's surrounded by trees and shrubs. If my memory serves me well, there's a little track that runs along the edge of the field behind it, so he could come and go without a soul seeing him.'

'Plus, he made sure that people like the gardener, who had never met him before, believed him to be the reclusive Mr Barton, the eccentric new owner. And when an estate agent's "sold" sign went up, courtesy of Mr Penny, who pocketed a nice little backhander from David, who would think any different? Another thing was the security cameras. Nikki, did you notice them when we visited? They were all over the place, every corner of the garden, and the main entrances and exits. Far more than you'd expect in a normal upmarket home. He kept a very close eye on anyone coming to his door.'

'But that would mean he knew *we'd* been there and talked to the gardener, wouldn't it?' Nikki said.

'I wouldn't get too uptight over that. He was a detective, don't forget. It would be standard procedure to check out his old home, and we picked a day when his gardener, who believed him to be Ian Barton, was there, which was perfect for Pelham.'

As they spoke, Nikki received a message in her inbox.

'That will be the sales brochure and floor plans of Cairngorm, Nikki. We'll need those if we are to go in and get Lynette out safely.'

'I think it's time we took this up to the MI room and brought the others up to speed, then I need to alert uniform,' said Cam. 'At the moment, we have the element of surprise on our side, and we still have hours to go before his deadline runs out, but we daren't waste a minute, in case there's a hitch. There's a hell of a lot to organise for a dangerous operation like this.'

Joseph didn't move. He had other ideas but wasn't sure what the super would think of them. 'Sir . . .'

Cam frowned. '"Sir?" That sounds ominous, it's usually "Cam" when it's just us.'

'Look, this isn't the sort of operation we're used to undertaking. In fact, it's more like something I'd have dealt with when I was with Special Forces. Yes, we need backup on hand, fully prepared to go in at a moment's notice, but I'm going to suggest that you let me, and maybe one other officer — two at the most — go in first and suss out exactly what's going on, and especially where Lynette is being held. I've done this many times before, Cam, and I know what to do and how to handle whatever I come across.' Joseph held his breath and waited.

Cam seemed to take an eternity to consider. Then he turned to Nikki. 'What do you think?'

'If Lynette is in there,' Nikki said at once, 'which I now believe she is, her best chance is Joseph, no question.'

'Then choose whichever officer you think best to accompany you, Joseph, and we'll go upstairs with these,' he picked up the materials on Cairngorm that Nikki had just printed off, 'while you work out the quickest and safest way to get that woman out of there.'

CHAPTER THIRTY-TWO

Cam hurried off, but Nikki held Joseph back for a moment and closed her office door.

'Two things. One, the security cameras all around the property. How the f—?'

Joseph smiled. 'Don't worry, I've thought about those. You know I mentioned maybe three of us going in first?'

Nikki raised an eyebrow. 'Ye-e-s?'

'Well, suppose I asked Vinnie Silver. Unless he's lost his touch since he got married, which I very much doubt, he'll be able to freeze those cameras just long enough for me to get inside. It would be a matter of minutes. Pelham would know nothing about it. Remember that Dutch case we investigated? On that occasion, it was the bad guys used that trick. They had us fooled for weeks.'

Nikki did remember. 'Then get hold of him right now. I'll authorise it and tell Cam later.'

Vinnie was an old army comrade of Joseph's, a good friend and also a very clever hacker. He was probably the only person in the world whom Nikki would trust with her Joseph's life.

'And the second thing?' Joseph said, his hand on the receiver.

'I want to be the one coming in with you. We have no idea how Lynette Sims has been treated. She might need a woman to be there with her.'

Joseph opened his mouth to refuse but instead sighed heavily. 'Okay, but for once in your life, you do absolutely everything I tell you, understood?'

She nodded. She wasn't used to deferring to anyone, but a life was at stake. He called Vinnie, who agreed, as she'd guessed he would. So, this was it, then. She'd have one of the best guys in the world beside her but the prospect was still terrifying.

'He's gathering up what he needs and he'll be here soon. I just hope you can square it with Cam.'

'Cam knows Vinnie well, Joseph, and he'll be aware that he's the only person who can get us past those cameras. He'll okay it. Now let's go and join the others and get to grips with those floor plans.'

All was silent in the Major Incident room as Cam delivered the situation report. He concluded by organising a small group to act as liaison should they require any assistance from the station. Another team would be a field party, on the ground and at hand to back up Joseph and Nikki should they need it. There would also be a contingent of uniforms, and a tactical armed unit had been put on standby in case the situation turned nasty.

Nikki listened carefully. If she didn't know they were dealing with a psychotic who could not be reasoned with, who had already murdered two men and was now holding a vulnerable woman and threatening to kill her, these preparations could have seemed excessive. As it was, she knew that these measures were the only way they'd have a chance of saving Lynette Sims's life.

At one point, she had wondered if David might simply give up once he realised they had found him, and within the deadline he'd set. It was a pretty remote hope, but could there possibly be a little of the old honourable policeman still lurking somewhere inside the deranged maniac he had become? She thought of him saying, 'Ah well, fair cop, you can have her, DI Galena,' and laughed at herself. *Yeah, sure.* The best outcome would be if she and Joseph found Lynette and got her to safety without David realising. It was a slim chance but worth taking. They could always storm the house but that could cost Lynette her life.

'Okay. Nikki, Joseph, and the backup team, over here, please.' Cam was standing by the whiteboards with an open laptop on the table in front of him, next to the estate agent's floor plans.

They gathered round. 'I'll hand this over to Joseph,' Cam said. 'He's going to head up this operation, so please listen very carefully to everything he tells you. I don't have to remind any of you what's at stake.'

To their low murmur of assent, Joseph accessed a satellite map of Lane End on the laptop. 'I'm thinking we access the garden from the rear, coming in from that farm track you mentioned, Nikki.'

She nodded. 'That's the least visible from the road and the house.'

Joseph zoomed in. 'Now, when we were there earlier, I noted that there are only two cameras in that area, which helps us. I also saw a ground-floor window that would be very easy to get in through. That would be my chosen method of ingress, but we might have to think on our feet. I'd dearly love to send a drone up so as to find where the heat sources are, but it would attract his attention. It's going to be down to sharp eyes and ears. Our priority is finding and bringing out Lynette Sims unhurt. If we can do that, while ascertaining if the place is safe to enter, uniform can go in and take Pelham.'

For the next ten minutes they studied the photographs of the interior of the house, and then the layout of the rooms.

'We have here an old Victorian property with a large kitchen, a big lounge, a dining room, a study, and various other smaller rooms as well as a utility room, a boot room and a cloakroom, all on the ground floor.' Joseph pointed to the boot room. 'That's the room with the window we hope to enter through. That's good as it leads into a hallway, not one of the rooms. I don't want us walking straight into Pelham. Upstairs on the first floor there are four bedrooms and a large bathroom, plus two other storage or box rooms above those on a third floor and a single staircase leading to an attic. There is no cellar, thank heavens.'

'If it was me, I'd hide Lynette in one of those, right out of the way.' Nikki pointed to the top-floor rooms.

'Normally, I'd agree, but when we were in the garden, I noticed that one of the first-floor bedrooms at the back of the house had some very heavy drapes pulled tightly closed. All the other windows had their curtains open, so I'm wondering if "Mr Barton" wasn't just protecting valuable paintings from sunlight or the interest of a passing burglar while he was away.'

'So, we aim to check there first,' said Nikki.

'Yes. And the sooner the better.' Joseph looked at Cam. 'We should decide how best to get the backup close, but out of sight. And most important of all is to approach in silence. If some idiot hits the blues and twos, Lynette Sims is dead.'

Cam nodded soberly. 'Uniform have been made aware. They're going to approach from both ends of Lane End, staying well out of sight of the house. They will virtually cut Cairngorm off. We'll have another crew a few yards behind your own backup team, out on the farm track. If he takes off, no matter which direction he goes, we'll get him.'

Nikki hoped that would be the case, but she didn't trust David Pelham in the slightest. He had been an ace detective, and before that, a damned good uniformed officer, so he would know how they'd likely proceed. However, he might not know about Joseph's Special Services background, and therefore about their covert attempt to gain access, especially when he believed he was protected by his surveillance cameras.

'Well, I guess we should get booted and suited,' said Joseph. 'Stabbies on and phones on mute, Nikki. And, Cam, we'll only use our radios if we need assistance or have anything to report, and only to you, okay? No one radios us unless it's life or death. We can't afford to have them bursting into life just when we're tiptoeing past a room with David Pelham in it.' With a final glance at the others, he turned to her. 'Okay, Nikki, it's time to shine.'

* * *

The three of them stood by the back entrance to Cairngorm. Joseph smiled rather grimly at the other two. 'Looks like it's the dream team in action again, and this time we have to prove that miracles can happen. You, Vinnie, are going to have to throw a cloak of invisibility over Nikki and me, just long enough for us to get across the garden and pop that window catch. Okay?'

Vinnie beamed. 'No sweat, old buddy, and it'll be like it never happened. I'm all organised and set up. I have all the data I need on this place and I'm ready to go whenever you are.' He looked wistful. 'I just wish I could come with you.'

So did Joseph. 'Sorry, mate, but you know the score — protocol and all that crap. But it's good to know you're here, so if things do go tits up, it'll be you I yell for and sod protocol.'

He turned to Nikki. 'Right, as soon as Vinnie says go, we head for that path with the shrubs and trees on either side, then branch off towards that window. Keep as low as you can, and stay immediately behind me, and if I deviate from the route, stick fast behind me because there'll be a reason for it, even if you don't know what it is. Got that?'

'Got it,' she said.

'Then over to you, Vinnie.' He glanced at Nikki, hoping she would understand the message he was silently sending her. They both knew he didn't want her there but for now, he needed to forget that she was the woman he loved. She was a trained police officer, doing her duty. He saw her slight nod, and understood the look she gave him. She was telling him she loved him but that they had a job to do. At this moment they were nothing more than two professionals, out to save a woman's life.

'Go!' Vinnie pressed a key on his laptop. 'And no pissing about.'

They ran.

Even though Joseph's attention was focused on getting to the house unobserved, he took careful note of their surroundings, especially that curtained window. That, he was certain, was where they would find Lynette. The curtains didn't hang in folds as they should, and it looked to him as if they'd been tacked to the window frame, preventing whoever was inside from opening them, and there'd be no gaps to see in through.

They arrived at the window they'd been aiming for and in seconds, with the help of a trusty implement he'd often used in the past, Joseph freed the catch. He took a tiny bottle from his pocket and sprayed the hinges with a fine mist of oil. He couldn't afford a tell-tale squeak from a rarely used hinge giving them away before they were even inside.

The window swung back smoothly and Joseph stood for a moment, listening.

During his years living on the edge, often in situations of the greatest peril, Joseph had developed a kind of sixth sense for anything that threatened danger. He wasn't picking anything up here. He frowned. What if he'd been wrong? Dismissing the thought, he swung his leg over the windowsill and jumped down, beckoning Nikki to follow.

The house was quiet. Quiet wasn't always a good thing.

They were in a small room that smelled of wet leather and boot polish. It contained a collection of outdoor clothing, all expensive brands, along with a navy Gore-Tex weatherproof jacket that Joseph recognised as one-time Fenland Constabulary police issue. Despite its utilitarian purpose, the room was spotless, almost scrubbed.

He stood listening for several minutes, then peered out through the partially open door. A long hall stretched away in front of him, a kitchen at one end, and next to it a room that the floorplans had given as the utility. Three other doors would lead to the dining room, the lounge and the study, but all were closed. Indicating for Nikki to hold back, he inched out into the hall and, moving stealthily, checked each room in turn. All were unoccupied, each as clean and as perfectly arranged as a showroom house. So, they hadn't been tidied up for the estate agent's brochure, this must be how David Pelham liked to live. Even so, there were small indications that the house was lived in. In the kitchen, the electric kettle was still vaguely warm, and there was fresh milk in the fridge. In the lounge, a recent local newspaper, carefully folded, rested on a coffee table. The hall table smelled of furniture polish.

But no sight nor sound of David Pelham.

How could they proceed if they didn't know where Pelham was? Joseph had envisaged locating him at some point, then having to find a way to sneak past whichever room he was in and get up the stairs. As it was, it felt like the *Marie Celeste*.

He turned back towards the boot room and beckoned Nikki over to the bottom of the stairs, where he waited for her. In seconds, she was by his side, looking up towards the landing.

'Wait here,' he mouthed silently and, one step at a time, he made his way up the staircase. He went slowly, placing his feet at the side of each stair, knowing that the boards would creak most at the middle.

At the top, a large open landing with a rather lovely pair of lattice casement windows. To the right, a closed door, and then a hallway to the left with several doors off it. His memory of the estate agent's brochure told him that the room to the right was the master bedroom with a large en suite attached. All the other rooms were off the hall. The one with the covered window would be the first on the right, and he would look there first. In case it was a trap, he looked back down the stairs to Nikki and held up two fingers, then pointed to his watch. She nodded. She would give him two minutes before joining him.

He almost smiled. For once in her life, Nikki Galena was actually doing as she was told.

Joseph inched his way across the landing. The door had a key protruding from the old metal lock, and a new modern bolt had been fitted to the outside, confirming his suspicions. His heart beat faster. Was Lynette inside that room? And if so, was she alone? He glanced at his watch. One more minute and Nikki would join him. As quietly as he could, he slid back the bolt and unlocked the door. His heart in his mouth, he opened the door and went in.

'Police. If you are in here, Lynette, say nothing,' he whispered urgently. 'We've come to get you out of here. Just stay silent.'

He hadn't been wrong. Light from the hall spilled into the room and he saw the lone figure of Lynette Sims, bound hand and foot, crouching beside a narrow bed.

Taking out his pocket knife, he ran over to her and freed her hands and legs. 'Don't try to walk immediately, you'll be stiff. Flex your hands and feet and then follow me, quietly as you can.'

Tears running down her face, she did as she was told. Joseph peered out on to the landing. All was quiet, Nikki hadn't come up yet. He couldn't believe how quickly they'd located Lynette. Maybe he was right not to believe it, it had all been just too easy.

'Do you know where he is, your captor?' he asked.

'I don't even know *who* he is,' Lynette breathed. 'I've never seen him.'

'Can you walk okay?'

She said she could.

'Then keep immediately behind me. We need to get down to my colleague and then we'll get you to safety. Just keep calm and follow me.'

They edged towards the stairs. Every moment he expected to see Nikki coming up, but when they reached the landing and looked down, the hall was empty.

Joseph's throat went dry. Where was she?

'As the saying goes, exchange is no robbery.' The voice that rang out was deep and menacing. 'Detective Sergeant Easter, you will do exactly as I say. First, you and Lynette will come down the stairs, slowly, a step at a time, and stand at the far end of the hall.'

Eyeing the police service pistol, a Glock 19, that Pelham was aiming at Lynette, Joseph complied. From his reading of Pelham's service history, Joseph recalled that Pelham was considered one of the best shots in his team.

'Where is DI Galena?'

David Pelham gave a little chuckle. 'That's for me to know and you to find out. For now, shut up and listen. This is what you are going to do. You are going to take this young woman outside, hand her over to your colleagues, who are no doubt waiting with bated breath, come straight back inside and lock the door. Do you understand?'

Joseph knew that getting Lynette away was paramount, although he had no idea why this deranged man was letting her go so easily. 'As you guessed, David, my colleagues are outside. In fact, we have the whole place surrounded, so you won't get away, no matter what.'

'First, my name is Oliver. Second, I don't give a flying fuck. This was only ever going to have one ending, so it's pointless threatening me.' Pelham laughed. It had a hysterical, unhinged edge to it. Joseph remembered Julia Tennant's words. *There is no reasoning with him.*

Still, he had to do something.

First, Lynette. He ushered the terrified woman towards the door, unlocked it and stepped outside, keeping her in front of him.

'Lynette, just walk towards that area over there.' He pointed to where the backup team would be waiting. 'Tell them what's happened and that they must surround the house but do nothing. Make that very clear. They do nothing until they hear from me. Now go!'

He watched her run to safety, saw Cat and Ben hurry forward to meet her, and turned back to face Pelham.

CHAPTER THIRTY-THREE

Cat and Ben listened to what Lynette told them with mounting horror. Cat then radioed the superintendent to apprise him of Joseph's request.

In no time at all, the house was surrounded, and the tactical armed unit was en route to Lane End.

Lynette Sims was taken to a waiting ambulance. She insisted she was unharmed, and wanted to remain at the scene until she knew the fate of the people who'd saved her. All she asked was that someone let her mother know she was safe, so Yvonne Collins volunteered to go and fetch Tessa.

There was nothing more to do now but wait.

Cat felt sick. The two people she most admired were shut in that house with a madman. A madman who also happened to be carrying a gun, and had once won a trophy for target shooting.

* * *

Joseph stepped back through the door and, as instructed, locked it behind him. Without waiting for Pelham to speak, he barked out, 'Where's Nikki?

'Oh, such concern!' Pelham mocked. 'But then again, you love her, don't you, and I understand all about that. Sit on the floor, I want to talk.'

'I'm saying nothing until you tell me where Nikki is and you've assured me she's unharmed.' Joseph was tempted to rush him, sod the gun, but had the common sense to realise that he wouldn't be of much use to Nikki dead.

Pelham gazed thoughtfully at Joseph. 'Mmm, you really do love her, don't you? My advice to you is marry her as quickly as you can. Forget your job and your career and put love first, or you might lose her and never get her back again. It would be a pity if she ended up as dead to you as Sharon was to me.'

Joseph sank down on to the floor. The last thing he'd expected from a murderer was to be treated to a lecture on love.

'DI Galena is fine, or she will be shortly.' Pelham looked at his wristwatch. 'I'd give her five or ten minutes more for it to start to wear off.'

'You drugged her?'

'It was the simplest way of dealing with the situation,' Pelham said, 'and the kindest.'

'David, what did you give her?'

'I've told you, Sergeant. My name is Oliver. That's not too difficult to remember, surely? David was a fool, what he did lost me my Sharon. True, he redeemed himself with the investigation, but now he's gone, so call me by my real name, will you?'

This seemed to be a different man to the one who had ordered him to take Lynette out and free her. 'Er, yes, of course, Oliver. But you were going to tell me what drug you used.'

'Oh that. Propofol.'

Joseph felt as if he'd been doused with ice-cold water. Propofol, used to keep you asleep during anaesthesia, was extremely dangerous in the wrong hands.

'Calm down. I know what I'm doing.' Oliver smiled gently. 'My father was an anaesthetist, you know, and I learned quite a bit from him. I like propofol because of its rapid onset and because it's quick-acting. Of course, you need to be careful with the dosage.' He grinned. 'After all, it's what killed Michael Jackson. It's a little like Rohypnol, inasmuch as she won't remember what happened. Some say it's like waking from a really refreshing nap. Sounds quite pleasant, actually.'

Joseph was starting to feel slightly unhinged himself. Oliver was now sitting on the floor opposite him, his back to the wall, the gun still trained steadily at his head, while they discussed love, and the merits of various anaesthetic drugs.

Wanting to buy some time, at least long enough for Nikki to be clear in her head if they needed to act fast, Joseph kept on talking.

'Why did you let Lynette go?' he asked, because he genuinely did wonder about that. Oliver had killed young Daryl Grayson so he wouldn't get in the way when he took her, and then he just let her walk out. What was that all about?

'Because I like her,' Oliver said simply. 'She's a really sweet kid. And I admire the way she stood up to that shitty family of hers when they tried to turn her against me because of what happened to Sharon.'

'But you abducted her, Oliver. You held her prisoner, tied up. She must have been terrified.'

Oliver shrugged. 'She had a bed. She had food. *Facilities*, if you get my meaning. She's tough, that one. What doesn't kill you makes you stronger, or so they say.' He sighed. 'I did it, as if you hadn't realised by now, to get at the family for putting all the blame on me. I decided to give them a little taste of what it feels like to be on the receiving end of an act of revenge.' He smiled almost angelically. 'And it was also a means to an end, since it brought you and your revered Detective Inspector Nikki Galena here to my door.'

A trail of icy fear slithered through his body. 'So, all along you wanted to take revenge on us as, what? Representatives of the police?'

'Give me strength! I thought you two were supposed to be bright.' He gave an exasperated hiss. 'No, Joseph. You are here to perform two specific tasks. One is to hear my confession. The other is to act as my witnesses. That's all. And then it will be over.'

There were several ways of interpreting that last statement, and Joseph didn't for a moment believe that Pelham meant handcuffs and the Custody Suite. Unless a miracle happened, it would be over when two out of the three of them came out of that house alive.

* * *

Seen from a distance, the house, surrounded with officers and emergency vehicles, resembled a scene from a movie. Most unnerving to Cat was the silence. It felt as if every member of the waiting teams was holding their breath.

It was not knowing what was going on behind those blank windows that was killing her. Cat had plenty of experience in witnessing the evil men could do, all of which added to the scenes her imagination conjured up. Somewhere in the midst of the waiting personnel, the super and other commanding officers would be calculating their next move. One option was to send in an elite team to overpower Oliver. Another would be to hand over to a negotiator and endeavour to talk him out. She prayed that they'd use neither of those options and do what Joseph had asked of them — nothing. And wasn't that the most difficult of all? Just to sit back and do nothing while people you cared about — and, yes, loved — were in mortal danger?

To Cat, Nikki and Joseph were family. Apart from Ben, no one meant more to her than them, yet she could do nothing but stand in front of a big old house and wait for the door to open. She wasn't a religious person, but Cat found herself praying.

She glanced at Ben and saw that his lips were moving. She edged a little closer and caught the whispered words, '. . . and deliver us from evil.'

The tears rose to her eyes. Well, what harm could it do? For the first time since her childhood, she joined Ben and whispered the only prayer she knew.

* * *

'You might have made one slight miscalculation, Oliver,' Joseph said evenly.

'Oh?' Oliver sounded amused.

'Nikki.' Joseph shrugged. 'You might have miscalculated Nikki's reaction to having been drugged.'

Oliver's face broke into a happy smile.

'So, it's true! I wondered if her legendary temper hadn't been exaggerated — you know, become one of those myths that gets passed around.'

'Oh, it's true all right. In fact, from personal experience, I'd say it's worse in reality.'

Just then, a muffled roar could be heard coming from a nearby room. This was followed by a series of dull thumps that he took to be violent kicks against a locked door. It appeared that Nikki had not experienced a refreshing nap at all. He gave Oliver a wry smile.

Oliver, meanwhile, looked amused, amazed, perplexed and, finally, angry. 'Shut her up!' He jerked the gun towards the boot room. 'I can't think properly with that row going on!'

Joseph started to get to his feet but Oliver swung the gun round. 'Stay on the floor! Crawl, but don't stand up. Talk to her, and I suggest you get through to her fast. That's a small room, and a few well-placed bullets through the door will shut her up if you can't.'

Gone was the man who, just minutes before, had spoken to him of love.

Joseph turned his back on the gun and crawled to the door.

'Nikki! Listen to me!' He could hear her swearing and grunting.

'The bastard fucking drugged me! He's tied me up! He's going to really regret this when I get ou—'

'Just stop it! Listen, will you? I'm here, I'm safe, and Oliver's here too. He has a gun, Nikki, and unless you calm down, he'll use it. Understand?' He lowered his voice. 'Please, Nikki, you said you'd do as I told you, so just get it together. Oliver wants to talk to us, and I think we should listen.'

The struggling ceased.

'Can you please get me out of here? I'm not talking to anyone, Oliver included, through a sodding locked door.'

Joseph turned, looked at Oliver and gave a slight shrug.

'Remain on the floor, Joseph Easter. One single outburst, the slightest rash move, and you're both dead. If she can agree to that, reach up and unlock the door. Leave her hands tied, but tell her to sit beside you, all right?'

Joseph nodded, and whispered through the door, 'No heroics, understand? We do everything he wants,' he put his lips close to the wood, 'for now.'

* * *

At first she didn't dare raise her eyes to look at Oliver in case her rage overcame her. She slid across the floor on her buttocks and sat next to Joseph. At least he wasn't tied up. Nikki guessed the gun had a lot to do with that, but Joseph being free still gave them a huge advantage, should an opportunity occur. *If* she could keep her cool.

It wasn't like her to lose it in a situation like this. Maybe it was because her own darling daughter had had her drink spiked with drugs, which ultimately caused her death. It made her see red, which was frightening for those around her, but it scared her too. She sometimes wondered what she was really capable of.

She raised her eyes to meet Oliver's gaze and hoped she never found out.

The sight of him shocked her. No wonder no one had connected him with David Pelham, the handsome, debonair detective with the playboy good looks. This man was haggard, so gaunt that his clothes looked several sizes too large. His eyes were deep-set and had a haunted expression. His hair was too long. She pictured the photo on their whiteboard and her fury began to dissipate. Had love done this to him? She could almost feel pity for the pathetic figure he had become.

'So, here we are,' said Oliver. 'At last.'

Neither she nor Joseph spoke. Nikki looked at him with interest, intrigued by the gamut of emotions that followed each other across his pale face. It was a bit like watching the ever-changing images in a photomontage. She was no psychologist, but she had an idea that these two persona — David Pelham and Oliver — had become inextricably intertwined, and each was vying for supremacy. Julia Tennant had said he was beyond reasoning with, and it appeared she'd been right.

'Where's Lynette?' she asked, for the sake of saying something. 'I seem to have missed that part of the action.'

'Safe,' said Joseph, sounding detached. 'Oliver let her go.'

'Because we inept coppers found her before our thirty-six-hour deadline was up, I suppose?' she said somewhat sarcastically.

Surprisingly, Oliver, or David, or whoever he was at that moment, laughed. 'You did indeed! Nice one, DI Galena. But no, it wasn't that. Frankly, there never was a deadline. I just threw that in to spice things up a bit. I enjoyed the thought of you all running round like headless chickens.'

'Thanks for that,' Nikki growled, recalling the stress and anxiety of everyone involved. All for nothing. It seemed that Lynette Sims was never in danger at all. She exhaled, relieved Lynette was out of his clutches, but also annoyed at what he'd put them through.

'Well, water under the bridge, as they say. So, Oliver, here we are. You wanted to talk to us.'

Joseph sounded oddly flat, and Nikki wondered why. Maybe he knew something she didn't. Or maybe he was warning her to be careful how she spoke to Oliver. Most likely it was both of those things, but in any case, she should follow his lead.

All at once, Oliver looked terribly weary. If it hadn't been for the gun, which never wavered, they might have risked taking him down.

'I've been working towards this moment for many years now,' he said softly. 'It's been a tortuous journey, but at last it's over.' He looked around the big spacious hall. 'I was born here, you know. This house has always been special to me, that's why I've always looked after it so well.'

His tone took Nikki aback. He was talking like some old man, ready to shuffle off his mortal coil. Of course. That was it, wasn't it? Not old, but he *was* planning on topping himself! It was what she had missed when she'd been under the influence of that damned drug. Oh no, he wasn't getting out of it that way! Sad or not, he had still murdered two men and ruined several people's lives, principally that of Sharon Kelly. No matter how sorry she felt for him, she still wanted to see him in court and hear the judge pass sentence. And it wasn't just retribution — this man needed help, badly.

Then she had another thought. Did he intend to take them with him? Was that why they were here? Well, that wasn't going to happen either. Not if she had anything to do with it.

She tried to formulate a plan, but any attempt to get at Oliver would come to nothing if her hands remained bound. All they could do was sit where they were, listening, and watching for his mood swings.

'Did you enjoy the special investigation I devised for you? It was a great honour, wasn't it?' He was beaming like a child. 'Did it excite you? Challenge you? Did you enjoy the thrill of the chase?'

Nikki wasn't sure how to respond to that. *Honour?* It made her want to stuff his bloody airmail envelopes down his throat.

Joseph answered for her. 'Everyone involved was awe-struck, Oliver. The way you solved those old cases was nothing short of brilliant. Or was it David who did that? Given the extraordinarily clever detective work involved, I think it was David, don't you? David, the detective who left the force when he should have gone on to higher things.'

Oliver gave him a withering look. 'I'm tired, I'm exhausted, but I'm not stupid. Don't treat me like a headcase. I know exactly who I am, and who I was. Come on, if I was a nutter, I could hardly have solved four cases that had been baffling the Fenland Constabulary for years.'

He sounded petulant, childish. Oliver made her very nervous indeed, but she wondered what would happen if she were to speak to the real David Pelham.

Well, she'd lose nothing by trying. 'DS Pelham!' she shouted. 'My sergeant was talking to you! Please pay attention!'

Oliver looked baffled. He cast a quick glance around the room as if he wondered where he was.

Beside her, Joseph stiffened. He too had seen Oliver's confusion. If it happened again, there might be just enough time for him to make a move. Oliver's confusion lasted only seconds, but seconds could be all he needed. Nikki nudged him very slightly to indicate she understood, and continued to address Oliver as if he were a police officer.

'You were being complimented on your exemplary work in solving those cold cases, David. Even I have to admit to being more than a little impressed, but I did wonder why you did it.' She stared hard at him. 'What impelled you, and why did you insist that I had failed those poor girls? You said, "*You failed me.*" In what way?'

David Pelham stood up and stretched, the gun still trained on them.

Nikki thought he appeared taller, less ravaged and more in control. When he spoke, his voice was deeper and stronger.

'It's complicated, DI Galena.' Yes, there was a little of the old police officer still there, and he responded as if addressing a senior officer. 'It wasn't personal, it never was. The truth is, I knew that you and DS Easter, along with

351

your team, were the only detectives capable of rising to the challenge.' He looked at her thoughtfully. 'You knew Sharon too, didn't you, ma'am? You even helped her.'

Nikki nodded. 'Yes, I did. When I knew her mind was made up and nothing would stop her going, I found her a sponsor, he was a distant cousin of mine.'

'Then thank you. At least that would have made things easier for her.' He shook his head. 'I couldn't have said that a while ago. I was angry then, jealous too, I guess, of the fact that you still held a warrant card. But it's different now.'

So, he never did bear her any deep ill-will for her part in Sharon's departure for Australia. Nikki was both surprised and relieved. Despite herself, it had profoundly upset her that someone could hate her so much.

David Pelham was slowly pacing the floor at the far end of the hall. 'I loved her so much that when she left it stole my reason, and when she died, I almost lost the little I had left. I needed something to stop the remaining tatters of my life from shredding altogether, and it had to be an undertaking of some magnitude. It was out of the question for me to remain in the force, I'd have been retired out as psychologically unfit to serve.' He uttered a hollow laugh. 'So, I pre-empted that and resigned. I can't recall exactly when I had the idea of finding all those missing girls, but I do remember thinking that it was most likely an impossible task.' He stopped pacing and leaned back against the wall. 'The more I considered those cases the more they began to call to me. I heard the voices of those young women, women that we had failed to find justice for. I kept seeing them as people who'd been loved, like my Sharon was, people who deserved better than a cursory review every six months or so. One night when I couldn't sleep, I actually heard the voice of Alexandra Cornfield begging me to find her. I still hear her sometimes . . .' David shook himself. 'But that was the pivotal moment. From then on, it defined my life and gave it meaning. I would find those girls and show an inadequate police force what good detective work really was. I, David

Pelham, would shake up the entire agency, right from the woodentops to the Chief Constable.'

'You did that all right,' Nikki said, smiling grimly. 'And some!'

David gave a slight bow. 'You realise, don't you, that I had to have a single person to focus on, especially for the mail.'

'*Par Avion*,' she said. 'Did you use airmail as a clue, indicating that if I really put my detective's hat on I'd make the connection with Sharon's flight to Australia?'

'Well, if it was, it wasn't conscious, though Sharon never left my thoughts. Oh, and one of the other things I wanted to achieve with my project was to get back at the Kelly family for the blame they threw my way after my darling Sharon died. They deserved some form of punishment for what they put me through, and a perfect way to achieve it was to take Lynette, the only girl in the family.' David exhaled, long and slow. 'The thing is, I undertook this journey as a form of catharsis, but that's not how it worked out. Something went wrong. Terribly wrong.'

His face set and he looked suddenly grim. Nikki was afraid he'd slip away from them before he could say more. 'Neil Weldon? Was that what went wrong, DC Pelham?'

David nodded, his gaze on the floor. 'He was a pervert, ma'am. He showed no remorse for what he did to Alexandra. When I found him . . .' He passed his free hand across his face. 'Someone else seemed to take over. Looking back, I realise that I changed at that very point. I couldn't wait for justice to take its course, because I knew that with the way the CPS operated, it might never even happen. So I, I—'

'Bypassed the system and executed him,' said Joseph calmly.

'And bypassed the point of no return,' David added. 'I continued my enquiry, but it wasn't the same as before. It was as if someone else was now doing the work. I started having odd ideas, crazy thoughts that felt like revelations. That's when I took the name. Sharon loved Oliver. Sharon loved Oliver . . .'

He turned his gaze on Nikki, and she saw bewilderment steal across his face, heralding the departure of DS Pelham. She acted fast, knowing that Joseph would understand that this was his chance. 'Oh God! I'm going to be sick! Those drugs! Oh . . . aargh . . .' She lurched away from Joseph, making retching noises.

'No! Not here! Not in my precious home! Oh, my clean floor! Please, no! You can't!'

David's excessive reaction played straight into their hands. Nikki upped the dramatics, loudly pretending to vomit, while Joseph took immediate advantage of David's horror and his momentary lack of attention to his gun.

It was all over in a moment, but not before the gun had discharged.

* * *

Outside, a cry went up to move in, and the gathered officers leaped forward. There was no need for stealth this time, it was all speed and noise. Doors were sent crashing in, while shouts rang out of both command and response.

Cat and Ben weren't far behind the initial wave of black-garbed men and women. With her heart in her mouth, Cat pounded across the garden towards the window where they'd last seen Nikki and Joseph.

They tumbled inside and almost fell into the hall.

She would never forget the scene that confronted her. It continued to haunt her for months afterwards, and never failed to arouse a feeling of intense emotion.

Nikki, Joseph and David Pelham were sitting on the hall floor together.

Nikki, from whose wrists still dangled the cords that had been cut but not removed, was clasping a sobbing David to her, whispering soothing noises as if to a frightened child. 'I know, I know.'

Beside them, Joseph still held a pocketknife in his hand, while a gun, emptied of ammunition, lay next to him. All three were apparently oblivious to the furore of the siege.

Around them, armed police officers stood in silence, their semi-automatics lowered.

Cat took a step forward, but Nikki gently shook her head. 'It's okay, just leave us for a minute or two.'

Everyone in the room appeared to be frozen in time. Apart from David's pitiful sobs, and the quiet murmur of Nikki's reassurances, the room was extraordinarily peaceful. Cat wondered how that could be, crowded as it was with sweaty policemen, bulletproof vests, and cocked firearms.

For Cat, it was one of those sublime moments that, once experienced, never leaves you. For once, all their efforts had come together for the greater good. There had been no shoot-out, it hadn't all gone out with a bang. Instead, there was a strange kind of stillness that to her signified closure. She would have considered it peaceful, if it had not been the final scene of a drama that had seen people murdered and a young woman abducted.

Later, when it was all over and they were driving back to the station, Cat began to wonder about that prayer she and Ben had offered up. She had no idea if it had had anything to do with the outcome, but just in case, she found herself issuing a quiet thank-you.

Ben glanced at her and smiled.

EPILOGUE

Three weeks later

Yvonne sat opposite her friend Dinah at the kitchen table. She had sneaked out for an hour to escape the heaving pile of reports on her desk that seemed to grow taller no matter how hard she worked on them. 'I was wondering how Lynette is,' she asked, helping herself to another chocolate biscuit.

'Remarkably good,' replied Dinah. 'She went through all the stages in a very short time — upset, angry, you know the score. It helped to be able to explain a little of the man's story. Lynette is a very understanding woman, and now she's back in the classroom and doing just fine.'

'I thought she seemed a pretty resilient person,' said Yvonne. 'But getting drugged and kidnapped — well, something like that could have had awful consequences.'

'She told me that David, who she certainly didn't recognise from her childhood, had approached her saying a kid had fallen and hurt herself and could she help him get her into the school. After that, she remembers nothing until she woke up in a dark room with her hands and feet bound. She admitted to being terrified at first, then she became frustrated at not being able to free herself.'

'She said that in her statement,' added Yvonne. 'I'm not sure I'd have been quite so brave. I take my hat off to her, I must say.'

'Young Amber is back in class too, and is a different girl altogether now her cousin is no longer there. She's got good grades and is thriving again. Ruby is being moved to another school, a sensible move now that she's having therapeutic treatment. I think new surroundings and a new start could be the making of her. She is very intelligent, so hopefully they can get her on to a course of medication that will allow her a decent future.' Dinah shook her head. 'What a shock that was. I'm so glad it's over and we're getting back to normal.' She drank a mouthful of tea and glanced at her friend. 'It's been a right baptism of fire for you, Vonnie, moving into CID and straight into the heart of a storm.'

Yvonne gave a dry laugh. 'You can say that again, though I have to admit I'm enjoying myself, and my old skills are proving useful to the team, so what more could I want?'

'Well, good luck to you!' Dinah lifted her mug, and they made a toast. 'To new beginnings, after retirement!'

All at once, Dinah slammed her mug on the table, leaped up and rushed to the back door, grabbing her water cannon as she went. 'Bloody squirrel!'

Yvonne burst out laughing. Things really were back to normal.

* * *

Two months later

Joseph rose early, pulled on some joggers and, leaving Nikki still sleeping, wandered down to Knot Cottage.

The morning was strangely still. For once, there wasn't the slightest breath of wind off the Wash. Even the birds were quiet, and as Joseph strolled along, he felt unusually contemplative.

It seemed that no matter what was happening, the David Pelham case lay in wait for him, ready to highjack his thoughts. It was hardly surprising. It had taken David years of painstaking work to discover the whereabouts of four missing women, now it looked as if it would take them even longer to clear up the aftermath and get it to court.

A couple of months had passed by now, but it was still the main topic of conversation around the station. Opinions were divided. Some were incensed that a police officer should stoop to murder, while others were in awe of his investigatory prowess in solving four old cases as well as taking matters into his own hands and killing a murderer and a predator. To these latter people, he was something of a dark hero.

Joseph looked out over the marsh to the early light that glinted like polished silver off the pewter of the ocean beyond. He realised that it wasn't the case itself that had disturbed him, it was their getting Pelham's reasons for acting as he did so very wrong. It was quite understandable that Nikki should have believed the whole thing to be a threat against her in person, especially as he'd addressed all his correspondence to her. Even so, Joseph berated himself for falling in with the rest and assuming Pelham's campaign to be a vendetta, motivated solely by revenge against a copper. Why hadn't he considered less obvious scenarios? He prided himself on taking a broad view of the cases he handled, but not this time. He wondered why. Was he getting stale? Losing his edge? Or was he just tired of constantly seeing the things they were faced with, daily occurrences that would send most people reaching for the bottle?

Watching the light change in the early morning sky, he realised that this case had affected him on an unbelievable number of levels. The forensic evidence, sacks of it, especially Rory's precious pollen and spores, had correctly placed everyone in given locations. It added up to all, bar one, of the suspects in the old and new murders, including their murdered stalker, being proven guilty beyond reasonable doubt. He regretted the fact that they'd been unable to prove that

Martine Knight was involved in the death of Ruth Baker. He still believed that she was as guilty as hell, but no matter how hard they tried, there was just not enough actual evidence. Still, apart from her, and considering David's own confession, it was pretty well case closed.

And that was the problem. It wasn't any of that. Joseph had been affected by the more intangible elements, not the hard facts or the good old hard graft of police work.

He walked on down the lane, a weak sun doing its best to break through the multitude of shifting clouds. A particular image kept playing out in his head. He saw Nikki, her face enraged and her voice full of venom, saying 'I will get the bastard!' That was replaced by the sight of her sitting on the floor in the hall at Cairngorm, cradling the "bastard" in her arms, while he sobbed piteously, a broken man.

Joseph would never forget that scene as long as he lived. It served to remind him that they weren't always right, and that he should endeavour to look further than the obvious.

Still deep in thought, he let himself into the cottage and went about the few jobs he had come here for, collecting and sorting his mail and putting out the waste bin for collection. It was mainly for show, but it was important to keep up the charade that he still lived there. He loved the old place, but it had become nothing but a repository for some of his old things, and a part of him felt it deserved more than an occasional visit.

He locked up again, wheeled the bin to the road edge, and started out for Cloud Cottage Farm.

The sun was now breaking through the clouds, and streaks of pink, orange and pale blue heralded a bright morning. A new day, he thought, and sighed. One particular moment came back to him. He heard David Pelham say, "My advice to you is marry her as quickly as you can. Forget your job and all your career plans and put love first, above everything."

He stared at the sky and squinted into the brightness. The birds were singing, vying for the sweetest, or maybe the loudest song.

Should he heed the words of a murderer? A man who had lost all reason because of love?

Deep in thought, Joseph walked slowly back towards Cloud Cottage Farm and Nikki.

THE END

ALSO BY JOY ELLIS

THE BESTSELLING NIKKI GALENA SERIES
Book 1: CRIME ON THE FENS
Book 2: SHADOW OVER THE FENS
Book 3: HUNTED ON THE FENS
Book 4: KILLER ON THE FENS
Book 5: STALKER ON THE FENS
Book 6: CAPTIVE ON THE FENS
Book 7: BURIED ON THE FENS
Book 8: THIEVES ON THE FENS
Book 9: FIRE ON THE FENS
Book 10: DARKNESS ON THE FENS
Book 11: HIDDEN ON THE FENS
Book 12: SECRETS ON THE FENS
Book 13: FEAR ON THE FENS
Book 14: GRAVES ON THE FENS

JACKMAN & EVANS
Book 1: THE MURDERER'S SON
Book 2: THEIR LOST DAUGHTERS
Book 3: THE FOURTH FRIEND
Book 4: THE GUILTY ONES
Book 5: THE STOLEN BOYS
Book 6: THE PATIENT MAN
Book 7: THEY DISAPPEARED
Book 8: THE NIGHT THIEF
Book 9: SOLACE HOUSE

DETECTIVE MATT BALLARD
Book 1: BEWARE THE PAST
Book 2: FIVE BLOODY HEARTS
Book 3: THE DYING LIGHT
Book 4: MARSHLIGHT
Book 5: TRICK OF THE NIGHT

STANDALONES
GUIDE STAR

Thank you for reading this book.

If you enjoyed it please leave feedback on Amazon or Goodreads, and if there is anything we missed or you have a question about, then please get in touch. We appreciate you choosing our book.

Founded in 2014 in Shoreditch, London, we at Joffe Books pride ourselves on our history of innovative publishing. We were thrilled to be shortlisted for Independent Publisher of the Year at the British Book Awards.

www.joffebooks.com

We're very grateful to eagle-eyed readers who take the time to contact us. Please send any errors you find to corrections@joffebooks.com. We'll get them fixed ASAP.

Made in the USA
Las Vegas, NV
09 December 2022